Julie Miller is an award-winn author of breathtaking ror National Readers' Choice A Maurier Award, among other prizes. She has also earned an *RT Book Reviews* Career Achievement Award. For a complete list of her books, monthly newsletter and more, go to juliemiller.org

Beth Cornelison began working in public relations before pursuing her love of writing romance. She has won numerous honors for her work, including a nomination for the RWA *RITA*® Award for *The Christmas Stranger*. She enjoys featuring her cats (or friends' pets) in her stories and always has another book in the pipeline! She currently lives in Louisiana with her husband, one son and three spoiled cats. Contact her via her website, bethcornelison.com

K-9 DEFENDER

JULIE MILLER

TARGETED WITH A COLTON

BETH CORNELISON

MILLS & BOON

First Published in Great Britain 2024
by Mills & Boon, an imprint of HarperCollins*Publishers* Ltd
1 London Bridge Street, London, SE1 9GF

www.harpercollins.co.uk

HarperCollins*Publishers*
Macken House, 39/40 Mayor Street Upper,
Dublin 1, D01 C9W8, Ireland

K-9 Defender © 2024 by Julie Miller
Targeted with a Colton © 2024 by Harlequin Enterprises ULC

Special thanks and acknowledgment are given to Beth Cornelison for her contribution to *The Coltons of Owl Creek* series.

ISBN: 978-0-263-32246-0

0924

This book contains FSC™ certified paper and other controlled sources to ensure responsible forest management.

For more information visit: www.harpercollins.co.uk/green

Printed and Bound in the UK using 100% Renewable Electricity at CPI Group (UK) Ltd, Croydon, CR0 4YY

K-9 DEFENDER

JULIE MILLER

For the trainers and staff at Dog Stars.
Thank you for helping our one-eyed Doodlebugs,
Daisy & Teddy, become all-star dogs.
Your expertise and kindness
were greatly appreciated.

Prologue

"You'll always be a stupid country girl!"

Mollie Di Salvo couldn't brace for the next blow when it came. She was still woozy from the hands that had squeezed around her neck until she'd nearly passed out and collapsed to the kitchen floor. She couldn't pull her legs up fast enough and curl into a ball. She swore she heard a rib snap when Augie kicked her in the stomach.

She'd always thought anger was a fiery emotion. But as she squinted through her swollen eyelid at the eyes of her husband, she knew that anger was ice-cold.

This was the worst beating yet.

All because she'd served her granny's biscuits at the dinner party with Augie's parents, the Brewers and Mr. Hess and his date. Delicious, yes. But poor folks and country bumpkins ate biscuits. Augie was embarrassed to see them on his table. Embarrassed that the investment bankers he worked with might think he was a poor country bumpkin, too, with no sense about handling their clients' money.

Embarrassed by her.

Was she trying to sabotage this business deal? A faux

pas at this level on Kansas City's social registry could cost him and his company millions of dollars.

Or something like that. To be honest, once she'd drifted away from consciousness, she hadn't heard much of his tirade.

Now all she knew was pain.

Mollie's lungs burned and her throat throbbed as she fought to catch a deep breath. She watched as Augie knelt beside her and clasped her chin in a cruel grip, surely leaving bruises, forcing her to face him. "I'm going out." His spittle sprayed her cheek. "The staff has gone home for the night, so clean up this mess. And don't wait up for me."

She watched the polished black Italian oxfords on his feet, making sure that they were walking away from her and heading out the side door into the garage. She heard men's unintelligible voices, a car door slam, and then Augie's latest fancy sports car revving up and driving away.

Mollie pushed herself up to a sitting position and leaned back against the oven. Breathing in through her nose and out through her mouth, she mentally assessed her injuries. There'd be bruises and swelling, yes—maybe even a cracked rib. But she could survive without a trip to the ER, without telling lies to the doctor and nurses, without explaining why it wasn't safe for her to talk to the police. She just needed to catch a deep breath.

She reached beneath the neckline of her dress to clutch the engraved silver locket she always wore. To her it was more beautiful than the obnoxiously large sapphire and diamond ring on her left hand. The wedding and engagement rings were all about Augie and showing off that he was wealthy and generous. But her locket was the real prize. It had been a gift from Granny. The one link left to her past when she'd been happy and the world was full of possibilities. She'd been so naive.

She had no more illusions of love. Her Cinderella story had ended just over a year ago, only five months into her marriage. The first slap that Thanksgiving night after an endless extravaganza at his parents' estate with his entire family and many of their important friends still rang through her memory. She was an introvert by nature, and the days of prepping and late-into-the-night dining, drinking, and partying had left her physically and emotionally exhausted. When they got home, Augie wanted to celebrate their successful evening. He informed her he was horny and ready for sex. She'd kissed him, explained how tired she was and promised that, after a little rest, she'd give him a very good morning.

He'd slapped her, the move so sudden she would have thought she'd imagined it if not for the heat rapidly replacing the shocked nerves on her cheek. No one said no to August Di Salvo, especially not his low-class hick of a wife. She should be grateful for every little thing he did for her. Augie took the sex he wanted that night, and Mollie knew her dream life had irrevocably changed into a nightmare.

Between the family attorney and his parents' influence, her report to the police the next day had mysteriously disappeared. And the one after that had been pleaded down to a public disturbance and dismissed with a fine.

So, she'd stopped calling the police. She stopped sharing a bedroom with her husband. And she stopped feeling hope.

Now, thankfully, Augie got most of his sex from the string of affairs he had. But Mollie didn't care that he was cheating on her.

She didn't have emotions anymore.

She drew in another painful breath. That wasn't exactly true.

She had fear.

Fear was her constant companion. If Augie wasn't with her, then she knew one of his friends or beefy bodyguards or even someone from the office or their home staff was watching her. The beautiful trophy wife who straightened her hair and dyed it blond because her husband didn't think her natural dark curls looked sophisticated. Who wore heels that pinched her feet because he thought they made her look sexy. Who'd married a man because she'd believed the Di Salvo family taking her in, and Augie supporting her through the worst time of her life, meant they loved her.

How could a smart woman be so foolish? Her loneliness and despair had led to some disastrous choices.

Her granny must be turning over in her grave to see how frightened and abused she had become. She'd grown up without parents, thanks to a rainy-night highway accident when she was four. But she'd been raised with love and enough food to eat, and she'd been taught a solid work ethic and some old-fashioned common sense by her grandmother, Lucy Belle Crane. She was the girl who'd overcome the poor circumstances of her Ozarks upbringing to earn scholarships and work her way through college at the University of Missouri. She had a degree in math education, a year in the classroom under her belt, and a semester's worth of classes toward her Master's degree.

Yet here she was, huddled on the kitchen floor of August Di Salvo's big, beautiful house, afraid to stand her ground with Augie, afraid to call the police, afraid to ask anyone for help, afraid to pursue a teaching job or further her education, afraid to leave, afraid to stay. Afraid. Afraid. Afraid.

Feeling an imagined warmth radiating from the locket in her hand, she pressed a kiss to the silver oval and dropped it inside the front of her dress. Then she braced one hand on the oven behind her and reached up to grasp the granite countertop on the island across from her.

The door to the garage swung open. Mollie gasped in fear and plopped down on her butt. The movement jarred her sore ribs, and she grabbed her side, biting down on a moan of pain and bracing herself for another round of degrading words and hard blows from her husband.

Only, she didn't recognize the man in the black uniform suit and tie who wandered into the kitchen, surveyed the entire area, then rushed to her side when he saw her on the cold tile floor.

He reached for her with a big, scarred hand. "Let me help you."

"No, I..." But he was already pulling her to her feet. He wound a sturdy arm around her waist and led her around the island, where he pulled out a stool and helped her to sit.

"Looks like you took a pretty good blow to the head." His gaze darted to the placement of her hand above her waist. "Did you hit your side, too? Do you want me to call 9-1-1? Or I could drive you to the hospital myself."

"No. I'll be fine. I'm just—" the well-rehearsed word tasted like bile on her tongue "—clumsy."

She smiled until she saw his gaze linger on the marks she knew would be visible on her neck. "You didn't fall."

The man was too observant for his own good. The others had been trained to look the other way. Mollie realized she was still holding on to his hand, where it rested on the countertop. She popped her grip open and turned away to pull her long golden hair off her cheek and tuck it behind her ear. "You're new here."

Although he frowned at the cool wall of diversion and denial she was erecting between them, he thankfully retreated a step to give her the distance she needed to pull herself together. "I'm Mr. Di Salvo's new driver. He took the convertible out himself, said he didn't need me tonight. But I'm on shift until midnight. It's kind of chilly just sitting out in the garage waiting to work. I was told I could come into the house to get some hot coffee."

"Of course. Everything you need is right here. Regular, decaf. Cream, sugar." Moving slowly, but with a sense of purpose, she climbed off the stool and showed him the coffee bar tucked in beside the refrigerator at the end of the row of cabinets. Ever the consummate hostess, she opened the cabinet above the coffee makers, but winced when she reached for the mug above her.

He was at her side in an instant, grasping the mug and pulling it down for her. "Ma'am, you don't have to wait on me. Can I at least make you an ice pack for that eye? I do have first aid training."

Ignoring his concern, or perhaps taking advantage of it by continuing this conversation at all, she asked for the smallest of favors. "Would you pull down another mug for me?"

"Sure."

When he set the mug in front of her, she poured herself some decaf coffee and cradled its heat between her trembling hands. She scooted off to the side, leaning lightly against the counter. "Please. Help yourself."

"Thanks." He poured himself a mug, fully loaded with a shot of cream.

While he fixed his drink and took a couple of sips, Mollie felt curious enough to make note of his looks. He wasn't as tall as or movie star handsome as Augie, but then, *tall, dark, and handsome* wasn't necessarily attractive in her opinion. Not anymore.

Her would-be rescuer had brown hair and golden-brown eyes that made her think of a tiger. Despite the breadth of his shoulders beneath his black suit jacket, and the unflattering buzz cut of hair that emphasized the sharp angles of his face, the man had kind eyes. Kindness was such a rarity in her small world that the softness of his amber eyes woke a desire in her that she hadn't felt for a long time now. The desire to step outside herself and do something for someone else—the way she might once have helped a friend in need—the way no one had helped her for more than a year now. "Let me give you some advice, Mr…?"

"Uh, Rostovich." Had he hesitated to share his name? "Joel Rostovich."

"Listen, Joel Rostovich. Get out. Get out of this house. Leave your job. Get away from this family as fast as you can."

He set down his coffee at her dismissal. "You need an ice pack or a raw steak for that eye. If you won't let me drive you to the ER or a police station, at least let me make sure you get to your room safely, and I'll bring you an ibuprofen." He started to pull out a business card. "If you change your mind, you can call—"

"And if you won't get out, then stay away from me. Don't talk to me unless you have orders to. Don't smile. And sure as hell, don't you be nice to me again." She tucked the card into the pocket of his jacket and rested her hand against his chest in a silent thanks for his humanity and compassion. Then she turned and slowly made her way out of the kitchen. "It'll be safer for you that way."

Chapter One

Present Day.
Summer...

"You stupid waitress." The young man swore and shoved his chair back to avoid the milk dripping off the side of the table.

"I'm sorry, sir." Mollie Crane righted the glass she'd bumped when she'd been clearing his plate and quickly pulled the towel from the waistband of her apron to mop up the spill before any of the liquid got on the customer. This was more about saving the chair and keeping the floor dry than making sure the grumpy customer wouldn't get anything on his Arabia Steamboat T-shirt from the tourist shop down the street. Nor would he slip on any wet surface.

She always carried a towel with her now. While she was more than willing to put in the hours, step out of her comfort zone to interact with customers, and ignore her aching feet, it turned out that waitressing wasn't her best thing. She startled easily, got distracted by anything or anyone unfamiliar to her, and tended to withdraw inside her head when she got stressed. Although she'd been raised in her Granny Lucy Belle's kitchen and loved to cook, serving food outside the kitchen seemed to be a skill she was still acquiring after ten months on the job. But, it was a job, she had an understanding boss, and she needed both. And when her shift wasn't a train wreck like this one, coming in a few hours early to help out while her friend and fellow server Corie Taylor went to an OB-GYN appointment to monitor her ninth month of pregnancy, she actually made pretty good tips.

Not that this self-entitled bozo would be leaving her much, if anything, now. "I'll bring you a fresh glass of milk," she offered, trying to remember that the customer was always right—even if he was being a jerk about it.

"No, you won't." His morning must have been longer than hers to see how easily he got riled over a simple accident. She wasn't even certain this was her fault. Hadn't he been pushing his plate aside when she walked up with the glass he'd ordered to go with his pie? "You'll bring me a new plate of food. Everything here is swimming in milk. It's ruined."

Everything? The man had already eaten his patty melt, save for the bottom bun, and all but two of his French fries. And the spill wasn't anywhere near his chocolate cream pie. Mollie bit down on the sarcastic retorts she wanted to spew at him. *Ungrateful man. Scammer. Spoiled rotten.* But talking back to anyone, especially a man with a short temper like this one, had been beaten out of her long ago. She might have left August Di Salvo and her nightmarish, dangerous marriage behind, but the rules of survival were too deeply ingrained in her to do anything but apologize again. "I'm sorry if there was a misunderstanding. I thought you were done with your lunch."

"Darrell, we were almost finished." His wife or girlfriend, who sat across from him, tried to placate him with a gentle reprimand.

But with a snap of his fingers, the woman fell silent and sank back into her chair.

Oh, God. Not this. Darrell wouldn't be hurting the woman later for contradicting him in public, would he? Because of Mollie's mistake? Her body tensed and her pulse thundered in her ears at the potential for violence. She quickly dropped her gaze to the woman's bare wrists, her neck, and face, looking for any subtle signs that she was being physically abused by her husband. Mollie eased a silent breath through her nose. She didn't see any obvious bruising or that the woman was holding a wrenched joint tenderly so as not to aggravate a hidden injury. But that didn't mean he wasn't verbally abusing her.

"You don't understand the kind of stress I'm under." Augie spat the words at her, bending her backward as he tugged roughly on her hair, snapping a few strands and sending pain burning across her scalp. She'd been dressing for dinner with his parents when he walked into her bedroom to announce he was ready to leave. He'd taken one look at her carefully coiffed hair and dragged her into the bathroom to shove her face into the mirror. "I said I liked you blonde. Brown hair makes you look cheap."

And the bottled bleach color he insisted on didn't?

"The stylist said I needed to give my hair a break from all the dying and straightening chemicals," she whispered, even though the truth wouldn't make a bit of difference to her husband. *"My hair is breaking."*

Mollie watched the reflection of his hand down at his side to make sure it stayed there. Although dinner with Edward and Bernadette Di Salvo wouldn't be a picnic,

*at least she knew Augie wouldn't leave any marks on her
that his parents could see. Not that they'd chastised their
son or supported Mollie in the past when he'd hurt her—if
anything had happened, it must have been her fault. They
were old money and all about appearances. So, she might
be safe from his fists and feet for the time being, but that
didn't stop Augie's cutting words.*

*"Your stylist doesn't have to look at your hair day in
and day out. I do." He finally released her, giving her a
chance to ease the crick in her neck. "You'll be wearing a
sack over your head next time I take you to bed."*

*An idle threat, since she knew he'd be sleeping with his
administrative assistant at the loft apartment he kept her
in in downtown Kansas City. But the words still hurt.*

*"I can't stand to look at you like this." Augie literally
wiped his hands on a towel, as if her natural curls had
contaminated him somehow. "You used to be so smart. I
don't understand why you can't get simple things like this
right." He tossed the towel at her and pivoted to stride out
of the room. "You'll stay home tonight. I'll tell Mother and
Father you're ill."*

Mollie sucked in a shallow breath and squeezed her eyes
shut to tamp down the urge to run away from her memories and real-life stressors to safety. Wherever that illu-
sion might be. Leaving her husband didn't mean leaving
her fears behind.

But she *was* smart. She was slowly amassing the tools
she needed to do better than simply survive. And beyond
her own gumption, the best tool she had was right here in
the diner with her.

Forcing her eyes open, Mollie looked across the diner
to spot her service dog, Magnus, lying in his bed at the far

end of the soda fountain counter. The sleek Belgian Malinois with the permanently flopped-over ear looked like the sharp, muscular dog that was his breed standard. But in the weeks she'd been training with him at Jessica Caldwell's K-9 Ranch just outside of Kansas City, she'd learned that, despite his athleticism, her boy was more couch potato than intimidating working machine.

"Magnus...?" She mouthed his name through trembling lips. She held out two fingers in a silent *Come* command. He was supposed to watch her, comfort her. Obey her.

Mollie frowned. Great. Magnus was facing the kitchen. He seemed to be happily relaxing, his teeth clamped around the tattered teddy bear he carried everywhere, instead of paying attention to her and hurrying to her side to calm her when she was on the verge of a panic attack, like she was now. She wasn't exactly sure what it was that Magnus responded to when she was about to lose it. But clearly, her pulse pounding in her ears, the cold, clammy feel to her skin and the short, shallow breathing weren't it.

Some therapy dog. Shouting for him wouldn't do any good. Being deaf in one ear, he might not even hear her over the noise of clinking dishes and chatty patrons. And if he did happen to look her way and respond to the visual signals she'd been practicing with him, the former K-9 Corps washout would probably frighten some of the customers when he loped across the diner to reach her.

Mollie dropped her hand to clutch the dripping towel to her chest. When she got her break later this afternoon, she'd be calling Jessica, who ran the K-9 Ranch where Mollie had gotten Magnus, and where they'd gone through several training lessons together. Jessica and she had worked hard to train Magnus to be an alert dog for Mollie. But other than that first morning on the ranch, when the partially deaf tan dog with a black face had trotted up onto the porch and lain across her feet, indicating that he knew she needed some help—even when her own brain was too stressed out to recognize it—Magnus's responses to Mollie seemed to be hit-or-miss. Jessica said she wasn't being assertive enough, that Magnus didn't see her as his pack leader and wasn't cued in to serving her needs reliably. Mollie imagined the dog saw her as the same weak fool her ex-husband had. That she wasn't worth his time and energy to take care of, so long as she met his basic needs. In Magnus's case, that meant having food, his teddy, regular exercise, and a comfy bed to sleep in.

How did she end up so horribly alone again? She had no family, an ex-husband who'd rather see her dead than pay her one dime of alimony, no friends outside of work and dog training, and a washed-up K-9 Corps dog who seemed to think she was his service human instead of him catering to her.

"Hey!"

Now the fingers were snapping at her.

Mollie startled and swung her gaze back to the table in front of her. "I'm sorry. What?"

"Are you going to go put in the order for my lunch again?" the rude customer asked.

"No, she won't." Mollie saw the flash of movement between tables a split second before her boss, Melissa Kincaid, stepped up beside her. Although shorter than Mollie's five feet six, and looking like a fairy princess with her golden hair and delicate features, despite the scar on her face, Melissa was a tough cookie when it came to running her restaurant. "I'll happily gift you with the slice of pie, but I'm not in the habit of comping meals that have already been eaten and clearly enjoyed. Would you like me to box your pie up to go? I'd be happy to," Melissa strongly suggested. She turned and smiled at Mollie, indicating she had the disgruntled customer well in hand. "Go on. Take a break. I'm sure Herb will have another order up for you in the window by the time you get back on the floor."

"I'm sorry." She mouthed the words to her boss.

"Don't be," the older woman reassured her, squeezing her shoulders in a sideways hug before nudging her away from the table. "Take five minutes. Find your calm place. Then get back to work. We're shorthanded and I really need you."

"Thank you." Mollie quickly retreated while Melissa dealt with the demanding customer. At least he hadn't put his hands on her, she reasoned, knowing she would have had a full-fledged meltdown if he had. The public knew Pearl's Diner as an eatery with a cute, nostalgic decor that served filling, yummy comfort food and award-winning desserts from early morning until late at night. But Mollie knew the truth behind the scenes—that Pearl's was a haven for women working to get back on their feet again after surviving a difficult or traumatic situation. Melissa Kincaid's first husband had been an abuser, and the original Pearl had practically adopted her, giving her a job and a way to start rebuilding her life some fifteen years earlier. Corie Taylor had been a struggling single mother whose ex was in prison. Since inheriting the diner from Pearl, Melissa had paid Pearl's generosity forward, hiring Corie and allowing her to bring her son to sit in a corner booth when she needed childcare. Both women were now happily married to good men—a KCPD detective and a KCFD firefighter, respectively—and had started new, healthy families of their own.

Mollie had once had a dream like that. But after her grandmother's death and her subsequent marriage to Augie, she was content to simply be alive and have a job. She might want more from life, but for now, survival was all that mattered. She was grateful to Melissa for giving her an apron after the Di Salvos had blackballed her name and kept her from getting a teaching job—or just about any job involving education. She was even more grateful that the petite, nearly fearless woman looked out for her when it came to rude customers, and that she allowed her to bring Magnus to work with her—even if he was the worst service dog in the history of K-9 companiondom.

Once at the sink behind the soda fountain counter, Mollie rinsed out the milky towel and draped it over the drying rack beneath the sink. Then, mostly out of sight from the customers, she knelt beside her furry partner. "Hey, baby," she cooed, making sure the dog was aware of her presence before she touched him. At least, he seemed pleased to see her. When he raised his sleek head and focused his dark eyes on her, Mollie smiled, chiding him even as she absorbed the affection he doled out. "How's my big Magnus? Taking it easy today, are we?" She scrubbed her palms along his muzzle and scratched around his ears when he turned his head into her touch. "You know, you failed rescue dog 101 a few minutes ago. Mama needed you."

As if he understood her words and wanted to apologize, he tilted his head, turning his good ear toward her and placing one big paw on her knee. He whimpered softly and laid his head in her lap. She continued to stroke the top of his head as she absorbed his body heat and focused on the inhales and exhales in his strong chest, willing his calm, currently devoted presence to seep into her psyche.

"That's it. Good boy. That's my Magnus. Mama about had a panic attack with the rude man. She needs some of your attention." She rewarded him for his supportive behavior now by picking up his teddy bear and playing a gentle game of tug-of-war with him behind the counter. She wondered if he was losing more of his hearing, or if it was her training that wasn't working out. "We're going to review our skills tonight. I need you to put your paw on me or your nose in my hand every time I'm on the verge of losing it. You keep Mama with you in the here and now, okay? Don't let me get lost in the scary places in my head." She talked softly to him, explaining his job to him as if she were teaching a student in her classroom, and he understood every word she said. "You're being such a good boy right now. We're going learn a new word this week—*consistency*." Magnus tilted his head, as if he was curious to expand his vocabulary. "*Consistent* means every, single, time. Not just when you're in the mood to pay attention. The whole idea of being an alert dog is—"

"Hey, girlie." Herb Valentino, the perpetually grumpy septuagenarian who ran the kitchen during the daytime shift stuck his head through the order window and waved her back into the kitchen. "Stop talkin' to that mutt of yours. If you're just sittin' around, I can use some help back here gettin' orders out. I'm swamped."

Mollie cringed at the cook's nickname for any female under the age of fifty. But she'd been called a lot worse. And, it was probably better for her to stay busy and focused on something other than thoughts of Augie, violence, and a service dog who'd failed her again. Besides, she felt a sense of comfort when she worked in a kitchen—even if it was beside grumpy Herb instead of her darling late grandmother. She'd learned the old man's bark was much worse than his bite. She even had a feeling he kind of liked her working beside him, so long as she obeyed his orders and didn't mess with his recipes. Mollie gave Magnus one last pet and pushed to her feet. "Sure. Melissa only gave me a short break, but I can help get some plates out."

"Wash your hands, girlie. After pettin' that mutt, I don't want you touchin' any food."

She was already at the sink, soaping up her hands, by the time he'd finished his warning. She grabbed a towel to dry her hands and pulled on a pair of plastic gloves before moving up beside the tall, lanky man with bushy gray eyebrows and faded tattoos from his time in the Navy several decades earlier. "Reporting for duty. Put me to work."

He winked at her and did just that. Mollie spent the next several minutes loading condiments onto burgers and putting side dishes onto plates. They worked side by side, with Herb cooking and Mollie finishing plates and setting them in the warming window. She made eye contact with one of the other waitresses. "Order up!"

While the other woman filled her tray with the hot lunches and carried them out to the diners, Mollie swung her gaze over to her own section to see if Melissa was still doing okay covering her tables. She was relieved to see the rude tourist had left the diner. Everyone else at least had their drinks. She'd better get back out there to make sure their food orders were in the queue. But she stopped and stared when she spotted Melissa at the hostess stand near the door, chatting with a man who looked unsettlingly familiar.

Joel Rostovich.

Not quite six feet tall. Muscular as she remembered, yet thinner somehow. Short brown hair with beautiful golden-brown eyes that reminded her of a tiger. He needed a shave, but somehow the beard stubble that shaded his jaw and neck looked intentional—and gave his face an animalistic vibe. He wore a light blue polo shirt that exposed his beefy arms, some intricate tattoos on his forearms that disappeared beneath the sleeves of his shirt, and a mile of tanned skin that was broken up by several pale pink scars that made him look like he was no stranger to violence. He looked like a mixed martial arts fighter who'd come out of the cage on the losing end of things.

He'd worked for her husband.

He'd been kind to her.

But there was a hardness to him now. Even with the length and noise of the restaurant between them muting the actual words, she could hear a snap to his tone. She could see the wariness in his eyes that hadn't been there two years ago in the middle of the night in her kitchen prison when they'd met. And when he stepped around the hostess stand to follow Melissa to a table, she saw the badge hanging from a lanyard around his neck and the gun holstered to the waist of his khaki pants.

And she saw the cane.

Mollie frowned, a fist squeezing around her heart when she saw him move. He hadn't used a cane when they'd met two years ago. He hadn't had that slow, uneven gait, either.

She'd met him here at Pearl's Diner once again a few months back, during one of her first shifts at the restaurant. No limp then, either. He hadn't been at one of her tables, but there'd been another rude customer, a uniformed police officer who'd grabbed her, and she'd had a full-blown panic attack. Several customers had tried to come to her aid that night, including Joel. She realized he was a cop for the first time that night because he'd been wearing a standard blue KCPD uniform. She'd been too shocked to acknowledge him, although she had a feeling he recognized her, despite her different hair color, hairstyle, and working-class clothes. At least, he'd sensed something familiar about her.

Mollie gasped when Melissa turned down the long aisle of tables and booths near the front windows. *No, no, no. Do not seat him in my section. Do not...*

A compactly built man with short black hair streaked with silver at his temples stood and held out a hand to greet Joel. With a nod, if not a smile for the hostess, Joel shook the other man's hand before sliding into the booth across from him.

Mollie exhaled a worried sigh and wondered if she could get away with spending the rest of the day in the kitchen, instead of waiting tables and interacting with a man from her past.

Only, she couldn't get it out of her head that the man who'd just been seated at her table wasn't the same man she'd known before. It didn't have anything to do with him wearing a polo shirt instead of a KCPD uniform or chauffeur's suit and tie. *Softer* wasn't exactly the right word, but that man two years ago had been willing to help if she'd asked.

This man didn't look like he wanted to help anybody, like he wasn't even happy to meet the man who appeared to be an old friend for lunch. Like he wouldn't be happy to run into her again.

"Mollie." Herb's gruff reprimand made her jump and pull her gaze back to the faded gray eyes beneath his gray, bushy brows. "You're fallin' behind, girlie. Finish these plates and get back out there. Melissa's giving you the high sign."

Mollie acknowledged her boss's wave to get back out on the floor before dropping her gaze to the three plates in front of her, all waiting for fries and a bowl of whatever side they'd ordered. She checked the computer screen beside the window and dished up coleslaw and cottage cheese. She salted the fries and set the plates in the window. "Order up!"

"What's your mutt up to now?" Herb asked. He nudged his arm against hers and nodded through the pickup window.

Mollie watched Magnus pace behind the counter, his dark eyes focused on her. He scratched at the swinging door that separated the soda fountain area from the kitchen, then raised up on his hind legs, bracing his front paws on the edge of the metal sink and stretching his neck to get his nose closer to her. He repeated the entire process, whining as if he was calling her name.

Now he picked up on her stress?

Yes, baby. Come to Mama before I completely freak out in the middle of the lunch rush.

"His job," Mollie whispered. "He's finally doing his job."

Chapter Two

Joel Standage didn't think anything good could come from being summoned to a lunch meeting with his covert division supervisor, A. J. Rodriguez.

Not that he didn't like or admire the hell out of the short, muscular man who was a legend in undercover work at KCPD. A.J. had taken down more perps in his twenty years with the department—either working his own undercover operation, or training and providing support for the younger UC operators he now supervised—than just about any other detective on the force.

But Joel was barely a cop of any kind anymore. After blowing his last assignment—losing the woman he'd loved but apparently couldn't trust, and damn near his life—he'd been relegated to desk duty at the Fourth Precinct offices. And hell, it didn't seem that he was much good at even that. Poring through case files, running background checks, babysitting perps who were cooling their heels in interview rooms, and providing info support to the men and women on the front line was what cops who were turning gray or losing their hair near the end of their careers did. Intellectually, he understood those jobs provided vital services to every person wearing a badge. But emotionally, it made him feel like he was on his way out, too.

He'd made his way back after injuries that would have taken out a man who was any less fit than he'd been. But even with months of physical therapy, he knew he'd never be 100 percent again. The trouble was, he didn't know if he was at 90 percent, 75 percent or even a lousy 50 percent. And the sad fact was, he wasn't sure he wanted to find out.

He wasn't sure he cared much about being a cop anymore.

He was pretty damn sure no one else did, either. He had no close family who cared, and certainly no girlfriend, anymore.

Joel leaned his cane against the bench beside his new knee and toyed with the rolled-up napkin and silverware in front of him as he summoned a wry smile. "So, boss. To what do I owe the honor of having lunch with you?"

A.J.'s dark eyes sparkled with an amusement Joel didn't understand. "I wanted to get you out of the office, amigo. Have this meeting someplace where you couldn't hide behind your desk or computer and act like an invalid."

"I died on the operating table, A.J. I've got more metal in me now than that cherry Trans Am of yours. Technically, I *am* an invalid."

"Boo-hoo." The black-haired man leaned forward, resting his elbows on the table and steepling his fingers together. "Frankly, Joel—I wanted to see you get off your ass and get back to being the good cop I know you can be."

Well, that was straightforward enough.

He was on the verge of telling A.J. that any faith in him was misplaced when the waitress walked up to their table.

Not just any waitress. *Her.*

Mollie Di Salvo. "Hi."

Joel tilted his face up at her quiet greeting and watched her set two glasses on the table in front of them with a barely there smile. She'd changed her hair. It was shorter, curlier, darker—earthier and more natural than the straight blond tresses he remembered. But it made her big blue eyes pop like pools of cobalt against her pale skin. He'd recognize those blue eyes anywhere.

What was the ex-wife of one of Kansas City's wealthiest men doing waiting tables in the City Market District? When he'd seen her here last October, he'd assumed it was a stopgap job until her alimony money came in or she found herself a better job. But that was nine months ago. Why was she still here?

"Welcome to Pearl's Diner." Her gaze moved carefully between A.J. and him, taking in the badges and guns they wore. And the cane. And the scars. Joel shifted uncomfortably in his seat and pulled his arms beneath the table. Did she recognize the pale shadow of the man he'd been when they met two years ago? Did she feel pity for him? "Can I get you anything else to drink? Iced tea? Coffee with cream, right? Or something from our soda fountain? It *is* hot outside."

"Mrs. Di Salvo." Joel's greeting was gruff and terse. "You know how I drink my coffee? I haven't been to Pearl's in months. And you didn't wait on me then."

She shrugged. "Actually, I remember from that night at…" The barely there smile disappeared completely.

"The Di Salvo estate." They'd talked for all of ten minutes that night. Either she had an eidetic memory, or she had the kind of brain that simply recalled random details about the people she met.

"I didn't know you were a police officer then, Mr. Rostovich." She clasped her order pad between her hands and hugged it against her chest. Although her voice said cool and polite, her posture screamed tension. Maybe even fear. "Not that it would have made it easier for me to trust you. You worked for my husband. That alone meant I couldn't trust you."

Looked like she still had her survival skills down pat. Underplay her knowledge. Hide her emotions.

Joel curled his hands into fists on top of his thighs, surprised by the urge to take her hand and give her a reassuring squeeze. Or even hug her as tightly as she clutched that pen and order pad—if that would ease the discomfort radiating off her in waves. "You were doing what was necessary to protect yourself." He reassured her verbally since touching her was out of the question for far too many reasons. "And it's Standage. Joel Standage. Rostovich was a role I was playing."

"To investigate Augie?"

"Yes, ma'am." Not that it had done them any good. In the end, August Di Salvo had walked away from his trial a free man, thanks to conflicting witness statements and a technicality that had rendered other testimony—like his own—inadmissible in court. And the DA's office wasn't willing to prosecute Di Salvo again until they could put together an airtight case against him. "I'm sorry we couldn't keep him in jail."

Her soft, rose-tinted lips pressed together in a tight frown. "Augie's parents spent a lot of money to make his troubles go away."

So, the rumors of witness intimidation and bribery were probably true. Did she include herself as one of those *trou-

bles? But again, why would she be waiting tables at a home-spun diner if she'd been paid off with Di Salvo money?

A.J. drummed his fingers on the Formica tabletop, joining the conversation. "Di Salvo? You're Mollie Di Salvo?"

Her blue gaze swung to A.J., then moved on past him to the soda fountain at the back of the seating area. Joel narrowed his gaze when he saw the blur of brown and black fur pacing behind the counter. Was that a dog in the restaurant? He looked like one of the Belgian Malinois dogs that worked in the K-9 division. Joel's frown of confusion deepened when Mollie raised her hand beside her shoulder as if she was taking an oath, and the dog sat.

The dog's dark, nearly black, eyes remained focused on her as she looked back at A.J. "That's not my name anymore. And I'd appreciate you not repeating it out loud. I'm Mollie Crane now."

More curious and faintly disappointed than he wanted to be, Joel asked, "You got remarried?"

He glanced at her ten unadorned fingers. Although, she might not be wearing a ring because of the work she did here.

"Divorced," she answered, clutching the order pad to her chest again. "Not that it's any of your business. As you might remember, that was a...bad situation for me. I went back to my maiden name."

Bad situation was an understatement. Bruises the size of a man's hands around her neck. A black eye that was swollen nearly shut. Struggling to catch her breath against the pain of a gut punch or kick. Her husband had been a bully and a bastard with work, his staff, and the woman he supposedly loved—and Joel hadn't been able to get enough intel to keep the man in prison after his arrest for a myriad of white-collar crimes. Yeah. He remembered her *bad situation*.

Although she had shadows of fatigue under her striking blue eyes, and she needed to put a few pounds on her skinny frame, he didn't see any obvious signs of violence on her today. "You okay now?"

He was obliquely aware of A.J. watching the whole interchange with curiosity.

Mollie tapped her pad with her pen, ignoring his question. "Drinks?"

Did that mean no, she wasn't okay and needed help? Or, was she dismissing him as in, *It's none of your business, Standage*?

Joel sank against the back of the booth, wondering why he cared one way or the other about her answer. He acknowledged the flutter of concern that quickened his pulse at the idea she could still be in danger, knowing he was a man who could help her. He was equally aware of the dark cloud of colossal failure that settled like an ice-cold storm front in his brain. He had no business rescuing anybody. Not anymore.

If only he'd picked up on those signs of rejection from Cici before that fateful night. He'd felt the distance growing between him and his fiancée. He'd been working too much, and he'd suspected she'd gone back to using again. But he'd been trying to make things right. He'd been in rescue mode, determined to save her from her addiction and remind her of the relationship that had once flourished between them.

Meanwhile, Cici had been using her knowledge about Joel's job as payment for the opioids that ruled her life. And when information alone was no longer enough for her suppliers, she'd fingered him as a cop working undercover in their organization. Cici hadn't survived the hell they'd put her through for keeping his identity a secret for so long. And Joel had literally died trying to save her one last time.

Joel was lost in the painful memories when A.J. spoke again. "You're right, ma'am. It's too hot for coffee today. I'll take iced tea. Plenty of ice. No lemon."

Those big blue eyes looked at Joel, and he nearly forgot the question. Drinks. *Get your head in the game, Standage.* "Same."

"What can I get you gentlemen to eat?" She jotted down their order, gathered their plastic menus, and left as politely and quietly as she'd come.

Joel watched her every step of the way, as she stopped and picked up some empty plates from one table, set them in a tub in a window to the kitchen, then put in their order on a computer at the far end of the soda fountain. The dog he'd noticed earlier followed her every step, then sat on his haunches beside her while she tapped the order onto the screen. Mollie's left hand slipped down to pet the dog's head. She murmured something, and the dog leaned against her. After she tapped in the last item on the screen, he watched a real smile blossom across her mouth as she dropped to her knees and hugged the dog around the shoulders. Definitely her dog, judging by the attachment the two shared.

Joel nearly smiled himself at the tender moment, when he noticed the vest the dog wore. It was more than a harness to connect a leash to. The vest had a handle, reflective tape, and the words *Service Dog* emblazoned on it.

Why did Mollie Crane need a service dog? Was she in some kind of trouble? Had she been left with a medical condition from the injuries August Di Salvo had repeatedly given her? It wouldn't be a stretch to suspect she'd been left with some kind of post-traumatic stress after surviving that marriage, either.

Joel straightened in his seat, the rusty urge to find out what was wrong and what he could do to help sparking through his veins. Only, he wasn't really much help to anybody these days. He dug his fingertips into his rebuilt legs, remembering pain without truly feeling it. He was a thirty-two-year-old man, hobbled up like he was decades older, and unable to fully trust anybody—not even himself.

What the hell kind of help did he think he could offer the prickly waitress?

He watched the tough woman push to her feet and order the dog to his bed at the end of the counter before washing her hands and carrying a tray out to another table. She'd been clear about not wanting his help two years ago. Why should he think anything had changed since then?

A.J. drew his attention back to him. "You two have a connection?"

"We met when I was working undercover for August Di Salvo. I was his driver. She was the missus. He beat the crap out of her, and I tried to help. Without success." Joel's gaze continued to track Mollie as she moved around the diner. "I couldn't get her out of that situation. To be honest, after that first night I found her with choke marks on her neck and a black eye, I didn't have much contact with her. Di Salvo kept her isolated from staff like me. I drove her a few places, but someone was always with her—Di Salvo, his parents, security. They didn't let her say much. She must have gotten herself out of the marriage somehow after I left."

"She remembers you."

"I ran into her one more time last year. Here at Pearl's. She must have just started working. A customer—one of our boys in blue, sadly—was getting handsy with her." Joel shook his head at the memory. "Rocky Garner? He works patrol."

A.J.'s laugh held little humor. "I know him. He's not doing KCPD any favors in the PR department."

Joel knew the veteran cop's reputation, too, having researched him after the incident. He couldn't recall the exact number of times Garner had been put on report for using excessive force or being inappropriate with female suspects. But it was enough to keep him from advancing in rank. Garner had to be a decade older than Joel, and he'd yet to make sergeant or earn his detective's shield. "I tried to help, but Mollie acted like she had no clue who I was. It wasn't too long after that I went on my...last assignment." The one that had nearly got him killed, gutted him emotionally, and left him sitting at a desk at KCPD. "Didn't expect she'd still be here after all this time. I figured waiting tables was a stopgap measure for her. Until her alimony came through, or she got hired for another job." He briefly replayed that encounter in his head. "She didn't have the dog with her then, either."

Joel felt A.J. studying him and met his dark gaze with an arched eyebrow. "Think you could rekindle your acquaintance with her? Develop a friendship?"

"What?" Oh, no. His boss couldn't be asking what he thought he was. "I don't do UC work anymore, A.J. Besides, she saw me in uniform last year." He fingered the lanyard and badge hanging from his neck. "She knows I'm a cop."

"You don't have to pretend to be anything but a cop. I'm

not asking you to marry the woman or infiltrate this place as a fry cook. But it couldn't hurt to chat her up and find out what she knows about Di Salvo's operation. Word on the street is that he's courting some new business associates. And not the respectable kind." A.J. leaned in again, dropping his voice to a low-pitched whisper. "We couldn't make the charges stick the last time. I'd love to have dirt on his lawyer, who got him off with a slap on the wrist, and find out how his parents got our witnesses to recant their testimony. And I'd love to find out about his dealings with Roman Hess. That guy's as dirty as they come. If we could tie those two together, we could make an arrest stick on both of them."

Joel couldn't believe what he was hearing. A.J. wasn't playing. "You want to go after the entire Di Salvo empire?"

"They play at being pillars of the community, but I think they're all dirty. At the least, they're laundering money for a half dozen criminal organizations across the country. At worst, they're making a play to control this city on the scale of Tom Pendergast in the 1920s and '30s, or the Meade family in the 2000s." The senior detective relaxed back in his seat, as if this ambitious assignment was a done deal. "I've talked this over with Chief Taylor. He's all in for launching another investigation into the Di Salvo family."

And now this meeting made sense.

"Did you know Mollie worked here when you invited me to lunch?"

A.J. didn't try to deny it. "One—you don't belong behind a desk. You've got good instincts about people—"

"That's crap."

"With the glaring exception of your ex. Otherwise, you read people. You read situations. I bet I could ask you about any person in this diner, and you could tell me their location, what they're doing, and if I need to be worried about any of them."

Maybe he could. Although, the only thing alarming him right now was this conversation. "Two—you can keep your cool when things go sideways. That's a natural talent you're wasting shuffling papers behind a desk. Three—your detective's badge is going to get rusty if you don't start actively working cases again. I don't want to lose you. KCPD doesn't want to lose you. What your woman did to you is every undercover cop's worst nightmare. But you survived. I'm sure you've got some PTSD from everything you went through—and I hope you're seeing Dr. Kilpatrick-Harrison or one of the other department counselors for that."

He was. Although he'd missed one appointment because of a conflict with his physical therapy schedule. And he had simply skipped the last two because he hated talking about the damn feelings he couldn't yet put into words.

"Did she report me for not showing up?" Joel asked, wondering if that was another reason for this meeting.

"Dr. Kilpatrick-Harrison said she was worried about you. Brought it to my attention that you keep putting off your appointments."

"Maybe I'm not interested in passing her psych eval and getting back out on the streets."

A.J. scowled. "I'm not just talking as your supervisor here, Joel. I'm talking as your friend. Don't let those bastards break you. Don't let them change the good man you are. Take this assignment. Prove to yourself that you're still a good cop. That you're still a good man who deserves to be happy. Who needs to feel useful. Who has to learn how to trust again." He paused to let his words sink in. "Like I said, this is not deep cover. You don't have to be anything but a KCPD detective. But if you could get close to Mollie Di Salvo—"

"Mollie Crane," Joel corrected.

A.J. nodded. "All I'm asking is that you get close enough to Mollie *Crane* to find out what—if anything—she knows about her ex-husband's criminal activities. If she's in the dark about him, then you're done. If you find out she can help us in any way, then we'll have another discussion about what our next step is at that time."

He'd been physically cleared to return to active duty, but he wasn't sure he was mentally ready. There was a part of him that wanted to get back into the game, but he was equally leery of misjudging the people around him so badly that he'd be setting himself up for a world of hurt. Again. Or worse, letting someone else down the way he'd failed his late girlfriend.

He visually tracked down Mollie and found her fussing impatiently with her dog, using hand signals and looking a little flustered. "I wouldn't know how to start a relationship, anymore. Real or fake."

"Find out what she cares about." A.J. turned to follow Joel's focus as Mollie fell to her knees and petted the dog, then teased him with a large gray toy that looked suspiciously like a teddy bear. "Never mind. I think your first step is pretty obvious."

"What's that?"

A.J. grinned. "Ask her about the dog."

THE MAN WITH the binoculars merged into the shadows inside his parked car. Although there was still some sun warming the sky on this late summer night, he was an expert at blending in and being overlooked, underestimated. When he did want someone's attention, he knew how to get it. But the time wasn't right for that yet. He learned so much more, was far more successful in getting things done, when he hung back to assess a situation first—learn the players and what he might be up against. Knowledge was power. Knowing his enemy's weak points and how to exploit them gave him the control over others that he craved.

He watched the woman walking her mutt across the street, dumping the plastic bag of excrement she'd dutifully picked up in the public trash can on the sidewalk as they hurried past his position. Although her gaze was on a swivel, looking for any threats, she didn't see him.

"There you are, sweetheart." He glanced down at the crumpled photograph in his lap, then lifted his gaze to study her again. Mollie Di Salvo could change her hair color and the quality of her clothes, but she hadn't changed her face. Even without makeup, he'd know her anywhere. She exuded that natural, all-American country girl vibe that he found so prosaic. "I've got you now."

It hadn't been hard to track down her place of work. But with an unlisted, pay-by-the-minute phone number and address, it had been harder to identify where she was hiding herself these days. Her apartment was in an older, well-maintained three-story red brick building, just a few blocks from Pearl's Diner and the pocket park at City Market, where she'd exercised her dog.

His lips curled with an arrogant smile. Once, she'd been at the top of Kansas City society. Now her world had shrunk to three city blocks.

She pulled a key card from the purse slung over her shoulder before crossing the street and approaching her building. He'd get inside another time to locate her exact apartment. For now, he was learning her routine. Did she work the same schedule at the diner every day? Walk the same route home every night? Did she drive a car? Take public transportation? Was she seeing anyone? Who were her friends?

Was that mangy wannabe police dog with her 24/7?

Did she think that reject of a mutt was going to protect her? When the time came, if he couldn't distract the dog with a steak, he'd shoot the mutt. He had plans for Miss Mollie, and he didn't want to be interrupted by man or beast.

She'd dishonored the Di Salvo family. Maybe she even thought she had outsmarted them. No Di Salvo, and no one who had ever worked for them, would tolerate what she'd done for long. If she didn't know there was a target on her back, she was sadly oblivious.

He could play this game for a while. Have fun with her. Edward and Bernadette would be so pleased with his initiative. And if he wasn't amply rewarded by the people who were supposed to respect him, then he'd take what he was missing out of Miss Mollie's hide.

He might get in trouble for it. But the satisfaction would be so worth it.

Besides, he'd have to get caught first.

And no one had ever been able to take him down.

Chapter Three

Even though it was his day off, and Joel could wear jeans and a T-shirt and forgo shaving his morning scruff, he still looped his badge around his neck and strapped his gun to his belt to remind himself that he didn't have to play any undercover part. If he was going to do this, he intended to be straight up-front with Mollie Crane about who and what he was.

After locking the door to his small gray bungalow, he paused for a few moments to scan up and down the block. He acknowledged his widowed neighbor out watering the flowers blooming in a riot of pots on her front porch. He recognized the cars parked in driveways, and took note of the people driving past he didn't know. His heart revved a little and his fist closed around the handle of his cane when one young man turned in the driver's seat and made eye contact with him.

But the guy kept on driving until he turned into a driveway farther down the block. One of the teenage girls who lived there charged out the front door and hurried to climb inside the passenger side of the car. The two teens kissed, then waved to the girl's father standing in the doorway before backing out of the drive and heading on their way.

Not the enemy. Not a contact from his past. Not a threat marking him for death.

Forcing his heartbeat to slow, he headed down the concrete steps and crossed to the faded red Chevy pickup in the driveway. Mentally, he knew the older neighborhood of Brookside, south of downtown Kansas City, was a decent, safe place to live. He'd hoped to move Cici in one day, get married, and start a family together. But she hadn't wanted him to save her. Emotionally, he still felt the loss of that pipe dream—she'd loved the drugs more than she loved him. He understood now not to take anything or anyone at face value. Everyone had secrets they were willing to die for—or kill for—to keep. And he wasn't going to be blindsided by putting his trust in the wrong person again.

He opened the truck door and shoved his cane across the bench seat. The plain metal stick was more of a mental crutch than a physical one these days, but when his muscles got achy from overuse or a change in the weather, he liked to have it with him to keep from limping along like an old man, or worse, falling flat on his face. He'd briefly considered playing up his wounded warrior status to gain Mollie's sympathy and develop a relationship in which she felt compelled to take care of him and thus spend more time with him.

But the small print on his man card didn't want her to see him that way—weak, damaged, something less. He wanted to be the man he used to be around her—sharp, confident, a few steps ahead of everyone else in the room. He thought Mollie was pretty. She seemed quiet and sweet, if understandably skittish about men. And though she wasn't acting much like it now, the woman he'd met that night at the Di Salvo estate had a backbone of steel. All things he would have been attracted to if he hadn't been burned so badly by Cici—things he was *still* attracted to if he was honest with himself. It was his faith in his own judgment and ability to handle a relationship that he needed to shore up before he got involved with another woman.

Not that he was getting involved with Mollie Crane.

Not an undercover op. He didn't have to watch his back or keep an eye out for whomever might trade his life for another fix. He was a cop, straight up. Just a cop following up on his supervisor's strongly worded suggestion that he strike up a friendship with one Mollie Crane, previously Di Salvo, and see if he could get any inside information on a man who'd gotten away with breaking numerous laws and hurting too many people for way too long. Joel had to remember to look at this as if he was cultivating a CI, a confidential informant, who might be able to help the department build a case against her ex.

This absolutely was not a date. Or the prelude to one.

But he had to admit he was a little bit excited—and a little bit nervous—about cultivating a relationship with Mollie. Not unlike the way he'd felt years ago in high school when he'd worked up the courage to ask the girl he liked out on his first date.

Not a date!

Reminding himself to stay in the moment and not worry about any suspicions or self-doubts, Joel climbed inside the pickup that was as up-to-date and well taken care of under the hood as it was beat-up on the outside. He loved how the engine purred with power when he turned over the ignition. His face relaxed with a genuine smile. At least one part of him hadn't been shredded by the incident with Cici. He loved working on engines in his spare time and had done a bang-up job restoring his truck and keeping it running like a dream under the hood. Giving himself a mental slap on the back, he backed out of the driveway and headed toward the City Market north of downtown. Ten minutes later, he was pulling into a parking space around the corner from Pearl's Diner.

Leaning on his cane, he took a couple of deep breaths. He'd timed his arrival for what he hoped was the end of the lunch rush so that Mollie wouldn't be too distracted by work. Plus, there'd be a smaller audience to see him and give him grief back at the Precinct offices, if his efforts to get better acquainted with the blue-eyed waitress crashed and burned. There always seemed to be someone from KCPD here, thanks to the diner's location, its early and late hours, and its delicious, homestyle food.

Taking one last deep breath, Joel pulled open the door to the diner and walked up to the petite blonde who was wiping down menus at the hostess stand. "Mrs. Kincaid?"

She looked up and studied him from head to toe, taking in his casual dress, his gun and his badge number before she met his gaze again. "Detective Standage, is it?"

"Yes, ma'am. I wasn't sure you remembered me."

"You're A.J.'s friend."

He smirked before correcting her. "He's my boss, actually. But yes, I met him here the other day."

"I remember." She tucked the menus away, save for one. "You're here by yourself today?" When he nodded, she turned away and headed toward a small table. "This way."

"Could you seat me in Mollie's section?" With a quick scan of the diner, he didn't immediately spot the curly-haired waitress. A brief moment of panic that he hadn't been smart enough to check to see if she was working today quickly passed when he saw the Belgian Malinois curled up asleep on his bed behind the soda fountain. He smiled. The dog wouldn't be here unless Mollie was. "I'd like to talk to her. But I'll order food if I need to. I don't want to get her in trouble."

The diner owner faced him again. "Does she know you're coming?"

"No, ma'am. To be honest, I had to work up the courage to come here and talk to her." He tapped his leg with his cane. "I'm a little out of practice with polite society."

The petite blonde crossed her arms in front of her and canted her hips to one side, studying him again. He got the sense she was looking for something different this time. "You're interested in Mollie? In the nine months I've known her, she's never dated anyone. FYI? You've got a tough hill to climb if that's your goal."

She didn't know the half of it. "We're old acquaintances. The last few months have been tough for me. I'm looking to rekindle a friendship with someone from before that time." None of that was a lie. Although, it sure sounded like he was interested in more than a friendship with Mollie Crane.

"Are you a good man?" Melissa asked bluntly.

Joel stood up a little straighter. "I try to be. I don't know exactly what kind of man I am anymore. Like I said, I'm out of practice."

"It doesn't matter what your social skills are, Detective. You're either a good man or you're not." She arched a golden eyebrow at him. "Don't be offended if I ask my husband about you."

"Sawyer?" He'd worked some cases with the decorated detective and believed the respect he felt for Sawyer Kincaid was mutual. "I think he'd give me a decent recommendation. But I'm glad you're looking out for the people who work for you. Makes me believe Mollie's safer now than she was before."

"Good answer." Her lips curled into a full-blown smile. Strong and beautiful. No wonder his coworker was so head over heels with her. "Come on. I'll seat you at the counter. You can catch Mollie when she goes on her break in a few minutes."

"Thank you, ma'am."

She waited until he was seated on the red vinyl stool before sliding the menu in front of him. "Uh-uh. I appreciate you being polite, but I'm not old enough to be a 'ma'am.' If Sawyer vets you, and Mollie okays it, then I'm Melissa, and you're welcome here anytime."

Joel summoned a smile of his own. "Thanks."

"I'll let her know you're here."

The diner's owner pushed through the swinging door into the kitchen. She came back out a minute or so later, nodded to him, then went back to her work at the front of the restaurant.

It was another minute or so before it swung open again and Mollie stepped out. She stood there a moment before looking to her dog and summoning him to her side. The dog leaned against her thigh, and she rested her hand atop his head before taking a deep breath and finally crossing to the opposite side of the counter from him. The dog followed right beside her and sat when she stopped. "Joel?"

He stood and hooked the handle of his cane on his side of the counter. "Hey, Mollie."

Although she continued to pet the dog's head, her blue eyes tilted up to meet his. "Melissa said you wanted to speak to me?"

Joel frowned at the pulse he could see beating in her neck. "Do I make you nervous?" he asked, refusing to acknowledge that his own heart rate had increased the moment he saw her.

"Lots of things make me nervous," she confessed, twisting her lips into a wry smile. She tipped her head toward Magnus. "That's why I keep this guy with me." He was surprised when she elaborated on what exactly was making her nervous now. "I don't like surprises. I didn't know you were coming today. Is this police business?"

"Why would it be police business?" He frowned at her question. Technically, he wasn't working on an active investigation. This was more of a fact-finding mission, finding out for A.J. if there was any new, compelling information that warranted launching a new investigation. Unless *Mollie* was expecting to be contacted by someone from KCPD? "Did something happen? Do you need a cop?"

"No," she answered quickly. "If you aren't working a case, why do you need to see me?"

Joel gave himself a mental reminder that Mollie Crane was an intelligent woman who'd proved herself a survivor. She might be nervous around him—around men—but that didn't mean she wasn't smart. He had a feeling she'd see right through any story he'd try to put over on her.

Admiring her courage to explain her reaction to him, Joel gestured to the stool beside him. "Melissa said you were ready to take a break. Would you like to sit down and have a coffee with me?"

Her uneasy reaction gave way to suspicion. "You mean like a date?"

"I mean like two people getting better acquainted, maybe even becoming friends." He leaned toward her and dropped his voice into a whisper. "I have a feeling I didn't get to meet the real Mollie two years ago. I know you didn't meet the real me."

She considered his invitation for a moment before tucking a loose curl beneath the headband she wore. "I need to take Magnus out for a walk to do his business and get some exercise."

"Around this neighborhood? By yourself?" There were a lot worse places in the city. But a woman alone on the streets of K.C.? Especially during the height of the tourist season this close to the City Market when there were hundreds of strangers, including the pickpockets and muggers who often accompanied large crowds, visiting the neighborhood? Wouldn't be his first choice if he was responsible for her safety.

But...he wasn't. *Not a date!*

"It's safe enough during the day." She offered him a slight smile that blossomed into something beautiful when she pulled a fuzzy gray teddy bear from beneath the counter and the dog danced in place beside her. "Magnus. Leash." The Belgian Malinois trotted over to his bed and came back carrying his leash in his mouth. He stood still for Mollie to attach it to his harness and was rewarded with words of praise and a short game of tug-of-war with his toy. "Besides, Magnus looks pretty scary, so no one bothers me."

Scary? With a teddy bear in his mouth? Although, the toy did look pretty mangled from where Joel was standing, so anyone who accosted Mollie might take the dog's energy, sharp teeth, and the strength of his jaw into consideration before approaching them. Instead of disparaging the ferociousness of her dog, Joel picked up his cane. "May I come with you?"

"To walk the dog?"

Ask her about the dog.

Remembering A.J.'s advice, he nodded. "I like dogs. Grew up with them. Although I haven't had one of my own since leaving home. My..." *late girlfriend didn't like them.* Nope. He wasn't going there with Mollie. He suspected the fact that he hadn't been able to keep his last girlfriend safe wouldn't earn him any trust points. "I miss being around one," he said, instead, dredging up his rusty skills that enabled him to say the right thing to the right person at the right time.

Mollie must have heard enough truth in his explanation to agree to his request to accompany her. "Okay." She thumbed over her shoulder to the kitchen. "We'll go out the back way. The alley comes out right across from the dog park where I take him during the day."

Joel nodded and followed Mollie and Magnus through the swinging door. He was inhaling the tantalizing scents of baking fruit pies and some Italian sauce sort of magic when a gravelly voice barked out, "What the hell is that mutt doin' in my kitchen? And who's this guy?"

"Language, Herb!" Joel had already stepped between Mollie and the grouchy shout when a woman with a blond ponytail waddled out from behind a bank of ovens. Her cheeks were flushed from the heat of the kitchen. She was about the same age and height as Mollie, and her arms were hugged around her very pregnant belly. She smiled at Mollie. "Whew! I wish I was going on your walk with Magnus. I feel like I'm the one baking in here."

Mollie nudged Joel aside to take the other woman's hand and squeeze it. "Didn't the doctor say you were supposed to stay off your feet as much as possible?" she chided gently. "I told you I know how to bake a good pie. My granny taught me."

The blonde woman kept hold of Mollie's hand. "Believe me, it's a lot easier to sit back here on a stool and work with the food than it is to wait tables. This little one will be here any day. I swear he's already half the size of Matt. Matt Taylor—that's my husband," she explained to Joel. "He's six-five." She rubbed her belly with her other hand as she smiled at him. "Who's your friend?"

A lanky older man with bushy gray eyebrows and an old USN tattoo on his forearm stepped up between the women. "Not my fault. I can't keep her sittin' down like she's supposed to be." He was where the growly voice had come from. "I swear to God, girlie, if you have that baby in my kitchen, *I'm* the one they'll be taking to the hospital." The words were complaints, but Joel thought he detected more of a protective papa bear in the man's stance. "You're sure he's a friend?" he asked Mollie. "You ain't never brought a man back here before. Hell, I ain't never seen you with a man, period. He ain't forcin' you to go somewhere, is he?"

Definitely a protective papa with the women who worked at the diner. "No, sir," Joel assured him, holding up his badge. "I'm one of the good guys. We're taking the dog for a walk."

"I'd like to hear that from her," he insisted.

"He's a friend, Herb." Joel glanced over to see Mollie smile at the older man. She put Magnus into a sit position, then made introductions. "Detective Joel Standage, this is my friend, Corie Taylor—responsible for all the delicious pies you've eaten here, and she's due to give birth to her second child next week."

"Not in my kitchen," the grouch with the bandanna tied around the top of his head insisted.

"And this grump is our chief cook and all-around ray of sunshine. Herb Valentino."

While Joel wanted to savor the unexpected snark in Mollie's comment and bask in the soft beauty of what he suspected was a rare smile, he remembered he was here hoping to earn Mollie's trust. Making friends with her friends seemed to be a good way to start. He extended his hand to the older man and nodded toward the faded black tattoo on his forearm. "You're a Navy man. Thank you for your service."

Herb seemed a little flustered to be acknowledged for his time in the military. But like the Navy men Joel knew best, he was proud to claim his ties to the letters and anchor inked on his arm. He reached out to shake Joel's hand. "I served twenty years on boats. Ten years on an aircraft carrier. I ran a tight mess."

"My dad was in the Gulf during Desert Storm. Marine. Demolitions expert. Defused a lot of land mines."

Herb's grip on Joel's hand tightened with a begrudging mutual respect. "He make it home?"

"Yes, sir." By the time they released hands, the cook seemed to see him as less of an intruder in his kitchen. "He stuck with it for twenty years. Now he's an accountant here in K.C. Just a few years away from his civilian retirement."

"You didn't follow him into the service?"

Joel shook his head. "No mom in the picture. She left when I was eighteen. I was the oldest of three boys. I raised my younger brothers while Dad finished up his commitment. Both my brothers serve now, though. Army National Guard and a career Marine."

"You serve our city as a police officer," Mollie pointed out from beside him.

"Yeah, I do." He glanced over at her and nodded his thanks for her support. "Dad remarried a few years back. Sweet lady. Another accountant in his office."

Corie pointed to Mollie and grinned. "Mollie is our numbers guru here. She tutored my son through his HAL math class, that's High Ability Learner, meaning I didn't understand his pre-Calculus, and she worked out a huge snafu in the books here at the diner. The cook who was here before Herb was ordering food on the sly to supply his own pop-up restaurant—on Melissa's tab."

"Fired his ass," Herb added. "Good thing I came along when I did. These two little ladies were trying to run this kitchen on their own. With no clue how to do it for paying customers. Slow as molasses."

Corie linked her arm through Herb's. "We make good food, but we're nowhere near as fast as this guy. Like he said, he runs a tight kitchen."

"Don't make me blush, girlie," the older man groused before shooing Joel and Mollie toward the back door. "You two get on with whatever you're doin' and get that mutt out of here."

"He's a service dog," Mollie reminded the gruff cook. "I'm allowed to have him with me wherever I go. He's never bothered anything in your kitchen."

"Well, I don't have to like it. And don't be late comin' back because I'll need your help gettin' prepped for the dinner shift." He patted Corie's hand where it rested on his arm. "I'm sendin' this one home."

Mollie nodded. "I'll help until Melissa needs me out front. And Corie? Listen to Herb. Go home if you need to.

Put your feet up. I can pull the pies out of the oven and do the prep work when I get back."

"And have my darling husband hovering over me 24/7? The baby's room has been ready for a month. My grand-mother-in-law gave me that great baby shower. At least here I'm allowed to do something." Corie shooed them on their way, too. "Go. No matter what this guy says, the baby and I are fine. Not my first rodeo."

Mollie glanced over at Joel and tweaked her lips into an-other wry expression, as if she was rethinking saying yes to spending a few minutes with him. He needed to move them along before he failed his first assignment out of the office since coming back from his medical leave. "Maybe I should—"

"We'd better get going before your break is over," Joel pointed out. "Magnus needs his exercise."

Mollie nodded. "Of course, he does."

"Don't forget your key so you can get back in," Corie reminded her.

Mollie patted her apron pocket. "I've got it."

Joel nodded to the cook and baker. "Nice to meet you both." He automatically brushed his fingers across the small of Mollie's back to turn her to the back door and tried not to take it personally when she scooted away from his touch.

She peeled off her sweater and tied the sleeves around her middle, unwittingly accenting her narrow waist and the flare of her hips, before tucking the teddy bear into the waistband created by the sweater. Giving a slight tug on the leash, she urged the dog into step between them. "Magnus, heel."

More distance. But considering who she'd been married to, Joel could understand how she'd be reluctant to have a man anywhere near her. He had his work cut out for him to earn her trust. But as long as she was willing to have a conversation with him, he'd take it as a win.

Chapter Four

Joel held open the heavy steel door that led into the alley behind the diner. Magnus leaped over the concrete step onto the asphalt and Mollie followed quickly behind him.

While he was instantly assaulted with the heat and humidity of the July afternoon, goose bumps pricked along his forearms. A potential ambush was his past talking, not the here and now. But it was second nature for him to check up and down the thoroughfare between two busy side streets, ensuring it was empty of traffic and pedestrians. The dumpster and recycling bin behind the restaurant gave easy places for someone to hide, as did the light poles and recessed doorways leading into the building across the alley.

He quickly shook off his suspicions and jogged to catch up with Mollie as she and Magnus headed toward the end of the alley at a fast clip. He couldn't help but check each hidey-hole as he passed it. But there was no enemy hidden here. And despite the sketchiness of a back alley, this one was remarkably clean. Other than a collection of cigarette butts on the ground at one back door, indicating a smoking area for employees, no doubt, there was no overflowing trash piled up beside the bins and dumpsters. And it looked like it would be well lit at night, judging by the lights on the centermost pole and above every door.

His nostrils flared with a steadying breath. He should be aware of his surroundings, but being paranoid about the bogeyman or some drug dealer's enforcer lying in wait to take him down would just mess with his head and keep him from being able to protect Mollie or himself if there was a real threat.

Of course, he wasn't here as her protector. The skills were there, but they were rusty. Thank goodness, this was all about striking up a friendship. *Not a date. Not a UC op where he had to be on guard around the clock. Just get reacquainted with the woman and talk. Then set up another time to talk again.*

Mollie looked over at him when he stepped up to the other side of Magnus. "You're moving pretty well without your cane," she pointed out.

He shrugged. "It's more for emergencies—in case my leg gives out."

"Does it give out a lot?"

He didn't want to read anything in her concerned tone. "Not really. Not anymore. I've had a lot of physical therapy to rebuild my muscle tone. It's more of a mental thing. For security."

She reached down and stroked Magnus's fur. "I understand that. Here's my security blanket." They stood in awkward silence for another minute, waiting for the light to change at the corner and allow them to cross safely. "I hope Herb didn't offend you," she said. The dog had dutifully stopped when she did, although he was panting with excitement at the outing. "It took me a while to figure out his bark is worse than his bite."

Glad for the change in topic, Joel smiled. "They're protective of you. Everyone who works at the diner is."

"We're protective of each other."

The light changed, and they waited for a black Lexus with tinted windows to turn at the corner and drive past before they stepped off the curb and crossed the street to the pocket park. A couple reading a walking tour map skirted around them on the sidewalk. An older gentleman walked his miniature schnauzer out of the dog park across the street and latched the gate behind him before heading down the opposite sidewalk. Although Magnus's head swiveled on alert to both the tourists and the dog, he remained at Mollie's side unless she clicked her tongue behind her teeth and ordered Magnus into step beside her.

Although the grassy area of the dog park was only about twelve feet deep between the fence lining the sidewalk and the brick building on the opposite side, it stretched from one end of the half block to the other. There were benches and a leafy maple tree at either end, plus a waste bag dispenser and covered trash can chained to the fence near the gate.

"An urban dog playground," he mused, watching as Mollie unhooked Magnus from his leash and gave him permission to run and be off duty for a few minutes.

"I suppose so." Mollie wound his leash in her fist and headed for the shade at one end of the park. "Local fundraisers added the fake hydrant, agility ramp, and plastic barrel just last month. I imagine every dog in the neighborhood loves to come here and sniff and mark their territory."

She perched on one end of the bench and watched Magnus check out every object that was geared toward dogs, as well as the tree and bench at the far end of the park. She busied her hands with the woeful teddy bear and gave Joel a sideways glance to see if he was going to sit beside her. Taking the cue from her guarded posture, he sat at the far end of the bench, beyond arm's reach, and she inhaled a deep breath. At the same time, her tummy growled. "Oops. Sorry about that."

"Am I keeping you from eating your lunch?"

"No," she answered a little too quickly for him to believe her.

His concern was genuine. "I don't want to be the reason you don't get enough food to eat today." He thumbed over his shoulder across the street. "We can head back."

"I'll eat dinner before I go home. Or I'll box up something to take with me." She paused long enough for Magnus to come trotting back to her for pets before he nudged at the teddy bear with his nose. "Silly boy. Go get it." She tossed the bear across the grass and Magnus tore out after it. "I've lost weight since the last time you saw me, haven't I."

"Yeah. But you've still got curves in all the right places." She raised her eyebrows at that comment. Maybe he should apologize, but he'd meant what he'd said. When Magnus returned and dropped the bear into her lap, Joel held his hand out for it. "May I?" Dark brown eyes followed the bear from Mollie's hand to his. "Go get it, boy!" He hurled the bear halfway across the park and watched the athletic dog chase it down and retrieve it. "Not that I should be noticing. But hey, I'm a guy. And I just want you to be healthy."

She chuckled softly, and Joel couldn't tear his gaze away from her gentle smile. With coffee-colored curls catching in the breeze and drifting across her cheeks and jawline, her skin flushed with the heat, and not a stitch of makeup that he could detect, he was struck full force by her natural beauty.

He felt himself smiling, too. "What? What did I say to make you laugh?"

"I heard my grandmother's voice in my head when you said that. *Are you healthy, Mollie Belle? Are you taking care of yourself? Eating right?* She was a fabulous cook, and she always fed me too much. When I went off to college, those questions came up in nearly every conversation we had." She tossed Magnus's teddy bear one more time, then tucked those loose curls back into the headband she wore. He could guess by the smile, and how it wistfully faded away, that her grandmother was a special, yet sad memory for her. "I'm not starving, Joel. Admittedly, when I first started working here, I didn't have a lot of money in my bank account." She shook her head. "Who am I kidding? I didn't even have a bank account back then. But Melissa took pity on me. She fed me breakfast during the job interview. Hired me before I'd finished my coffee. I'm not the best waitress, but I can put up with Herb, so I think she keeps me around for that reason alone." Joel grinned as he was meant to. "Plus, she has a soft spot for a hard-luck case like me and Magnus. Pearl—the original owner of the diner—gave Melissa a break when she needed one. I hope to pay her generosity forward one day, too."

Any urge to smile faded. Where was Mollie's money from her divorce? Joel made a mental note to research some court records to find out if there was some sort of legal issue with her alimony. Or if Di Salvo's slick lawyer had gotten him out of paying anything, just like he'd gotten August Di Salvo off on the major charges that had been brought against him. But instead of pressing for info related to her ex right this minute, he asked, "You have enough money for food now?"

Mollie nodded. "I have an account at the Cattlemen's Bank extension over by the City Market now. And a studio apartment down the street that allows dogs. It's just stress. I don't always feel like eating."

"You have to eat to keep your strength up, Moll." He left his cane leaning against the bench and stood to play a vigorous game of tug-of-war with Magnus. Once he'd won, the high-energy Belgian Malinois danced and drooled, eager for Joel to throw the toy again. "Go get it!" Joel looked down at Mollie. "It was just an observation. I sure hope I don't sound like your grandmother."

Although it was barely a noise in her throat, he loved that she laughed again. "My granny was five foot nothing. You're a giant compared to her. Heck, so was I, and I'm only five-six. She had a beautiful, melodic voice. Not like that gravelly tone you have." She nodded to the ink sticking out beneath the sleeves of his T-shirt. "And, absolutely no tats on Granny. So, no worries that I'm confusing the two of you." He liked that she'd noticed some details about him. He also noted that the moment she started talking about her grandmother, her shoulders relaxed their stiff posture and she'd pulled a silver locket from the neckline of her uniform and was rubbing it between her fingers. "It's having somebody worrying about me that made me think of her."

Her smile disappeared abruptly, and she tucked the locket back inside her dress. "You look like you've lost weight, too. I mean you've still got muscles in all the right places, but…" She blushed as she realized she'd echoed the compliment he'd given her earlier. "Does it have something to do with your injuries?"

Joel grabbed his cane and sat again. The topic was bound to come up. And since he'd probed into her health issues, it was probably only fair that he share a bit of his recent past, too. "I was in the hospital for a couple of months. Multiple surgeries on both legs." He turned his left arm in front of him, pointing out the pink puckers of skin that marred the lines of tribal symbols and motivational words that curled around his forearm. "Some of the cuts got infected."

"That sounds horrible. What happened?" Gunshot to both his knees. A couple of thugs trying to butcher him alive while he was incapacitated. Beating what was left of him and then literally dumping him in the trash. He'd lost so much blood by the time he reached the hospital that his heart had stopped. Drug dealers didn't take kindly to cops who infiltrated their operation. When he didn't answer, Mollie came up with her own explanation. "Sounds like you were in a horrible accident."

"I got hurt working a case," he responded vaguely.

She looked as though she suspected there was more to his injuries, but he wasn't going to share the gory details. He was here to get her to talk—not the other way around.

But she had an inkling that he'd suffered more than a car accident. "Did Augie's men do that to you?" she asked in a strained whisper. She reached toward one of the scars but pulled away before making contact, and Joel regretted missing the chance to find out what her skin felt like against his. "He had a man who worked for him, Beau Regalio. Augie called him his bodyguard, but he could be—"

"I know who Beau is." An enforcer of the first order. He'd confiscated one of Beau's guns that he'd turned in as evidence, but somehow Di Salvo's lawyer had gotten the forensic report tying the weapon to a witness tampering crime tossed out on a technicality. "No, he didn't hurt me. I was done working your ex-husband's case when this happened." He hated the words coming out of his mouth. "Did Beau ever hurt you?"

Her skin blanched, and she shook her head. "That was Augie's prerogative. But Beau never looked away. It was almost like he…enjoyed the violence. You're the only one in that house who ever tried to help me."

Joel swore beneath his breath. "I should have done something more."

"No." He flinched when her compassion finally overcame her fear, and her fingertips brushed across his forearm. Her touch was soft and cool against his warm skin, but she didn't linger. "You couldn't risk blowing your cover and jeopardize your investigation. I know that now."

He nodded. "Plus, money buys a lot of loyalty. We couldn't make the major charges against your ex stick because witnesses changed their testimony and evidence simply disappeared."

"If I could have stopped Augie from hurting people…" A warm breeze caught her hair and dragged a curl across her cheek. Joel clenched his fingers around his cane to keep from reaching out to tuck it back behind her ear. "Defying him was never really an option. He made so many business deals that were shady. I'm a math teacher, not a forensic accountant. But I could tell that some of the arrangements made at meetings I overheard weren't legit. The numbers simply didn't add up. And some of his investors who reneged on a project…? They'd be at a dinner party at our house one night, and the next week I'd see their name in the business pages of the newspaper, losing their company or closing shops and laying off workers. There was even one man…" Her voice faded away. "I saw his name in the obituaries. He…killed himself."

Yeah, he knew about the man's suicide—and probably some other cases of violence related to her ex she *didn't* know about. He reached over and lightly wound his fingers around her wrist. Her wide eyes locked on to his. "Nothing August Di Salvo did is on you. You were a victim as much as anybody. I'm glad you got away from him."

It was on the tip of his tongue to ask her exactly how she had gotten away from the Di Salvo family. But even in the heat of the afternoon, he could feel the skin beneath his grasp chilling. Her cheeks paled and she reached into the neckline of her uniform again and tugged on the long silver chain to reach her locket.

As gentle as it was, he popped his grip open and pulled away. "I'm sorry. I remember that night in the diner a few months back. You don't like men touching you."

"That's not it. Well, that customer was a jerk." She moved her fingers and focus to the top of Magnus's brown and black fur. "Actually, I miss having someone touch me. But... I need to be in control of what's happening. I need time to know who the person is and why they're putting their hands on me."

He remembered her warning in the diner. "No surprises."

Visibly calming herself, she tilted her gaze back to his. "Granny used to hug me all the time. I miss the warmth and the comfort of that physical contact. Back when I was a naive newlywed with Augie, I liked when he put his arm around me, or when we'd make out—" Nope. He did not want that image in his head. "And then, he changed. Or rather, he let the real Augie out." He'd seen plenty of proof of the real Augie Di Salvo. "I hate that he ruined hugs and cuddling and even holding hands for me."

With the urge to reach for her pulsing through his fingers, Joel hated that, too. Mollie Crane was a pretty woman with a wry sense of humor and a quiet intelligence that he longed to get to know better. But understanding that his touch might be more frightening than comforting, he wrapped all ten fingers around his cane and changed the subject. "That's a pretty locket. Looks antique."

"It was Granny's. She raised me. It's one of the few things I have of hers." Her nostrils flared with a deep breath as she paused. "Augie sold, threw out, or burned the rest of the things I brought with me into the marriage. Including the house where I grew up."

Clearly her grandmother had meant the world to her. "I'm so sorry."

"He didn't see cute and adorable and a tribute to early twentieth-century architecture the way I did. He saw *old*. And *small*. He said a Di Salvo would never live in a dump like that. He didn't want anyone connecting the property to him once we were married. I didn't know he had done it until after we'd been married for a while. I was feeling homesick and had driven out to see it. He took great pride in explaining how that part of my life was over, that I was a Di Salvo now, not a hick from the Ozarks."

"He can't erase your memories. Or what your grandmother meant to you."

"It was a beautiful little cottage. Granny took such good care of it. She planted a huge garden in the back. During December, she put up enough lights and decorations to rival the Plaza lights. I loved growing up there." Tears glistened in her eyes, and Magnus rested his head in her lap, nudging at her hands. She leaned over to touch her nose to the dog's, then scrubbed her hands all around Magnus's head. "I'm okay, boy. Mama's okay."

Joel wanted to comfort her, too. But while the dog's touch was welcome, his was not. He needed to keep the conversation moving before he did something stupid like hunt down Di Salvo and burn *his* house to the ground. "So, Magnus? He's your service dog?"

She nodded, sitting up straight before tossing the teddy bear and letting Magnus chase it again.

"Post-traumatic stress?"

"He alerts when I'm about to have a panic attack. So I can get somewhere safe, make sure I pull over if I'm driving, or to comfort me to keep it from happening, like he did just now. He's supposed to, anyway. He's still in training, I guess. I feel safer when he's around, too. He can be scary when he gets fired up. Although, he's hard of hearing. He misses a few things. That's why he couldn't qualify for KCPD's K-9 Corps." Magnus trotted back and dropped the slobbery bear into her lap. "I'm sorry. I'm going on about stuff you're probably not interested in."

"Mollie, I'm interested in anything you have to say. You can talk to me. Tell me things. I'm not the bad guy here."

"I didn't think you were." She glanced up at him. "Why *are* you here?"

Suddenly, this assignment he hadn't wanted was becoming way too personal. How much truth did he share without blowing the most interesting and meaningful fifteen minutes he'd had since the night he'd lost everything? Partial truths weren't exactly a lie, were they? "I was surprised to see you still working at Pearl's Diner. I wanted to know how you've been, if you're okay. Just because I haven't seen you in a while doesn't mean I haven't thought about you. I felt guilty that I didn't do more to help you."

"I'm okay," she answered quickly in a tone he didn't

quite believe. "I honestly never expected to see you again. I thought I'd left Augie's world behind me. That's my goal."

"I'm not part of that world. I'm a cop. A detective with KCPD."

"I know that now."

"You seeing anyone?" Well, hell. Where had that question come from?

She shook her head, stirring the curls against her jawline. "I don't socialize much. I go to work, go home. Go to dog training or run errands, go home again." Her question proved even more surprising. "Are *you* seeing anyone?"

That made him go to the dark side. "My girlfriend... died."

"Oh, Joel. I'm so sorry. Was it the same accident where you got hurt?"

She held his gaze for the longest time as he worked through his personal hell to find some civilized words he could share about that night. Before the words about betrayal and loss and a wasted life could come, Joel was startled from his thoughts by Magnus rising on his hind legs and propping his front paws against his chest. Instead of blue eyes, he was looking straight into the darkest of brown eyes and feeling the dog's warm pants of breath against his face.

"I'm so sorry. Magnus! Sit!" Mollie tugged on his leash, but the dog plopped down on Joel's feet and rested his head atop his thigh. "You're *my* comfort dog, you big goof."

Pulling a rusty laugh from his throat, Joel scrubbed his hands around the dog's ears and neck. "He's okay."

"I'm sorry. He must have sensed your distress." Her bottom lip disappeared briefly between her teeth as she offered him an apologetic smile. "Honestly, I could, too."

"I do get stressed thinking about Cici and everything that happened. She had an addiction to opioids. Wish I could have saved her. Wish I'd done a lot of things differently the night I lost her." He was talking to the dog as he continued to pet his warm fur. He was beginning to see how a good therapy dog could truly help someone dealing with tragedy and trauma. A warm, living, breathing distraction. Something to focus on besides stress and pain. "Good boy. Thanks. Go to Mama." Nudging the dog's muscular shoulder, he guided Magnus back to Mollie. "I thought service dogs were supposed to focus on their owner."

"They are. Apparently, I've got the one reject who can't seem to remember that his job is to take care of *me*."

"Shouldn't he be more reliable than that? If he's supposed to protect you?" Maybe he was doing Mollie a disservice by interacting so much with Magnus. But he was smart, all boy, and pretty hard to resist.

"I'm meeting with our trainer tomorrow to see if there's more I can do to make him bond with me. He's deaf in one ear." She explained the flopped-over ear that seemed at odds with the Belgian Malinois's sleek lines. "I wonder if he's losing hearing in the other ear, as well. If he's looking at me and focused on me, he does fine. But he gets distracted too easily."

"I think he's just a friendly guy with a big heart. Trying to help as many people as he can."

"That's not how he's supposed to work."

"Look at how he's rubbing against your hand," Joel pointed out. "He's devoted to you."

"I guess. I'm still taking him in for a refresher course at K-9 Ranch."

"I've heard of the place. Just outside the city." He'd heard the owner had recently married a sheriff's deputy who sometimes helped KCPD with investigations that crossed jurisdictions with the county. "They do good work there. Rescuing dogs. Training them to be companion or service animals."

"I went there looking for a small dog, a little noisemaker who fit my little apartment and could give me the help I needed. But this big guy latched on to me from almost the moment I set foot on the ranch."

"He picked *you*."

"That's what Jessica, the ranch's owner, said, too. Sometimes I think he was just anxious to be adopted, and I was the first sucker to come along who'd take him."

"Don't sell yourself short." He leaned over to pet Magnus again. "This guy's a smart dog. I don't think he'd make a mistake and choose the wrong person."

She rolled her eyes in a *Whatever* retort, and Joel got the idea that Mollie Crane had once been full of wry humor and attitude—before August Di Salvo had beaten the spirit out of her. Parts of his body that hadn't cared about much of anything for a long time perked up at the idea that he could get to know the old Mollie—the real Mollie—if he played his cards right. He was actually excited by the challenge of proving to her that he was someone who was safe enough to be herself with.

With anticipation still sparking through his veins, he stood as Mollie checked her watch and hooked up Magnus's leash. He needed a plan. He needed to spend more time with her. He needed to be the man who could rise to the challenges that A. J. Rodriguez and Mollie herself had unknowingly set before him.

"My break is almost up, and Magnus has done both his

businesses," she announced. "I'd better be getting back before Melissa sends out a search party."

Joel helped clean up after the dog. He was racking his brain to come up with something more they could talk about as he held the gate open for an elderly couple bringing a pair of miniature poodles into the dog park. The three dogs sniffed each other as if they were all old friends, and the couple exchanged polite greetings with Mollie. Once she gave the order to *heel*, though, Magnus came right to her side and followed her through the gate. They crossed to the curb and stepped between two parked cars, waiting for the traffic to stop.

Not ready to end their conversation yet, Joel asked, "Melissa is married to a guy I know at KCPD. Sawyer Kincaid?"

Mollie nodded, watching the cars, as well as the pedestrians on either side of the street go by. He was glad to see her be so aware of her surroundings. "He comes in a lot. Sometimes with their kids, sometimes with his partner. He's very protective of her."

He detected the note of wistfulness in her voice and tamped down the urge to be just as protective of Mollie. It wasn't his place. It might never be. "I've seen her at police functions, like the softball game with KCFD."

She smiled, her gaze watching every vehicle that drove past. Gray car. White car. Public works truck. Car with out of state plates. "Yeah. We've got a friendly in-house rivalry at the diner. Melissa is married to a cop, and Corie is married to a firefighter. They've all come in to eat after a game. They tease each other a lot. I don't always like big, rowdy crowds like that. But it's all in fun. And the tips are great."

He could imagine. "You're more the stay home and read a book or watch a movie on TV kind of gal?"

"I used to enjoy a good celebration. But now I like quiet and predictable, which I guess makes me sound pretty boring, so yes."

Sounded a little bit like undercover work. "Too many people to be on guard against in a crowd, right?"

She looked up at him, perhaps surprised at his understanding, and nodded.

Blue minivan. Gray SUV.

"Still, those softball games are a hell of a lot of fun. You should come watch one." He thumped his thigh. "Not that they're going to ask me to play on the team again anytime soon."

For the first time since he'd known the dog, he heard Magnus growling a low-pitched warning in his throat.

At first, he assumed Magnus was making his presence known to one of the other dogs. But his dark eyes were tracking movement out on the street.

Joel felt his own hackles rise to attention. Black car driving slowly past. Tinted windows. Sunglasses and a lowered sun visor kept the driver's face from being visible. The car flashed its left turn signal and paused at the light. *Yeah, buddy, I notice it, too.*

"Magnus?" Mollie tugged on the dog's leash to turn his attention to her, and the growling ceased. "I don't know what's wrong with him."

"He's protecting you."

"From what?"

Joel was too paranoid to ignore anything suspicious in the people around him. Maybe if he hadn't ignored the danger signals when he'd run to Cici's aid that night, she'd be alive and he'd still be the cop he once had been. The black car stopped at the traffic light and he instinctively put his hand on Mollie's back and urged her forward. "Let's go."

When she arched her back away from his touch, he quickly pulled away. "I don't mean to flinch every time you touch me."

"My fault," he quickly apologized. "Didn't mean to startle you. Shall we?"

Even without sharing contact, she was moving across the street beside him. "It was good to see you again, Joel."

"Same here." He made sure the car turned the corner and drove away before relaxing enough to continue their conversation. "Is it okay if I stop by again to see you?"

"Why? You've checked up on me." She stopped at the end of the alleyway. "No bruises. No abuser. I'm fine. I don't blame you for anything that happened to me, so you shouldn't blame yourself." She gestured to the cars on the street. "I'm assuming you parked somewhere around here? You don't need to walk me back to the diner."

"Uh-uh. A man makes sure the lady gets safely inside before he leaves her." Especially when the hairs on the back of his neck had been standing on end ever since Magnus had growled.

"Okay, Sir Galahad," she teased. "You may walk me to my alley door."

He fell into step beside her. "While I appreciate you letting me off the hook, I've enjoyed our conversation. I'm fascinated by your dog, curious to know if his training works out. And, I don't want this to come out as an insult—but I feel comfortable with you."

"Why would that be an insult?"

"I should be telling you how pretty you are. That I like

your dark hair better than that fake blond look you were sporting two years ago. I should tell you how brave I think you are." He shrugged. "Something more personal and profound than you make me feel comfortable."

"Do you feel comfortable around a lot of other people?"

He pondered her insightful question and gave her an honest answer. "No. Not anymore."

Mollie stopped and tilted her gaze up to his. "Then that was a compliment. And I'll take it as one. Thank you." He saw the whisper of a smile before they walked beside each other once more. "You're welcome to come by the diner anytime. We're a public place, and you can't deny the food is delicious."

"As much as I love the burgers, I actually want to know if I could come to see you."

"Oh. Like a date?"

"Maybe you'd let me take you out to lunch or grab a coffee."

"I'll think about it. I haven't dated anyone since Augie."

They passed one door and then another. "It wouldn't have to be a date. But we could hang out. Talk some more. Be comfortable together."

They were nearing the dumpster behind the diner when she finally nodded. "Okay. But just as friends. And you can't surprise me like you did today. I don't do well with surprises."

"Magnus will save you."

"I'm not holding my breath."

"Give the guy a chance. He might surprise you." Why did that feel like he was trying to sell his own worth, and not the dog's? Joel stopped and pulled out his phone. "Could

I have your number? That way I can call or text before I stop by, so it won't be a surprise."

Mollie studied the badge at the middle of his chest, then met his gaze. "I suppose that's the smart thing to do." She pulled out her phone. It was a cheap, pay-by-the-minute style, but it got the job done. "Now text me, so I can program your name and know it's you."

The message he sent was simple and honest. And maybe a little bit hopeful.

You can trust me, Moll.

Her shoulders lifted with a deep sigh. His phone dinged when she texted him back.

I'll try.

Any attempt to confirm that they now qualified as something more than acquaintances fell silent when Magnus barked and lunged forward. "Magnus! What is he doing?" Mollie jerked on his leash. "Magnus. Come."

Oh, he was loving this misfit of a dog. Magnus had sensed the threat even when Joel's guard was down.

The same black car had pulled into the far end of alley. "Do you know that car? Who drives it?"

"No. I—"

"I'm going to take you by the arm now," Joel warned, so Mollie wouldn't be startled. "Get your key out. Walk faster."

Although she quickened her pace and didn't pull away from his hand above her elbow, she still questioned his concern. "Joel, what's wrong?"

"I see that car one time, I don't worry about it. I see it twice, I dismiss it as somebody circling the block because they're lost or looking for a parking space." The windshield reflected the afternoon sun, blinding him to the driver or any passenger inside. "But three times?"

"He's following us?"

The car revved its engine, shifted into gear, and hurtled down the alley toward them. Joel cursed. "Move!"

They ran. But they weren't going to be fast enough. The car nearly clipped a dumpster as it drifted toward their side of the alley.

"Get the door unlocked." He tossed his cane aside, clamped his hands at either side of her waist and lifted her onto the concrete step. While she worked to jam the key into the lock and turn it, he pressed up behind her as the car barreled toward them. "Hurry!"

Magnus nearly tore the leash from her hand as he lunged toward the approaching car. His furious barking echoed off the brick walls like a pack of hounds warning off an intruder.

"Magnus!" Mollie clamped down on the leash to keep the dog from bolting, turning her attention from the door.

"Mollie—lock!"

Leaving the relative safety of the recessed doorway, Joel scooped the dog up in his arms. And with seventy pounds of squirming dog sandwiched between them, he pushed them all forward the second he heard the key turn the lock.

The steel door swung open and the three of them tumbled inside as the heat of the car rushing past swept over them like a crashing wave.

They landed in a tangle of legs and fur on the kitchen floor. He cursed the *oof* of air from Mollie's chest as he landed on top of her. Magnus woofed and scrambled to one side as Joel rolled to the other. When he saw the dog clambering to his feet and heading for the door, he kicked it shut. "Magnus. Stay." He gave the order, having no idea if the dog would obey him or not. "Mollie?"

Joel reached for Mollie to see if she was injured, but she was already pushing herself up to her hands and knees. She glanced over her shoulder, breathing hard, maybe from adrenaline as much as any physical exertion. "Are you all right?"

"Are you?" She'd lost her headband in the fall, and he reached out to push her hair off her face. She snatched his wrist to pull his fingers from her silky curls. "I'm sorry."

"What is going on?" He jumped at the worried female voice above his head. "I heard the commotion at the door and tried to get back here to open it as fast as I could, but... baby belly." Corie Taylor's cheeks blanched as they heard the squeal of brakes and the unmistakable sound of a car jumping the curb and painting rubber across the pavement as it made a sharp turn at high speed. "What is that guy doing? Is he drunk? He could have hit you."

Mollie squeezed Joel's wrist before she pushed him completely away. "Go, if you need to." She turned her head the other way. "Magnus?"

"I got the mutt." Herb had joined the party and had the dog's leash wrapped around his bony fist. "He's fine."

Mollie reached for her dog and wrapped her arms around his neck before nodding to Joel. "Go."

He pushed to his feet, ignoring the twist of pain above his right knee at the sudden movement. He nailed Corie with a look as the pregnant woman leaned over to squeeze Mollie's shoulder. "Stay with her. Make sure she's all right."

He gave the next orders to the Navy vet. "Keep this door locked. I'll knock when I'm ready to come back in."

"Okay. Should I—"

But Joel was already out the door, giving chase, pushing his rebuilt legs as hard as they could go. The car was already out of sight, but he easily followed the tire marks where the car had turned left across traffic. The noise of horns honking and the jumble of cars in the intersection told him the car had cut through a red light. But which way had it gone?

Joel ran to the corner. He held his badge up and stepped between the cars to reach the center of the intersection. He was breathing hard, and the nerves in his right thigh were sparking through his muscles like a shot from a Taser. Joel spun three hundred sixty degrees, looking down every street. But the car had disappeared. The angle had been wrong to even glimpse a license plate number between the parked cars along the sidewalk and uptown traffic.

But he knew cars. And a late-model four-door Lexus RX with tinted windows, gold trim, and a 6-cylinder engine under the hood wasn't one he'd soon forget.

The lights changed and horns honked. He waved an apology to the vehicles that were waiting and jogged back to the sidewalk. He kept his eyes peeled for anything else that pinged his suspicion radar as he hurried back to the diner.

After he checked to make sure Mollie and Magnus were okay, he needed to get to Fourth Precinct headquarters to see if he could get a hit in the system with just a make and a model. He needed to know who was driving that car, and why the driver had been watching Mollie.

Because that "accident" was no accident.

Chapter Five

"Something's wrong with Magnus." Mollie unhooked the dog's harness and sent him off to play with the boy who was tossing balls across the backyard for some of the residents at K-9 Ranch before turning to their training supervisor, Jessica Bennington Caldwell.

The older woman carried two glasses of iced tea across the deck, where it had become their habit to sit for a few minutes and chat after one of Mollie and Magnus's training sessions. Jessica shook her silvering, blond braid down her back and eyed the Belgian Malinois racing ahead of a Black Lab and an Australian shepherd to retrieve the ball. "Wrong? He looks fine to me."

"Penny! Tobes!" The nine-year-old boy called each dog by name and tossed a ball, so each dog had the chance to run and retrieve successfully. Magnus skidded to a stop in the grass and almost knocked the boy down in his enthusiasm for playing the game. "Good boy, Magnus."

"You're doing a good job, Nate," Jessica called out to her foster son. He beamed at the praise and went back to exercising the dogs. Then Jessica handed Mollie one of the glasses and invited her to sit in one of the deck chairs. She leaned down to pet her own service dog, Shadow, a German shepherd mix with a graying muzzle, who seemed content to supervise the activity from his shady spot on the deck, before taking the seat beside her. "Do you think he realizes he's helping me with a chore to earn his allowance?"

Mollie couldn't help but smile at the boy's joyous laughter as he rolled on the ground with the dogs licking his face and silently pleading with Nate to throw the balls again. She looked across the deck to watch Jessie's foster daughter, a sweet blonde girl named Abby, pet and feed treats to a spotted Australian shepherd puppy as she mimicked the training she'd seen Jessie do with the other rescue dogs in her care. "Nate and Abby are two lucky children to have found a home here." She'd heard some of the story of how Jessie had found the two runaway children and taken them in as foster children, and how she had guarded them like a fierce mama bear from a home invasion. "How's the adoption going?"

"We've jumped through all the hoops and filled out more paperwork than you can imagine." Jessie's face softened with a serenely beautiful smile. "But our attorney says they'll be ours before Christmas."

"That's wonderful. Congratulations." Mollie toasted her with her glass. She'd given up on having a family of her own. She had too many hang-ups to manage even a healthy relationship with a man, which she considered a prerequisite to starting a family. But she would dearly love to at least get back into a classroom to surround herself with young people again. If only she didn't have the specter of the Di Salvo family hanging over her. "I have to admit I'm a little jealous. You have this beautiful property, your amazing dogs, two children to love—and let's not forget the hunky deputy sheriff you married last month."

K-9 Defender

"You ladies talking about me out here?" The back door opened again and a tall, well-built man wearing a sheriff's department uniform walked out. Garrett Caldwell pulled a departmental ball cap off his spiky salt-and-pepper hair and leaned down to trade a kiss with Jessie. Then another one. Mollie politely looked away from the love shining between them.

"You're home early." Jessie's tone was happy, but her expression looked vaguely worried.

"Relax. Nothing's wrong." He pressed his thumb against the dimple of his wife's frown to ease her concern. "The county is relatively quiet today. I'm the boss of my department, so I decided to grant myself permission to spend an extra hour with my beautiful family." Mollie looked back as Jessie's husband straightened and pulled the tea from his wife's hand to steal a long swallow. "Mollie. How are you doing today?"

"I'm fine."

Garrett dropped his gaze to Jessie and the two exchanged a look. He handed off the sweating glass and put his cap back on his head. "I'll keep an eye on the kids. Looks like you two were in the middle of an important conversation."

"Thanks, sweetheart."

He winked a goodbye to Mollie, then headed over to Abby to scoop the giggling little girl up in his arms. He carried her down to the grass where he traded a fist bump with Nate and listened patiently as both children recounted the highlights of their day.

Jessie had inherited the seven-acre property that had once been a working farm and converted it into a dog training facility, as well as a spacious country home, allowing them the distance they needed to share a private conversation. "So…" Jessie sipped her tea. "You don't think Magnus is working out as service dog? I thought your training session went well today. Especially with the nonverbal cues. His reactions to you were spot-on."

Mollie nodded. It was hard to explain the difference in Magnus's behavior when he was here on the ranch to when he was with her in the city. She didn't want her boy to be labeled a failure any more than she wanted to feel like one when it came to their working relationship. "Do I need to get his hearing tested again? He doesn't always seem to be aware when I need him unless he's looking right at me."

"And…?"

"And what?"

"He's barely two years old. Just out of his puppyhood. Maybe it's taking him longer to mature, but I don't think so." Jessie turned her head to point out how responsive Magnus was to Nate's commands as he showed off his skills for his foster dad. "He's a clown, but he can also turn on work mode faster than any dog here. He wants to work. He wants to have a job and do it well. He wants to please you."

Mollie reached down into her bag beside her, where she'd hidden Magnus's toy. "What he wants is his teddy bear."

Jessie laughed. "That, too. He's definitely more reward driven than treat driven." The older woman set her glass on the table between them and leaned a little closer. "We can take Magnus to my vet again, if you think his hearing loss is a legitimate concern. But we already knew he was going to be more responsive to visual cues. Is he not answering your verbal commands when you're away from the ranch?"

"He went to this guy I was talking to yesterday and put his paws on him. Laid his head on his lap just like he does with me." Mollie wasn't sure if she was explaining her hit-

or-miss success with Magnus clearly enough so that the other woman would understand her fears. "*I* was stressing because I don't always handle social situations that well anymore. I was sitting right there, and he ignored me. He's supposed to be *my* dog, and he went and comforted someone else."

"Was this a one-on-one situation, or something with more people, like the diner when there's a run of customers?"

"I was exercising Magnus. He asked if he could go with me to talk. It was the two of us and the dog."

"Hmm… Maybe you weren't as panicked about being with *this guy* as you thought you were. Maybe there's something about *this guy* and having Magnus with you that made you comfortable enough to be with him."

Comfortable. There was that word again. Joel said he felt comfortable with her. But did she feel the same? Joel was a man—an attractive one at that, if a little beat up around the edges. And he knew about her time with Augie. How could she possibly feel comfortable with a man connected to the past she could never truly move on from?

Jessie's gray eyes narrowed as she pondered Mollie's story. She glanced out into the yard to see the three panting dogs sitting in front of Garrett and the children, eagerly waiting for the balls to go flying again. Magnus's razor-sharp focus was impossible to miss. Once the dogs took off, Jessie looked over at Mollie, nodding as if she had some kind of answer for her. "Was *this guy* in distress? Could he have been having a panic attack like you do sometimes?"

It was Mollie's turn to carefully think over her response. She'd asked Joel about his injuries, but he'd skimmed the details, either protecting her sensibilities or protecting himself from reliving a painful memory. He'd made a joke, but his knuckles were white where he gripped his cane. And then he'd mentioned his girlfriend dying. His tone had sounded so bleak. His golden-brown eyes had seemed so distant. And she thought he was going to snap that cane in two. That was when Magnus had targeted him. She'd had the urge to comfort him, too. If she was a toucher, she would have squeezed his hand or offered him a hug. But Magnus had stepped up and done what she hadn't been willing to do. "Yes. He was very stressed at the moment."

"It's rare for a service dog to respond to anyone but the human he's bonded with. Maybe our boy here is so smart, he responds to anyone in distress. My Shadow does that with the kids." Mollie sat up a little straighter, watching her dog with a sense of pride. Maybe there wasn't anything wrong with Magnus. Maybe her boy was smarter than she'd given him credit for. "Is there a personal connection between you and this *guy*?"

Surprised by the question, Mollie swung her gaze back to her friend. "Personal? With Joel?"

"Joel. Okay, at least I don't have to keep calling him *this guy*." Jessie smiled. "This Joel—have you been dating him? He's not your brother or a family friend, is he?"

"I don't have any family."

"So, you are dating?" Jessie continued before she could correct the misassumption. "Magnus may see you as a family unit, and he's responding to you both because he wants to protect his entire pack."

"I'm not dating him," Mollie blurted out. "I sat and had a conversation with him for fifteen minutes. Sure, we discussed some surprisingly deep stuff, but that's just where the conversation went. I've met him a couple of times before, and he was always nice to me. He doesn't look nice—I mean, he looks more like a thug or a street fighter or something dangerous like that. I think he must look that way for his work. But he was always nice to me."

Picking up on her rambling discomfort, Jessie reached across the table to touch the arm of the chair, where Mollie squeezed her fist. "I'm not your therapist—I rehabilitate dogs, not people. But it sounds like you have feelings for him."

Did she? How could she?

"I… I guess we share a connection." She vividly remembered Joel tackling her and Magnus when that car had nearly run them down. And when he'd come back after chasing the car, he'd come right up to Mollie to make sure she was all right before he called the near hit-and-run in to someone at KCPD. He apologized for the bruises on her knees, even though she assured him they were quite minor compared to the injuries she could have sustained if that car had hit them. As frightened as she'd been of that car racing toward them, she hadn't completely shut down in panic when he'd lifted her to safety and shoved her and Magnus into the kitchen ahead of him. Then she'd given him her phone number because he'd revealed some things that made her think he was just as broken as she was, and, like her, was trying to move on with his life and find his new normal. "I *am* comfortable with him. Yes."

He'd said those words about her, and now she was saying them about Joel. They both had a lot of emotional baggage to deal with, but it hadn't seemed to matter when they'd sat down and talked. It had all felt so normal, and she hadn't shared anything *normal* with a man for a very long time.

Jessie patted her hand before pulling back. "I'm not trying to put you on the spot, but I do need to understand what's happening so that I can evaluate Magnus's behavior and figure how to retrain him. Or if it's truly necessary."

"That makes sense." She thought she understood the point Jessie was making, even if she didn't find it completely reassuring. "Magnus protects my world. And if someone is part of that world, then Magnus thinks he has to protect that person, too?" Jessie nodded. "But Joel and I are friends. Barely that. I need Magnus to be there for *me*, not everyone else."

Jessie stood and crossed to the deck railing to watch the dogs interacting with her husband and foster children more closely. "Can you ask Joel to come to a training session with you? I'd like to observe the three of you together. Then I could tell if Magnus is switching loyalties, or if he's just being a typical Mal—" Jessie's nickname for the Belgian Malinois dogs she worked with "—who's looking for a bigger, more demanding job to do."

"You want me to invite Joel here?" Mollie wiped the icy condensation from her glass, then palmed the back of her neck beneath her hair to cool her skin. The late afternoon was hot with the sun high in the hazy blue sky. But it was the mix of nervous anticipation and a familiar dread at purposely developing a relationship with a man that made her temperature spike.

"Yes. If you're nervous about it, just remember that I'll be with you the whole time. Do you feel safe with Joel? I can make sure Garrett is home when you're here." Jessie turned to face Mollie, leaning her hips against the railing. "The kids will be here, of course, since they're off for the summer from school. That reminds me. Have you given any more thought to tutoring Nate on his math skills? He quali-

fied for the HAL program in math. But since this is a new
school, I don't want him to feel like he's out of sync with
the other students when he starts fourth grade this year."

Mollie finally set down her glass and joined Jessie at the
railing. "Sure. I'd love to repay you by helping him with
math. I miss working with students."

"Good. Then I'll see you, Joel, and Magnus tomorrow.
If that time still works for you?"

Mollie tried not to feel like she was being rushed into
this. Impulsive behavior had been smacked out of her by
Augie years ago. And the secrets she'd kept since her divorce demanded she be cautious about her dealings with
people. "I'll have to check with Joel to see if his schedule
allows him to get away in the afternoon."

Reaching over, Jessie squeezed her hand where she
clutched the railing. "Make it happen. It's as important for
Magnus as it is for you that we get this problem straightened out. Some dogs can't be trained to be more than the
family pet. And that's okay. Being the family pet is an
important job. But I've never met a Mal who couldn't be
trained to do more. Even without his hearing, he's a high-
energy dog. We need to focus that energy, or he could become difficult to control. Might even become dangerous
to himself or to others."

Mollie pictured Magnus going after that black car yesterday in the alley behind the diner. No one on the outside
needed to know that her dog was a happy boy who loved his
teddy bear and a good tummy rub. He looked and sounded
dangerous when he perceived a threat to her.

Augie had always driven black cars. For a brief moment
in that alley yesterday, her stomach had bottomed out at
the idea that not only had he tracked her down—a night-

mare she'd suspected would eventually happen—but he'd violated one of the few details of their divorce agreement by getting close to her again and threatening her.

Of course, the dangerous driver in the alley could have been a drunk driver. Maybe he thought he was still on one of the main streets. Or maybe the impatient driver had taken a shortcut and driven so fast the car had been nearly out of control.

Augie had always been an impatient driver.

Even before that first time he'd assaulted her, she'd seen glimpses of road rage when he was driving. She should have gotten a clue about his selfish, irrational, violent behavior long before that Thanksgiving night. His mother, Bernadette, had insisted he use a driver on staff as often as possible to protect the heir to the Di Salvo fortune—keeping Augie from behind the wheel in order to keep his name out of traffic court records and keep him in one piece.

A staff driver reminded her of Joel and the few months he'd worked for the family. Although he'd been at the periphery of her world, other than that first night they'd met, she'd sensed even then that he was a good man. Someone she should be able to trust. Someone who wanted to keep her safe.

He seemed a harder version of that good man now. Something about the accident he'd glossed over, as well as the girlfriend he'd lost to drugs had changed him. Not just the limp or the visible scars—but the scars on the inside. Oh, he was still very much a protector. The way he'd shoved both her and Magnus out of the path of that reckless driver, then run off to see if he could identify the man, proved that.

But was he still the man who'd spoken so gently to her, who'd tempted her to lean into his strength and allow someone stronger to stand between her and Augie? Mollie had sensed the reticence in him today. Maybe it was sorrow or guilt. Self-doubts that he'd failed the woman he'd loved. He'd been dealing with a lot of emotional stress. Clearly, Magnus had picked up on that, too.

"Mollie?" Jessica touched her arm. She startled but didn't shy away.

Magnus was staring at her from the middle of the yard, and when she made eye contact, he trotted up the steps to push his head into her hand and lean against her thigh. Mollie instantly breathed easier at the warm contact. She scratched around his ears and knew he'd become much more than her service dog. Maybe that was why she was honestly afraid that his loyalty wasn't to her. She had no one in her life beyond a few work friends and this dog. She needed someone or something to belong to her—someone who wanted her to belong to them, too. "Good boy. You're my good boy."

"You were a million miles away." Jessie asked permission before she petted and praised Magnus, too. "I don't think you need to worry about Magnus being your dog. But I still think it would be a good idea to bring your Joel to a training session tomorrow."

Her Joel?

She hadn't thought she could do a relationship again. So why wasn't she correcting Jessie's assumption about her friendship with Detective Standage?

"I'll talk to him. I really want Magnus to work out as my service dog. I… I'm getting attached to this big goof."

"I'm glad to hear that. Come on. Let's run him through one more set of commands before you head back to the city.

Hook him to his leash, and we'll go out to the barn, away from the distractions of playing children."

They went through one more session of basic dog commands, using both verbal and visual cues. Then there was another round of pets from Nate, a shy hug from Abby, and Mollie had a worn-out Magnus loaded into the back seat of her car where he stretched out on his blanket and cuddled with his teddy bear while she pulled out her cell phone.

She waved to Jessie and her family and held up her phone to show them she'd be sitting in their driveway for a few minutes while she contacted Joel.

Mollie stared at the blank screen of her phone for a full minute, working up the courage to text Joel. She hadn't purposely contacted a man for several months now.

When she heard a whine from the back seat, she lifted her gaze to the rearview mirror and saw that Magnus had raised his head to look at her, tilting his head as if to ask if she needed him. Mollie smiled, then reached back to pet him. "I sat here too long without speaking or moving, didn't I? I didn't mean to worry you." When she reached his flank, he stretched out and gave her full access to a tummy rub. "You're mama's good boy. You go ahead and rest now. You've earned a break."

When she faced the steering wheel again, she breathed out a determined sigh. She could do this for Magnus. She fingered her locket, summoning the confident young woman her granny had raised. Then she pulled up Joel's number. With only a few numbers on her phone, it was easy to find. She typed before self-doubts and second-guessing could get in her head again.

Hey, Joel. Is this a good time?

Only a few seconds passed before he answered.

For what? Miss my scintillating charm already?

Are you still at work? I can text you later if you're busy.

Sorry. Ignore my sarcasm. I try to be funny when I get nervous.

Why would you be nervous?

Because a pretty woman I like just texted me.

Mollie glanced at her reflection in the rearview mirror. Her hair was a windswept mess from spending the past two hours outside. Her cheeks were flushed from the sun, and the only makeup she had on was some pink gloss to protect her lips. Shorts, sneakers, and a faded Worlds of Fun T-shirt she hadn't even bothered to tuck in completed her look. She was a far cry from the perfect beauty Augie had demanded she be.

So why did Joel Standage saying she was pretty make her smile when Augie's praise had only made her feel trapped and on edge?

His three blinking dots turned into a message before she could answer.

I'm not taking it back. You're pretty. I like you. And you texted me. You can't argue with that logic.

I don't know what to say to that.

You don't have to say anything. Things are winding down here on my shift. This is a perfect time to chat. What's up?

She glanced back at Magnus. Her boy had fallen asleep already, with his muzzle lying on top of his bear. Poor guy had put in a full day. She needed to take care of him.

I need to ask you a favor.

Clearly, he'd been texting while he waited for her response.

I didn't have a LP# to ID the owner of the car that played chicken with us yesterday. But I did find out that Edward Di Salvo and your ex both own that make of car.

LP# must mean License Plate number. Sure, she could go off on a tangent with him. Besides, she'd already suspected that yesterday's incident had something to do with Augie. Confirming her worst fear or having another rational explanation for nearly being run down would at least tell her what she was dealing with.

Augie always valued what his parents said. If Edward said that was the kind of car someone of their station would own, then Augie would get one, too.

Sadly, they aren't the only drivers in the state who own that make of car. I can't even say for sure it belongs to a K.C. resident.

So, you're saying it's not much of a lead.

It's not even enough to get a warrant to look at their cars to see if they have the kind of scratches and alignment issues it would have sustained from jumping curbs and turning at the speed that guy was going.

Mollie shook her head. She really wanted it to be a drunk driver. She might not be able to identify who was behind the wheel yesterday, but she had a feeling she knew who'd sent him.

What's the favor? You can ask me anything.

Right. She didn't really want to be talking about the Di Salvos right now, either. She typed in her request.

Would you be willing to come to a training session with me and Magnus tomorrow at K-9 Ranch?

Yes.

She huffed a sound that was almost a laugh at his easy acquiescence.

Don't you want to know what time? Or why I need you?

I enjoyed our time together yesterday. Before someone tried to run us down. My schedule is flexible, so I'll make it work. You need me? I'm there.

Magnus is the one who needs you.

I'm still in. You two are a package deal. Besides, I like the guy. Wait. Is he okay?

He's snoring in my back seat right now.

:) Go Magnus. Play hard and sleep well.

Jessie—our trainer—wants to see how Magnus interacts differently when you're around. Why he doesn't focus on me when you're there.

He's your dog, Moll. I'm sorry if I screwed up his training.

It might be nothing. Maybe you're a distraction. Maybe he's creating his own job. Jessie can't help me until she sees the three of us together.

What time?

4 p.m.?

Yes. Do we drive together? Should I pick you up someplace? Work? Your apartment?

I don't know if I'm comfortable being alone in a car with you. It's not you. It's my own hang-up.

Augie hadn't even let her drive after the first few months of their marriage. She'd thought it was sweet at first, that he was taking care of her. But she eventually realized he was controlling where she went, and making sure she was never alone. And the punishment he meted out hadn't been limited to the closed doors of the estate, either. Being trapped in the back seat of a car with Augie wasn't an experience she cared to remember.

Her phone dinged, dragging her out of her thoughts.

I'm not your ex. But I can drive separately.

Making even a simple decision like sharing a ride had been taken out of her hands when she'd been Mollie Di Salvo. No more.

I don't want to be paranoid for the rest of my life.

I don't want you to be afraid of me. Ever. If that means you don't want to be shut up in a vehicle with me, that's what we'll do. I'll drive my truck and meet you there.

No. She was braver than this. Granny Crane would be pointing a stern finger at her right now if she let Joel think she was afraid of him, specifically. Inhaling deeply, she typed away.

Change of plans. Would you mind driving the three of us? I don't think we'd all fit in my compact car very comfortably.

You sure?

Yes. She could do terse and direct, too.

Magnus can sit in the seat between us.

Deal. She texted him her address. Just pull up in front of the building. We'll be waiting in the lobby and will come out when we see you. We'll need twenty minutes to get there.

I'll be there. Red pickup truck. It doesn't look like much on the outside, but she's a peach on the inside.

Sounded a little like Joel himself.

While she was smiling at that revelation, the surprisingly chatty detective texted her a new message.

See you tomorrow at 4. Thanks for asking me. It means a lot to me that you want me to help.

It means a lot to me that you said yes.

Are you driving?

Not yet. I'm still at K-9 Ranch.

Put your phone down and get yourself safely home. I'll see you tomorrow around 3:30.

See you then.

As if he knew she was still looking at her screen, savoring their rambling conversation, another text from Joel popped up.

Phone down. Drive safely. See you tomorrow.

Bossy much?

You have no idea.

Before she gave in to her curiosity to ask him to explain that response, Mollie stuck her phone into the cup holder between the seats and started her car. She replayed their conversation in her head as she drove down Highway 40, heading into Kansas City. She smiled when she realized that had been the longest conversation she'd had with a man in ages. Yeah, they'd covered some serious stuff, but they'd been silly, too. It felt good. And normal.

She liked normal.

She liked Joel, too.

She was still smiling as she parked her car in the private lot behind her building. She gave Magnus a few minutes in the grassy median, then they ran up the stairs to her second-floor apartment.

That's when the smiling stopped.

Mollie froze at the top of the stairs, pulling Magnus to a halt beside her. There was a newspaper tacked to her door—the weekend society page from the *Kansas City Journal*, with a picture and headline announcing the engagement of August Di Salvo to a woman she recognized, one of the family's attorneys and his longtime mistress, Kyra Schmidt. Kyra looked as blonde and beautiful and dressed to highbrow perfection as she'd once done for Augie.

But seeing her ex's face on her front door wasn't the thing that made her blood run cold. It was the message scrawled across the paper in black marker.

You know what I want. Make this right. Don't ruin this for me.

The door itself wasn't quite shut. She could tell by the scratches on the lock that it had been jimmied open. "Magnus, sit. Stay." Avoiding both the newspaper and the knob, she nudged it open with her elbow. The old, walnut-stained wood door creaked open to reveal careless destruction. "Oh, God."

Her apartment was small. The only interior doors were a closet and a bathroom. But they both stood open. The mattress where she slept had been flipped off the bed, the pillows cut open. And every drawer and cabinet were open or overturned on the floor. Even Magnus's bed had been torn open, its stuffing strewn about like cotton candy.

She heard Magnus whining beside her and looked down to find his nose tilted up to her. Right. Stay in the moment. Freezing up in panic wouldn't do her any good. She bent down to pet the Belgian Malinois around the head before patting his flank and pulling him away. "Magnus, with me."

Mollie instinctively touched her locket through her T-shirt as she retreated. When her back hit the opposite wall, she yanked the chain from beneath her shirt and opened the locket. She breathed out a sigh of relief when she saw the tiny, folded piece of paper opposite her granny's picture inside. Then she reached down and fingered the small pocket in Magnus's harness, nodding when she felt the small object hidden there. "Good boy. Good boy, Magnus."

She knew what the intruder was looking for. He'd never get his hands on it as long as she was alive. Keeping it well hidden and out of Augie's reach was the only thing *keeping* her alive.

Make this right? As if. August Di Salvo was never getting his hands on it. It was the only bargaining chip she had.

Why was this happening now? What had changed in Augie's world to prompt him to come after her like this? His engagement? While she pitied Kyra for saying yes to his proposal, Mollie was more than happy to see him move on to another woman and leave any connection with her behind. This had to be related to the car that tried to kill them yesterday. Or maybe the goal was to scare her. Or make her retreat so far into her fear that she'd be an easy mark for someone to complete the job.

But he wasn't getting his hands on what she'd taken from her ex-husband. It was the only leverage she'd had to get away from him, to get his signature on the divorce papers, to keep him from hurting her ever again. Augie didn't get to win this time.

She was deep into her mental pep talk when she heard the clanging of a ring of keys and an old metal toolbox coming down the stairs from the third floor. "What the…?"

Mollie cringed at the building manager's reaction to her door. She yelped when Mr. Williams swung around to face her.

"You okay, Miss Crane? Looks like somebody busted in." He set down his toolbox and moved closer to the door, inspecting the same damage she had. "I've been upstairs all afternoon working on that broken pipe between 304 and 305. I never heard a thing."

He scratched the back of his thinning gray hair. "How'd they get inside the building without one of the residents' key fobs?"

"Don't touch anything!" she warned, shaking herself out of her terrified stupor. "There may be evidence."

"You're right, ma'am. Goll-darnit." He unrolled the sleeve of his gray coveralls to cover his fingers before pulling the door closed again. "They busted my lock." Right. Because that was the worst of what had happened here today. "Good thing you weren't home, Miss… Miss Crane?"

Mollie was already charging down the stairs, swiping

away the tears that threatened to fall so she could dig her phone out of her back pocket and pull up a familiar name. When she reached the bottom step, she perched on the edge of it and typed.

Joel? I need a cop.

She stared intently at the screen, waiting for his response. Then she startled so badly when her cell rang that she dropped her phone. She quickly scrambled to pick it up from between her feet, sending up a silent prayer of thanks when she read the name and answered. "Joel?"

"What's wrong?" His gruff voice didn't sound at all like the jokester she'd been texting a half hour earlier. She threw her arm around Magnus's shoulders and reminded herself of the decision she'd made during that conversation. Joel Standage was a good man. Beat up by life and rough around the edges, but he made her smile, he liked her dog, and he made her feel safe. "Mollie?"

"I'm here."

Joel cursed. "Don't scare me like that. Where are you? Are you hurt? Are you in danger?"

She answered each question as quickly as he'd rattled them off. "My apartment building. No. I'm not sure."

"I'm on my way to you now. Tell me what's going on."

"He broke into my apartment."

"He? Di Salvo? Is he still there?"

"I don't think so." She heard a siren in the background of the call. Joel must have one of those portable models he stuck on the roof of his vehicle. "Augie or someone who works for him was here. They left a message, and it looks like they went through the whole place. I don't have much, but I think everything has been touched."

"Do you have something he wants?"

She glanced around the empty foyer and tuned out the voices in the hallway above her as Mr. Williams knocked on doors and asked the other residents if they'd had a break-in, too. She knew the answer was no. This wasn't a break-in. It was a targeted search. After nearly a year of so-called freedom, Augie was coming after her.

"Mollie?"

"Yes. I have something. He…he didn't find it. I didn't hide it in my apartment." She could hear a siren close by now. A black-and-white pulled up out front, sliding into the fifteen-minute loading zone at the curb. She didn't think detectives drove squad cars. "What are you driving?"

"My truck. Red pickup."

"Did you call for backup? There's already a police car here."

Mr. Williams and his rattling toolbox came down the stairs. "*I* called them. I read that heinous message on your door." He leaned over to pat her back or squeeze her shoulder, but Magnus put himself between her and the super and growled.

"Magnus!" She tugged him back to her side.

Mr. Williams gave them a wide berth as he stepped down to the foyer. "That dog's a menace. When I said you could have a pet, I didn't mean an attack dog."

"He can tell I'm scared. He's protecting me. You may have startled him because that's the side he can't hear on. He won't hurt you unless I tell him to." At least, she hoped he was that disciplined of a dog.

Joel's voice shouted in her ear. "Who's that? Who are you talking to?"

"The building super. He called 9-1-1."

"Don't talk to anyone until I get there. I'm only a few minutes away."

When she saw the two uniformed officers getting out of the car, she gasped and pulled her knees to her chest, instinctively folding herself into a smaller presence. "Joel?"

"Right here, babe."

"Remember that police officer who wouldn't keep his hands to himself at the diner last October?"

"Yeah. Rocky Garner. What about him?"

"He's here."

Joel swore again. "Do not talk to him. Magnus with you?"

"Yes."

"Good. Keep him between you and Garner."

"Okay."

"I'm in your neighborhood now. I'll be there shortly. You're going to be okay, Moll. You're stronger than Augie. You survived him. You'll survive this, too."

"You have a lot of faith in me."

"Hell, yeah, I do."

She took a deep breath at his words and pulled her shoulders back. "Don't get hurt driving over here. I'm okay."

"Damn right, you are."

She almost smiled. "You know, Joel, you cuss a lot when you're fired up."

"That going to be a problem for you?" Did that mean he was an emotional hothead? She wasn't a big fan if that was the case. Or was the problem that he intended to be around her more often?

She hoped it was the latter. "As long as you're not cussing at me."

"Never."

She watched Rocky Garner and his partner climb the front steps to the building. The handsy officer adjusted his protective vest, his gun, and his hat before he made eye contact with her through the glass. Then he smiled. He remembered her, too.

Mollie shivered. "Joel?"

"Yeah, babe?"

"Hurry."

Chapter Six

There wasn't a ball small enough Mollie could curl into. Officer Rocky Garner removed his hat and made a bee-line toward her spot on the bottom step. "You the one who had the break-in, sweetheart? Are you okay? You're not hurt, are you?"

The words were right, but the person saying them, and the slick way they were said, was wrong.

Mr. Williams stepped in front of Rocky before he could reach her. "I'm the one who called it in, Officer. We don't get a lot of break-ins here, but this one's serious."

Officer Garner seemed confused, then displeased, to have the gray-haired man impede his progress toward Mollie. But he pasted a smile on his face before patting the man's shoulder. "You the manager here?"

"Yes, sir."

"Fine. That's just fine." Officer Garner stepped back and gestured to the Black officer, who appeared to be his partner. "Why don't you give your statement to Darnell there, and I'm going to talk to the victim."

"I dunno. Miss Crane is a little shaken up. She knows me. I could stay…" Mr. Williams glanced back at her, then seemed to think better of going against Garner's suggestion and left Mollie to fend for herself.

"She's in good hands with me." The smarmy officer assured her super before propping his elbows on his holster and utility belt and facing her with a deceptively casual stance. "Mollie, isn't it? You're a mite prettier out of uniform. Sorry this happened to you. Want to show me your apartment where the break-in happened?"

She glanced out the glass doors at the front of the lobby, hoping Joel would make a miraculous entrance and save her from having to talk to Rocky Garner. But no such luck. The street was in the throes of rush hour traffic, and there was no place to park on either side. If he parked in the back of the building, he'd have to knock hard and flash his badge to get someone to let him in. If that didn't happen, he'd have to run around to the front, where Mr. Williams or one of her curious neighbors who were gathering to see what the police being there was all about, could admit him.

But no red pickup. No Joel. No miracle.

"Ma'am? Let's go." Any deception about casual or friendly disappeared when he leaned toward her and latched his fingers against her elbow. "You on the main floor or upstairs?"

Mollie jerked her arm, but couldn't immediately break his grasp. At the same time she breathed in his coffee and mint-scented breath, Magnus growled, low in his throat.

Officer Garner released her and held both hands up in mock surrender. "Your mutt has a mean streak in him. I'm afraid you're going to have to muzzle him or lock him in a neighbor's bathroom, so I can walk through the crime scene with you."

Mollie shook her head. "He stays with me. Always."

"Bet that puts a damper on your love life, don't it?" He snickered at his own joke.

"Please don't touch me again, Officer. I have panic attacks. I do better when the dog is with me."

His dark eyes narrowed at her attempt to stand up for herself. "You a mental case?"

She cringed at his crass comments. Either he thought he was being funny and was woefully mistaken about his level of charm or he was legitimately one of the biggest jerks she'd ever met. And that was saying something.

Anger surged ahead of her fear, and Mollie pushed to her feet, holding Magnus's leash tightly in her hands. "Are you married, Officer Garner?"

"Nope. Divorced twice."

"I can see why," she muttered under her breath, ducking her head.

"Excuse me?"

"I said this way," she answered in a stronger voice. With his blatant innuendos and touchy-feely hands, it didn't surprise her that marriage wasn't a strength of his. But she kept her comments to herself and headed up the stairs. "My apartment is on the second floor."

She felt the officer's gaze like laser beams on her backside as he followed her to the second floor. "Why'd you ask? You interested? You always seem like such a prickly thing at Pearl's. But I'm willing to try anything once."

Her granny would have slapped the man's face by now and lectured him up one side and down the other. Mollie was sorely tempted to do the same. Instead, she kept her cool and pointed out her front door before stepping aside and putting Magnus in a sit between her and the police officer. "That's my place."

He let out a long, low whistle before pulling his phone out and snapping a few pictures of the newspaper and threat. "Make *what* right? You know this Di Salvo dude? Looks like he's pretty pissed at you. Why would he threaten you?"

Threaten? Mollie blinked back the images that tried to sneak out of her memories. Hair literally pulled from her scalp. Vile words. A punch to the mouth if she dared to talk back.

The memories blended with the commotion down in the lobby, her neighbors whispering in the doorways, and Officer Garner pushing open her door. "Boy, he sure did a number on your place." He snapped a few more pictures. "You're lucky you weren't here. What did he take?"

Magnus was leaning against her leg and pushing his cold nose into her hand when she heard footsteps on the stairs and turned with an audible sigh of relief at the sight of Joel's muscular shoulders and golden-brown eyes. Magnus's tail thumped the floor with a similar anticipation. "Joel."

"You two okay?" were the first words out of his mouth. He crossed straight to her, his limp barely slowing his stride. For a second, she thought he was going to touch her face or hair with his outstretched hand. But at the last moment, he reached down and scrubbed Magnus around his ears. "Good boy. You keeping Mama safe?"

She wondered what his fingertips would feel like against her skin, and she acknowledged a moment of envy that he'd petted her dog instead. But she was beyond happy to see him here and felt herself take a normal breath under his watchful eyes. "We're fine." She glanced around at the neighbors peeking from their open doors before nodding to Rocky Garner and the officer talking to the super and more residents downstairs. "It got crowded pretty fast."

"And you don't like crowds." He raised the badge hanging from the lanyard around his neck and flashed it to the other residents. "I'm Detective Standage, KCPD. I need you all to go back to your apartments and lock your doors." He might look like he'd just climbed off a Harley with his tattoos and beard stubble, but he spoke with an authority that got the others moving from being curious onlookers to respecting her privacy. "Everything is fine. Miss Crane and her dog are safe and so are all of you. Thank you for your cooperation." He dropped his warm brown gaze back to her as the others did as he requested. "I didn't lie to them, did I?"

Mollie shook her head. "I'm okay. Magnus is, too. He's been great." She dropped her voice to a whisper. "He growled at Officer Garner when he tried to take my arm."

Joel grinned and reached down to give Magnus the praise he loved. "Good dog."

He gave her a nod before turning to the uniformed police officer standing in her open doorway. "What are you doing here, Garner?"

"What are *you* doing here? I answered a call from Dispatch about a B&E."

Joel looked beyond him to the open door and muttered a low curse. "And making terroristic threats. That's clearly a personal message on her door."

"Whatever. You may be schtooping the victim, but this is *my* call."

Joel moved toward the bigger man. "Watch your mouth, Garner."

"Butt out, you has-been."

"You're a patrol officer, not an investigator. Do. Your. Job."

Rocky Garner was a good four of five inches taller than

Joel, and he was squaring off as if he was looking for a fight. "I will be an investigator. I'm the one who's up for a promotion in two months. You're on your way out."

Mollie moved up behind Joel and brushed her fingers against the fist at his side, not wanting to be a part of any more violence today. She gasped when Joel's fist opened, and he laced his fingers together with hers and clasped her hand firmly in his, keeping her behind him out of Garner's line of sight, but maintaining the connection. Instead of panicking or pulling away, she followed her first instinct and tightened her grip in his.

"Your job is to secure and control the scene, calling for whatever backup you need. Not to go all cowboy and stomp all over the crime scene yourself. Be smart, man. You had at least seven witnesses on the scene besides Miss Crane. Do you know their names? Their locations? Did they see or hear anything? Are any of them traumatized by what happened here? Are they suspects?"

"Are you calling me stupid?" Mollie's breathing rate increased right along with Officer Garner's. He turned red in the face as his anger consumed him. "Telling me I don't know how to do my job?"

"I'm trying to keep the peace here, which is what you should be doing. Not upsetting people." Joel remained surprisingly calm, which made her feel better, but only seemed to aggravate the uniformed officer. "Especially not Miss Crane."

"I heard about you, Standage," Garner taunted. "How you blew your last assignment. People died."

Joel's grip pulsed around hers.

Uh-uh. She wasn't letting this man denigrate Joel or make her nervous any longer. She threaded Magnus's leash through the belt loop on her jeans and tapped 9-1-1 on her phone.

When the Dispatcher answered, she apologized for not knowing exactly who to call and gave the woman her name and address. "Yes, ma'am. There's a police officer who's arguing with a detective. I think he's trying to start a fight."

"Mollie..." She wasn't sure if Joel was warning her he didn't need her help, or if she was making things worse.

But she identified the threat when asked and read the badge number off Rocky Garner's chest. "I'm the victim whose apartment was broken into, and he's saying crude things about me. It's not the first time he's harassed me. Who can I report this to?"

Officer Garner broke his stare-down with Joel and nailed her with an accusatory glare. "Who are you talking to, lady?"

"9-1-1. They're giving me the number to call to file a complaint." Joel squeezed her hand, hopefully applauding her initiative in making the call.

"A complaint? Screw you, lady. I came here to help you. It looks like you've got some bad juju headed your way, and I put my life on the line to protect you. You should be grateful I answered the call." He shoved Joel away, cursed as Magnus shifted to his feet and growled, and headed down the stairs to the lobby. "C'mon, Darnell. We'll wait outside and let the mighty detective handle the hysterical female."

They both watched until Officer Garner stormed out the front door. His partner made some sort of apology to Mr. Williams before heading out after him.

"I'm not hysterical," Mollie whispered. "I'm pissed off." She raised her voice to a more normal tone and called after the retreating cop. "And who says 'bad juju' anymore, anyway?" She practically growled herself as her emotions surged through her. "He's so old-school. And not in a good way."

"There's a good way?"

"Yes. Chivalry and kindness. Not, men rule the world and women are their minions to do with and talk to as they please—and then expect us to be grateful for that kind of attention."

"I'll take angry over scared any day." Joel chuckled and held his hand out for her phone. "May I?"

"Oh." She felt her cheeks heat with embarrassment. "I forgot she was still on the line. Sorry."

Mollie handed it over and Joel took over the call, giving the Dispatcher his own badge number and explaining the situation. "The threat has been neutralized," he assured her. "A disagreement on jurisdiction. I've already called in for backup. I appreciate your help in calming my witness. Yes, ma'am. I think she's going to be just fine." His gaze remained locked on hers the entire conversation, reassuring her that, despite Garner's taunts and her outburst, he did, indeed, have the situation under control. "You bet."

Joel ended the call, and she tucked her phone back into her pocket. "Did I overstep?" she asked. "Make things worse for you?"

"For me? Hell, no. I hate the way Garner talks to you. To any female from what I've heard. I'm guessing the sensitivity training we all have taken hasn't rubbed off on him yet."

"I guess not." She huffed out a relieved breath that the officer had gone.

"That was cool to see you stand up to him."

Mollie shook off the compliment. "I didn't like how he was talking to you, either. I could only do it because you were standing between us. I would have been in full-on panic mode, hugged around Magnus and unable to think of any way to help if you hadn't been here."

Those tiger eyes gleamed with some sort of secret light as he held her gaze. "I'll take that job, standing between you and the Rocky Garners of the world."

She sensed he meant something more than simply protecting her from the crude cop. But she was too long out of practice to believe her intuition when it came to a man's words. "What happens now? I'm assuming since you're a detective, you'll want to ask me some questions or do some investigating?"

Joel shook his head. "Not me. I called in reinforcements. They should be here any minute." He held up their hands between them and grinned as if he was surprised to see her still clinging to him. "I won't lie and say that KCPD isn't interested in nailing your ex for a myriad of crimes. Not that what happened here isn't upsetting, but, they'd like to pin something bigger than breaking and entering and threatening his ex-wife on him."

Mollie felt the warmth in her body drain out through the soles of her sneakers. "That makes logical sense. Augie has been indicted before without much success." She glanced at the threat on her door. "But you'll still make a report on this, right? I know in abuse and stalking cases, it's important to document, document, document. Show a pattern of behavior."

"I hate that you know that." His smile disappeared. "My friends will actually be the ones looking into this. I'm probably a little too close to the situation to be objective."

"Too close? What does that mean?"

"You and me?" He shrugged, clasping both hands around

hers now. "I'm feeling something here. Between us. It's new, and we're still getting to know each other better. I'm more likely to do whatever is best for you than whatever is necessary to solve the case and arrest whoever did this. So, I called an objective third party—my boss and his partner. Two veteran detectives. They'll get answers."

"Joel, this is too much. When I called, I just… I wanted some backup. A friendly face who knows a little about me and what I went through with Augie." She was shaking her head as she spoke. "I'm not comfortable being caught up in the middle of a big investigation. I don't know why he's coming after me like this now. I don't care if he gets married again. The terms of our divorce won't change."

"He doesn't pay you alimony?"

"God, no. I want nothing from that man. I just want him to leave me alone." Maybe she was shaking. Maybe she'd gone pale. Maybe she was obsessively fixated on the angry threats. *You know what I want. Make this right. Don't ruin this for me.*

It sounded like a reckoning was coming her way.

Keeping their hands linked together, Joel pulled her aside and hunched down to put his face in front of hers. "Hey. Look at me, not at that message on your front door. Mollie?"

When he said her name, she stopped fidgeting and met his gaze. She tilted her head to keep her focus on him as he straightened. "I didn't know who else to call. Maybe because we just had that long text conversation, but you were the first person I thought of."

"I'm glad. That's what friends do. You need me? I'm here." He rubbed his thumb across the back of her knuckles, and the warmth of that simple caress seeped beneath her skin and calmed her, allowing her to stay in the moment and think more rationally. "Maybe I'll need your help one day, and I'll call you to return the favor."

"What could I possibly do for you? I'm a waitress with post-traumatic stress. I'm perennially broke and scared of my own shadow."

"No, you're not. If you were weak, you wouldn't let me stand here holding your hand when I know physical contact can be a trigger for you. You wouldn't have stood up to Garner and stopped him from being a bully." A grin reappeared in the middle of his scruffy face. "You made him go away. I'll always be grateful for that."

She pooh-poohed his joke, and she almost laughed. "That's all I'm bringing to the table? My ability to make a phone call?" And then understanding dawned. "Oh. My connection to Augie." She tugged against Joel's grip. "That's why you want to be my friend. Because you think I can help you build a case against him."

He released her hand the moment she struggled but refused to back up. "Hey. Hear me out. Please. Maybe that's why I approached you initially. But that's not why I'm here today."

She eyed his hands as he held them out to either side without touching her. Even now he was respecting her need to be cautious about physical contact. That alone made her want him to touch her. But she petted the top of Magnus's head instead. "Why are you here?"

He scanned the hallways, perhaps making sure they were still alone before he continued. "You make me smile. You asked me to help your dog." He reached down to pet Magnus, too, and the tips of his fingers brushed against hers. "You just showed me you can think on your feet, even when you're upset. That's strength, Moll, and I admire that. You make me want to be the man I used to be. No, you make me want to be better than that guy."

She didn't pull away when he slid his hand over the top of hers.

"I can feel your hand growing cold under mine. You're holding yourself so still right now, I'm guessing you're trying to placate me and not draw any attention to yourself." His mouth hardened into a thin line. "You probably did that with your ex. A survival mechanism. And I hate that. I hate that you think I could be anything like him."

"I know you're not Augie." Those words were true. "But I still don't understand what you think you can get out of a relationship with me if it's not part of some plan to capture my ex-husband."

He slipped his fingers beneath her palm and pulled her hand away from the dog's head. She didn't resist when he gently chafed it between both of his to bring some circulation and warmth back to her fingers. "The short version of the story is… I think I need you."

"You think?"

He glanced up and down the hallways before turning his focus back to her. "I'm a man looking for a reason to get up in the morning. A man trying to make sense of the past few years of my life and where I go from here."

"And you're saying *I'm* that reason?"

"I don't know. But I know I've felt more excited about the last two days of my life than I did the last two years before that. It's because I got to see you and talk to you and get to know you. Knowing that you like me enough—trust me enough—to ask for my help with Magnus or when you're scared or overwhelmed, tells me that I need to be strong again." When Magnus heard his name, he raised his nose and nuzzled it against the clasp of their hands. Joel released one hand to pet the dog and praise him for being so attentive. "I need to care about something beyond the guilt and anger and resentment swirling around in my head 24/7."

"Guilt, anger, and resentment?" Mollie gave Magnus some attention, too, centering herself before asking, "Are you okay?"

"I'm working on it. But not like I should." Joel pulled her fingers from Magnus's fur and clasped them within his own again. When she didn't protest, he tightened his grip ever so slightly. "Talking to you makes me feel a little less broken, a little less useless."

"You're not useless."

"My last girlfriend betrayed me. She disappeared one night. I thought I was going to save her, but it was a trap. She was already dead from an overdose of opioids laced with fentanyl, and I got hurt because of her. I literally died and had to be resuscitated because of her."

"Died?" Her hand squeezed around his again. "Joel—"

"I'm not telling you this for sympathy. Just the opposite, in fact. It's nice to have someone who believes in me enough to call me when she's afraid and needs a favor. Not someone who's using me or setting me up to get hurt."

She uttered a breathless apology. "But I *am* using you."

Mollie felt the callused pad of his thumb gently stroking her hand again. Did he even realize he was doing it? Was it weird to feel this sensual pull to the man simply by holding hands? Maybe it was the way she felt cocooned between him and Magnus and the rest of the world. Maybe it was the fact that his touching her wasn't sending her into a panic. Maybe it was the fact that she hadn't been touched so caringly in a long time.

"Asking me for help is not using me." Joel's voice dropped to that gravelly timbre that sounded so masculine to her. "Telling a drug lord that I'm a cop working undercover in his organization in exchange for your next fix is."

Her mouth dropped open, aghast at the meaning behind the words he'd so casually shared. "She did that to you? The woman you loved?" Her gaze dropped to his muscular forearms, and she traced one of the puckers of scar tissue there with her fingertip. "Is that how you got hurt?"

When she looked up again, his jaw was tight and he simply nodded. She suspected there was a lot more to his story he wasn't sharing. "Cici didn't need me. She needed her next fix. My life, my heart, meant no more to her than a wad of cash. The dealer and his thugs she was working with explained that to me in very painful detail. I was the most convenient way to get her drugs."

Mollie needed a moment to process what he was telling her. Because of his limp and scars, and hardened personality, she thought he'd been in a traffic accident. But he'd been attacked, viciously, possibly by more than one person. More than the miracle of him surviving, he'd managed to get back to his normal life and become a cop again.

She'd finally stood up to Augie. She'd put together a plan, and finally made her escape. But she hadn't moved forward from her trauma the way Joel seemed to be trying to.

"Did the police capture them?" she asked quietly. "Were they arrested?"

He answered with a scary lack of emotion. "Cici's murder? The attempted murder of a cop? Any number of lesser crimes? They're in prison for the rest of their lives."

He'd found justice for the monstrous crimes committed against him. He'd survived, got justice, and was trying to move on. She wanted to do the same. She wanted the proof of Joel coming back from deception and violence and shattered hopes and dreams to inspire her to do the same. To do better than simply survive the way she had been. "Sounds like we're both searching for what's next or closure or something to make us feel a little less broken. Augie didn't need me, either. Lied to me all the time. He wanted a trophy wife who fit the standards of what he considered beautiful and accomplished to be a benefit to his career. To show his parents that he could find a good girl and settle down and take over the family business." The more she talked about what she'd been through, the easier it was to talk about it. "And the parts of me that didn't fit— my rural upbringing, a job he considered beneath him, sarcasm, brown hair—he changed or eliminated."

"He's an idiot for not embracing and protecting the treasure you are." *A treasure? Right.* She hadn't felt like anybody's treasure for a long time, and Joel's vehement defense made her a little uncomfortable. He must have sensed her retreating from him, and hastened to add, "Just continue to be real with me. Don't hold back your snark on my account. Don't lie about what you're dealing with or how you feel. Trust me to be there for you. To be enough to take care of whatever you need. I'll do my best to earn that trust. That's the only favor I ask."

"I'll try." She shook her head. "I don't know if I'm enough for anyone anymore—"

"That's your ex talking."

"—but *you* are." She reached down to pet Magnus, who seemed more relaxed now that she was alone with Joel. Smart dog. *She* was more relaxed with Joel here, too, even with the difficult conversation they'd just shared. Then, with that same hand, she reached up and rested it against Joel's chest. She felt his skin quiver beneath her touch, the warmth of finely sculpted muscle. She watched his nipples tighten into hard nubs and push against the cotton T-shirt he wore. The instinct to pull away from his body's natural reaction to being touched, to brace herself against the possibility of an unexpected blow blipped through her mind but quickly dissipated. This wasn't Augie. This was Joel. Her friend. He wasn't going to hurt her for reaching out. She could do something as normal as give him a reassuring pat on the chest, and she would be safe. "I will try to be the friend that you need, too. I promise. But I don't know how much help I can be with Augie. That's scary territory for me."

When she would have pulled away, Joel reached up and covered her hand with his, keeping it resting gently against him. "We'll figure it all out. Whether we stay friends or become something more? Who knows? Just give me a chance, okay?"

She considered what he was asking of her. And though they'd gotten off to a rocky start, she had to admit she wanted that same chance with him. "You didn't have to tell me about KCPD investigating Augie. You could have kept quiet and just used me to get what you needed."

"I'm not using you," he stated without equivocation. "The department isn't going to use you."

She heard a low-pitched conversation punctuated by a laugh and nodded to the two men coming up the stairs behind Joel. "The decision may not be yours."

Mollie pulled away from Joel and reached for the comfort of Magnus instead. She recognized the short, wiry man with the graying sideburns as Joel's friend from the diner.

But the man with him was as big as a house. His blond hair receded slightly at the points of his forehead, but the creases beside his eyes were laugh lines. She tried to focus on those, and that he'd been laughing a moment ago, and not on the fact that he towered over both the dark-haired detective and Joel.

Joel turned to greet them. "Relax. I know these guys, and they're the best detectives I've ever worked with." He extended his arm to shake hands with both men.

"Boy, you don't get out much, do you, Standage," the big man teased. "Better introduce us quick before your lady friend decides big ol' me is one of the bad guys."

"I don't think that." She didn't sound very convincing even to her own ears.

Joel reached back and snugged his hand around hers, somehow finding her hand without even looking, as if a magnet drew his hand to hers. As if he felt that same connection she'd imagined earlier, too. As if they hadn't just shared a conversation that had knocked her sideways and given her a whole lot to think about. "Don't give her any grief, Josh. Rocky Garner was just here being his usual pleasant self. This is Detective Josh Taylor, and his partner—my supervisor—Detective A. J. Rodriguez. This is Mollie Crane."

"I apologize for anything Garner said." The big blond man nodded a greeting before tucking his hands into the pockets of his jeans and assuming a casual stance. "Please know he's not representative of most of KCPD. Guys like him on the front line give the rest of us a bad name."

Mollie arched one eyebrow. "He's not doing you guys any favors."

Josh Taylor laughed. A. J. Rodriguez smiled. And Joel

looked at her as if he was proud that she'd let her sarcasm peek out from her typically closed-off demeanor.

"I appreciate you two taking the lead on this," Joel said. "On the surface it looks like a typical B&E. But the picture, the threat, and the way it has been tossed inside makes me think the intruder was looking for something. Full disclosure? Mollie is August Di Salvo's ex-wife." Knowing it was necessary to share that information, she still shivered at being tied to the biggest mistake of her life. "With complications like that, I'm not ready to handle my own investigation."

"That's a crock—"

"I also have a certain prejudice against Di Salvo." Joel cut off his supervisor's protest. "If he is behind these terroristic incidents, as I suspect, then I want to make sure we build a case against him that can't be thrown out of court this time. I can provide any backup you need, but I feel better knowing you're running the show."

"Backup?" Josh smirked at A.J. "You going to set him straight, or should I?"

A.J. was clearly the more subdued partner. He nodded. "Josh, you see to Miss Crane, and I'll have a chat with our *amigo* here about resigning himself to being a paper pusher for the rest of his career."

Joel nodded toward Mollie. "This is too important for me to screw anything up."

A.J.'s face lost a bit of its cool demeanor. "You're gunshy, Joel. Not incompetent. You need to find that badass cop I know you are again."

"This is gonna be an unpleasant conversation. Ma'am?" Josh gestured toward the apartment door with his big hand.

"Have you had a chance to look around to see if anything was taken?"

She was hesitant to go with the larger man, even though he seemed polite and professional enough. "I didn't want to mess up the crime scene. I don't have much. The things I do value were with me."

"That's good." He thumbed over his shoulder to her apartment. "You want to just come hang out with me and skip the fireworks?" When Mollie didn't immediately respond, Josh Taylor nodded. "That's okay. I'll go scope things out and wait for a team from the crime lab to get here." With a nod from A.J., the blond detective took pictures of the newspaper and threats, as well as the splintered wood and scratches around the lock.

A.J. decided to postpone his lecture to Joel and turned his dark eyes on Mollie. "I'm not sure how long the crime lab will need to process the scene. Unfortunately, since the Di Salvo name is involved, this could be connected to other crimes we're looking at. You got a friend you can stay with tonight, ma'am?"

Other crimes. Oh, yeah. She knew Augie and some of his associates were involved in crimes far more serious than breaking and entering. But she wasn't ready to volunteer that kind of information. Her silence might be the only thing keeping her alive.

Although that threat on the door seemed to indicate that her time might be running out.

She pulled herself from the abyss of her thoughts and heard Joel answering A.J.'s question for her. "She'll be staying with me. Once the scene is cleared tomorrow or the next day, I'll come back with her to salvage what we can and clean up the place."

Mollie tugged on Joel's hand. "Do I get a say in this?"

"Give me a minute, A.J.?" The older detective nodded. Joel pulled her aside. "Told you I was bossy. You weren't saying anything, and I thought maybe this was all getting to be too much. I should have asked and not decided for you. And after I just dumped all my emotional baggage on you, you may not want to spend any one-on-one time with me. *Do* you have a friend where I can drop you off tonight?"

"Corie's due date is tomorrow, so I'm not calling and imposing on her."

"Melissa?"

"They're at a family reunion with Sawyer's mom and brothers and their families this weekend. And Jessie Caldwell isn't really that kind of friend. Maybe more of a mentor, but I don't want to put her out. She's already help-ing me with Magnus." She didn't know if she was sad or embarrassed when she added, "I don't know who else I could impose upon."

"You're not an imposition. I have a fenced-in backyard. Plenty of room for Magnus to run off-leash. It's a safe neighborhood. My coffee maker works, and I've got beer in the fridge."

"Trying to sell me on your offer with beer and coffee?" Her gaze dropped to his waist and chest before meeting his eyes again. "I suppose you do have a gun and a badge."

He smiled at her subtle teasing. "There is that."

Mollie's hand found the top of Magnus's head, and she drew in a calming breath, her decision made. "Do you have a spare bed?"

"Yes. Nothing fancy, but it's clean and comfortable."

"I come with a dog. I don't need fancy." She peeked around Joel's shoulder to A.J. "I'll be staying with Detective Standage tonight. You can call me there or on my cell phone if you need me."

"Sounds good." A.J. offered her an apologetic smile. "I really do need you to do a quick walk-through with Detective Taylor to see if you think anything is missing, or if there's another message besides what's on the door. Pack a bag if you need to. He'll let you know what things are safe to touch. I need to talk to Detective Standage for a few minutes." She nodded and headed for the door. "Sorry, but, the dog should probably remain out here. So, he doesn't accidentally disturb anything."

Her pulse leaped in a moment of panic. She didn't want to face anything Augie had left for her on her own. "But Magnus is my service dog."

Joel held his hand out for the leash. "I'll keep an eye on him—if you'll be okay without him for a few minutes. You've got this, Moll." She debated for a moment, then put her precious boy's leash in his hand and ordered the dog to stay. "We'll be at the door, so he can keep an eye on you."

Trust me to be there for you. To be enough to take care of whatever you need.

Baby steps, Mollie. She'd made huge strides in reclaiming some of her confidence and independence over the past two days. If she didn't want to be the prisoner of her fears the rest of her life, she needed to keep taking those steps forward. She could trust this man with her dog, at least. Right? "Okay."

Carefully finding her way around overturned chairs and food dumped from her cabinets and refrigerator, Mollie entered her apartment. She looked back to see Joel in a terse sotto voce conversation with his boss. About the crime scene? About her? About Augie?

Although the conversation was slightly heated, Joel
sensed her looking, and turned to make eye contact with
her. He winked before glancing down at Magnus. Her Belgian Malinois was lying down like a sphinx in the doorway,
his tongue lolling out the side of his mouth as he panted,
his dark eyes following her as she moved through the apartment after Detective Taylor.

Relaxed. Not concerned. Surrounded by people he
seemed to trust.

Could she trust these men, too?

She was spending the night with a man. She hadn't done
that since her divorce. And those first few weeks when
she'd been staying at a homeless shelter, trying to save
enough money for the down payment on this apartment,
was the last time she'd had any kind of roommate besides
Magnus.

She wasn't worried about staying with Joel. She didn't
fear that he would try to hurt her, didn't worry that he had
an ulterior motive for being kind to her and Magnus. She
didn't dread the idea of sharing a meal with him and dropping her guard enough to be able to sleep.

Joel Standage was her friend. He'd answered her call for
help twice today. And she got the feeling that he was just as
leery of where this relationship might be going as she was.
She was honest enough with herself to admit that there *was*
a relationship developing here. And that was okay. With
her. With Joel. And apparently, with Magnus.

Chapter Seven

The After Dark gentlemen's club wasn't in the best part of town. But the appointments of green leather, mahogany, and etched glass gave it the feeling of wealth and privilege. The place had been raided and closed down more than once in its checkered past, but under the new management of entrepreneur Roman Hess, After Dark had become less of a strip joint, and more of a place where wealth and discretion were the norm. The liquor was top-shelf, and the booths were appropriately secluded for meetings such as this one.

The host shooed away the server who had brought their drinks and welcomed the big man who slid into his seat on the far side of the table.

The big man downed his whiskey in one gulp, then wiped the back of his hand across his lips as he leaned back against the green leather with a self-satisfied sigh. "That went well."

"Is the cop you saw her with going to be a problem?"

"No. He's gimpy and washed up. I hear he's been stuck behind a desk for the past few months. He got lucky with the car yesterday. If you'd wanted me to actually hit them, I could have." He smirked a laugh. "Should have clipped the dog, though. I'm not a big fan of that mutt."

Although the host wanted to be there to witness first-hand how Mollie Di Salvo got knocked off her high horse each and every step of the way, there was the practical matter of distancing oneself from the crimes to maintain plausible deniability. That's what willing employees like this one were for. "How did she look when you saw her today?"

"Scared out of her mind."

"Serves her right. I haven't had a moment's peace since she dared to defy the Di Salvo name."

The big man rested his forearms on the table and fisted one hand within the other. "I didn't find what you're looking for."

No apology was necessary. "I didn't think you would. That country bimbo is smarter than she looks. I imagine she has more than one copy and a couple of contingency plans to keep them hidden."

A smug smile spread across the big man's expression. "I did put my hands on everything she owns in that ratty little apartment—from dumping out the dog food to slicing up her boring cotton panties."

"She really has fallen a long way from the life she once had with us."

"I'll bet she misses everything she gave up."

"Threw away, you mean." It was hard to compare the beautiful, polished blonde who'd lived at the mansion for two years with the ragamuffin brunette who waited tables at a diner—poorly, too, if reports were accurate. "I've worked too hard to get where I am. I'm not about to let her get her grubby waitress hands on any of it. And I won't allow her to ruin what the Di Salvo family has built."

The big man nodded his agreement. "What's the next step?"

"We keep her off-balance, punish her for her disobedience. When the time is right and I do get my hands on her, I want her to fall apart and beg to give me everything I want."

"Right before we kill her?"

The host gave a firm no. "I'm not getting my hands dirty. That's what I'm paying you for."

"I appreciate you giving me this opportunity. Done wonders for my bank account. I'll be waiting for my next assignment."

"Soon. I'll let you know." An envelope thick with cash exchanged hands. "I reward loyalty like yours. Mollie Di Salvo doesn't know the meaning of loyalty. That was her mistake. Keep up the good work."

The big man tucked the envelope inside the front of his jacket, understanding that he was being dismissed. "What about her dog?"

"Expendable."

"And the cop?"

"Also expendable." The host held up a hand for the server to return with another drink. "All that matters is getting what's mine. And making her pay for causing me so much trouble."

MOLLIE STOOD ON the front porch of Joel's gray bungalow as she hugged her arms around herself and watched the rain fall from the night sky. Lightning flashed, momentarily lighting up the clouds above her, and the drumbeat of thunder rumbled in the distance. The hairs on her arms pricked to attention with the electricity in the air.

Some people might find the storm unsettling or even frightening, she supposed. But she loved being out in nature like this. After the intense heat of the past few days, a thunderstorm had been inevitable. She loved the normalcy of it all. Hot, moist air rose into cooler air higher in the atmosphere. The moving air charged the atmosphere. Water vapor formed as the air cooled, lightning flashed, and rain fell from the sky. The process repeated itself over and over. Everything felt right in Mother Nature's world tonight.

She missed nights out in the trees and hills of the Ozarks, where she could smell the rain and feel cocooned from the rest of the world by a summer storm. Her vandalized apartment had no balcony, and the metal fire escape outside her window wasn't where she wanted to stand when there was lightning. And outdoor activities beyond a stuffy garden party were generally frowned upon at the Di Salvo estate. Joel's home might still be within the city limits of Kansas City, but the old neighborhood with the charming small houses and well-tended yards felt a lot closer to the country than where she lived in the City Market area north of downtown.

She breathed in the ozone-scented air, closed her eyes, and savored the damp mist from the rain splashing her cheeks and frizzing her hair.

"I'd feel better if you two came inside." Joel's gravelly voice matched the rumbles of thunder and darkness of the night.

She smiled at the unexpected sense of familiarity and security she felt here. She spread her fingers across the limestone rocks that still held some of the heat from the day. "I love your front porch. These rock pillars make me think of Granny's house. We used to sit out on her porch when it rained. It was always so cool and refreshing. No central air."

"It's not the storm I'm worried about."

"Oh." She turned to see him waiting in the shadows behind the screen door. He was leaning heavily on a metal cane tonight. She wondered if the same barometric pressure changes she'd been enjoying made his injuries ache more than usual. "Do you really think Augie's men are out in this?" She pointed to the porch lamp beside him. "I left the light off."

"Good call." He pushed the door open wider and gestured for her to come in. "But my gun and badge still think inside and out of sight is a safer place for you to be until we can figure out what your ex is up to. Come on, boy." Magnus immediately rolled to his feet and trotted indoors to find a drier, softer place to snooze, no doubt. Mollie hesitated at the threshold, saddened to be reminded that every decision in her life seemed to go back to her ex-husband and his impact on her life. "Unless you're afraid to be alone in the house with me."

"That's not it." Mollie tilted her gaze to Joel's, marveling at how his beautiful eyes gleamed in the lamplight from inside his living room. She couldn't help but notice, too, that while she was dressed in sweatpants and a long-sleeved shirt in deference to the weather and the air-conditioning in his house, Joel wore a pair of gym shorts and a faded gray KCPD T-shirt that clung to his biceps and gave her a glimpse of more of the tattoo swirling around his left arm. Her pulse beat at a faster tempo as she imagined pushing his sleeve out of the way and tracing her fingers completely around the intricate markings.

Good grief. She'd never been obsessed with any man's body the way she was with Joel's. Not even Augie's back when she'd been happy with him. When she realized her nostrils were flaring as she breathed in the clean, spicy scent of his skin and damp hair after his shower, she turned away and hurried through the front door.

She sat on the tweedy black and tan plaid couch where she'd been reading a book while he showered and changed after dinner. The throw blanket he'd offered her earlier was piled on the oak floor beside her feet, and Magnus was stretched across it with his head resting on his teddy bear. With Magnus's dog bed out of commission, Joel had been kind enough to give the dog permission to make himself at home with his things, although she'd drawn the line at letting the dog up on the couch. Dog hair and drool weren't the easiest things to clean up.

Mollie heard the screen door latch and two locks engage on the interior door before Joel spoke again. "Then what is it? Do you need something? I'd rather not run to the store in this weather, but I will. I can loan you a sweatshirt if you're cold. Or, I've got a spare toothbrush from my last trip to the dentist if you forgot yours."

Wincing in sympathy, she watched pain jar through his clenched teeth as he limped around the black leather ottoman that served as a coffee table and practically fell into his seat at the far corner of the sofa. He leaned the metal cane against the armrest and immediately dug his fist into the scars of his thigh above his right knee. "How much pain are you in?" she asked.

"Answer my question first. Are you okay being in here with me tonight?"

"Joel," she protested.

"Moll," he mimicked right back.

She would have laughed at his teasing delivery if she wasn't worried about him. "On a scale of one to ten, what's your pain level right now?"

"You're not my nurse."

"No. But I do have some experience dealing with healing fractures and sore muscles."

Joel nailed her with a look that conveyed a depth of anger he thankfully held in check. "I'm never going to let that man touch you again."

Yeah, yeah. Augie was a monster who'd screwed up her life and left her a fragile shell of her former self. But one thing she *could* still do well was focus on someone else, especially if that someone was in pain, and she could help. "One to ten?"

The grin that softened the angles of his face made her think she'd imagined the anger from a moment before. "You were a handful for your granny growing up, weren't you. Sarcastic. Stubborn. Strong. That's the real you, isn't it."

She faced him on the couch, settling her back against the armrest and curling her legs beneath her. She plucked at an imaginary piece of lint on the butt-hugging sweats she wore and nonchalantly responded. "I can neither confirm nor deny any worrisome late nights I might have caused Granny."

He laughed out loud.

THAT WAS THE moment when Joel realized he was in deep trouble with this woman.

At first glance, Mollie Crane was fragile and scattered and in need of a rescuer—just like Cici Martin had been. And yeah, she triggered his need to help and protect her, to be needed by someone. But unlike Cici, who'd lost her way to drugs and a quick fix for her pain, Mollie had courage and a sense of humor and was fighting for her own salvation every step of the way. She turned to a dog, not drugs, to cope. She worked hard at a job she might not love, found herself a decent place to live, bought herself a rattletrap of a car he fully intended to check out before he let her drive another centimeter in it, and made her own way in the world. She'd escaped her violent prison, and still had the strength to make a joke and care about others. He'd seen her interact with the people she worked with at the diner. It felt as if she might even care a little bit about him.

"That's the Mollie I like. Do you mind if I put my feet up?" She didn't protest when he turned sideways and stretched his legs across the couch. It was a big piece of furniture, and with her curled up like that, his toes barely touched the edge of the cushion where she sat. "Storms like this and changes in the weather wreak havoc on my rebuilt knees. Plus, I lost my favorite cane in your alley yesterday, so I've been walking and running without it too much today. I'm probably at a four or five. The hot shower helped. I'll take a couple of ibuprofens when I go to bed. Mostly, I just need to get off them for a while."

"Do you have enough room to stretch out?" she asked.

"Yes. Now, answer my question." He was really hoping for an answer that wouldn't make him feel guilty for issuing the invitation earlier that evening. "Are you okay here? Or is being with me stressing you out?"

"I'm fine."

He suspected as much after she'd put her foot down about his pain and teased him with a silly answer about her childhood, but he still breathed a sigh of relief to hear her say the actual words. "I'm glad."

"I certainly don't want to be in my apartment with a busted lock tonight. Even with Magnus, I wouldn't feel safe. I'm sure I wouldn't sleep." She shrugged. "I don't know if it's the house or the storm isolating us from the threat that's out there, or you, but I feel safe. I enjoy our conversations. I know there are some heavy issues we have to discuss regarding Augie. But I appreciate that you're not pushing me. To be honest, I haven't felt this…normal…with a man in a long time."

"Normal?" Was that akin to *comfortable*?

"It's hard to explain." She tucked a dark curl behind her ear and caught her bottom lip between her teeth in a soft smile that zinged straight to his groin. He wanted to taste that bottom lip for himself, soothe the spot where she nipped it with the stroke of his tongue. But she continued to talk, and he wasn't going to do a damned thing to scare her away from the easy conversations they'd been sharing all evening. So, he continued to rub at the knotted muscles in his thigh and pretend that this was how every evening between them might go. "The storm reminds me of where I grew up. I love your house. It's small, but it feels like a home. It's easy, relaxed here. I don't feel I have to dress for company or choose the right fork to eat with."

"We had pizza and beer and used our fingers," he reminded her. "I'm not that fancy."

She patted her tummy, indicating that she was still full from the takeout meal they'd picked up on the way here. "My ex-mother-in-law would have had a coronary if she caught anyone eating on the couch watching the ball game like we did tonight. And pizza was food for the hired help, not the Di Salvos. If Bernadette caught me eating anything but a canapé or hors d'oeuvres with my fingers, she would have told Edward. Edward would have told Augie. Then there'd be a conversation about me forgetting my station and embarrassing him."

"Did your in-laws live with you?" She was talking about her past. This was the information he needed. He knew he should keep her sharing intel about her previous life, but hell if he wanted to talk about anything except the two of them.

"The Di Salvo estate where you worked for a few months belongs to Augie's parents. *We* lived with *them*. Separate wings of the mansion, but still…" She sighed heavily. "Unless they were traveling, or he was on a business trip, Edward and Bernadette were there."

"Nothing says *honeymoon* like having your in-laws on the premises."

But his joke didn't elicit a smile. "Edward and Augie had offices in the city. But they conducted a lot of their business at the house. Dinner parties were contract negotiations. Business associates would stay in a guest room and use the home office for strategy meetings. Late-night drinks were for problem solving."

"What kind of problems?"

"Augie could be a loose cannon." Obviously. "He'd alienate clients with a temper tantrum or sleep with someone's wife. I learned too late that marrying me was supposed to clean up his reputation." She pumped her fist as if she was repeating a familiar cheer. "Sweet, all-American girl. No family to speak of, but a straight-A student who hadn't gotten herself knocked-up before graduation or caused any scandals. Pretty enough to be arm candy, but not ambitious enough to be a threat to the family." She shook her head, no doubt recalling what a sham her marriage had become by the time he'd met her. "I was in a vulnerable place when I met him. Granny had just died. I thought I was gaining a devoted husband and a loyal family who cared about me.

But I was just window dressing. Once I got to know the real family, I became a prisoner, a puppet to play whatever part they needed from me."

"I'm so sorry. You deserve so much better."

She nodded. "Because I was so unhappy, *I* became the problem sometimes."

"You?" Since she'd been isolated from him during most of his assignment there, he hadn't realized just how much of the family business pertained to her. She could be a gold mine of information for KCPD. But the more he got to know her, the less he liked the idea of looking to her for a lead on their investigation. "What possible problem could they blame on you?"

She plucked at that invisible piece of lint again. "Volunteering for the wrong charity. I'm trained to teach. I wanted to volunteer with schoolchildren, but that didn't have the client base the Di Salvos were looking for. I needed to schmooze with wealthier people. Set them up for meetings with Augie."

"I'll bet you're a good teacher. Do you miss it?"

She gave him half a smile. "I keep my hand in it by tutoring Corie's son, Evan, and Jessie Caldwell's foster kids."

"Why are you waiting tables? Isn't there a demand for good teachers?"

Her gaze dropped to the dog snoring at the foot of the sofa, and he knew he'd hit a sensitive spot for her. But before he could turn the conversation to something less upsetting for her, she answered. "Edward is friends with one of the school board members. He got a note slipped into my personnel file that says I'm a danger to children. That I'm mentally unstable."

"No way." Joel fisted his hand on the back of the sofa

and scooted closer to her. "You have panic attacks brought about by a traumatic marriage that they're responsible for. People with disabilities work in schools all the time, and yours is minor compared to some of the stuff I've heard about. They're all good people. Good teachers. Just because they're in a wheelchair or blind or need a service dog doesn't make them a threat to anybody."

She gaped at him through his entire defense of her. Too late, he realized he was probably scaring the crap out of her.

"I'm sorry," he quickly apologized. He opened his fist and pulled it back into his lap. "What you said pissed me off. I didn't mean to yell at you."

"You weren't yelling at me. You were angry on my behalf. I can tell the difference." She didn't leave the room. She didn't reach for her dog. She didn't even flinch away from his toes pressed against her knee. His brave, backbone-of-steel girl simply nodded and quietly answered. "That's the kind of power they have. If they want something, they know someone or pay someone to make it happen. Or they pay someone to make it go away."

"Like you?"

She was silent for so long, Joel thought he'd pushed too hard, got too emotional, and the conversation was over. But her words surprised him. "I left on my own terms. I didn't take a penny from them." Her fingers rubbed against the outline of the locket she wore beneath her long-sleeved T-shirt. "The break-in at my apartment? I'm sure they were looking for something I took from Augie." She reached down to pet Magnus now, as the conversation became more stressful for her. "I had to blackmail him to get him to sign the divorce papers and then leave me alone. He threatened to kill me if I ever left him. And I believed him. I had to do something to get the advantage over him."

Blackmail? Forget the fact that technically Mollie had committed a crime if what she was saying was true. This could be the mother lode of information A.J. thought she could give them. "What could you possibly take that would inspire the kind of violence you've seen the past couple of days?"

"Evidence of illegal activities. Money laundering. Pay-offs. Intimidation tactics."

Bingo.

But there was a catch. She nibbled on her bottom lip again, and it was all Joel could do not to slide across the sofa and take her in his arms and tell her she never had to talk about any of this again. "I know that's what you want from me. That's what A.J. and Josh want from me. But I can't give that to you. The moment I hand over the information I have, I lose any leverage I have over Augie and his family. They'll come after me. They'll silence me. The only advantage I have is that they don't know where I've hidden the information, or how many copies I've made, or who I've arranged for it to be distributed to should anything happen to me. I'm sorry, Joel, but I can't do it."

Magnus sat up and laid his head in her lap, no doubt sensing the same fear he felt radiating off her in waves.

"You have evidence that can implicate the Di Salvos?" Joel felt compelled to point out the same facts A.J. and Josh would. "Withholding evidence is a crime."

She continuously stroked Magnus's head, but her pretty blue eyes were focused squarely on him. "So is blackmail. If it helps any, I never took any money from them. Just the divorce and my freedom. Arrest me if you have to, but keeping the evidence hidden is how I'm staying alive."

And that's where the facts he needed for this investigation ended.

After a few moments, Mollie gave Magnus permission to lie down again. "Good boy. You go night-night with Teddy, okay?" Joel imagined the dog was giving him the stink eye for upsetting his mama before the Malinois stretched out again on the floor in front of the couch.

That was probably his cue to shut up and get to bed himself before he said or did anything else that would scare Mollie away from the tentative trust they shared. "I'll re-check the windows and doors, make sure everything is secure before we turn in."

"You're not going to ask me any more questions about Augie?"

She was frowning when he met her gaze. She didn't yet understand that her well-being was more important to him than any investigation. "No."

Joel started to pull away. But Mollie grabbed his ankles and stopped him. "The round, puckered scars on your knees. Are those bullet wounds?"

He tugged against her grasp. "You don't want to hear my story tonight."

Her grip tightened almost painfully, and he suddenly had the insight that maybe she needed to talk about something else besides August Di Salvo so she could fall asleep and not have nightmares. Or simply fall asleep at all. Once she realized she was still holding his legs, she eased her clutch on him and stroked her fingers along the sides of his calves. Her fingertips felt like heaven against his skin. But she suddenly pulled them away. "Is it okay if I touch you?"

He nodded. "You don't have to ask. You can touch me anytime you want."

"But you're so respectful of my needs. You always ask, or make sure I know it's you."

"Those are your boundaries, and I'll respect them as long as you need me to. Mine are different. Not everybody gets permission, but you do." He held out his hand until she rested her fingers against his palm. "Yes. I've been shot in both legs."

Her grip tightened around his for a moment before she pulled away to settle her hands back against his legs. "You've had surgery to replace both knees?"

"Yes."

"You sound so cold and clinical when you talk about your injuries."

"My therapist says that, too." Her eyes opened wide at the news he'd been seeing the KCPD psychologist. Well, that he was supposed to be reporting for more sessions with her. "But that's how I cope. I keep my emotions pinned down, so they don't get in the way of doing my job."

She arched a skeptical eyebrow. "Your job pushing papers?"

He poked her knee with his big toe. "Smart-ass."

Thankfully, she let the topic drop and resumed her curiosity and concern about his pain.

"I always found that alternating a hot washcloth and cold compresses helped when my injuries were healing." She climbed up onto her knees and scooted between his feet, forcing his legs apart. "Once the bruising had faded, a good massage stimulated the blood flow and helped the aches feel better." She leaned forward and wrapped her hands around the thigh he'd been rubbing himself. When she dug her thumbs into the ligaments and muscle above his knee, he winced. But it was a good kind of pain. The initial rebellion of his knotted muscles calmed a bit with each pass of her fingers across his skin. "Wow. You're tight as a crossbow. You've been overcompensating for your painful joints. No wonder you're limping."

"Crossbow?" he bit out through his tightly clenched jaw. Her strong hands and nimble fingers created a friction that warmed his skin and settled into his muscles. The massage hurt at first, but he exhaled sharply when the cramp unknotted itself and the pain finally eased to an ache rather than the stabbing sensation that had practically crippled him.

She inclined her head to the book on the ottoman. "You had a copy of the first Bonecrusher Chronicles on your bookshelf. I love that series."

He nodded. He liked that they were both fans of the high fantasy series. "Larkin Bonecrusher carries a crossbow."

She smiled in a pretty apology as she continued to work the kinks out of his leg muscles. "Don't take this the wrong way, but you don't look like a reader. Yet you've got a ton of books over there."

Genuinely curious now, he asked, "What does a reader look like?"

"You know. Skinny. Glasses. Socially awkward." She slapped a hand over her mouth and blushed. "I am so sorry. That was a terrible stereotype." She went back to the massage, focusing intently on her work and refusing to meet his gaze. "Readers come in all shapes and sizes and personalities, of course. I just meant that you seem more like a man of action, that you prefer to be outdoors rather than curled up on the couch reading like I was." He grinned when she waved her hand at him, indicating his face and body, without looking at him. "With all your badness and spiky hair and scars and scruffy face and all."

His badness? Joel chuckled and extended a hand toward her. "May I?"

She nodded when she understood his intent. "You don't have to ask every time you want to touch me, either. As long as I know it's you."

"Thank you." He reached out with one finger to tap her chin and tilt her gaze up to his. "I'm an old pro. I had a lot of time to read during my recovery. Besides, that's how I got my brothers to sleep every night. I'd read stories to them. It's still how I get myself to sleep most nights."

"I like that. I read, too, to escape reality long enough to calm my thoughts and relax."

He pulled back and leaned against the arm of the sofa, savoring her willingness to touch him and truly appreciating the massage. "I don't know what kind of badass you think I am. Blending in and looking like every other guy on the street is my stock-in-trade. Yeah, I work out and take care of myself. But I've always had a forgettable face. Brown hair, brown eyes. I'm easy to overlook. Makes me a perfect candidate for undercover work."

Her hands stilled above his knees. "That's not true."

"No, I was pretty good at UC work. Right up until my last case."

"What I meant was that there's nothing about you that's forgettable. Your eyes are more golden than brown. That first night I met you, I thought of a tiger. And tonight, they're reflecting the light the way a cat's would. Your voice is sexy—low and gravelly, like you just woke up or you just had…"

Her eyes got wide, and she blushed. *Sex*. She was thinking about him and sex together in the same sentence.

Joel adjusted his position on the couch to hide his body's
reaction to her innocently provocative words. He was in
more trouble than he thought. He wasn't just attracted to
Mollie's sass and vulnerability. He was falling hard and
fast for a woman who'd been so damaged by her previous relationship that she might never be able to love again.

She curled her fingers into her fists and pulled away
to hug her arms around herself. Just as quickly, she was
gesturing to him again. "You're funny one minute and
over-the-top manly the next. You've got muscles and tats.
Not everyone is into those, but they give you that bad boy
vibe—unless those words on your arm are a Shakespear-
ean sonnet."

"They're not. If you want to read my ink, all you have to
do is ask. I just didn't think you were the kind of woman
who would be into tattoos."

Her eloquent hands landed on her hips, and she gave him
a confused look. "What kind of woman do you think I am?"

"Very high-class. Out of place in a working-class neighborhood like the City Market or Brookside. A lady through
and through. Way out of my league."

"And you claim I misread *you*?" Any trace of embarrassment was gone. Now she was just huffy, and it was
cute as hell. "Joel Standage, I was raised in the country by
my granny. Not my grandmother or my grand-mama. We
lived in a little town in the Ozarks. I went from kindergar-
ten through twelfth grade, all in the same building. I can
make biscuits and gravy from scratch that would make your
daddy weep. I can change my own tire on a car and fix a
toilet. I played second base on my high school softball team,

and we made it to State my senior year and I had the best double-play completion stats in the entire state that year. I had a twang in my voice until I met Augie in college, and he convinced me I could go further in life without it. But it sneaks back in now that I don't have to watch every word I say. I try to be a lady, but I'm not some prissy girlie-girl with a stick up her butt like you're describing."

Food. Cars. Softball. Snark. He was so hot for her right now.

He realized his mouth was hanging open, and he snapped it shut. "You can make biscuits and gravy?"

She puffed out a breath that stirred the wavy bangs on her forehead. "That's what you got out of my impassioned speech?"

"I love biscuits and gravy."

She smiled and shook her head. "You come off as a streetwise bad boy, most of the time. But you're just a little boy inside."

"A little boy who likes biscuits and gravy," he mock pouted. She laughed out loud, and Joel smiled, thinking she didn't do that nearly often enough. "And if I'm around, you won't be changing your own tire or fixing the damn toilet. You don't have to change who you are to meet some society standard that the Di Salvos want you to be. That's not what makes you a lady."

She uncurled her legs from beneath her and scooted back to the far end of the couch, pausing as she considered his words. He could see the expression on her face change when she made a decision.

Leaning toward him, she rested her hand lightly over his shinbone. "Do you want me to fix you breakfast in the morning?"

"Yes. If you can find something more than a box of cereal in my pantry, I would love to eat anything homemade."

"You don't cook?"

"I fix cars."

"Huh? I don't get the connection."

"I never learned how to cook. Mom left us, remember? I learned how to fix cars. I'm good with engines, not ovens."

"How did you feed your brothers when you were taking care of them?"

"I can grill burgers or hot dogs outside, and whip up a mean box of mac and cheese. And I can zap anything in the microwave. But I don't have the kind of skills you're talking about."

He was suddenly, vibrantly aware of her hand on his leg. "I'm sure you have other useful skills, Detective."

Well, hell's bells. Was that sexual innuendo from Mollie Crane? Or did he just want it to be? The part of him swelling inside his shorts voted yes. Joel swung his feet to the floor, grabbed his cane, and stood before he embarrassed her with his physical reaction to her. "It's late. You must be getting tired. Does Magnus need to go out one more time? When do you need to get up for work? You can use the alarm on your phone, or I've got an old clock in my dresser."

Mollie stepped over Magnus and hurried to block his path on the other side of the ottoman. "Did I say something wrong? You act like you're trying to make a quick getaway."

When this whole assignment started, he promised himself not to lie to her. He wasn't going to start lying now. Feeling like the luckiest man in the world to know she'd given him permission to touch her, he reached out to capture a tendril of rich brown hair that had fallen over her cheek. He watched the tendril curl around his finger before he brushed it back and tucked it behind her ear. Then he sifted his fingertips into the silky weight of her hair at her nape and cupped the side of her neck and jaw. "I like you, Mollie Crane. More than a guy you need as a friend should. Some of tonight feels like flirting, like we're on a date and really getting to know each other because it's leading to something… I'm trying to be a good guy and walk away while I still can."

"A date? Can you imagine how out of practice I am at picking up signals and flirting after being married to Augie? And you have no idea how good it feels to have somebody touch me, and be able to touch him, and not freak out." Instead of pulling away, she turned her cheek into his palm. Her skin was warm and soft against his. "I'm sorry if I made things awkward or you thought I was leading you on."

"I don't. You have nothing to apologize for."

She smiled at being let off the hook so easily. "I've been scared for so long, it felt good to relax with you tonight and be comfortable enough with you to resurrect a little of who I used to be. I mean, I do have brains and a personality. I have history besides being a Di Salvo. I care about people. I haven't always lived from one panic attack to the next."

He picked up on the same word he'd been feeling since the moment they'd reconnected at the dog park. "You're *comfortable* with me?"

"Yes. I'm surprised at how quickly I'm learning to trust you. It's like I've known you for a lot longer than a couple of days and a couple of random meetings in the past."

"It's like fate kept trying to push us together, but we

weren't in the right place in our lives to do anything about it until now."

Nodding her agreement with his fanciful notion, she wound her fingers around his wrist, holding his hand against her face, linking them together. "Full disclosure? I think I also have the hots for you, and I'm wondering if I can ever be *normal* with a man again. If I can build the kind of trust necessary to be intimate with someone."

Joel burned with the implication of what she was saying. "Did Di Salvo...?"

"Yes. He forced me. Whether or not I was in the mood didn't matter if Augie wanted sex. Thankfully, he always had a girlfriend or two on the side, so it didn't happen too often."

Not too often? That didn't make it any easier to hear how that bastard had brutalized her. "I'm going to kill that son of a bitch."

She shifted her hand to cup his unshaven jaw, mirroring the hold he had on her. "No. You're not. If I'm lucky, you're going to be very patient with me, and you're going to conduct a thorough police investigation. And then we're going to put him away in prison, where somebody else can kill him for us."

Joel's eyebrows rose at the quick addendum. She'd not only calmed his need for retribution, but she'd said *we* and *us*, letting him know that she was feeling the bond growing between them, too. "Yes. To all that. I shouldn't like your vindictive streak, but I do."

She glanced down at the tent in his gym shorts and pulled away without putting any distance between them. "Thank you for being stronger than I am tonight. Maybe one day you won't feel you have to hide that from me, and we can make out on your couch. Hopefully, I won't freak out on you and be a disappointment."

"No way could you disappoint me. We're *comfortable* with each other, remember? That's our motto now. Making out with you will blow my mind, I'm sure. Anything beyond that will be a true gift. And if it never happens, that's okay, too. We'll go as hot and heavy or slow and careful as we need to, and I will treasure every moment."

He was surprised when she grasped his forearm and turned it so she could read the words inked there. "Are you sure this isn't a sonnet on your arm? You spout some pretty sweet poetry when you want to."

"Nah." He pulled up his sleeve so she could read the full message. "It's part of the Armed Forces prayer. I got it in honor of my father and brothers."

She read the words out loud. "'Teach us not to mourn those who have died in the service of the Corps, but rather to gain strength from the fact that such heroes have lived.'" Tears glistened in her eyes when she tilted her gaze back to his. "Oh, Joel. This applies to you, too. It's beautiful. Your family must be so proud." She stunned him when she leaned in and kissed the words above his elbow. Then she lifted her gaze to his. Keeping her hand braced against his bicep, she stretched up to gently kiss his stubbled jaw, his cheek, and finally the corner of his mouth.

He couldn't have held back the groan of desire that rumbled in his throat if his life depended on it. Mollie was kissing him. Battered by life, but never broken, she sweetly, boldly slid her lips against his. She'd put her hands on him and stirred his body to life. But her soft, sweet lips were stoking a fire deeper inside.

Joel dropped his cane to the rug and cupped her face with

both hands, tunneling his fingers into the silky weight of her hair. He kissed her chastely at first, pressing his closed mouth against hers, not wanting to frighten her just as much as he *did* want to claim everything she offered him. She didn't protest when he angled her head from one position to another, seeking the perfect link between their lips. And each new taste was as perfect as the last.

He felt each fingertip digging into the muscles of his arm, and her open palm skimming along the textures of his scratchy stubble and the short, damp hair at the back of his head. When her lips parted to capture his bottom lip between her own, Joel felt his temperature spike. In response, he stroked his tongue along the plump arc of her lower lip and the sculpted arch of her pliant upper lip, asking for permission to enter. Her warm gasp across his skin was more of a turn-on than the most seductive words. Her lips parted and her tongue tentatively reached out to touch his. Their tongues danced around each other for a few seconds before he slipped inside her mouth and claimed the generous gift of her willing mouth.

He tasted a slight tang of beer on her tongue, or maybe that was his own. He breathed in the delicate flowery scent of whatever lotion or soap she'd used on her face. Their bodies never touched. It was hands in hair and lips and tongues, exploring and claiming, giving and demanding, and absolute heaven.

This woman was brave yet fragile. She was strong but delicate. She was generous yet cautious. She was more than everything he wanted in a woman. With this kiss? This moment? He knew that she was everything he needed.

With a nervous chuckle in her throat, Mollie broke off the kiss. He felt the gusts of her uneven breaths against his neck and knew he was breathing just as erratically. But he didn't try to re-engage her. He didn't pull her into his body the way he longed to. He didn't tug on her hair to tip her head back so he could kiss his fill of her. Any physical contact between them needed to be on her terms.

Mollie tilted her dark blue eyes up to his. "Sorry. I liked that. I loved it. I've never kissed a man with beard stubble before. It's…sexy…like a hundred extra little caresses against my skin." Her hands had settled on his shoulders, and her gaze dropped to his lips. "You're a really good kisser. Or, maybe I've never been kissed right before… You probably wanted something more, but I'm feeling a little overwhelmed…"

"Hey." He pressed his thumb against her slightly swollen lips to silence her rambling and keep her nerves from spiraling out of control. "Treasure. Every. Moment." He whispered the heartfelt promise before planting a silly kiss on the tip of her nose and another to her forehead, where he lingered long enough to inhale the fragrance of her skin and hair once more. "I don't think I've ever been kissed that right before, either. Thank you."

He bent down to pick up his cane. His gaze swept past her taut nipples poking against the thin cotton of her shirt and he smiled. It was nice to know he wasn't the only one whose clothes felt a little confining right now.

Mollie stepped back and called Magnus to her side. "Magnus is fine for tonight. I'll use my own alarm. Good night, Joel."

He reached out and tucked her short hair behind her ear, tracing his fingertips around her delicate earlobe before pulling away. Knowing he could touch her like this soothed him, even as the possibility of getting closer to her excited him. "Good night, Moll."

She gifted him with a smile before turning away and ordering Magnus to heel. Joel watched her walk down the hallway to the guest bedroom. He was still leaning on his cane and watching as her door snicked shut behind her.

What the hell was he doing here? He wasn't the best man for Mollie's protection detail. He probably wasn't even the best man to be her friend. She needed someone who wasn't as broken as he was. She needed better.

But after tonight, after getting close to her, he wasn't giving the job to anybody else.

So, he was damn well going to figure out how to be a better man for her.

Protector, friend, dog walker, lover—whatever she needed, he wanted to be able to give that to her.

And that meant getting rid of his cane, getting out from behind a desk, and getting back to being the cop—and the man—he'd been before his world had imploded.

Chapter Eight

Joel holstered his weapon, counted down from three, then pulled out his Glock and fired the last three bullets in rapid succession into the outline of a man on the downrange target.

Then he dropped the magazine from the butt of the gun and opened the firing chamber to make sure both were empty before setting them on the shelf in front of him. He was aware of the dark-haired man waiting patiently behind him in the booth at the firing range in the basement of the Fourth Precinct building. But he wanted to complete this round of training to make sure he was good enough to be responsible for Mollie's safety. He was trying to find his way back to being good enough for her, period.

He'd known when A. J. Rodriguez had slipped into the back of the booth a few minutes earlier, but he was focused on the task at hand. He appreciated his boss's inimitable patience and knew that was half the reason A.J. had earned his legendary reputation at KCPD. Joel removed his safety goggles and earphones and pushed the button to bring the target forward.

A.J. pulled off his earphones and hung them on the hook beside Joel's safety gear. "Working off some steam? Or getting your skills in shape so you can go back to your real job?"

"I'm trying to come back from being an idiot and dying. I *need* to come back."

Joel studied the paper target hanging in front of him. Most of his shots hit center mass. But there were three wide shots that would only wing a perp he was trying to bring down or annoy him with the boo-boo on his arm.

A.J. stepped up beside him to check the results, too. "Looks like your aim is drifting a shade to the right. You still favoring that leg?"

Joel felt almost normal right now, but he hadn't gone for his morning run or taken the stairs to the third floor more than once today. He was still relishing the fabulous, unexpected massage he'd gotten from Mollie last night. Although he hated knowing how she'd become such an expert in pressure points, pinched nerves, and massages, she could do some amazing things with those hands. "It's doing better. I don't think it's a hundred percent yet. I don't always need the cane. I just have to be careful about wearing myself out."

"You'll get there."

"Or I'll learn to compensate."

A.J. waited while Joel reassembled and reloaded his gun and secured it in his holster. "I got your message you wanted to meet. Is this about Miss Crane, or you?"

"Both."

"Walk me to my office?" A.J. pushed open the door and gave a salute to the officer on watch while Joel checked out of the range. "We can talk on the elevator ride up."

They walked past the locker rooms, and Joel remembered hiding out there his rookie year when a tornado had come through the city. The building had gone through an extensive remodel since that time, both for architectural and security purposes. But for a long while, it had been just a place to stow his stuff and hang out before his shift upstairs. But that was about to change. He wanted to get back out into the world and be a cop again. Maybe he wasn't ready for the pressure and isolation that came with under- cover work. But he could be a detective. He could run an investigation. He could help Mollie.

He followed A.J. into the empty elevator and waited for the doors to close before he spoke. "I talked to Mollie Crane last night. She does have evidence against August Di Salvo."

"Yeah? She tell you what she has on him?"

This was where Joel needed to tread carefully. "It sounds like something in a file or on a flash drive. She took it to blackmail Di Salvo into signing their divorce papers."

Although his posture looked relaxed as he leaned against the back railing of the elevator, A.J.'s full attention was ze- roed in on Joel. "She gonna work with us?"

Joel shook his head. "Mollie is in a very vulnerable po- sition. I don't know if we should continue working this in- vestigation through her. There has to be another avenue we can pursue."

"We tried that already. We couldn't get any witnesses to stick to their original testimony against him. His attor- ney, Kyra Schmidt, got him off on time served and a fine for obstruction of justice. We need hard evidence and a reliable witness."

Imagining Mollie up on the witness stand while Di Salvo stared daggers at her, and Kyra Schmidt glibly made her look like she was too scared to know her own mind, wasn't an easy picture to stomach. "If she turns it over to us, what's to stop him from going after her? He's threatened to kill her more than once. She claims it's her only leverage to keep him out of her life."

A.J. straightened as they neared the third floor. "Keep him out of her life? What do you think the car in that alley and the break-in at her apartment are about? I'd say Di Salvo or someone who works for him is back in her life already."

The elevator stopped, and Joel followed A.J. through the check-in desk and cubicles of detectives to reach his office in the back hallway. "Those are the angles I want to pursue. If we can tie either one of those crimes back to Di Salvo, we can at least get an arrest warrant and get that guy off the streets so she can breathe a little easier."

A.J. unlocked his door and invited Joel to one of the chairs in front of his desk while the supervising officer circled around to his own chair. "You're going to need a lot more than a B&E and reckless endangerment to keep a Di Salvo behind bars."

"But if we have more than just what she brings to the investigation, doesn't that lessen the threat to her?"

A.J. eyed him for a moment before sitting. "How close are you getting to her?"

"She's staying at my house."

"You up for a protection detail like that?"

Joel paced to the window and looked down on the parking lot below. He scrubbed his hand over the trimmed stubble on his chin that he'd decided against shaving off completely this morning because Mollie had said she liked how it felt against her skin when he'd kissed her last night. He considered A.J.'s question. Clearly, his emotions and desire were already getting tangled up with Mollie Crane. But was he ready to put his life on the line to save someone he cared about again? His heart would do anything to protect her. But his brain wasn't so sure he was the best man for the job. "I don't know, A.J. I've been sittin' a desk for a few months now. That's why I was at the shooting range this afternoon. I know there's a gap between being fit for duty, and being fit enough to hold my own on the street the way I used to."

"Maybe you're a step slower than you used to be. Or you hurt more at the end of a long day. But you were one of my best operatives out on the streets. A lot of people are serving time because of the work you've done. Even the cowards who tried to kill you. You can think on your feet. You're aware of everything going on around you. You know when to hide, when to run, and when to fight." A.J.'s dark eyes drilled into Joel's gaze, making sure he understood what the veteran detective was saying to him. "Even beat-up around the edges, you're a good cop. You need to own that."

Joel returned to his seat across from A.J. He braced his forearms on his knees and clasped his hands together. "The instincts are still there, but I find myself second-guessing almost every decision I make. I'm not sure I know who to trust. I'm not sure I even trust myself."

"Let your training get you past those doubts. You trust me?"

"Yes, sir."

"Then I'll be your handler. I'll get you whatever you need as fast as I can." A.J. picked up the phone on his desk, as if he was about to make a call and get the ball rolling on him becoming an active investigator again. "You trust Mollie?"

Joel hesitated.

A.J.'s thumb ended the call before it had even connected. "It's your decision. You want me to assign someone else to work the case? To protect her?" He leaned back in his chair. "I think Rocky Garner's available."

"That's a low blow." He pushed himself upright. His boss probably wouldn't be giving him a hard time on this if he didn't think he could handle himself successfully.

"Think on it, Joel. Until Miss Crane decides to give us and the D.A. a statement on this evidence she has, Di Salvo will always be a threat to her. What if she decides never to let us help her nail her ex? Can you be on alert 24/7 the rest of your life?"

"If that's what she needs."

"You have to sleep sometime. You're gonna need some backup." A.J. pointed the phone at him, sending the message that even though he was supportive of his team, he was still the man in charge. "I'd have a lot easier time budgeting the extra manpower with the brass if we were getting useful intel from her."

Joel leaned back in his chair, still needing some time to make his decision. "What did you and Josh and the crime lab determine about the break-in at Mollie's apartment?"

"I believe it was as much about intimidation as it was finding this evidence you say she has. It wasn't just a search—it was personal. No more written threats, but..."

Joel wasn't sure he wanted to hear the details, but he needed to. "But what?"

"The intruder went through her lingerie and shredded it. A picture of an old woman with Miss Crane had been cut up, too."

"Her granny?" Joel cursed. "He's trying to break her.

He's trying to get in her head and punish her for having the strength and resourcefulness to outwit him and play hardball with him so that she could get away from the family." The only time he'd seen an obsession like the one Di Salvo had for Mollie was when he witnessed Cici's addiction to drugs firsthand. The thing he wanted the most—to hurt Mollie—was the most important thing in his life. "He probably believes that if he can victimize her again, make her afraid, he can force her to give up the evidence and stop anything incriminating from getting to us and the D.A."

"You think her ex can break her with his intimidation tactics?"

"No. She's a strong woman. I just don't think she always believes it."

"Sounds like somebody else I know, *amigo*." A.J.'s dark eyes narrowed with a piercing stare before he waved him on his way. "Now, get out of here so I can get some work done."

Joel rose from his chair and crossed to the door. He paused with his hand on the doorknob. "May I ask a question?" A.J. nodded. "I heard that you went undercover with your wife, before you married her. Because she was a witness to a murder?"

"That's right." A.J.'s gaze drifted to the picture on his desk of his wife and two boys. "Claire and I met when I was working that case. She was the only person who could identify the hit man."

"Would you have trusted her protection to anyone else but you?"

"That was a different situation. She was already under my skin, and I was falling in love with her. It was my honor and my duty to protect her."

"Would you put her life in anyone else's hands?"

Dark eyes studied his. "No." Then A.J. opened a file and picked up his phone, already going back to work. "Talk to her. See if you can get her to open up to you. And watch your back out there." Knowing he was dismissed, Joel nodded, stepped out, and closed the door.

Under his skin and falling in love. That was exactly where he stood with Mollie.

His decision was made.

JOEL ENJOYED THE training session with Magnus and Mollie. And now, as he watched Jessie and Garrett Caldwell's foster son, Nate, play with Magnus and a myriad of other dogs of all sizes and breeds—from a lumbering Newfoundland to an active Jack Russell terrier, who was darting amongst the other dogs in search of the balls the boy was throwing—he could see the benefits of having a pet or partnering with a working dog.

He drank a long swallow of the tea Jessie had served to the four adults watching the dogs and boy play from the back deck. "Man, I miss having dogs around." He took a seat in the Adirondack chair next to Mollie and pressed the icy glass to his forehead to cool off from the ninety-degree heat. "I wish I could bottle that work drive. I would have graduated from physical therapy and been cleared for active duty a month sooner if I could have focused like Magnus does."

"You recently suffered a trauma, too, Detective Standage?" Jessie asked.

Back to reality. His lighthearted mood vanished. He'd been treating this early evening session like a date when he should have been thinking about how to move the Di Salvo investigation forward while keeping Mollie safe.

The thick, humid air weighed heavy in his lungs as he took in a deep breath and set his drink down. "Yeah. I was injured in the line of duty."

Garrett Caldwell was still wearing his Jackson County deputy's uniform since he'd gotten home from work just before the training session had ended. "Sorry to hear that. What happened?"

Mollie reached over and squeezed Joel's hand. He was grateful for the gentle touch and lightly curled his fingers around hers. Jessie noticed the contact, too. Since he'd figured out that these training sessions were like therapy for Mollie, he wanted to help her get the answers she needed about Magnus. That meant opening up about himself, too, apparently. Still, he opted for sharing the barest of bare-bones versions of his story. "I was working undercover. Got made as a cop."

"That's rough," Garrett sympathized. Judging by the silver in his hair and the chevrons on his badge, he'd had considerable experience in law enforcement. He understood the dangers a man with a badge faced when meeting the enemy face-to-face.

But Jessie wanted details. "What else?"

Joel pinned her with a look. That woman was as intuitive about reading people as she was dogs, it seemed. He must have been staring at her for too long because Garrett moved to sit on the arm of the chair beside his wife and drape a protective arm around her shoulders. "Jessie's just trying to understand the complete picture so she can make an accurate assessment of what's going on with Magnus."

"Sorry." His grip pulsed around Mollie's, and his raw

feelings settled to a manageable level with that simple connection to cling to. "I was betrayed by my last girlfriend. She set me up with her dealer. Told him I was a cop."

Mollie leaned forward to add, "She's gone, too. Drug overdose. Joel tried to save her."

A stark look temporarily darkened Garrett's gray eyes, and he leaned down to kiss Jessie on the crown of her hair. The older woman's hand squeezed her husband's knee, and she gazed up at him until he nodded, and the fiercely protective expression finally eased. "Yeah. Drug dealers can be tough SOBs to deal with."

Joel nodded, thinking Garrett and Jessie and possibly that little boy they were both studying so tenderly now had some personal experience with a drug dealer. Jessie inadvertently confirmed it when she looked up at her husband. "They're okay now, Garrett. Just remember, Nate and Abby are going to truly be ours by Christmas."

"Damn right, they are." He tipped Jessie's chin up and kissed her gently on the mouth. Then he stood, apparently satisfied that his wife was safe without him beside her. He pointed to the house. "I'm just going to check to make sure Abby and her puppy are doing okay upstairs." Joel stood when the older man extended his hand. "Good to meet you, Detective. Mollie."

After he'd gone into the house to see to their foster daughter, Jessie smiled. "Garrett's such a protective father. That little girl isn't going to be allowed to date until she's well into her thirties if he has his way."

Joel smiled as he was meant to, although he felt a little lost when Mollie released his hand. Jessie stood and invited both of them to join her at the railing to watch the dogs eagerly chase the balls and bring them back to the boy, who rewarded them with pets and praise and throwing the balls again. "So, what's the verdict, ma'am?" Joel asked. "Magnus seemed to work just as well with me as he did Mollie, once she showed me the commands. Am I a bad influence on the dog? Am I preventing him from helping her?"

"I don't think so. Mollie, you said Magnus stayed by your side when you had the break-in?"

She nodded. "And he growled at the man who made me feel so uncomfortable."

Jessie tilted her gaze to Joel. "And Magnus came to comfort you when you were telling your story to Mollie."

"That's right."

Jessie pulled her long, blond braid from her shoulder and tossed it behind her back. "I think I know what's going on."

"Please tell me," Mollie urged.

"Magnus sees Joel as part of your pack, and he's protecting the pack," Jessie explained. "Mals are overachievers. Why just take care of one human when he can take care of two? He sees the two of you together as a unit he's in charge of. Basically, he wants to be a service dog for you both. He wants to please you both. I hope you two are serious because he thinks you are."

"Serious?" Mollie echoed. "Like a couple?"

"Yes."

Joel reached down to capture her hand again and lifted it to his lips to kiss it, taking a moment to rub his chin across the back of her hand, giving her some of those hundred little caresses she'd liked so well last night. Her blue eyes darkened, and her lips parted with a sharp intake of breath. Yeah, that kiss last night hadn't been a fluke. These feelings that were hitting him hard and fast seemed to be mutual. "We're working on it."

Mollie's gaze locked on to his. "We are. We have some issues we're still working through, but I care a great deal about Joel."

"Ditto."

She rolled her eyes in that beautifully snarky way she had at his eloquent response, but she was smiling. Then she looked out at Magnus charging across the yard to reach the ball first. "So, you think he's okay? There's nothing wrong with him?"

Jessie shook her head. "I'd keep up your regular training—both of you now. And let him do his job. I think he'll continue to alert when you have a panic attack and—" Jessie glanced up at Joel "—he'll offer you comfort when you're stressed about work or events in your past. And he'll probably be protective of you both."

"Okay. Then I'll try not to worry." Mollie stepped in front of Joel and embraced the other woman. "Thank you, Jessie. I was so worried that either I was a failure or Magnus was."

Joel settled his hand at the small of Mollie's back as they hugged, letting his fingertips slide beneath the T-shirt she wore to touch a strip of soft skin above the waistband of her jeans. Mollie didn't flinch at the modest contact, and since she seemed okay with it, he didn't pull away. But they'd just crossed an emotional hurdle by admitting they cared about each other, and he needed to touch her as much as she needed to hug the woman who had given her a way out of constant fear and stress with Magnus.

"No way is either of you a failure." Jessie smiled, and he was pleased to see Mollie smiling back as the women parted. He was even more pleased to feel Mollie slide her arm behind his waist and hook her thumb into the belt loop of his jeans. "You just have a very smart dog," Jessie continued. "You know, sometimes, I think with his hearing loss, that Magnus feels broken, and he feels he has to do more—be more—to prove that he's important and loved and necessary."

"I understand that," Mollie said, surprising Joel. "I think that's why the two of us bonded."

"You're not losing that bond," Jessie assured her, squeezing Joel's arm to include him. "You're just enriching it by adding Joel to your pack."

Was she talking about dogs or his relationship with Mollie now?

Mollie seemed to ponder the same question for a few seconds before she pulled away and gave Jessie another quick hug. "We'd better get going. It's dinnertime and you have hungry children to feed. Thanks so much."

Jessie frowned. "This isn't the last time I'm seeing you, is it?"

"Of course not. You and your family have a standing invitation at Pearl's Diner. I make to-die-for milkshakes that your kids will love."

"I'd love one, too."

Mollie nodded toward the aging German shepherd mix that had been napping by Jessie's chair. "And bring Shadow with you. Service dogs are welcome there."

"I will."

"Magnus! Come!" Although the Newfoundland had tired of playtime and lain down in the middle of the yard, the other dogs were running circles around him and Nate.

When the Belgian Malinois didn't immediately respond to Mollie's summons, Joel thrust his tongue against his teeth and let out an ear-piercing whistle. The dogs all stopped and turned as one. "Magnus!" Joel put two fingers down at his side, and the black-and-tan dog came running right to him. He touched his wet nose to Joel's fingers, then sat beside him, heavily panting from his exertion. When he saw Mollie crossing her arms and glaring up at him, he quickly apologized. "I didn't think he heard you."

"I can see we're going to have to work on exactly who the pack leader is," Mollie teased before handing him the dog's harness and leash.

Jessie laughed along with Joel. "As long as it isn't Magnus, you two will be okay. Come on, I'll walk you out to your truck."

Chapter Nine

Following another round of goodbyes and a promise to keep in touch, Joel pulled his truck past the gated entrance and security cameras and turned out onto the road leading to Highway 40 into Kansas City. Since there was no center console on the wide bench seat of his truck, Magnus was stretched out between him and Mollie, resting his head on Mollie's lap. She stroked her left hand along the dog's back, more out of habit, he hoped, than any nervousness she was feeling about being alone with him again.

He waited at the light before turning onto the highway. Because they were headed into Kansas City, they were driving against the rush hour traffic heading out to the countryside and small towns east of the city. And since 40 was a divided highway out here in the county, they were pretty much the only vehicle on their side heading west.

He replayed the words she'd said to Jessie. *I care a great deal about Joel.*

Ditto might not have been the snappiest response, but he meant it. He cared a great deal about Mollie. And he had an idea that Magnus had spotted right away what the two of them had been reluctant to recognize, much less act on. He and Mollie meant something to each other. And if she gave him the chance, they were going to mean something to each other for a long time to come—maybe for the rest of their lives.

But he'd start small. He had a feeling knowing when to be patient and when to push would be key to any long-term relationship with Mollie. "Speaking of dinner..." Not the smoothest start to a conversation, but he had Mollie's attention. "We'll drive past about any kind of fast-food restaurant you want when we get to K.C. We can drive through one of them and get dinner to eat at home. Are you in the mood for anything in particular?"

"You're not going to zap something in the microwave for me and show off your cooking prowess?"

He loved it when she teased him. It felt healthy. Normal. A special way to communicate between just the two of them. "Nah. I'm saving that for our third or fourth date. I don't want to spoil you."

She laughed with him. "So, we're dating now?"

Joel sobered up, not wanting any misunderstanding between them. "I'd like to. Maybe I just needed Jessie to put things into perspective for me, but I like you, Moll. A lot."

"You said that last night."

"Yeah, well, maybe it's more than a lot." He glanced across the cab to find her listening intently to his words. "When you told Jessie you cared about me, something seemed to click inside." He skimmed the rearview mirror and took note of a couple of cars on the highway behind them before turning his focus to the road in front of them. "Even when you were still married to the jackass who hurt you, I was attracted to you."

"I was black-and-blue, and I had a split lip and cracked rib."

"You were glorious. Strong. Brave. Not afraid to set

me straight when you told me the rules of the house." He glanced her way again. "Di Salvo would have made things worse for you if I had tried to help you then, wouldn't he."

"Yes. He would have hurt you, too. If not physically, you'd have lost your job, for sure. Of course, I didn't know then that chauffeuring wasn't your real job."

"I was involved with Cici then, so I wouldn't have acted on my attraction. I felt guilty for not being able to help you then, but I admired you." She turned away to look out the side window, and he took note of the SUV behind them, slowing and turning left into a tire and auto repair business between the east and west lanes of the highway. With the hills, curves, and trees along the highway, there was only one other vehicle in sight behind them, and that one disappeared into a valley, and they were alone again. "Then I met you again that night at the diner when Rocky Garner put his hands on you, and I was struck all over again by how much I was attracted to you. I wanted to punch his lights out for upsetting you like that."

"I was a mess, Joel," she reminded him. "I'm still a bit of a mess."

He shook his head. "You're a work in progress. So am I. We've both been through some stuff, but we're getting better. The chemistry between us gets my blood pumping, just like it always has. You mentioned that you miss human contact. But when you hold my hand or reach out to me, it soothes something inside me. Knowing you trust me enough to be the man you can do normal, touchy-feely stuff with makes me feel like a stud."

She chuckled at that description. "You *are* a stud, Joel Standage."

He tried to explain himself in a way that didn't make

him sound so egotistical. "Spending time with you makes me feel better about myself. I feel grounded. You settle things inside me."

"We're comfortable with each other."

"Yeah. I think *comfortable* for us means we're good for each other. Maybe I sensed that potential bond when we first met two years ago." He shifted his grip on the wheel, wishing he wasn't doing so much of the talking here. "Please tell me I'm not the only one feeling this connection between us."

"You're not," she answered quietly.

"We're both free of our exes now, in one way or another. We can do something about how we feel."

"I'm not free of Augie."

"You can be."

He heard her pained gasp above the hum of the truck's tires on the pavement. "If I turn over what I know to you and KCPD."

"Think about it, Moll. If we could get him behind bars where he belongs, and you've got the evidence to keep him there, then you'd be free of him. His parents are only going to bail him out so many times. His lawyer can't charm a judge or dispute hard evidence. His so-called business associates won't let the Di Salvos touch another dime of their money if he goes to prison." He remembered her vindictive wish from last night. "They might not want him alive in prison if they think he's going to turn state's evidence and implicate them in exchange for a lighter sentence."

Magnus whined in her lap now, and Joel hated that he was causing Mollie any kind of distress. "What about those weeks or months between handing over the flash drive that got me out of that house and testifying against him? He'll kill me, Joel. Or he or his father will hire someone to do it for him. Then you've got no witness, and Kyra Schmidt can refute or discredit any evidence you got through me, and I'll still be dead."

He wanted to reach across the seat and be the one she turned to when she needed comfort. But he kept his hands on the wheel and let Magnus do his job.

"I'd be with you the whole time. We'd go to a safe house. There'd be backup in place. A.J., Josh, a SWAT team. Whatever we need to get you through the trial and sentencing. I'll keep you safe. If you'll let me." He took a deep breath and put his heart on the line. "I want a future with you. We can move as slowly as you need to, and I'm okay with that, I swear. As long as I know you want that future, too."

"I do." Her words were hushed, but he heard them loud and clear. "But I'm scared, Joel. So much."

Her blue eyes were hard to look away from to concentrate on his driving. "You think I'm not scared? I lost everything once. But I'm falling in love with you, and I don't want to give up without fighting for us."

"You want me to fight for us, too." It was a statement, not a question.

"Can you? Will you give us a chance?"

She considered his challenge for several seconds. "Will you give me some time to think about it?"

The volume of his sigh of relief was almost embarrassing. Magnus's tail thumped against his thigh, and he considered it a good sign. "I'll give you as much time as you need—"

His gaze caught a blur of movement in the rearview mirror, and he swore. How the hell had that car caught up to them so fast? The driver must be breaking all kinds of speed limits.

And then it topped the hill behind them.

"Son of a…"

"Joel?"

Black Lexus. Gold trim. A dent in its fancy grill from where it had bounced over a curb at high speed.

He pushed a little harder on the accelerator, needing to put some distance between them. "Moll, are you buckled up?"

"Of course."

"Magnus is in his harness, secured in the seat?"

"Yes." Those questions naturally made her suspicious. "What's wrong?"

"We're being followed. I know that car and he's gaining speed." She whipped around to look behind them, but he urged her to face forward again. "Don't look. I don't want to alert him that we're onto him yet." He nodded toward her door. "Check your side-view mirror."

She looked out her window and sat up straighter. "That's the same car that tried to run us down in the alley. What is he doing?"

He tightened his grip on the steering wheel and channeled every bit of training he'd had into doing what was necessary to get them out of what he suspected was about to happen. "Any chance you can get a read on the license plate?"

"Uh. It's a Missouri Bicentennial plate, with the red and blue squiggly lines?" Her fingers curled beneath Magnus's harness, and she braced her other hand against the dashboard to steady herself as they picked up speed to peer more closely into the mirror. "He's coming up awfully fast." She glanced back at Joel. "How fast can this old truck go?"

"This old truck can outrun that engine he's got any day of the week. He looks stylish, but I've got substance."

"That's right. You fix engines."

"Can't cook an omelet like that one you made this morning, but I can make this baby run like a Mack truck."

Their words came out faster and louder as they raced up one hill and down another. She leaned over Magnus and rested her fingers on his forearm. "I like substance."

"Me, too, babe. License plate."

"M-X—I don't know if that's a three or an eight." They hit a bump and all three left their seats for a split second. "I lost him behind that hill."

"Grab my phone off my belt." He gave her the security code to unlock it. "Find A.J. in my contacts. Give him our location, the three digits you got off the plate, and tell him we're being pursued." Joel swore as the car reappeared behind them. He couldn't make out the driver through the sun reflecting off the windshield, but he could see the arm and the gun sliding out the driver's side window. "Tell him there's going to be shots fired."

"What?"

"Do it!"

He nudged Magnus's butt to get him to sit up and move over, and Mollie curled her arm around him while she rattled off information to A.J. like a seasoned dispatcher. "He's sending backup and calling the sheriff's department. Says he's not clear on jurisdiction."

"Tell him to notify Garrett Caldwell." They sank into their seats at the bottom of the next hill before the truck kicked into a stronger gear and flew up the next hill. "We may need a friend to smooth things over for us because this is about to go down outside city limits."

He saw the first flash of a gunshot and knew the driver had fired his weapon. They were going too fast to get an accurate aim—he hoped. Hell. He *heard* the next pop of gunfire and knew the guy was getting too close.

"Shots fired, A.J!" he yelled for his boss to hear. "He's going to try to run us off the road."

"He says 'Affirmative.'"

Lowering his voice, he risked sliding his hand over hers where she clung to Magnus. "You okay?"

"No. I'm scared out of my mind. But I'll do whatever you tell me." She checked her side-view mirror again a split second before a bullet shattered the reflection. She jerked back in her seat. "Joel!"

He eyed the road up ahead. This guy had a plan. But Joel was onto his game. He had a plan, too. "He waited for this straight, empty stretch of road. We need to do this before we hit that curve at the end and those trees up ahead."

"Do what?"

"Hang up. Hold on."

"Gotta go." She ended the call and tucked his phone into the front pocket of her jeans. The black car swerved into the left lane and crept up beside his truck. "Damn it." The passenger side window was open. Was there a second shooter in the car? Or was the driver going to pull the incredibly foolish stunt of shooting through the car at breakneck speed and risk a ricochet inside the vehicle if his aim was off? "Get down!"

"Down, boy." Mollie pulled Magnus down and leaned into the middle of the seat with him while Joel reached for his holster. When he couldn't immediately free his Glock, he felt nimble fingers brush against his and unhook the clasp to free his weapon. "Be careful, Joel."

He breathed deeply—once, twice—then steeled himself for the coming confrontation. "I got this."

Mollie squeezed his thigh. "That's what A.J. said."

And then there was no talking. There was speed and gunfire. The black Lexus drifted onto the far shoulder, then the driver overcorrected and nearly clipped the side of the truck. He heard one ping off the bed of the truck. Another bullet smacked into the door panel. *Damn that loser. He's messin' up my truck!* Mollie gasped as another shot shattered his mirror and he felt the nick of something sharp pierce his forearm. *And you're scaring my woman!*

The truck sat up higher than the Lexus so he couldn't see into to car to know who was shooting. But he knew the guy was firing wild. A stray bullet could come right through his open window if the shooter leaned over far enough to angle his shot up. But that wasn't happening at this speed.

But that also meant *his* shots wouldn't hit their intended target, either.

Plan B. Think on your feet. Know every detail of your surroundings. That's what A.J. said he had over other cops. They were barreling toward the curve and the thick grove of trees beyond. No cars up ahead. No vehicles close behind. What he wouldn't pay to be a lefty right about now. But he could make this work.

"This is gonna be loud," he warned Mollie a split second before he eased up on the accelerator and the black car surged ahead of them. The shooter had actually done him a favor by taking off his side mirror. It made it easier for Joel to twist his body and brace his right hand outside the doorframe. He took a bead on the black car and fired off five shots in rapid succession.

He hit his target with bullet number four.

The right rear tire exploded, sending the Lexus into a tailspin. The car swerved from one side of the road to the other, leaving traces of rubber and sparks from the bare rim on the pavement. When it sailed past the shoulder and hit the ground that had been softened by last night's rain, the car flipped over and rolled three times before it plowed into the trunk of one of the stately pine trees that had been planted ages ago when Highway 40 was still a two-lane road.

Joel pumped his brakes to a stop and pulled off onto the side of the highway, turning on his warning blinkers before he shut off the engine. He ripped off his seat belt and holstered his gun before reaching down to palm the back of Mollie's head. "You can sit up now, babe. Are you okay?" She was pale and breathing hard as she pushed herself upright, but Mollie nodded. Spine of steel, this woman. He spared a quick scratch around the ears for Magnus. "How about the big guy?"

"He's fine. We're both fine." She reached up to cup the side of his jaw. "Are you okay?" Then she saw the blood trickling down his forearm. "Joel!" She grabbed his wrist and pulled it across his lap to inspect the small cut. "You *are* hurt."

"It's just a scratch." He could barely feel the sting with her hands moving so tenderly around the injury.

"No more bullet holes or shrapnel wounds, okay?"

He wished he could make her that promise.

"First aid kit?"

"Under the front seat. I'm good for now," he assured

her, pulling her fingers from his arm. "Can't say the same for my truck, but I can fix that. I need to check the other driver."

She'd been so helpful in following his orders when he needed to keep her safe, that she hadn't seen the devastating crash. But she saw the aftermath. Her fingers went to the locket that hung inside her shirt and she whispered a soft prayer. Gouges of sod were torn up along the car's tumbling path. Scratches of silver bled through the black paint. A headlamp and part of the grill had snapped off and were scattered along with a hubcap and shreds of the rubber tire in a debris field. Steam or smoke was spilling out from the crumpled hood.

There was no sign of the driver. But whether he was unable to get out of the car, or he was lying in wait to shoot them, Joel couldn't know until he got eyes on the perp.

He was relieved to see the color flooding back into her cheeks. "Should I call 9-1-1?"

Joel nodded. "Backup is already on the way, but we'll also need an ambulance and someone to reroute traffic around the accident."

"I can do that."

He massaged the back of her neck and let his fingers tangle in the curls of her hair for a moment before releasing her. "Stay in the truck with Magnus."

She pulled out his phone and handed it back to him before unbuckling and pulling her own phone from the back pocket of her jeans. "We're good, too."

Taking the woman at her word, Joel opened his door. His gun was in his hands, and he was carefully making his way to the wrecked vehicle.

"KCPD! Drop your weapon and put your hands out the

window where I can see them." He should have put on
the protective vest he kept in his go bag in the back of the
truck. But he hadn't planned on making a traffic stop today.
And this guy—this loser—was definitely stopped. With the
tinted windows in the back still intact, he steeled himself
for approaching the car. "KCPD! I said to get your hands…"

The last of his adrenaline whooshed out on a frustrated
curse. The driver wasn't lying in wait to shoot him. The
driver wasn't doing anything ever again.

He identified the location of the man's gun on the floor
in front of the passenger's seat. Then he holstered his own
weapon and reached in to press his fingers against the
man's neck. The driver had been battered around inside
the car. The blows to the head or even his chest smacking against the steering wheel would have been enough to
stop his heart.

Joel wasn't sure if he was angry or saddened by the loss
of life. It had been a damn foolish stunt to try to pull off.
But he needed to know why this particular man had been
targeting Mollie.

He spared a moment to reach inside the car and turn off
the engine before stalking back to his pickup. He opened
the door on Mollie's side of the truck and held out his hand
for her phone. "We're not getting any answers out of him."

"I'm handing you over to Detective Standage, ma'am,"
Mollie explained to the Dispatcher before surrendering her
phone. "He's dead?"

Joel nodded. He requested to be patched through to Deputy Caldwell. He was amused, and stunned again by Mollie's determination, to see her open the first aid kit to clean
and doctor the cut on his arm while he talked on the phone.
Once he explained the situation to the deputy sheriff, he

felt a shade better about what he needed to ask of Mollie. "Thanks, Garrett. I'll see what I can find out. See you in a few. Standage out."

Joel waited in the open triangle between the open door and the body of the truck while she taped gauze over the cut and tucked her phone back into her jeans. "Jessie's Garrett is coming?"

"We're still in the county. We're not in KCPD's jurisdiction. But I want someone I know backing us up on scene." Perched on the seat above him, Mollie had watched him through the entire conversation. He braced his palms on the seat on either side of her thighs. "How squeamish are you?"

Her eyes got wide, then narrowed with a question. "After surviving Augie? Not much."

"Any triggers?"

"A few." She looked beyond him to the car and understood what he was really asking. "If you're worried about a lot of blood, though, I'll be okay."

"I really need you to confirm the ID on this guy."

"Is it Augie?"

Joel shook his head. But if he was right, she wasn't going to like what he'd found.

"Can I take Magnus?"

"Yes. And you'll take me."

"Then I'll be fine."

She scooted to the edge of the seat to climb out the door, but he stopped her and planted a quick, firm kiss on her lips. "Bravest woman I've ever met."

Her gaze skimmed across his face, his shoulders, and chest, before blue eyes met his. "Kiss me again, Joel."

Although he was surprised by the request, he didn't hesitate to tunnel his fingers into her hair and lean in to cover her mouth with his. Her taste was sweet. Her touch was tender. And Joel knew he'd never shared a kiss that meant as much to him as these few stolen moments of shared support did. She stroked his face as she pulled away. "This grounds me, too," she whispered. Then she braced her other hand against his bicep and climbed down. "Magnus, come."

He waited for the dog to take his place beside her, then captured her hand in his and led them to the wreck.

When they reached the passenger side of the crumpled vehicle, Joel took her by the shoulders and turned her to look at him a moment. "Take a deep breath." She did. "It's not pretty. Looks like he hit his head more than once."

"You're positive he'd dead?"

More than. "Yeah, babe."

Mollie inhaled another deep breath before she stepped up to the driver's window. She quickly spun away and buried her nose against his chest. "Oh, my."

Joel willingly wrapped his arms around her and pulled her farther away from the body. "Tell me that's who I think it is."

Shock seemed to chase away her fear when she looked up at him. "Rocky Garner. He's not in uniform, but that's him."

"There's been some bad blood between him and me, so I didn't want to make the identification. And I'm not touching the body until the M.E. gets here."

"Garner's been after me? I mean he's a jerk, but…trying to kill me? Us? That doesn't make any sense. Can a cop even afford a car like this?"

Joel pointed to the sticker on the rear window. "It's a rental. Stay here." He circled around to reach through the open window of the passenger door. He pulled the rental agreement from the glove compartment. He read the information and cursed. "Leased to Kyra Schmidt. The lawyer who makes trouble go away for Augie."

"And his new fiancée."

Chapter Ten

Mollie awoke to a cold nose nudging her hand, followed by a whine and several warm licks across her skin.

It wasn't the first time Magnus had awakened her in the middle of the night. But it was the first time she hadn't been in the throes of a nightmare when he forced her out of her horrific memories and fear that sometimes never left her, even when she slept.

The moment her eyes opened, Magnus crawled up on the bed beside her and licked her cheek. He was whimpering in earnest now, and Mollie wondered if she'd been dreaming something awful and had simply forgotten it the moment she was awake. Only she wasn't covered in a cold sweat, and she wasn't shaking with the terror that usually accompanied the panic attacks that could take hold of her even in her sleep.

She sat up to embrace the dog. His eyes were almost invisible in the blackness of his face and the darkness of the room, but she could feel his strength and warmth and smell his treat-scented breath. "I'm okay, good boy. Mama's okay. Did I scare you? What's wrong?"

And then she heard the headboard in Joel's bedroom thump against the wall of the guest room where she slept.

This time she did startle and jumped to the middle of the bed. "What the...?"

She petted Magnus, timing her breaths to each stroke and slowing both until she was fully oriented in the bedroom that was illuminated only by the bathroom light Joel had left on for her across the hall. Her sweats had been pushed up to her knees and the long sleeves of her T-shirt were nearly up to her elbows. Maybe she'd gotten hot during the night, or maybe she had been unsettled in her sleep.

But when the headboard thumped against the wall again and Magnus woofed, she knew she wasn't the one in distress tonight. The dog gently mouthed her hand, urging her to move. Someone less accustomed to violence and nightmares might have thought she was overhearing the sounds of sex. But she was far too attuned to the insidious ways fear could overtake one when they were at their most vulnerable in sleep.

"I'm coming. I'm coming." She pushed Magnus off the bed and scooted to the edge. She shivered when she stepped onto the cool wood beyond the small rug and blanket where she'd been sleeping. Tugging her sleeves down to her wrists and smoothing her pants down her legs, she put her hand on Magnus's head and followed him down the hall to Joel's room. "Show me."

Magnus led her unerringly through the shadows to the open door of Joel's bedroom. She stopped to let her eyes adjust to the near total darkness. "Magnus!" she called in as loud a whisper as she could without disturbing Joel.

Instead of sitting next to her when she stopped, the dog trotted into the room and propped his front paws on the bed. He dodged and dropped to the floor when Joel kicked his foot out from the covers twisted around his legs, but he had his paws right back up on the bed a moment later. Magnus wasn't the only one concerned about the man who was thrashing in his sleep as though his life depended on it. Besides the sounds of him twisting in the bed and pummeling his pillows, she could hear guttural vocal sounds coming from his throat that nearly broke her heart. That had been her more nights than she could count.

"No. Stop." Those words and her name were words she could make out.

But it was the strangled whimpers that had her whispering his name from the doorway. "Joel?"

Magnus trotted back to her and tugged at her sleeve again. Not sure exactly what she was supposed to do in this situation, she listened to her heart instead of all the damaged memories in her head. She let Magnus pull her into the room. "Good boy. You're Mama's good boy."

She cautiously approached the bed and raised her volume to something more than a whisper. "Joel."

She turned on the lamp beside the bed, blinking against its soft illumination. Wow. Joel Standage, in the middle of summer, at least, slept in nothing but a pair of gym shorts. And with the covers down around his ankles, she could see every inch of muscle across his chest, and the whole of the tattoo circling down his left arm. He had an innie belly button and those V-shaped muscles at his hips that pointed down to that most masculine part of him. Mollie gulped at the hard beauty of his body and felt an answering heat of feminine awareness between her thighs and at the tips of her breasts. How could this man ever call himself *forgettable*?

And how had she ever believed that she'd never be attracted to a man again? Her body, her heart—and her dog—kept drawing her toward this one.

But hearing the keening sound in his throat and watching him clench every muscle in his body against the terrors in his mind shook her out of her hormonal stupor. "Joel," she called in a louder, firmer tone. Still no response. But she knew who had a stronger voice. "Magnus, speak!"

At the same time Magnus barked, Mollie touched Joel's shoulder. "Joel—"

Suddenly Joel was awake. She screeched in surprise when he snatched her wrist and flipped her beneath him on the bed. Her breath lodged in her chest at the weight of him crushing her, the feel of her wrists cinched within his grip and his hips cradled intimately against hers. She knew a brief moment of panic. But that awareness was followed just as quickly by the realization that she wasn't caught in a bruising grip, and there were certainly no insults or profanities being hurled at her. *Not Augie. Not Augie.* "Joel?"

Those golden eyes blinked, then opened wide in horror.

She inhaled a deep breath as Joel scrambled off her. "Damn, Mollie. I'm so sorry. Did I hurt you?"

"Startled me." She slowly sat up, curling her legs beneath her. "But I'm okay. I'm more worried about you."

He slid to the edge of the bed, his head bent, elbows on his knees, his fingers raking through his short hair. "I had you pinned under me. I didn't bruise your wrists, did I?"

His voice sounded as agonized as those senseless mutters in his throat had.

"I'm okay."

"I didn't remind you of him, did I?" His tortured gaze sought out hers.

No. No way could this rough-around-the-edges man with

the sense of humor and addictive variety of kisses ever remind her of the cold polish and selfish evil of August Di Salvo.

She scooted to the edge of the bed beside him. She caught the wrist closest to her to pull his hand from the punishing assault on his head. He flinched with the instinct to pull away, but he purposely relaxed his arm against his thigh as if he might hurt her by struggling, and she kept hold of him. She reached out with her left hand to cup his stubbled jaw and turn his anguished face to her. "Joel. Look at me. Take a deep breath. I'm okay."

He did as she asked, much the same way he'd calmed her in the past. "I'm sorry I woke you. I never want to add to your stress."

"You woke Magnus. He was worried about you and came to get me." He glanced down at the dog trying to wedge himself between Mollie and Joel's knees. Mollie moved her hand to the middle of Joel's back and rubbed what she hoped were soothing circles there. "Do you think I'd feel better knowing you were in here suffering, fighting some demon in your sleep, all alone? Magnus did what he was supposed to do. He sensed you were in trouble, and when he couldn't take care of you, he went and got help."

"But *I'm* supposed to be taking care of *you*."

"No. You're supposed to be *protecting* me. And I do feel safe with you. But I'm not an invalid, Joel." She kept one hand on Joel's back—his broad, smooth, incredibly warm back—and petted Magnus with the other. "One of the things I like about you is that you treat me like a normal woman. I've had some experience with nightmares, and I'm a terrific listener. I *am* someone who can help. Please let me. Now praise your buddy here. He did his job."

Joel reluctantly reached down and scrubbed the dog around his ears and muzzle. "Good boy, Magnus. Good boy." Magnus's tail thumped against the floor at the bit of roughhousing. She was relieved to see the hint of a smile at the corner of Joel's mouth. It reached the other corner when Magnus pushed his head into Joel's hands, and they shared some more gentle wrestling. "That's my good boy."

She let the boys bond for a few moments before asking, "Do you need to talk about your dream? It seemed pretty violent."

Joel shook his head. When the wrestling stopped, Magnus stretched out across their feet.

She suspected that Joel appreciated the contact as much as she did. "Should you talk to your therapist about it?"

He glanced at her, then focused on the dog again. "I stopped going."

That might explain why his emotions had manifested themselves in his dreams. "I'm willing to listen to anything you want to tell me. I care when you're hurting like this, but a police psychologist would be able to give you some specific strategies for coping. I talked to a therapist at the shelter where I stayed for a while." She pointed to her canine savior at their feet. "Hence, the service dog. Would you do me a favor and call tomorrow morning to make an appointment?"

He considered her request for a moment, then nodded. "Thank you."

Joel brushed the backs of his fingers across her cheek and played with her hair, smoothing the tendrils that refused to stay in place off her forehead. While she enjoyed the soft caresses, he seemed to think better of touching her and pulled away. "The nightmare was about you. It was you in that car, battered and bleeding, not Garner. I couldn't save you. Then it was you in that drug house where I found Cici, and they were hurting you." His gravelly voice was raw with emotion. "And then you were in that dumpster with me, and I couldn't save you. I'm going to fail you the same way I failed Cici."

"That's a crock," she muttered. "You *did* save me, Joel. You have saved me. More than once." She pulled her toes from beneath Magnus's warmth and faced Joel, lightly clasping his forearm. "Today on the highway. In that alley. Two years ago when you were undercover. When I was too scared to function, you came, and suddenly I could think again and do what I needed to do. The fact that I'm sitting here with you now and I'm not panicking is a testament to how many times you've saved me. You've given me back the gift of human touch. You've reminded me that I once was a pretty sweet catch."

He folded his larger hand over both of hers. "You still are in my book."

"Nightmares are wicked things, preying on our fears and worries and stress. Our lives haven't been easy. But we're here. And we're both okay." She turned her hand to link her fingers together with his. "Sometimes, you just need the reassurance of someone holding your hand or hugging you or making love, to *feel* that you're safe and cared for. That you're going to be okay."

One eyebrow arched when she said the words *making love*, but he didn't comment on it. "Magnus does that for you. You ground yourself in reality when you pet him or hug him, or he nuzzles his cold nose in your hand."

She smiled at how well he knew her and her dog. "May I do that for you tonight?"

"You want to nuzzle your cold nose in my hand?" His stab at humor reassured her more than anything else that he had recovered from the nightmare and was feeling more like the good man she cared for so deeply.

With that thought foremost in her mind, Mollie asked, "Could I sleep with you and hold you while you sleep?"

"Only if I can hold you, too." He lifted her hand to his lips and gently kissed her fingers. "I'd really love to *feel* that you're safe, even when my mind is trying to tell me otherwise."

Mollie nodded and crawled to the middle of the bed, where she straightened the mess he'd made of his pillows and sheets. Then she lay down and patted the mattress beside her. "Do you have a preference which side you sleep on?"

"The one where you're within arm's reach." He urged her to lie on her left side and snuggled in behind her. With one arm under his head on the pillow, he curled the other arm around her waist. He tugged at the hem of her shirt, and she gasped when she felt his warm, callused fingers splay across her bare skin underneath. "Is this all right?" When she didn't immediately answer, he started to pull his hand from under her shirt. "I'm sorry."

"Don't." Mollie caught his hand and laced her fingers with his to put it right back on her belly and hold him against her. "I like the feel of your hands on me. It's not sex, but this feels intimate to me. I miss intimacy. Lying like this feels good to me."

She felt his lips near the crown of her hair. "Me, too."

They lay together like that, as close as two people who still had their clothes on could be, for several minutes. Mollie felt her own heart rate calm to a contented rhythm, and she relaxed against him, eventually feeling the tension in him begin to fade, too.

Soon after, Joel's voice vibrated against her eardrums. "You know, as much as I love holding you—as much as I need this to settle myself down—I'm having a little trouble with an audience watching us sleep."

Mollie blinked her eyes open to see Magnus resting his head on the bed, those dark, steady orbs indeed watching them. She laughed softly and smiled at the dog. "Give me your hand." She put both their hands on Magnus's head. "Good boy, Magnus. Your pack is safe."

"Good boy," Joel echoed, as they pulled away. "I owe you one, buddy."

"Night-night, Magnus." If a dog could pout, she had a feeling that's what the whiny sound he made meant. "Go night-night, you big goof."

Joel raised his head, and in his firm, gritty tone ordered, "Magnus, night-night."

The dog finally got down, and she could tell by the scratching noises and circling flag of his tail that he was gathering up the throw rug on her side of the bed and making himself a nest to lie down in. Once the dog had obeyed and settled close by, Mollie rolled onto her back and looked up at Joel hovering beside her in the lamplight. She gently poked his chest and chided, "*My* dog, Standage. I don't like that he responds to your commands faster than he does mine."

He captured her hand against his chest, and she felt the heat of his skin branding her. "*Our* dog, Crane. *Our* energetic, overachieving, too-smart-for-his-own-good dog."

She smiled, more than happy to keep her hand pressed

against the ticklish dusting of chest hair and the warm skin underneath. "Maybe it means I'm getting better. That taking care of me isn't enough work for him, anymore."

"Are you still willing to go to the Precinct offices tomorrow morning and talk to A.J. and Josh and the assistant district attorney?"

Her nostrils flared with a deep breath, and she dropped her gaze to where her fingers clung to a swell of pectoral muscle. They'd had this conversation in one form or another several times. She'd done her best to make Joel understand the risk she'd be taking by surrendering her evidence against Augie to the ADA. And he'd done his best to make her believe that she would never be alone against the Di Salvo family again. She met Joel's gaze again and nodded. "I haven't made my decision yet. But I'm willing to talk to them. As long as you make that phone call to your therapist in the morning."

"I will. I promise. I need to do better taking care of that part of my recovery."

"Thank you." She raised her head to press her lips against his, rewarding him with a gentle kiss. She lingered when his lips moved tenderly against hers and reached behind his neck to slide her hand across the spiky mess of his hair. He touched his nose to her face and moved his lips along her jawline, inhaling deeply as if he was learning and memorizing her touch and scent. He nipped at her earlobe, and the zing of desire that arrowed down to the juncture of her thighs caught her off guard. Who knew she had an erogenous zone there? After Augie, who knew she had any erogenous zones left?

Sensing her sudden hesitation, if misreading the cause,

Joel pulled away and flopped down on his back beside her. "Maybe this isn't a good idea. I can't guarantee that the nightmares won't come back. I'd never hurt you if I was fully conscious. It kills me to think that I could frighten you or be too rough with you when I don't know what I'm doing."

But Mollie wasn't going anywhere. "I'll have Magnus to protect me."

Joel pushed up on his elbow beside her to talk over her and the edge of the bed. "You take my head off if I hurt her in any way, buddy." Magnus answered with a stuttered snore. Laughter vibrated in Joel's chest beneath her hand. "Yeah, that's backup I can count on," he muttered sarcastically. "Still, if I did anything to remind you of him…"

"You don't remind me of him at all." Mollie dropped her voice to a whisper and purposely brushed her lips against his ear. "Augie never liked to cuddle."

She knew Joel got the message behind her words. His eyes glittered with something possessive just before he turned her to her side, slid his arm around her and pulled her into his chest. Her butt nestled into his groin and his legs tangled with hers. "Do you need the covers?"

She shook her head. "You'll keep me warm."

She clutched his forearm between her breasts and sighed at the gentle press of his lips against her hair. "Sleep well, my love."

She smiled at the whispered word and dipped her head to kiss his hand. "You, too."

It was too soon for her to fully believe that she could fall in love again and trust her heart and body to another man. But it wasn't too soon for her to know that when she was ready, it would be with this man.

They fell asleep holding each other, with the cadence of a snoring dog curled up on the rug filling the room with a quiet sense of security.

MOLLIE HAD AWAKENED from the best night's sleep she'd had in ages. The only way she and Joel could have been closer was if they'd been lying skin to skin. And she was surprised to realize that the idea of being with Joel in that way didn't frighten her. She was nervous about being that intimate with any man again, but if the erection pressing against her bottom when she woke hadn't bothered her— and, in fact, had made her feel cherished and desirable— then she had a feeling making love with Joel would be a good experience for her. If he'd enjoyed cuddling so closely with her through the night as much as she had, then she knew he'd be patient with her. Possibly even more patient than she'd be, judging by her own off-the-charts reactions to the man's damn fine body.

But that was this morning, cocooned in the homey sanctuary of Joel's Brookside house, where Joel and Magnus were the only personalities she had to deal with. She trusted both implicitly, and she felt safe with them.

Here, in the tight confines of the Fourth Precinct conference room, surrounded by some heavy hitters in Kansas City law enforcement and the district attorney's office who were analyzing her life and breaking down every detail that could possibly be used against the Di Salvos, she was having a much harder time holding on to that sense of calm and security. It almost felt as if she'd been summoned to a command performance at a Di Salvo dinner party, where she was expected to say certain things and play her part well. Only, these guests weren't talking big bucks and making themselves look good in the worlds of business and culture and KC society. These men and one other woman were strategizing ways to build a case against her ex-husband and redeem the fiasco of the last time they'd gone up against Augie in the courtroom.

There was a big, stocky man in a suit and tie. And though Chief of Police Mitch Taylor's graying hair and authoritative demeanor confirmed that he was the man in charge, he leaned back in his seat at the opposite end of the long, heavy table from her and slowly rubbed his fingers back and forth across his chin while he listened to the intense conversation around the room.

The Black man next to him, Joe Hendricks, was the captain of this Precinct. Apparently, he and the chief were old friends, as he'd been sharing pictures of his grandchildren with Mitch before the meeting started.

The woman, Assistant District Attorney Kenna Parker-Watson, looked like the woman Augie and his parents had tried to transform her into. Straight blond hair. Tall and poised. Her tailored designer suit said she had money, and her pointed comments and quick wit put her on equal footing with the men in the room. She was also happily married, judging by the gold rings on her finger and the smile and kiss she'd shared with a handsome dark-haired detective out in the third floor's main room when she'd arrived.

Of course, she recognized A. J. Rodriguez and Josh Taylor, who was somehow related to the chief of police. She'd missed the exact connection in the flurry of introductions. A.J. was fixated on his laptop on the table in front of him, while Josh paced back and forth, occasionally stopping to jot something on the whiteboard on the wall across from the door.

Joel sat in the chair beside her, doodling pictures on a yellow legal pad and drawing lines from one symbol to the next before scratching the whole thing out, flipping the page and starting the design all over again. Magnus sat in the space between their chairs, his head resting atop her knee. So many big personalities. So much talking. She clung to Magnus's leash and burrowed her fingers into the fur on his warm head. She didn't even care that he was panting, and some drool was trickling down the leg of her jeans and seeping through to her skin.

In fact, she found herself tuning out much of the conversation and focusing on the sound of the dog's breathing and the warmth of him against her when she got too stressed. The air conditioning in the room was working just fine. But Magnus was slightly overheated and panting because he was working so hard to keep her calm.

Joel circled two of the doodles on his paper several times and tapped the pad with his pen sharply enough that she looked over to see what he had drawn. "I found a tracker on my truck when I was checking the damage. There was one on Mollie's car, too. Mine has only been there a few days. It's still shiny new. Hers was there for some time. It showed signs of salt damage from driving in the winter." So, the doodling was how he organized his thoughts? "I removed them both and bagged them as evidence."

The blonde ADA on the other side of Mollie leaned forward. "If the crime lab doesn't come back with Garner's prints on one of them, we can't prove he put them there."

Mollie realized that Joel had drawn a map of every location where she'd had an encounter of some kind with the man they now suspected was Rocky Garner. He could be placed at the diner, the alley behind it, the dog park, her apartment and Hwy. 40, where he'd met his death trying to kill them. Joel pointed to the symbols where he'd written *RG*. "Then how else do you explain him lying in wait for us when we left K-9 Ranch? We were fifteen miles out of the city, and I know he didn't follow us there."

Kenna leaned back in her seat, shaking her head. She glanced around the table to include everyone in her question. "What else do you have?"

A.J. looked up from his computer. "Garner recently bought himself a thirty-thousand-dollar fishing boat. Paid for in three installments of ten thousand dollars each. The last one was paid yesterday." He turned the screen around to show an invoice from the sporting goods store where Garner had bought the boat. "He's bleeding money in alimony payments to his two ex-wives. No wonder he was keeping the payments out of any bank account. Their attorneys could go after him for more."

"Can we trace the cash?" Kenna was persistent in documenting each fact.

"Not yet. It's already changed hands a number of times. The dealer deposited the payments in his account, and it left the bank shortly after that." A.J. turned the computer back to him and pulled up a different screen. "We can trace the car rental agreement back to Kyra Schmidt. She charged almost six hundred dollars on a credit card to have the car for a week."

Mollie's fingers flinched around the leash. "He's been following me that long?"

"Possibly longer." A.J. looked apologetic when he met her gaze across the table. "There's evidence of other deposits to Garner's account—five hundred dollars, a thousand—some more, some less—over the past two years.

It's not overtime pay, because that's direct deposited like his paycheck. It's not from moonlighting as security for a reputable company like a store or sporting venue. The deposits came from Garner himself. That means he took cash to the bank."

Joel reached across the arm of her chair and covered her trembling hand with his own. "Any chance there was a deposit nine months ago?" he asked his supervisor. "That's when he was harassing Mollie at the diner."

"Last October?" A.J. scrolled through the numbers, then nodded.

Mitch Taylor pounded the table with his fist and Mollie jerked in her chair. "I had a dirty cop on my force?" He pulled out his cell phone. "I'm calling Internal Affairs to do a deep dive into Garner's financials."

Joe Hendricks seemed equally disappointed by the proof of Garner's misconduct. "They already have a file of harassment complaints leveled against him."

Mitch muttered a curse. "I have over two thousand employees on the payroll here. And it just takes one bad seed like Garner to give us all a bad rep."

Mollie could appreciate how Garner's actions were an embarrassment to the department, but she had a bigger threat to worry about. "But nothing about Officer Garner ties back to Augie? August Di Salvo?"

It was Joel who answered. "Not yet."

She felt the eyes of everyone in the room looking at her, possibly with pity, but mostly with expectation. It was more than clear that without her help, the Di Salvos would remain untouchable. She tightened her grip on Joel's hand and stroked the top of Magnus's head. "They're setting Kyra up to take the fall if things go south. It's a classic Di

Salvo move. With Garner's death, if he was the man they paid to follow me, I think we can safely say things have gone south."

"We'll need a court order to look at Kyra Schmidt's financials." The ADA nodded in agreement with Mollie's assessment. "I'll work on that today. If she's paid Garner to do odd jobs for her and the Di Salvos from her personal account, we can track the timelines to see if they match Garner's deposits. But she could just as easily have paid him petty cash from her law firm, and investigating the firm's financials would be a harder sell to a judge."

Josh Taylor had made a list of crimes on the board. "So, we can prove Garner is guilty of harassment, breaking and entering, and the attempted murder of a police officer and potential witness. We can prove he had some kind of working relationship with Schmidt—"

"Who could get her connection to him tossed out of court by claiming he stole the rental car. Or that she had no idea what he was going to do with it when she hired him for a different job, like escorting an important client to the airport," Kenna countered. "He can't defend himself, thanks to your detective here."

Mollie spun her chair toward the attorney. "Joel saved our lives. If Officer Garner hadn't been driving so recklessly—"

"Easy, Mollie," Kenna apologized. "I'm just repeating what Kyra Schmidt would probably say in the courtroom."

"Don't insult Joel when I'm around. Please. He's a good man. And a good detective. He does whatever is necessary to protect the people he cares about."

"It's okay, Moll." Joel squeezed her hand. "We're just talking through what we know on the case, looking at what all our options are." Then he leaned in more closely and whispered against her ear. "But thank you for sticking up for me."

If they'd been alone, she imagined he would have added something about Cici choosing her drugs instead of protecting him. But they were hardly alone.

"I didn't mean to upset you, Mollie," Kenna apologized, and her blue eyes looked sincere. "I could use someone like you on the witness stand. You speak from a place of strength. You don't come off as someone who's angry or frightened and desperate. You have a calm demeanor."

"Calm?" When was the last time anyone had used that adjective to describe her? "That's because of Magnus."

"It's not just because of the dog. But you could have him in the courtroom with you. You were clearly the wronged party in your marriage, yet you don't sound bitter or brokenhearted."

"I'm more embarrassed that I fell for him in the first place. Trust me, he was easy to get over."

Joel chuckled behind her. Kenna smiled and rolled her chair closer. "I think I like you." For the first time, Mollie felt as if the attorney was speaking to her woman-to-woman, and not as the secret weapon who could make or break her case. "I'd like to take a look at your divorce papers."

"The ones I printed off the internet?"

Kenna nodded. "Sounds like you negotiated yourself a hard deal. And you said it was vetted by an accredited attorney and filed properly, which was a smart move on your part. But maybe I can do better by you."

"I don't want anything from Augie."

"She'd like to be able to teach again," Joel interjected.

"Can you get the false report on her record cleared with the school board?"

"I'll waitress for the rest of my life if I have to. I just want my freedom."

"Do you feel free of him?" Kenna asked. "Or are you going to be looking over your shoulder for the rest of your life?"

"Kenna..." Joel warned.

"I'm sorry, Detective. But if I'm going to prosecute this case, and win, I need more than what any of you have shown me." She turned to include everyone in the room. "Garner, I could have put away with my eyes closed. But the DA doesn't prosecute dead men. Maybe I could get Kyra Schmidt fined, or even disbarred, if I could tie her to Garner's harassment campaign. But I've got nothing— nothing—that conclusively links any of this to the Di Salvo family."

"Except me." Mollie felt a little like a soldier being prepped for a suicide mission.

"Look," Kenna began, "I've been in a situation where I wasn't safe. That's how I met my husband, in fact. He saved my life. Twice. That whole situation convinced me to leave the dark side of defense and go to work for the prosecution." She laid her hand on the table close to Mollie, understanding and respecting that she wasn't comfortable being touched by someone she didn't know well. "My point is, I understand your reluctance to put yourself in a position where you feel threatened again. Let me play devil's advocate for a moment. Do you think you're the only person the Di Salvos have threatened? Cheated? Or worse? What about those people who will continue to be hurt by them if nothing is done to stop them?"

"I feel for them, but… Augie said he'd kill me if I left him. I countered with the offer to keep what I took from him out of police hands, so long as he let me leave. And live. If anything happens to me, I've willed it to go to KCPD and the DA's office."

"You're not going to die before we take that bastard down," Joel griped.

But Kenna Parker-Watson seemed eternally cool and unruffled. "It doesn't sound as if he's keeping up his end of the divorce agreement."

Suicide mission. "*If* you can prove he's behind the harassment and Garner trying to kill Joel and me." Mollie offered another explanation. "Kyra Schmidt might have decided to eliminate me to protect her new fiancé and all the money she stands to gain by marrying Augie."

"Possibly," Kenna conceded. "But that just means she knows there's something there she has to protect. You know, the thing about bullies is that they only keep their power when no one stands up to them."

Mollie had heard that argument before. She believed it herself once. "Yes, but the person who stands up to the bully usually gets the crap beat out of them, or worse."

Kenna's hand inched closer. "I'm willing to stand up with you against your bully. You wouldn't be alone this time."

Mollie looked to Joel. He tucked a stray strand of hair behind her ear. "You know I'm with you all the way."

There was a chorus of support from around the room, from A.J. and Josh, as well as the two senior officers. Finally, Magnus put his head in her lap and turned his dark eyes up to hers, promising his unflinching support.

Mollie smiled down into those faithful eyes. Then she lifted her gaze to Joel's handsome golden eyes. She wasn't alone against the Di Salvos. Not anymore. *Not a suicide mission.* Instead, she was the veteran survivor who could lead this makeshift army into battle. She just prayed she wouldn't be a casualty along the way.

She turned to Kenna's blue eyes and nodded to the yellow legal pad in front of her, warning her to get ready to write. "I have documented evidence of money laundering and racketeering from internal servers on the Di Salvo computers. I can show payoffs to enforcers and bribes to officials that probably coincide with the witnesses who backed out of testifying against Augie in his previous trial."

This part was harder. She turned to Joel but couldn't quite meet his eyes. Her gaze landed on the Armed Forces prayer inked into his arm and she replayed the words in her head. *Teach us not to mourn those who have died in the service of the Corps, but rather to gain strength from the fact that such heroes have lived.*

She had to be the hero now. But could she trust that these people would be there for her when she needed them?

Joel tapped a finger beneath her chin and tilted her face to his. "What else, Moll?"

"I don't want you to see them. But I have dated pictures of my injuries and my copy of the first police report and medical exam that disappeared after the first assault. And, there's an audio recording of one of the times Augie...hurt me. There's no video. I hid my phone in a drawer, but it was running the whole time."

She heard deep-pitched curses in two different languages, and gasps of admiration for her and contempt for the Di Salvos from around the room. But her eyes were glued on Joel and the muscle ticking in his jaw at the evidence she'd described. "Hell, babe, you had the presence of mind to record him?"

"That's how desperate I was to get away from him."

His gaze caressed her face. "Strong as steel."

"It's in a lockbox at my bank." She patted Magnus's shoulder. "I keep the key with me at all times. And the false account numbers are in—"

"Your locket." She nodded at Joel's deduction. "And Magnus guards your key." His eyes remained shrouded in sadness, but he smiled. "Brilliant, brave, and beautiful."

There was a respectful moment of silence before Kenna spoke. "Please tell me you'll let me see that evidence."

She hadn't looked away from Joel. "You'll keep me safe?"

He pulled her into his arms and hugged her as tightly as the chairs allowed. "Twenty-four seven."

"He'll have the backup of the entire Precinct," Joe Hendricks promised.

"Of the entire department if needed," Chief Taylor added. "I'll assign a SWAT team to you to and from the courtroom."

"Are you afraid to testify against your ex?" Kenna asked.

"Yes. But I'll do it anyway. I want..." She reached over to squeeze Joel's hand. "I want to fight for *us*, too."

Chapter Eleven

Joel's head throbbed with a mixture of fatigue and forcing his eyes to concentrate on the pages of the book he wasn't really reading.

For the umpteenth time that night, he let his gaze slide over to the opposite corner of the couch, where Mollie was curled up with her book. He could tell she was deep in thought because she hadn't turned a page in the last ten minutes.

Giving up the pretense, he set his book aside and clicked on his phone to check the time—11:00 p.m. He also pulled up his messages to see if there was any news on what progress the DA's office was making in going through the flash drive, photos, and recording Mollie had turned over when they'd opened her lockbox at the bank the afternoon after that strategy meeting at Precinct headquarters. Nothing there.

He typed a quick text to the undercover officer stationed somewhere outside the house to make sure the neighborhood was as quiet as it seemed to be. Nothing to report there, either.

"Any news?" Mollie finally closed her book and set it on the ottoman in front of them. He hated that there was no hope in her eyes when she looked at him, just polite curiosity.

"No." He tucked his phone into the pocket of his shorts and stood. "It's getting late, though. Maybe we should turn in."

She nodded. "I do have an early day tomorrow."

Mollie had barely slept the past three nights, even with Joel's arms wrapped around her and Magnus snoring on the rug on her side of the bed. There'd been an officer somewhere near them around the clock, and a squad car made regular passes through the neighborhood throughout the night. When they left the house, they both put on protective vests, but here, he thought they were safe enough that they could stay indoors without the vests. Still, he checked the locks on the doors and windows to make sure everything was secure while Mollie roused Magnus and headed back to his bedroom.

He wished there was something more he could do for her to ease the seemingly endless wait for justice to happen.

All she did was work at Pearl's, lie in bed with him, where he'd distract her with kisses and some making out until she fell into an exhausted, if troubled, slumber, and run Magnus through his training paces in the backyard while Kenna Parker-Watson pored over each piece of evidence. Every time she called with a follow-up question, the ADA assured Mollie they were putting together arrest warrants and restraining orders that should put the Di Salvos away for a very long time and give her back the normal life that her marriage had denied her.

Earlier this evening, Joel had declared she needed a break, and he had driven her to Saint Luke's Hospital to visit Corie Taylor and meet her new baby boy, Henry Sid Taylor. Somehow, Chief Taylor and his wife were there visiting, too. But Joel knew the timing was about more than visiting their new grandnephew. Mitch Taylor was armed when he told Joel he'd stand watch outside the room while they visited with Corie, her husband Matt, older son Evan, and baby Henry.

It was a treat to watch Mollie hold Henry, who was a strapping eight pounds and twenty-two inches long, and chat about some of the adventures Corie was missing at the diner. Herb was grumpier than usual with the change in his routine, now that Mollie had stepped in to take over pie baking duty and help with morning prep work. Melissa was looking to hire two new waitresses, with Corie going on maternity leave and Mollie finding a home she was better suited to back in the kitchen. The tourists weren't tipping as well as the regulars, and—thanks to some scheduling by Captain Hendricks—there seemed to be three or four more police officers than usual coming in for lunch or dinner this past week.

Joel loved seeing Mollie smile and laugh with her friend. And watching her hold baby Henry twisted his heart with longing. Mollie would make a great mother with her intelligence, strength, and gentle ways—and he desperately wanted to be the man who put a baby in her belly. If she could ever trust him enough to let him love her.

He'd kept his promise and gone to see Dr. Kilpatrick-Harrison to talk about his nightmares and fears that he wasn't the man that Mollie needed to get through this investigation and trial. Mollie seemed genuinely pleased and relieved that he was taking care of himself.

But it killed him to see the shadows beneath her beautiful blue eyes. Mollie wasn't thinking about babies and a future with him. Until this nightmare was settled, and the Di Salvos were no longer a threat to her, her world was a tiny, confining thing filled with fear and anxiety about living long enough to testify against her ex.

After letting Magnus out for one last run and securing the back door, Joel followed Mollie back to his bedroom. By the time he finished brushing his teeth and pulling off his T-shirt, Mollie was sitting up on the edge of the bed. He walked past her to plug his cell phone into his charger on the bedside table and secure his Glock and holster with his badge in the drawer there.

"You want to get up at 4:00 a.m. again?" he asked, setting the alarm.

She nodded. "I'm still not used to getting to the diner so early. I don't trust myself to wake up on my own."

He smiled down at her. "Then we'd better get to bed now."

She scooted back to the middle of the bed. "You don't have to stay with me. Herb will open the kitchen, and you can drop me off and go on to work or come back home for a nap while I help with prep."

"Twenty-four seven, remember? Where you go, I go." Joel settled in beside her and pulled her into his arms. He loved that she didn't even hesitate to curl against his side and rest her cheek against his chest. When she started tracing lazy circles across his chest with her fingers, he had to capture her hand and spread it flat against his heart to stop his body from reacting to her innocent caresses.

He lay in silence for several minutes, waiting for the tension to leave her body and for her to finally drift off to sleep. But she wasn't relaxing. And neither one of them were sleeping.

"Make love to me, Joel," she murmured against his chest.

"Looking to relieve some stress?" he teased.

But she didn't laugh. "I feel so disconnected from the life I wanted for myself. A career, a man who loves me, a family, a home. I'm this brittle, wishful shell of everything I used to be. But I feel connected to you. I feel closer to who I'm meant to be when I'm with you."

"And you think making love will strengthen that connection?"

"I wouldn't be using you to escape what I'm feeling." She pushed herself up to rest her chin where their hands were clasped and look him in the eye. "I want to be with you because you make me feel stronger."

"Are you sure?" He released her hand to tuck a coffee-colored tendril behind her ear. "Sex could be a trigger for you, and I don't want to make you afraid of me."

"I'd never be afraid of you," she vowed. "And, something might trigger a horrible memory. But I've never wanted to try with anyone else. I've never wanted any man the way I want to be with you."

"I feel the same way. I would be honored—and ever so grateful—to make love to you."

"I can't guarantee I'll be any good."

He pressed a finger to her lips to silence that nonsense. "We're both a work in progress, remember? I might not be any good, either."

She rolled her eyes. "I doubt that. All you have to do is kiss me, and I want you."

"I get the same feeling when you put your hands on me." He raised his head to kiss her gently. She joined the kiss as he rolled her onto her back and he positioned himself beside her. "I expect there to be a lot of talking while we do this. You tell me what you like, and you, for sure, tell me anything you don't like."

"I will." She swept her hands along his biceps and across his shoulders before cradling his jaw between her hands and rubbing her palms against his stubble. "But you need to tell me stuff, too. I want it to be good for you."

"It will be." When she started to protest that he couldn't know that, he silenced her with another, deeper kiss that required several minutes of heated contact before he could pull back and explain. "Because it's with you. Because you trusting me with this is the biggest turn-on and best gift I've ever been given."

She stroked her fingers across his jaw and his heart raced with desire. Her brows arched with an apology. "Protection? I stayed on the pill while I was with Augie because I couldn't imagine bearing his child. But I went off them when I ran out. I've never been with another man, so there was no need to pay for them."

He smoothed his thumb across each eyebrow until she relaxed. She had nothing to apologize for. He'd be honored to take care of her protection in this way, too. "I have condoms."

"Thank you." Her lips were slightly swollen and a seductive shade of pink from their kisses. "I want this so badly. But it scares me, too."

"If you decide you don't want to go through with it, I'll be fine. I'll cuddle with you all night the way we have been."

Her gaze ran down his chest to his belly before she met his eyes again. "Could I touch you?"

"You *are* touching me, babe."

"I mean…" Her hand followed the path her eyes had taken, skimming over his stomach toward the evidence of his arousal tenting his shorts. *"You."*

"You touch me however you want."

He loved it when she laughed like that. He loved when she bravely pushed the boundaries of her growing self-confidence, too. "You'd give me that kind of power over you?"

He loved her, period. "Yes. Don't you know, babe? You always have that kind of power over me."

"You'd better kiss me now, Joel."

"Happy to oblige."

The next thing he knew, her bold hand was slipping inside his shorts and curling around his manhood.

Joel sucked in a harsh breath and gritted his teeth against the jolt of anticipation thundering through his blood. He rested his forehead against hers while he tried to even out his breathing.

She smiled, showing him the woman she'd been before her ex and violence had ever touched her life. "I think we have on too many clothes."

Joel made love to her mouth with his and pulled up the hem of her shirt, taking his time to learn the shape and feel of her breasts plumping beneath his hands. She squirmed beneath his touch, then gasped and arched against him when he plucked her rock-hard nipples between his thumb and palm.

When he lowered his head to lick the exposed peak and draw it into his mouth, her fingers stroked along his shaft. Joel's mind blanked for a moment at the absolute perfection of Mollie's hand on him. "You're going to be trouble for me, aren't you?"

He reclaimed her mouth and gave himself over to her needy hands.

Yeah. So much trouble.

THE MOMENT MOLLIE stuck her key into the back door to the kitchen at 4:50 a.m. the next morning, she knew something was horribly wrong.

It wasn't locked.

She looked up to the man beside her, fearing the worst. "Joel?"

He pressed a finger to his lips, warning her to be silent, even as he unholstered his gun. He pulled his phone from his belt and pressed it into her hands. "A.J. Backup. Now."

Mollie nodded her understanding. She was as afraid now as she'd been that first night Augie had assaulted her. Only this time, her fear was for Joel and the unknown threat that might be waiting on the other side of that door. He gave Magnus a silent hand signal to stay by her side, then wrapped his fingers around the door handle.

She grabbed his arm before he could open it. "Be careful. I don't want to lose you."

He mouthed two words. *"Love you."*

Then he nodded to the phone, pulled open the door, and disappeared inside.

She gaped at the steel door for a moment, processing those last words. Then she snapped herself out of her stunned freeze, galvanized by the emotion filling her heart and spilling over into every cell of her body. Joel loved her.

She loved him.

The rightness of that revelation chased away the self-doubts and second-guessing that had ruled her life for too long. She was fighting for her future, fighting for the man who loved her. She pulled up A.J.'s number.

He answered on the first ring. "Rodriguez."

She didn't bother with a greeting, either. "Pearl's Diner.

Something's wrong. Joel armed himself and went inside to check it out."

"Are you safe?"

"Joel is in there by himself." She articulated every desperate word.

"Easy, Mollie. Backup is en route." He said something to someone on his end, and she pulled the phone away from her ear at the shrill of a siren. "Josh is notifying the UC man assigned to you this morning. We're spread a little thin. Josh and I and a SWAT team are at the Di Salvo estate to take your ex into custody. We've got Mom and Dad in a squad car, but there's no sign of August, Beau Regalio, or the lawyer."

Mollie's heart sank when she heard the jumble of overlapping voices from inside the diner. "That's because they're here."

She jumped back from the door when she heard Joel shouting. "KCPD! Drop your weapon! Hands where I can see them!"

She heard three distinct gunshots. Magnus leaped to his feet and barked. She heard a crashing sound, some indistinct voices...and her name, shouted in a voice that was sickeningly familiar. "Mollie! Where is she?"

She wrapped Magnus's leash around her fist.

"Mollie?" She heard A.J.'s voice over the phone again.

"He needs help. Now!" she shouted.

She disconnected the call and pulled open the door. "Magnus, heel!"

The drops of blood on the floor leading from the back door to the freezer didn't frighten her as much as seeing Beau Regalio dragging Joel's limp body. Was that blood on his shirt beneath the edge of his flak vest? Was this his blood on the floor? Where was Herb?

"Joel!" She would have moved to help, but the gun pressed against her scalp froze her in place.

"There's the little woman." Augie stood at the stainless-steel sinks, wiping his hands on a dish towel. "You've caused me a lot of trouble."

There was no teasing, no love, no regret in his dark eyes as he crossed the kitchen toward her.

The feeling was mutual.

Magnus growled and lunged to her left, nearly pulling her arm from its socket as she fought to keep him at her side. The gun was jerked away from her head as Kyra Schmidt dodged the Belgian Malinois in full protector mode. "I hate dogs!" The blonde backed up several steps until her back hit the row of ovens. "August. We need to take care of business and get out of here now. We need to get to the airport."

"Shut up and keep your gun on her."

Kyra circled around until she was standing in front of Mollie, well out of the furious barking dog's reach.

It was enough of an interchange for her to see Beau dumping Joel inside the freezer and shutting the insulated door. "Joel! What did you do him?" she demanded.

That was definitely blood on the sleeve of Beau's jacket as he pulled up the back of his suit jacket and tucked a Glock 9 mm—probably Joel's gun—into the back waistband of his slacks.

"Did he shoot you?" she taunted. "Maybe Herb went after you with one of his kitchen knives."

"You don't get to talk unless I ask you a question."

She saw it coming, but there was no way to dodge the

fist that came flying at her face. Mollie stumbled back from the blow, and would have landed on her bottom if Magnus hadn't been tugging so hard in the opposite direction. She immediately put her hand up to cup the pain blooming across her cheek. "The police are on their way, Augie. You can't escape."

"I said no talking." He might have hit her once, but Magnus wasn't going to let him hit her again.

Augie cursed. "Get that dog away from me!"

"Shut up, mutt!" Beau kicked Magnus, knocking him off his paws. But he was instantly up and lunging for the bigger man this time.

"Don't you hurt my dog!"

"Put him in the cooler with the others," he ordered Beau. But when the Di Salvo bodyguard tried to grab Magnus's leash, the dog bared his teeth and snapped at him.

When Beau pulled his gun to shoot the dog, Mollie put up her hand, pleading for mercy. "I'll put him in the freezer."

Augie grabbed Kyra's gun and pointed it at Magnus. "Try anything funny and I'll shoot him myself."

Although Magnus fought her every step of the way, she led him through the kitchen. Beau was close enough that she could feel the heat of his big body when he reached around her to open the freezer. When she glanced inside, she saw Herb Valentino lying on the floor, unconscious. There was blood oozing from the bandanna tied around the top of his head. Her heart lurched when she saw Joel lying face down on the floor beside him. A small pool of blood stained the floor beneath him. He was still wearing his protective vest, but one of those gunshots could have hit him in the neck or caught him low in his belly beneath the bottom edge.

Please God, don't be dead. I love you, too.

He'd been shot and left to die once before. Even if she didn't make it out of this, she prayed that backup would come, and Joel would get whatever medical help he needed.

"Quit mooning over your dead boyfriend. Get rid of the dog now!"

Augie's command spurred her into action. "I'm sorry, baby," she apologized to Magnus, forcing him to go against months of training that told him to stay by her side, to be there for her whenever she needed him. "You stay here with Daddy."

He was still barking and lunging for the armed men when Beau shut the freezer. Then he was on his hind legs, frantically scratching at the door to get back out.

Augie grabbed her by the hair. But since she kept it short now, he lost his grip and she fell to the floor. That only seemed to anger him further. Before she could scramble to her feet, Augie took her arm in a painful grasp and dragged her through the kitchen.

"Nobody's coming to save you, Mollie. You're mine. I told you what would happen if you left me."

"Shoot her," Kyra insisted, hurrying after them, her high heels clicking on the tile floor. "We need to make this clean and fast and get out of here."

"I told you to let me handle this."

"I'm a damn good lawyer, August. But even I can't refute a former Di Salvo testifying against you."

"Shut up!" He swung around and backhanded Kyra. *Welcome to the club, lover girl.* "That cop you paid off couldn't finish the job, but I will. I want her to suffer for the embarrassment she's caused me. I lost investors. Father threatened to disinherit me if I didn't get that evidence back. If I'm convicted, we all go down." He barked an order to Beau. "Bring the car around. We'll finish her off at the dump site. Then make sure the charter jet is waiting for us. I intend to be in Belarus where they can't extradite me before any other cop finds me."

Augie's first mistake was that he didn't kill her outright.

His second mistake was in thinking that Magnus was just a dumb, annoying animal of no consequence.

His last mistake was underestimating how determined Joel was to keep her safe.

The emergency latch inside the freezer suddenly unfastened and the door swung open. In three long strides, Magnus was across the room. He leaped at the man holding on to her, his vicious snarl even making Mollie cringe. He hit Augie in the chest with enough force to knock him to the floor and free Mollie. His long teeth clamped around Augie's wrist as he grabbed the dog to fight him off. The gun went flying, clattering across the kitchen and sliding beneath the sink.

"Shoot him! Shoot—" Augie's command ended in a high-pitched screech as teeth tore through flesh.

Beau trained his gun on the dog, but pulled it back just as quickly. "I don't have a shot!" He swung the weapon around at Mollie. "Call off your damn—"

Beau crashed to the floor with a hard thud as Joel tackled him. "Joel!"

The two men fought for control of the weapon. Beau landed a punch in Joel's side that made him groan. But then Joel was on top. He hit the bigger man once, twice, in the jaw, stunning him long enough to flip him onto his stomach, drive his knee into the middle of his back and handcuff him.

Then he pulled his own gun from the bodyguard's belt and turned to Mollie. "You okay?"

She moved behind him as he aimed his gun at Augie. "I'm fine. You got shot."

"Clipped me in the side. Second shot hit my vest and knocked me down. Hit my head. Magnus licked my face. He was quite insistent that I get my ass back out here to protect you."

Augie cried out again.

"Better call him off."

"Magnus! Come!" When the dog didn't immediately respond, she spoke in a louder, firmer tone. "Mama's okay. Come!"

Augie cradled his bleeding arm and writhed in pain as Magnus trotted back to Mollie's side and sat. She picked up his leash and praised him. "Good boy, Magnus. Good boy."

As Joel trained his gun on Augie and ordered him to roll over and put his hands on top of his head, Kyra made a run for the back door. But she was knocked flat on her ass when the door swung open and five fully armed SWAT officers streamed in. They were followed closely by A.J. and Josh, who quickly moved to cuff both Kyra Schmidt and Augie.

Standing down from superdetective mode, Joel holstered his weapon. He reached for Mollie, but she was retrieving a clean towel from the sink shelf. And instead of returning his hug, she pressed the folded towel against the wound in his side. "You're not dying, understand?"

"I'm okay, Moll." He gently grasped her shoulders.

"No, you're not. This is blood. Your blood."

A.J. pulled a whining Augie to his feet while the SWAT

team secured the kitchen and the rest of the diner and helped Herb out of the freezer.

"I see you got yourself shot again, Standage," A.J. commented dryly.

Joel chuckled. "Any bullet you can walk away from..."

"You two, stop it!" Mollie didn't find their cop-to-cop teasing very funny at the moment.

"Don't worry." A.J. handed Augie off to another officer. "An ambulance is on its way. I doubt the bullet hit anything vital or his color would be off, and he'd be unconscious by now. I'm guessing your ex is in worse shape with the damage your dog did to him."

"Magnus did his job. He was protecting me."

A.J. held his hands up in apology. "You'll get no complaints from me. I'm putting that dog in for a medal." Then his eyes darkened with sincere admiration. "Thank you for saving this guy. I need him on my team."

Mollie nodded. "Thank you for being here to back him up."

"Thanks, A.J." Joel pried her hand away from the towel and kept it in place there himself. "Come on. Let's go out front and have a seat somewhere out of the way while they secure the scene."

When she saw that he was limping again, she slipped her shoulder beneath his arm and helped him through the swinging door. Magnus saw his familiar bed at the end of the counter, and she released him so he could sniff it out and lie down if he wanted. Mollie guided Joel to one of the vinyl stools and climbed up on the one next to him.

When she started fussing with the abrasion at his temple, he caught her fingers in his free hand and kissed them. "I'm fine. You just sit here with me and keep the towel pressed against my wound." He frowned when he saw her face, and brushed her hair away from the bruise he must already be able to see discoloring her swollen cheek. "I want them to look at you, too."

"A souvenir from Augie. I've had worse."

"Not on my watch, you haven't."

Tears stung Mollie's eyes as the fear and adrenaline left her body. "You told me you love me, and then you got shot and I thought you were dead."

Joel gently cupped her cheek and swiped away the tears that spilled over with his thumb. "I've been dead. Didn't like it. I've never been more alive than when I'm with you."

Then he slipped his hand behind her neck and pulled her closer until he could cover her lips with his. Mollie reached up to stroke his stubbled jaw and returned the gentle kiss with all the love and hope blossoming inside her. A few moments later, she pulled away to look him in the eye and speak her truth. "I love you, too. I can't wait to testify and put the Di Salvos and their greed and evil out of my life forever. Because I want to start a new life with you."

He smiled. "You want to be part of my pack, Mollie Crane?"

"You'll be part of *my* pack, Joel Standage."

"I accept those terms."

A cold nose nudged her arm, and a warm, furry head nestled in her lap as Magnus squeezed between the two of them.

They both laughed and reached down to pet the dog who had brought them together. "Fine, you big goof," Mollie conceded. "We'll both be part of *your* pack."

* * * * *

TARGETED WITH
A COLTON

BETH CORNELISON

For Kasey—mental health professional extraordinaire and sweet friend. Thank you for answering my questions!

Prologue

One year ago

First Sergeant Wade Colton stood behind the young Marine private, watching as the other man worked through the steps of setting a charge, learning the proper techniques for using munitions. The sun beat down on the back of Wade's neck, and he used his hand to wipe sweat from his brow. Private Sanders was perspiring, too, Wade noticed. Beads of moisture were popping up on the younger soldier's top lip. The private's hands were shaking as he moved through his training.

"Private Sanders, a word?" Wade said, motioning for the private to come closer to speak to him.

Private Sanders approached, then stood stiffly before Wade, his chin raised. "Sir?"

"Is there a problem, Private? You seem rather nervous."

"No problem, sir. I can do it."

"Because before you're allowed to work with live munitions, you'll have to get your jitters under control. Shaky hands and volatile explosives are not a good combination." Wade added a half smile, hoping to ease the private's tension with a degree of humor. "Wouldn't you agree?"

The other trainees who were gathered in a circle around Wade and Sanders chuckled.

Private Sanders twitched a grin. "I agree, sir."

"Okay then. Take a breath, still your hands and try again," Wade said, hearing a truck engine and the squeak of brakes behind him. He turned to see who was arriving and snapped to attention as his superior officer climbed out of the front seat. "Sergeant Major Briggs," Wade said, saluting.

Briggs strode forward, returning a salute. "How is the training going, Colton?"

"Very well, sir."

"Good," Briggs replied, "because I received word this morning that Colonel Meyers will be visiting the base today and wants to observe your training after lunch."

Now it was Wade's turn to feel a spurt of jitters. Though he knew his team was ready, having any officer observing always put his men on edge. Which gave Wade qualms. Nodding his understanding, he said, "We'll be ready, sir."

Briggs asked a few more housekeeping questions before returning to the truck where his driver waited. "Look for the colonel around fourteen hundred."

Behind him he could hear the murmur of his men. A few guffaws. Whispers.

Wade had only turned a half circle back toward his men when he was hit by a blast of heat and energy that knocked him backward. Searing pain blazed over his right side, his face. His ears rang. His men yelling. Fire. Smoke. Burning flesh.

His vision dimmed.

The materials were supposed to be inert, he thought numbly. Then darkness swallowed him.

Chapter One

"Welcome to another edition of *Harlow Helps*," the beautiful brunette woman on Wade Colton's laptop screen chirped. "In honor of May being Mental Health Awareness Month, I'm doing these live events with my friends to answer a few questions and highlight the importance of mental health and mental health professionals." Harlow Jones smiled at her audience through the screen. Wade's attention was drawn to her dark brown bedroom eyes—eyes that Wade remembered with heartbreaking clarity shining with tears as they stared at him in disbelief.

His heart clenched seeing Harlow's face again, and he almost left the Facebook Live event then and there. But a powerful yearning and possibly self-destructive curiosity made him stay with the broadcast.

"...and have a few laughs along the way. While mental health issues are no laughing matter," Harlow said, "it is also true that laughter is medicinal, and keeping a sense of humor is always helpful."

Keeping a sense of humor? Wade furrowed his brow, an

action that tugged at his new scars. He tried to remember the last time he'd really laughed. The day of the accident flashed in his mind's eye. Joking around with the recruits. A teasing exchange with Sanders before—

He squeezed his eyes shut as the sights, sounds and smells of the tragic explosion replayed vividly for him. He gasped and shuddered as he tried to shake off the memory, but wave after wave of adrenaline sent tremors to his core, a cold sweat to his brow and nausea to his gut.

"Hello, caller! What is your name and where are you calling from?" Harlow's bright voice cut through his derailed and terrifying thoughts.

"Uh, it's Cindy. You asked me to call so you didn't have dead air, remember? You know where I live," the new female voice said.

Harlow pulled a face and made slashing motions at her throat. "Ah, ixnay the commentary. We're live on the air, *Cindy*. How can Harlow help you live a better life?"

Wade took a breath and, out of habit, raised a hand to pinch the bridge of his nose. When his fingers encountered the eye patch that now covered the damage to his permanently blinded right eye, he muttered a curse word under his breath. He hated his eye patch. It felt like an affectation. A costume. A flashing billboard sign that screamed "damaged" to the world. But the injury the explosion had caused to his eye was more unsightly than the patch, and he'd vetoed the suggestion of a prosthetic eye, so he sighed in resignation to his new accessory.

"Yeah, um, I've been hearing voices lately, and I'm worried what that might mean," the caller told Harlow.

Harlow arranged her face in a thoughtful moue. "Voices? What are they saying to you?"

"Strange but oddly comforting things. First I hear crying, which is pretty freaky. Then I hear a woman saying, 'Ahh, it's okay. I'm here. Who's a good girl?' and the crying stops."

Harlow arched an eyebrow. "Cindy, do you have a radio of some sort on in your house?"

Wade groaned, already seeing where this silliness was going.

"Yes. I drive a taxi and have my dispatch radio here at the house."

"I see. And do you know if one of your neighbors recently had a baby?" Harlow asked with a half grin.

"Oh, uh, yeah. My downstairs neighbor had a baby two months ago. Why?" Cindy's voice cracked with a chuckle as she gave her obviously staged response.

"Don't worry, Cindy. You're fine. I think you're hearing your neighbor's baby monitor through the dispatch radio."

"Oh, right!" Cindy said as they both chuckled over the lame act.

"Hearing baby monitors is not a sign of mental illness," Harlow said, sobering a bit, "but if you or a loved one is hearing unexplained voices or sounds, it is important to get the help of a trained psychiatrist for further evaluation. Today, many once unexplained or misinterpreted mental health conditions are better understood, and help is available from a variety of resources."

Wade rose from the wooden table that bore even more scars than he now had on his own chest, shoulder and face and shuffled to the refrigerator to get a beer. Twisting off the cap, he took a long pull and glanced at Harlow's face on his laptop. Why was he torturing himself this way? Harlow was gone. Part of his past. His family, doctors and friends were all telling him to focus on the future, to accept his new normal and forgive mistakes of days gone by.

"Letting Harlow go is a mistake, man," his big brother Fletcher had said years ago. "One you'll regret."

"What choice do I have? She wants no part of my life in the Marines. I leave for training Friday. She put me in a position to choose her or my dream of the Marines."

"You're burning bridges you may want a year or two from now. That's all I'm saying." Fletcher clapped him on the shoulder and gave him a dark look. "You will regret losing Harlow."

"Hello, caller! What's your name and where are you calling from?" Harlow's voice pulled him out of his melancholy reverie.

Fletcher had been right, of course. But Wade hadn't needed a year or two to regret breaking up with his high school sweetheart. He'd regretted losing Harlow before the harsh words severing ties with her had even left his mouth. He'd missed her, longed for her and hated his choice every day since telling her that he didn't love her when he announced he was leaving Owl Creek for his new career in the Marines. Now he was back in Idaho, in his small hometown, and Harlow was the one who had left for bigger, brighter things. Los Angeles, according to Hannah, who'd kept up with Harlow's life and career moves through Facebook. Hannah had been the one to tell Wade about Harlow's *Harlow Helps* Facebook presence and her new live broadcasts to promote mental health awareness. Wade had pretended not to be interested. Pretended he was over Harlow. Pretended he wasn't desperate for any morsel of guidance or help navigating his own mental health crisis. Because he'd gotten really good at denying he had a mental health crisis, to others and to himself. All he needed, he told himself, was fresh Owl Creek air, quiet and solitude to decompress. In time, his memories and his scars, glaring reminders of *that day*, would both heal and fade.

With another sip of beer, Wade put his hand on the laptop lid, prepared to slam it closed. Harlow's face and voice were not helping him feel better. They only reminded him of loss. Pain. Hollowness inside him.

"I need your help, Harlow. I have nowhere else to turn," the trembling voice of her new caller said.

Wade hesitated, removing his hand from the laptop when he saw the subtly startled look on Harlow's face. She blinked once, her mouth twitching slightly. He knew her well enough to realize something significant was amiss. Harlow had been caught off guard and was confused. Concerned. And trying to hide it.

"Yes, caller. I'm here to help." Only someone who knew Harlow as intimately as he did would have recognized the tension in her voice. "Can I have your name and where you're calling from?"

"I, uh… Janet. I'm in my car. I—I want to die. I c-can't—" A sob stifled the caller's words.

Wade dropped heavily into the kitchen chair, his heart pounding as he imagined Harlow's was, given the way the color had leached from her face. He studied her body language, seeing the moment she lifted her chin the slightest amount and firming her shoulders with resolve. The color returned to her face along with an expression of honest compassion and concern.

"Janet, I know things look bad right now, but we can work through whatever is wrong together if you'll trust me. Will you let me help?"

A broken hum of agreement answered Harlow.

Wade leaned toward the computer as if he could bolster Harlow, as if drawing nearer to her would give her the courage, strength and wisdom to handle this distraught caller.

"I think you want to find a way through this bad time. Isn't that why you called? You want to live, and you want me to help guide you through whatever's happened, whatever has left you feeling hopeless. Am I right?"

"I…" Janet sniffled and was silent for several tense seconds before saying, "I guess. I'm just…so lost. So alone."

"You are not alone, Janet. I'm here, and I will not leave this call until you are ready. I'm one hundred percent with you now and any time you want to call me."

"Okay," Janet squeaked.

Wade held his breath. He couldn't imagine what must be going through Harlow's mind right now. The pressure to get things right. The worry for the hurting woman. The panic knowing this whole thing was playing out live through her Facebook page.

Wade narrowed his gaze on Harlow's face and modified the last assumption he'd made. Harlow's intensity and attention were razor sharp. The set of her brow, the slight tilt of her head, the keen focus of her eyes on some fixed point off-screen. She was fully locked in on Janet's plight, the live broadcast and other viewers forgotten.

Harlow had had that same intensity and fervor during sex. Wade's blood heated just remembering. When she committed to something she was all in. Which was why he'd had to be so harsh, so clear about breaking things off with her. So decisively, painfully final when he left Owl Creek for the Marines at nineteen.

"Now, Janet, you said you are in your car. Are you driving or are you parked somewhere?"

"Parked."

"And where are you parked?" Harlow asked.

"In my garage."

"Is your engine on?"

Wade leaned even closer, his hand fisting as the silence stretched.

"Janet, are you there? Is your engine running?"

"Yes. I just want to go to sleep and never wake up again."

Heart sinking, Wade dragged a hand over the "good" side of his face. The unscarred left side. Unshaven stubble scraped his palm. He could remember feeling the same despondency in the earliest days in the military hospital when he learned he'd lost an eye. Lost a fellow Marine. Lost his career. Those black moments could really suck at your soul and drag you down. He still fought the pull of those moments at random times. Unexpected triggers. Days when the doubt demons seemed to hound him harder.

"Don't do it," he whispered to Janet. To himself?

When he turned his attention back to Harlow's voice, she was cajoling Janet to turn off the engine, step outside for fresh air. The sounds and responses Janet gave indicated she had complied. Wade released the breath from his lungs. *Well done, Harlow. Well done.*

He sipped his beer again and listened with rapt wonder as Harlow eased the conversation skillfully through the maze of tragedy and grief that surrounded Janet. Her tone was compassionate, earnest. Her focus was steady and her advice sage.

"Life can feel so overwhelming when you have such big things to deal with in your life. But, Janet, be kind to yourself. You didn't make these things happen, and no one expects you to snap back from such hardship and loss overnight."

Wade clenched his back teeth as ripples of recognition washed through him. His doctors had said much the same to him.

"Give yourself the grace to take each moment, each breath, each step as it comes. Do one tiny thing, even if that is just getting out of bed, and give yourself credit for making that step. Celebrate that step. Tell yourself that you did a good thing with that step. It counts. It matters. You matter."

Wade's cell phone rang, and caller ID showed it was Hannah. He considered ignoring it, but in the past months, ignored calls had been interpreted as flashing red beacons to his family, who all seemed to feel the need to walk on eggshells around him.

He swiped to answer the phone, anticipating the reason for the call, and saying, "I'm fine."

"Are you? Really? I swear I had no idea the broadcast would take such a serious turn. I was worried you might think…" Hannah didn't finish saying what she'd thought. "I guess I shouldn't have even mentioned Harlow's show to you at all. I'm sorry."

"Don't apologize. I'm a big boy, and I can decide for myself whether I want to look in on my ex-girlfriend's live show or not."

"Then work toward taking a shower. Then toward getting dressed," Harlow was saying to Janet.

"Is that Uncle Wade?" a tiny voice said in the background at Hannah's house. "Can I talk to him?"

"Have you brushed your teeth?" Hannah said, her voice

muffled as if having placed her hand over the phone. "Okay, but just for a minute. You have school in the morning."

Wade rolled the cursor on his laptop to pause Harlow's live broadcast as his five-year-old niece came on the line.

"Hi, Uncle Wade! Guess what?"

"Hi, Lucy Goose," he replied, his chest filling with a welcome warmth as he pictured his niece's bright smile. "I can't guess. You tell me what."

"My best friend, Bella—well, I guess she's not my *best* best friend. Ginger is my *best* best friend. I guess Bella is my next best friend. At school. Hilary is my next best friend in the neighborhood. We both like the same TV shows, and Mommy says having things in common and shared int— Um, shared—"

"Interests?" he prompted.

"Yeah! Shared interests is part of making friends."

"She's right."

"Anyhoooo," Lucy intoned, imitating the expression she'd doubtlessly heard the adults in her life use.

Wade bit back a chuckle over the five-year-old's precociousness. God, he loved this little girl and the innocent joy she brought to his life.

"So… Bella—wait for it!"

Wade smiled brighter. "Waiting…"

"Got. A. Puppy!" Lucy's squeal of excitement was so long, loud, high-pitched, he had to pull the phone away from his ear.

"Wow! A puppy? That's pretty cool. Have you met the puppy yet?"

"Yes! It's so soft and squirmy, and it licked all over my face! She hasn't named it yet, but I think she should name it Yippers cause when it barks it goes, 'Yip yip yip!'"

Wade chuckled as his niece imitated the puppy bark, then heard his sister telling Lucy her time was up and she had to go to bed.

"Awww," Lucy whined. "But I haven't even told him about the end-of-school program."

Wade cast his gaze to the frozen computer screen, where Harlow's face had been caught in a worried frown. A beat of impatience, a need to get back to Harlow's conversation with Janet, rippled through him. As much as he adored Lucy and her sweet lift to his spirits, he couldn't help wondering how Harlow was managing the suicidal caller.

"Mommy says I have to go. Bye, Uncle Wade. Mu-ah!"

"Mu-ah," he said in return, imitating the sound of blowing a kiss. "Sweet dreams, Lucy Goose."

Hannah came back on the line. "I have to put Lucy to bed now, but…you're sure you're okay?"

He sighed and repeated the line he'd said to his family a thousand or more times in the last several months. "I'm fine."

"Okay. I'll call you later. Bye, Wade."

"Bye, sis." He disconnected the call and started the live broadcast playing again. The video playback skipped forward, catching up to what was currently airing.

"Look up at the stars," Harlow was telling Janet. "Fill your lungs with air. Allow yourself to notice little things that can help you root yourself and feel a bit of control over this moment in time. We're not going to think about tomorrow or an hour from now. Just here and this moment in time."

"Okay."

"What can you hear?"

"Crickets. Tree frogs. The wind in the leaves."

"Good. What do you smell? Fresh air? Gosh, I don't know how fresh the air is where you live. Here in LA, fresh air is relative." Harlow gave a gentle smile for her quip. "Where do you live, Janet?"

"Omaha."

"Oh, the Midwest. I visited Omaha once. Beautiful place," Harlow said.

He continued listening and marveling as Harlow continued to calm Janet. Eventually she got her caller to reveal her home address in a private message to Harlow. When Harlow's eyes flickered briefly to something in her lap, Wade could guess what that something was, what Harlow was doing. It was the same thing he'd be doing—calling emergency services in Omaha.

"Smooth," Wade said with a nod. He raised his beer in salute to Harlow. She had handled every aspect of the obviously unexpected crisis call with aplomb and composure.

When it was clear that emergency services had found Janet, Harlow made sure that Janet was referred to local counselors and promised to follow up with her in the coming days.

Taking a deep breath and feeling rather like he'd run a marathon, Wade finally leaned back in his chair and tried to shake the tension from his limbs. He couldn't even imagine the relief and emotional fatigue Harlow must be feeling.

Harlow rubbed her eyes and, as if suddenly remembering that her computer camera had just captured and broadcast live the exchange with Janet, she rallied and address the audience. "Friends, that was obviously not what we had planned for tonight. Ideally, I would not have conducted such a personal emergency so publicly, but I didn't want to risk losing my connection with Janet even for a second." She swallowed hard and exhaled. "Emergencies don't give us a chance to plan or schedule—" she raked fingers through her thick dark brown hair, clearly deciding what needed to be said "—which is why it's so important to constantly be addressing your mental health, paying attention to what's happening with your family and friends, taking measures to promote mental wellness just as you take steps to protect your physical health."

Wade picked at the label on his beer bottle. *Emergencies don't give us a chance to plan or schedule.* That was an understatement. His own recent disaster had altered his life in a fraction of a second. A stray spark. A faulty blasting cap.

Harlow was staring straight into camera now, her eyes so piercing not even Kevlar could have protected him from their impact on his heart. "This is exactly the point of highlighting mental health in May. Your mental health is every bit as important as your physical health and cannot be ignored. There is no shame in asking for help if you are struggling."

Wade grunted. He'd heard that line, too, several times since waking up in the hospital a year ago. But that advice was antithetical to his Marine training in so many ways. Needing such personal help was not something a member of the Marines Special Forces unit could easily admit. He'd been trained to be self-sufficient in the direst of circumstances, to endure the most difficult environmental conditions, perform the most dangerous and difficult military operations, and shove his personal comfort, wants and desires aside. The mission came first. Suck it up and do the job. *Oo-rah!*

"So until next week, this is Harlow Jones with *Harlow Helps.*"

Wade squeezed the beer bottle, not wanting the live feed to end. He wanted to sit there all night and stare at Harlow's beautiful face, wallow in the dulcet tones of her voice and remember how, with her, he'd once felt complete.

But instead, he listened as she said, "Be kind to yourself and others, and join me next time as we continue to talk about how to protect your mental health." Then with a wave to the audience, she ended the live feed.

Wade closed the laptop, drained his beer and released a sigh. Had it been a mistake to watch Harlow's live broadcast? He'd told himself he wanted the closure of seeing her and knowing she was doing okay. That she'd moved on and was fine.

Instead, he'd reopened the hole in his soul that had never healed when they split up. He'd only reinforced for himself how alone he felt and in so many aspects, how far away from him she was.

In Los Angeles, Harlow's phone was blowing up—texts, calls and Facebook messages. She answered a call from her friend Yolanda, who had been the *planned* guest for the broadcast, with a softball question about the importance of exercise for mental well-being.

"Wow," Yolanda said. "Just...wow."

"Yeah." Putting Yolanda on speakerphone, Harlow moved from her desk chair to lie supine on the floor and stretch her back and arms. Her black cat, Luna, took that as an invitation to walk on Harlow's chest and curl up on her stomach for a nap.

"You were amazing. I mean, I'm sorry I didn't get my call in before she rang in, but...big picture, that was fate, I think. You saved her!"

Harlow didn't want to go down that thought path. As soon as she'd realized what was happening, she'd shifted into counselor mode, shut everything else out, and just… followed her instincts and training. "Alexa, remind me to follow up with Janet tomorrow," she said to her Echo device. She rubbed Luna's head and let the rumble of her cat's purr soothe her. She took a few slow breaths, steadying her nerves.

"Holy cow, Harlow! There are *already* like two hundred comments on your Harlow Helps page. Most are support and encouragement for Janet, but a lot are commending you for how you handled the situation." Yolanda chuckled with awe in her tone. "This is amazing. You need to follow up."

"I intend to. I mean, I know I referred her to a counseling group in Omaha, but I don't want her to think I've abandoned her, that I don't care." Harlow closed her eyes, pointing and flexing her toes to stretch her calves.

"Well, that's good, too. I wouldn't expect otherwise from you. You're nothing if not conscientious and caring. What I meant was this could be the start of something big. What a launch pad for your platform!"

Wrapping an arm around Luna, Harlow sat up, frowning at her phone. "Hang on. You're not suggesting I exploit Janet's call, her pain, for commercial gain, are you? Because that would be…too reprehensible for—"

"No! Of course not! I just mean…if you want to reach more people with your show, help more people, increase the exposure of your message…"

Yolanda fell silent, letting Harlow fill in the blanks. "Well, of course I want to reach as many people as I can. The whole point of using social media is to try to reach a larger audience. More people reached means more lives helped. In theory."

"Well, you certainly have a great start tonight," Yolanda said. "You saved Janet's life. And you have…geez, five hundred comments now and two hundred shares already."

Disturbed from her attempt to cuddle, Luna sauntered off, tail high, and Harlow rolled her shoulders. She'd been so tense, so tightly wound during her conversation with Janet, and her muscles were still in knots.

"Say, you know who could help you make the most of this momentum? My friend Nadine. She's in public relations and is great with maximizing social media exposure. Want me to put her in touch with you?"

Harlow laughed tiredly. "Yolanda, jeepers! My brain is still numb from talking with Janet, and you're already planning my next career moves?"

"Strike while the iron is hot, my grandma used to say," Yolanda replied without an ounce of remorse in her tone. "I'm texting you her number now. You'll love her. She's the best."

"Thanks, but if I decide to hire a PR consultant—big *if*, that seems way premature—I'd probably call a friend of mine from Idaho. Vivian's got her own company, and I like to support small businesses."

"Okay. Your choice. But if you change your mind about—Oops, gotta go. I hear the baby waking up. Love ya, girl! And congrats again. You were great tonight!"

"Thanks, I—" But Yolanda was gone. The buzzes and pings of incoming messages and texts continued, and she lifted her phone to mute it. She'd answer the barrage of attention tomorrow. Right now, she needed a hot bubble bath and a chance to decompress.

Her brain replayed her conversation with Janet, and she examined every bit of advice and word of comfort she'd given the distressed woman, hoping she'd struck the right tone, said the most appropriate things, done everything she could.

And for the first time in several months, her thoughts traveled back eleven years and north a thousand miles to Owl Creek, Idaho, to a night when the scent of pine had filled the air and a warm spring breeze had ruffled her hair. The night Wade Colton had broken her heart and left her standing alone in her backyard, believing her life was over.

"I understand, Janet," she whispered as she turned on the bathtub taps and dumped in a generous dollop of lavender-scented bubble bath. "But you can survive it. I did."

But as she had many times before, Harlow renewed her pledge to herself to never give her heart to anyone so blindly and fully. She never wanted to risk that depth of heartache again.

Chapter Two

Los Angeles
The next January

"So, I've confirmed the interview with the local magazine in Boise," Vivian Maylor, Harlow's high school friend and current PR consultant, said. "They want it to be a 'local girl's rise to success' kind of article."

"Except I'm not from Boise. I'm from all over. The closest I ever came to Boise was Owl Creek, and you know I only moved there when I was in junior high. Does four years in a town make it your hometown?" Harlow asked, giving Vivian a wry grin.

On her laptop screen, via Zoom, Vivian waved off Harlow's concern. "Details, details. It's great exposure. I'm working on similar articles with a magazine in Boston and one in Savannah. You're going to be a household name when I'm finished, Harlow."

Harlow shifted uncomfortably in her chair. A household name? Was that what she wanted? Fame and national recognition had never been her goal when she hired Vivian to help boost her social media presence, and thereby increase her audience for the *Harlow Helps* live Facebook broadcasts.

Back in May, her emergency counseling session with Janet had gone viral. Taking Yolanda's advice, Harlow had seized on the attention to grow her audience, expand her online counseling program and reach more people in the name of mental health awareness. Sure, the attention of advertisers and increase in her income had been a boon, but it had never been her motivation.

Harlow sighed, reflecting on the past few months' whirlwind of business opportunities, growing exposure—and personal turmoil. Amid the excitement of her growing counseling program, Harlow's mother had died unexpectedly.

Grieving her mother, just two years after losing her father to cancer, had sapped much of Harlow's energy, but had also been a good reason to address grief and share her own experience with self-care after loss during her live broadcasts. The topic had struck a chord with a huge audience, especially when she highlighted how grief over pets, job losses and broken relationships were just as real and important to address as the sorrow following the death of a friend or family member.

Knowing how many people she was reaching, hearing from dozens of grateful listeners daily and learning how her program was making a difference both validated and inspired Harlow to keep going. She wanted to keep expanding her program, keep building her platform.

But only seven months into the exponential social media expansion, Harlow was already getting uncomfortable with the limelight. As her media presence grew and she attracted advertisers who wanted to share her high profile, critics lambasted her for selling out. Guilt had hit Harlow hard when those accusations were made. She'd never wanted to use her platform for anything but good. Promoting mental health services available in most communities, highlighting healthy practices and debunking myths that harm or hinder people with mental health issues had been her only agenda. That she was now making a good living with the Facebook Live programming and had advertisers and representatives from Spotify proposing a podcast deal were secondary benefits to Harlow.

"Speaking of households," Harlow said, rubbing her temple where a headache was building, "I still haven't done anything with my parents' place. Between the holidays and all the promotional stuff you have me doing, I haven't found five minutes to call a real estate agent to inquire about listing the Owl Creek house."

When Luna jumped up on the desk and walked across Harlow's keyboard, demanding attention, Harlow lifted her down with a chuckle. "Not now, Luna."

"Are you saying it's my fault you're procrastinating?" Vivian asked with a sassy lift of her eyebrow. "You know you can do your job from anywhere with a Wi-Fi connection, right?"

Luna jumped back up, and Harlow pursed her lips in a frustrated scowl. "Yeah, yeah."

"If you're putting off cleaning out your parents' home, that's on you."

"You're right, of course." Harlow bobbed her head in concession, scratching her cat behind the ears. "But it's more than a lack of motivation. I'm so mentally drained at the end of a day hearing about other people's problems that I don't have the bandwidth left to take care of my own." That, and she hadn't found the nerve to return to Owl Creek in person. Too many memories lived there.

But Los Angeles had begun to feel uncomfortable in recent weeks, too. Along with the popularity of *Harlow Helps*, her growing fan base also meant she'd gained some online trolls. And a stalker.

As best she could determine from the cryptic Facebook messages she'd started receiving, someone had taken exception to something she'd said in one of her live broadcasts. She'd initially engaged the man she knew only as Chris72584, in case he was open to mental health advice, offering help to the obviously distressed individual. Harlow had left lines of communication open, offering replies such as "How can I help you?" or "I'm here to listen. Tell me what is upsetting you."

But the angry replies were cold and had become threatening. "What gives you the right to judge me?" and "You're what's upsetting me. You've ruined my life," and then, "Want to help the world? Die. I wish I could kill you."

At that point, she'd stopped communicating with Chris72584. She'd blocked him as his threats grew more disturbing.

"Don't ignore me."

"I will find you."

"I'm coming for you."

"Sounds like the counselor needs to take her own advice and take a mental health break," Vivian said, drawing her out of her thoughts. "What do you say? A weekend on the beach? A quick trip to Mexico for margaritas and sun? I'll come with you!" Vivian added the last with a singsongy tone and an unabashed grin.

Harlow chuckled. "I'm sure you would. But no Mexico for me."

"Spoilsport. I was looking for an excuse to put this freezing Idaho weather in my rearview mirror for a few days."

"Sorry," Harlow replied. "I actually like winter weather. I miss cold days curled up by the fireplace and making snow ice cream and..."

Harlow let her sentence trail off as she glanced at her phone and read the notification of an incoming text. The message from an unfamiliar number simply read, "Boo, bitch!"

Acid curled through her stomach.

"Harlow? You okay? You look like you've seen a ghost."

"I, um..." She blinked, trying to clear her head, settle her gut. But then another text came through. A picture of her condo, her car parked on the driveway, and Luna visible, sitting in the open kitchen window.

I found you. Be scared.

A shudder raced through Harlow as she snatched her hand away from her phone as if it were a snake that could bite her. She *was* scared.

"Harlow?" Vivian's tone sharpened with concern. "What's wrong?"

"I—I think I'm going to take that break after all. And, uh, close up my parents' house. Getting that albatross off my mind will help my stress factor considerably."

"You're coming to Owl Creek?"

She hated the idea of returning to the place where her heart had been broken. But old ghosts were a safer bet than dealing with a potentially dangerous stalker—who'd somehow gotten her private cell phone number. Harlow's mouth dried.

"Y-yes," she said, hearing the tremble in her tone. "Could you pick me up at the Boise airport tomorrow?"

"Of course," Vivian said, chuckling lightly. "Tomorrow, huh? Once you make up your mind, you don't mess around! What time should I be there?"

"I'll let you know. I'm going to look up flights now."

"Can I ask what spurred this sudden change of heart?" Vivian became more serious, leaning toward her camera as if wanting to grasp Harlow's hand or trying to make a deeper connection despite the impersonal Zoom call. "Something spooked you just now. I can see it in your face. What happened?"

Harlow forced a stiff grin. "I just took your advice to stop procrastinating. No time like the present." *That, and the fact that my stalker has just upped the ante by a factor of ten.*

Her house, her life, Los Angeles, no longer felt safe. She would call the police as soon as she disconnected with Vivian. Tomorrow, she'd hop on a plane to the only place she'd ever truly felt at home. Owl Creek was haunted because of Wade Colton, but she could hide in the safe haven of her parents' home until the authorities caught the person who was so maliciously closing in on her.

Even as she set her plan to flee to Idaho, another text came in from the same unfamiliar number. Her breath stuck in her throat as she read the new message. It was as if the stalker had read her mind.

You can run, but you can't hide.

Chapter Three

Vivian pulled in the driveway of the ranch-style house that had been Harlow's first real home. After years of moving from one city to another as her father changed Army bases like he changed his socks, her family had finally settled down in Owl Creek. Her father's military retirement and the roots the family had planted in the small Idaho town had given Harlow a sense of permanence when she needed it most. Having reliable friends, a sense of security and the promise of consistency during her high school years had been a welcome relief.

"Looks just the way I remember it," Vivian said.

"If in need of a little TLC," Harlow countered, noticing a loose shutter on a front window and the faded paint on the trim. "It's like the house knows it's vacant and droops a little in loneliness."

From her travel carrier, Luna gave an impatient yowl.

"Poor girl." Harlow turned to poke her fingers in the carrier and scratch Luna's head. "She's been cooped up in this thing all day, other than the quick breaks for litter box and food at LAX and the Boise airports. Come on, girl. Let's go inside and get you set up in Grandma's house."

A twinge of grief plucked Harlow's heart as soon as the words were out. Her mother and father would never meet their real grandchildren, assuming she ever had any kids. That prospect was starting to look dim, considering her bleak love life of late.

Ticktock, said her biological clock, and Harlow firmly shoved those thoughts aside. Before she entertained any thoughts of romance and attracting the attention of a potential spouse, she had to rid herself of the unwanted and rather scary attention of her stalker. Harlow shouldered open the door of Vivian's car and yelped at the cold bite of the Idaho winter.

"Problem?" Vivian asked as she opened her car's trunk to get Harlow's suitcases.

"Only that I've apparently gotten spoiled by the mild California weather. I'd forgotten how cold it can get here." With Luna's carrier in one hand, Harlow hoisted her computer bag and the handle of her largest rolling suitcase and headed for the front door.

Vivian followed, rolling a smaller bag and carrying the tote bag with Luna's supplies. "I know you came up here to get your mom's house cleaned out and market-ready, but I'd love to put our heads together while you're here and brainstorm some promo ideas for this spring. Strike while the iron is hot, you know?"

"Um, sure. We'll do that."

"And lunch?" Vivian waited while Harlow keyed open the door and carried Luna inside. "Or maybe dinner and drinks with some of the old gang? Hannah and Lizzy are still in the area. Have you talked to either of them lately?"

Harlow turned on the lights in the foyer and living room and gave her mother's house an encompassing glance. She'd last been here for a quick in-and-out weekend for her mother's funeral back in the fall. The gloom of the gray winter day did little to brighten the homecoming. She unzipped Luna's carrier and stroked the cat's fur as her cat poked her head out with a suspicious sniff.

"No, I haven't talked to anyone," Harlow said, finally answering Vivian's question. "I didn't really keep up with many people after high school. Most of my closest friends were part of the Colton family, and after Wade and I broke up, I just couldn't…"

Vivian's expression lit with recognition before she winced. "Wade. Right. I can see how that might be awkward."

Excruciating, more like. Even the mention of him now sliced through her like barbed wire tangled around her soul.

Harlow rallied herself, pasting on a smile. "But I really shouldn't let bygones stand in the way of friendships. Right? I mean, that's what I'd tell a client. Don't let fear of the past stand in the way of important relationships."

"Amen!" Vivian said with a laugh. "So… I'll set something up and be in touch." She squatted and held her hand out for Luna, who was timidly creeping out of her carrier to check out her new surroundings. "Um…speaking of Wade…"

Throat tightening, Harlow said, "Were we?"

Vivian tipped her head to glance up at Harlow while stroking Luna's back and tail. "You know he's Nate's half brother, right? Robert Colton was living a double life with two families, including a son and daughter he didn't tell anyone in Owl Creek about."

"Seriously?" Harlow blinked hard, trying not to gape as she digested this news. Wade's father had a second secret family? Wade had half siblings he'd never known about? Clearly, she had missed a bit of drama in the years while she was away. She schooled her face and said, "No, I hadn't heard that. That's…wow!"

"Will it be a problem for you, seeing as how Nate and I are involved?"

Harlow scoffed. "Why should it be? You're my PR agent and friend. If your friendship with Wade's cousin Lizzy doesn't bother me, why should your relationship with Nate?"

Vivian gave her a silent scrutiny before nodding. "Okay. Just checking. I know this is an emotional enough trip for you without piling on because of my connections." She twisted her mouth, and her eyebrows dipped. "What do you think you'll say to Wade if you see him while you're here?"

Harlow's pulse jumped. "Why would I see him? He's in North Carolina or somewhere with the Marines, right?" Harlow saw something flicker across Vivian's face, and her insides grew cold. "Isn't he?"

"Um…no. He left the Marines a while back. He's been in Owl Creek ever since. He lives in a small rental cabin by Blackbird Lake and works for his uncle on the Colton Ranch now."

Harlow felt her knees tremble, and she moved quickly to a chair in the living room before she could slump onto the floor.

"Why can't you stay here and be a ranch hand or policeman or an accountant for your dad or something? Why do you have to be a Marine?" young Harlow sobbed, her voice tight with anger and hurt.

"Because that's not who I am. I'd never be satisfied being a rancher or accountant. You should know that about me. We've talked about this before!" Wade's eyes blazed with determination, chipping away another piece of Harlow's breaking heart.

"Harlow? Are you all right?" Vivian hurried into the living room and knelt by the wingback chair. "I thought you knew."

She shook her head. "No. But then I've intentionally avoided any news or reminders of Wade since we broke up." She met Vivian's worried look. "You're sure? He's here? He's...ranching?"

Vivian nodded. "According to Lizzy. I haven't run into him myself, but I hear he's been lying low since he got back in town. He works the ranch, then goes straight home."

Harlow drew and released a breath, gathering her composure. She gave her friend a wry grin. "Well, thanks for the...warning."

So Wade had changed his mind about ranching, about living in Owl Creek...

What else had changed for Wade? And why did the answer matter so much to her?

THE SUN WAS just cresting the ridge of distant mountains as Wade arrived at Colton Ranch. He took a moment to appreciate the peaceful sunrise, and once he'd parked his pickup near the front door of his Uncle Buck's barn-style home, he glanced around the ranch yard. He spotted extra vehicles near the horse stable and some unusual activity in the paddock. He hesitated a moment before heading up the gravel path to knock on Buck's door. He squinted, trying to determine if one of the people in the paddock was his uncle, but the figures seemed too petite and slim. Women?

He didn't see as well as he used to out of his "good eye," though as scar tissue healed and swelling receded, his vision was getting better, like the doctor had promised. He knew he needed to get a contact for his left eye, but in the past eighteen months, he'd had his fill of doctors and appointments and physical therapy. He just wanted to be left alone. No more doctors poking and prodding, and no more relatives and friends hovering like spy drones, watching his every move, expecting him to…do what? Have a meltdown? Grow horns to go with his new scarring? Find him abusing painkillers? Wade grunted at that possibility. He took pride in the fact that he'd purposely avoided narcotic pain medicines after leaving the hospital. He'd endured the excruciating pain of his healing wounds and physical therapy, specifically to avoid dependence on any drug. If he was hurting, if he lost sleep from the searing pain some days, he considered it a small price to pay to be alive. Private Sanders hadn't been as lucky.

The sound of laughter, male and female, sounded from behind Buck's front door. The woman's voice sounded *very* familiar. Very…familial. Wade weighed his options. Let his mother have her secrets or—

The front door opened, and his mother and Buck both pulled up short, their faces reflecting surprise at finding Wade on the front step and…was that guilt?

"Wade, uh…hello, darling."

Buck jerked a stiff nod of greeting. "Mornin', Wade."

Jenny Colton stepped over to her son for a hug and looked him up and down. "Why are… I mean, is everything all right? Are you okay?"

Wade gave his mother a quick squeeze, then stepped back, furrowing his brow. "I'm fine. I just had a question for Buck before I started work today."

"Oh. Right." Jenny's hand fluttered up to twist her stud earring. "I'm only here because I, uh, brought Buck some cinnamon bread I'd baked." She aimed a nervous finger over her shoulder to the kitchen and flashed a weak smile.

Wade nodded once. "You don't have to explain yourself to me."

"Of course not," Jenny said with a tight laugh. "I just… Well, I should go. Bye, darling."

"Bye," Wade and Buck answered at the same time, eliciting another nervous laugh from Jenny and putting an uncustomary flush in his uncle's cheeks. Wade chose to dismiss the obvious explanation for both his mother's presence at his uncle's house at this hour of the morning and the awkward vibe he was getting from the older couple. He had no interest in family drama or intrigue if he could avoid it.

His mother patted his arm and, tipping her head to a concerned angle, gave him another worried scrutiny. "You're sure everything is all right? You've been keeping to yourself a lot lately."

Wade gritted his back teeth, hunching his shoulders against the cold when a stiff winter wind buffeted him. "I'm fine, Mom."

Jenny looked unconvinced but hiked her purse strap onto her shoulder and moved past him before giving another awkward laugh. "Silly me. I parked in the back." She sidled past Wade again and shrugged as she passed Buck. "I'll call later. Okay?"

Buck folded his arms over his chest and mumbled, "Yeah. Bye." Then facing Wade, he shifted his feet before leveling a narrow-eyed gaze on his nephew. "You had a question?"

"Uh-huh. I was wondering if you'd heard anything back from the mechanic on the four-wheeler? I can take my truck to pick it up from the shop, if it's fixed."

"Oh, uh, no. Not yet." Buck exhaled heavily and dropped his hands to his sides. "Waiting on a part. Could be Friday before it's ready."

"Okay." Wade turned to leave. "Unless you have something of higher priority for me, I'll take Cactus Jack out to check fences."

"Sure. Ruby said she'd drop by this afternoon to give another round of vaccinations to the cows from the upper pasture," Buck said, meaning Wade's younger sister, a veterinarian. "You could give her and Malcolm a hand with that later."

"No problem."

Wade started to walk away when Buck said, "Wade? I think you should know…"

Facing his uncle, he shook his head. "Like I told Mom, I don't need an explanation."

"That's not…" Buck scowled. "I was only going give you a warning. Nate is here."

Nate. The half brother he only recently learned about. The half brother who had been excluded from their father's will.

"Is there a problem?" Wade asked.

Buck shook his head. "Naw. At least I don't think so. He's here with Lizzy…and Vivian."

"Oh. Right." Wade mentally connected the dots. Buck's daughter Lizzy was best friends with Vivian Maylor—whom Nate was now dating. "Makes sense." He gave a wry grunt at the tangle of linked relationships. He'd forgotten during his ten years in the Marines how close and interconnected the people of Owl Creek were. *Small towns...*

That explained the extra cars and people at the paddock, anyway. Wade lifted a hand to wave as he walked back to his truck. "Thanks for the heads-up, but I have no beef with Nate or his sister."

Half siblings. The legacy of his late father's double life. Wade groaned and cranked the truck's engine. He'd come back to Owl Creek for peace and solitude. A place to hibernate and lick his wounds until he figured out what he was going to do with the rest of his life. What he'd found in the last several months was an increasingly complicated web of family secrets and lies. His siblings and cousins had been caught in an unrelenting series of dangerous events and dramatic conflicts that made his life with the Marines seem like a vacation.

Big families always had some drama, Wade acknowledged, and the Coltons had known their share through the years. But the past several months had seemed especially thick with life-changing moments and new relationships.

As long as I don't get drawn into the spiderweb, Wade thought. Solitude and quiet was all he wanted until he could get his life back on track. What defined *back on track*, he couldn't say. He only knew he still saw no direction for his life beyond the next day of ranching, surviving each restless, nightmare-populated night and watching the glacial healing of his scarred body each morning in his mirror.

When he reached the stable, he parked his truck and stuck his keys in the cup holder in case someone needed to move the vehicle while he was out in the pastures. He ambled toward the dimly lit stable, and the warmth of the overhead heaters washed over him as he stepped into the alley. He glanced toward the sound of voices coming from a stall at the back, next to the stall where Cactus Jack was housed. He exhaled heavily. He didn't exactly avoid other people, but he hated the pitying looks and obvious questions that paraded over the faces of new acquaintances when they saw his eye patch and facial scars. The awkwardness of introductions was tedious and tiresome, even all these months after returning to Owl Creek. While he'd met everyone in the stable before, he didn't know Nate well and hadn't spent much time around Vivian since high school.

Mustering his best public expression, the polite one he'd employed in recent months that said, "I'm fine. No problem here. Just minding my own business," he marched down the hay-strewn alley toward Cactus Jack's stall. He'd almost reached the small cluster of visitors to the ranch when a female laugh wafted out from behind the wall of Sunflower's stall.

He stopped in his tracks. A chill shot through him, making his limbs tingle with recognition and...was it anticipation or dread?

Harlow? Surely he was wrong. Harlow had no reason to be here. Maybe he was just imagining—

But then the group moved out of Sunflower's stall, and the foursome—Lizzy, Nate, Vivian...and, yes, Harlow—drew up short, apparently startled to see him.

"Oh, Wade, hi!" Lizzy said cheerfully. "I was just showing these guys around a little. Vivian and Nate wanted to meet the new horses, and since Harlow was in town, Vivian invited her to come along."

Wade forced himself to make eye contact briefly with

Vivian and Nate as he jerked quick nods of greeting and muttered, "Yeah. Hi." Then his gaze returned to Harlow and stuck.

She stared back at him, clearly just as stunned to have run into him as vice versa. His tingle of dread morphed into a full-fledged jangle of self-conscious expectation. Harlow hadn't seen his injuries before now. If she'd heard about his accident, it hadn't been from him. He wasn't sure who from Owl Creek, which of his siblings or cousins, she'd kept in touch with. He hadn't wanted to know, hadn't wanted to be tempted to ask, *What do you hear from Harlow?*

He waited, holding his breath as he watched for the crinkle of her forehead or tightening of her mouth that reflected the dismay, the repulsion, the morbid curiosity, the sympathy he got from others when they first encountered his new look. The awkward glance away that said, *I'm not staring,* but also, *I don't know how to process the change in your appearance.*

He refused to be the first to look away, as if daring her to acknowledge the light ripple of scars that pocked half of his face. He drew his shoulders back, assuming a posture of confidence he had to dig deep to project. Let her grimace in pity. Let her frown and drop her gaze in discomfort. He could take it, he told himself. Everyone else in the family had been visibly distressed over his injuries and still treated him with deference. Why not Harlow, too?

But Harlow's expression said none of those things. All he saw in her dark eyes was the bittersweet shock of encountering the man who'd so cruelly broken her heart eleven years ago. She blinked and quickly shed the momentary surprise as she said, "Hello, Wade."

Harlow flashed him a smile that bore only the slightest tremble of nerves and nostalgia.

He swallowed hard and wrenched a terse, "Harlow," from his throat.

A soft gasp caught his attention, and Lizzy said quietly, "Oh my God. I forgot that you two dated! I—"

Vivian cleared her throat and said quickly. "It's nice to see you, Wade. Harlow and I were just making plans for lunch. You should join us."

Harlow sent Vivian a quick, silencing look.

Jamming his hands in his back pockets, Wade shifted his weight to his heels. "No. Thanks. I'm sure Harlow would rather I *didn't* join you."

Harlow tipped her head slightly and arched one sculpted eyebrow toward the edge of her knit hat. "Don't speak for me."

Wade inhaled slowly and flipped up a palm. "Am I wrong? Haven't you spent the last decade avoiding me?"

Her eyes widened, and he realized how cold his tone had been. Before he could apologize, she returned, in a more magnanimous voice than he'd used, "I could say the same of you."

Nate tugged Vivian's arm and hitched his head toward the front of the stable. "Viv, why don't we give them a moment alone? Huh?"

Lizzy and Nate were already edging away, and Vivian glanced at Harlow with a wrinkle of query on her brow. "Okay?"

Harlow flashed a smile at her friend. "Yeah, I'll be with you in a minute."

"Actually," Wade said, aiming a thumb toward Cactus Jack's stall, "I need to get to work."

"Work?" Harlow blinked and cocked her head slightly. "That's right. Vivian mentioned that you work here at the ranch."

Wade shrugged one shoulder. "For now."

The furrow of confusion on the bridge of her nose deepened. "But...what happened to the Marines? I thought you intended the military to be your life's work."

He didn't answer right away. He narrowed a gaze on her that asked, *Seriously?*

But her expression held no irony or duplicity that he could detect. He chuffed a sarcastic laugh and aimed a finger at his face. "This happened." He waved a hand indicating the right side of his chest and upper arm. "There's more of the same under here. Don't tell me your contacts here in Owl Creek didn't tell you about my career-ending accident."

Now her face fell with sympathy. "Career-ending? Oh, Wade. I am sorry. I know how much the Marines meant to you."

You have no idea, he wanted to say. *My service cost me the most important person in my world, and I've never forgotten that.*

Instead, he gave another shrug and mumbled, "Yeah. Well, stuff happens and...you deal with it."

She shifted her feet, and the inquisitive look on her face said she was going to drill him for more details, so he cut her off with his own question. "What are you doing here? In Owl Creek, I mean. I thought you lived in LA." He mentally kicked himself as soon as the words left his mouth. Did he want her to know he'd looked her up on Facebook, had listened to her show, had checked to see where life had taken her since he'd let her get away?

"I do live in LA," she said. "But I'm considering a change of scenery." She flapped a dismissive hand before he could ask for follow-up details. "Long story. I won't bore you. The short version of why I'm in Owl Creek is, my parents have both died, and it was time I dealt with cleaning out and selling their old house."

Wade took a turn sending a sympathetic frown to her. "I hadn't heard. I'm sorry."

Her smile of acknowledgment held a hint of regret and grief. "Thanks. I miss them but…stuff happens and you deal with it. Right?"

He couldn't help the wry grin that cracked his face when she tossed his words back at him. He could see the spark of deeper emotion in her eyes that said that she wasn't as glib or resigned to her loss as she pretended.

He balled his hands at his sides. He knew all about faking acceptance and well-being, showing the world the face he knew they wanted to see. The urge to reach for her, to hug her and offer her comfort kicked him in the gut, but he shoved it down. Consoling Harlow, holding her, wasn't an option anymore.

She tucked stray wisps of her chocolate-brown hair behind her ear, then tugged her knit hat back in place. "Truth is, I thought I could spend a long weekend getting the house in shape to sell, but it's proving a far bigger job than I'd imagined."

"How so?"

"Well, my mom had apparently put off some important maintenance on the house. I'll have to get some repairs made before it can be listed. And I'm finding a butt-load more junk in the attic and closets than I'd expected, stuff I'll need to sort before I toss anything."

Unsure what to say, Wade just gave a grunt of understanding.

"It seems my mom was something of a pack rat...or maybe the right phrase is super sentimental. She saved everything."

A strained silence fell between them. Harlow chafed her hands, red from the cold, before tucking them under her armpits to warm them. "Anyway, it's a big job, so I'll be busy with that for the foreseeable future."

In his stall, Cactus Jack nickered, drawing Wade's attention. He hitched his head toward the gelding. "Listen, I...should get going. Lots to do today."

"Oh. Right." Harlow motioned to the stall with both hands. "Didn't mean to keep you."

He shrugged. "You didn't. I just..." *Good God. Why was this so damn hard? So awkward? You used to tell her everything. You used to spend hours sharing your hopes and dreams...your body with her.*

Used to. Past tense. He'd forfeited the privilege of Harlow's confidence and companionship.

She raised a hand as she shuffled past him, flashing a half smile. "Well, good to see you, Wade."

He nodded and mumbled, "Yeah. You, too."

As he turned to open Cactus Jack's stall, Harlow said, "Wade." He turned back to her.

She met his gaze levelly, her expression sincere. "I mean it. It was good to see you. I'd...kinda dreaded running into you, honestly. But... I'm glad we did. I don't hold any grudges against you...just so you know."

He drew his shoulders back, startled by her admission. "You don't?"

"It's in the past, right?" She lifted a corner of her mouth, her dark eyes twinkling with humor as she added, "Stuff happens and you deal with it, huh?"

He gave a short laugh. "That's what I hear." He took a cleansing breath to loosen the tight grip on his chest. "It was good to see you, too, Harlow. Really."

"Thanks." She cleared her throat. "Bye, Wade." Her smile brightened, and after a few backward steps, she spun around and jogged down the stable alley.

"Harlow," he called after her, not knowing what prompted him and not pausing to analyze what he was doing. When she stopped and turned around, he said, "I could give you a hand at your mother's house, if you want."

Chapter Four

Harlow and Vivian spent some time later that morning buying all the cleaning supplies, trash bags and storage boxes Harlow would need to get started sorting through her mother's house, then headed to meet Lizzy at Tap Out Brewery for lunch.

As Vivian drove them through the streets of downtown, Harlow noted all the changes, the growth, the revival that had kept the small town vibrant and relevant. Some of the shops catered to the tourists who visited town year-round thanks to nearby ski slopes for winter fun and Blackbird Lake for warm-weather boating, camping and water sports.

Once Vivian parked and fed coins in the meter, they hustled into the brewery that smelled of spicy barbecue, handmade pizzas and yeasty beers. The lunch crowd was buzzing, and televisions spaced around the bar and dining room silently played sports channels from around the world.

"Wow. Popular place," Harlow said, scanning the full tables for an empty booth.

"Lizzy said this was one of the best places for lunch. Clearly most of the town agrees!" Vivian smiled as she craned her neck to search the crowd. "Oh, there she is."

With a tug on Harlow's coat sleeve, she started into the busy dining room to join Lizzy.

Harlow followed, noticing Lizzy was with two other women. Both were blonde. Both had their backs to her.

Both were Coltons. Even without seeing their faces, Harlow knew.

Her feet stopped as if frozen to the floor. Did she want to have lunch with Wade's family? How could she pretend—

And then the darker-haired blonde stood to greet Vivian and turned toward Harlow. Familiar green eyes latched on Harlow's and widened. Harlow's heart thudded a rhythm, half anxious, half joyful.

Hannah Colton—Wade's sister and Harlow's best friend for four years of high school. Later, she couldn't say who made the first move, but the next thing Harlow knew, she and Hannah had rushed to each other and embraced, laughing and crying at the same time.

"Oh my gosh! Harlow, I had no idea you were in town!" Hannah said, while Harlow could only repeat over and over, "I'm sorry. So sorry. I've missed you so much!"

Hannah levered back, meeting Harlow's gaze with a tearful, confused expression. "You're sorry? For what?"

Harlow dropped her chin, humiliated and ashamed of her treatment of her friend after high school. "I ghosted you. I cut you out of my life for no reason other than my own self-protection. It was cold and selfish of me, and I'm so sorry."

"You mean…it wasn't my fault?" Hannah's brow dipped, and her grasp on Harlow's arms tightened. "I thought I'd said or done something to make you mad. I thought—"

Fresh guilt stabbed Harlow's heart. "No! Oh, Hannah,

no! Now I'm doubly sorry. All you ever did was...be Wade's sister. You were just a too-painful reminder of what I'd lost in him. I was afraid of all the ways a continued relationship with you would keep the wounds he'd caused open and raw. But I... Hannah, I was wrong to walk away from our friendship!"

Hannah drew her back into a hug and said, "You're forgiven. I'm just so glad to know I didn't do something terrible to hurt you."

Harlow backed out of the embrace, stepping aside as a server with a loaded tray sidled past them. "No. Not you. Never you. Wade's the one who—" Harlow shook her head. "Never mind all that. I'm just...so glad to see you!"

"Same. Please, join us. We have so much to catch up on!" Beaming and wiping happy tears, Hannah led Harlow the last few steps to the table where Lizzy and Vivian sat with another of Wade's sisters, Ruby.

Ruby's face brightened as Harlow took a seat at the table. "Well, if it isn't Harlow Jones! Is this the *H* squared reunion tour?"

Vivian tipped her head. "*H* squared?"

"Harlow and Hannah. These two were like this in high school," Ruby said, holding up two crossed fingers.

"When Harlow wasn't like this—" Lizzy touched her index fingers together and made kissing sounds "—with Wade, that is."

A prickle of embarrassment heated Harlow's cheeks as Lizzy and Ruby laughed. Hannah shot Harlow a worried glance that Harlow waved off despite the sting at her core for the bittersweet memories.

Ruby sobered first. "Oops. Did we step in it? I'm remem-

bering now that things ended kinda badly between you."
She winced. "Sorry."

Harlow put on a brave face. "Ancient history. Life moves
on."

Lizzy handed Harlow a menu. "I'm sure seeing him this
morning was…awkward. I swear I didn't know he'd be in
the stable that early in the morning. He's not usually around
until later. I've never seen him out in the pastures or in a
pen working with Dad before eight."

Harlow forced a grin as the shock of having seen Wade
at the Colton stable earlier reverberated through her again.
Being at the Colton Ranch again for the first time in so
many years had been hard, had opened the door to so many
memories she'd closed away.

The color in Ruby's cheeks faded. "You saw him? Then…
you know about…his accident."

Harlow's gut clenched, and she jerked a nod. "I do now."

After his appearance in the stable, his eye patch, his facial scars, his uncharacteristically somber mood were the
next bombshells. She prayed she'd hidden her surprise at
seeing him, seeing his injuries, well enough. Knowing that
he was working at the ranch, a career he'd rejected in his
pursuit of his Marine commission, had been perhaps the
most painful revelation for her. He'd sacrificed their relationship for his dream of the Marines, and now his dream
was dead. The price they'd both paid had been for nothing.

Laying the menu aside, Harlow flattened her hands on
the cool tabletop. "When did it happen?"

The sisters glanced at each other, obviously searching
their memories.

"He moved back to Owl Creek about a year, thirteen
months ago," Ruby said, and Hannah nodded confirma-

tion. "Before that he spent several weeks in the burn unit at the military hospital."

"So like seventeen or eighteen months ago," Hannah said.

Harlow didn't want to spend the lunch talking about Wade, but she needed one more question answered before she moved the conversation in a new direction. "And is he...will he be okay?"

The pregnant pause that followed her question and the exchange of concerned looks among the other women told Harlow plenty. Wade was still hurting, somehow, someway.

"Physically, he's healing well, I believe," Ruby said.

"That is, considering he lost his right eye and had burns on twenty percent of his body," Lizzy added.

Vivian made a sound in her throat of sympathy and dismay, and Harlow's chest tightened. She'd heard that the treatment of burns was one of the most painful things a person could endure. Her soul ached for Wade, and she shied from the notion of his suffering. She couldn't bear to think of it.

"But..." Lizzy added ruefully, bringing Harlow's attention back to the conversation, "he's changed."

Harlow cut a glance to Hannah for confirmation. Or maybe hoping she'd deny her cousin's assertion.

Swallowing hard, Harlow asked, "Changed...how?"

Hannah's face brightened then. "That's right! You're a professional counselor! I've heard your show, Harlow. You're awesome! Maybe you could talk to Wade and help him find his path."

Around the table, the other Coltons seemed to warm to the idea and nodded their agreement.

Harlow held up a hand and shook her head firmly. "Whoa.

Slow down. I'm only in town for a few days to get my mom's house ready to put on the market. Besides, considering our history...well, it wouldn't be right for me to try to counsel him or—" She let her sentence drop off, seeing Hannah's face fall. "Of course, I'll do what I can to help him while I'm here, but my plan was to avoid him as much as possible. Things between us were civil this morning, but it's still raw, and picking at those scabs doesn't serve either of us."

Harlow could tell Hannah wanted to push the topic further, so she jumped in with her own question. "Ruby, what's happening in your life these days?"

Fortunately, the Colton women took the hint and let the topic of Wade drop. The conversation shifted to Ruby's new baby, her veterinary practice and engagement to Sebastian Cross, the owner of Crosswinds Training, a K-9 search-and-rescue training facility. Harlow could easily see how fulfilled and happy Ruby was from the glow on her face as she showed pictures of her baby and talked about Sebastian and Crosswinds. Lizzy had had much the same joy in her voice and expression this morning when they'd talked at the ranch about her new love, Ajay Wright.

Turning to Hannah, Harlow hoped to learn her best friend from high school had found the same happiness. Instead, Hannah's eyes held a degree of forlorn longing. "Hannah?" Harlow said, touching her friends arm lightly. "What is it?"

Hannah shook her head, rallying and fixed a smile on her face. "It's nothing." Pulling out her phone, she woke the screen and angled it for Harlow to see the picture of a cherub-faced little girl with light brown pigtails and an endearing smile. "This is the love of my life. Lucy. She's five going on thirty."

Harlow clapped a hand to her chest as happy tears filled her eyes. "She's precious, Hannah!" When Harlow glanced up at her friend, the pure maternal love and pride radiated from Hannah like spring sunshine. Harlow noticed no mention was made of Lucy's father, so she took the hint and let that pass.

"Between Lucy and my catering business, I stay plenty busy." Hannah took her phone back and gazed at her daughter's image a moment before stashing the phone in her purse again.

"Catering?" Harlow prompted, and Hannah detailed the business she ran and her satisfaction with the job. Still no mention was made of a husband or hint given regarding Lucy's father. Harlow tucked her curiosity away. If Hannah wanted to tell her that story later, she would. Today was about celebrating a reunion with old friends and shoving old hurts aside.

But as their server brought out their meals, Harlow felt her phone buzz in her pocket, and she dragged it out to check the text. She read the message from the real estate agent she'd contacted and made a note of the proposed meeting time. Before she put the phone away, she noticed she had a Facebook message as well. Heart in her throat, she opened the message. When she read the words on the screen, she froze.

You cannot hide from me.

The attached picture was from inside her Los Angeles condo.

Icy fear sluiced through her veins. If her stalker had

found and broken into her LA house, she'd been right to leave town.

"Harlow, are you all right?" Ruby asked. "Your expression looks like you're being chased by a demon."

She forced a grin to appease her friend. "I… I'm fine."

But Harlow was afraid Ruby's quip was far too close to the truth.

Chapter Five

When the doorbell rang the next morning, Harlow struggled to her feet amid a pile of clothes she was sorting on her mother's bedroom floor and scurried to answer the summons. "Coming!"

Knowing she'd arrived to a house with an empty refrigerator and pantry, her mother's neighbors had brought by a steady stream of casseroles and desserts. Harlow was moved by the outpouring of kindness from her mother's friends, neighbors she barely remembered from when she'd lived in the neighborhood with her parents. One neighbor had even taken it upon himself to keep the yard in shape without being asked, not wanting the street view of the home to shout, "Vacant!"

When Harlow peered cautiously through the peephole to see who was there—she hadn't forgotten that some creep was still sending threats via her social media—she was startled to find Wade waiting on her mother's porch instead of another food-bearing acquaintance. Surprise rippled through her, along with a jolt of something more...sensual. She yanked open the door and gaped at him. "Um, hi."

Wade had been fit as a high school senior thanks to his work on the family ranch and participation in a variety of team sports at school. But the Marines and time had transformed him into a solidly built and incredibly appealing man. No fleece-lined ranch coat could hide the wide set of his shoulders or the way his blue jeans hugged his muscled thighs and tight derriere. The new eye patch he wore, rather than detracting from his appearance, gave him a roguish, sexy aspect that stirred a tickle in her belly. She was imagining the pirate-centered role-play his new look inspired when she realized she was staring. She shook herself out of her daze and asked, "What are you doing here?"

Spying Luna at her feet, trying to sneak outside, she blocked the cat with her leg and gently nudged her back.

When she raised her gaze again, Wade was studying her, his gaze wary. "You did say you wanted my help with the house." He spread his hands. "So here I am. But if you've changed your mind…"

"No," she blurted as she grabbed his arm and tugged him inside from the frigid weather. "I just… I guess I'm surprised to see you this early in the day. Don't you have ranch work to do?"

She closed the door behind him, before Luna could escape, and held out her hand. "I'll take your coat."

As he shucked off his gloves and stuck them in a pocket of his coat, he pulled a different, smaller pair of gloves from his other pocket. "Here. These are for you."

She took the proffered gloves made of a buttery soft leather and lined with cottony fleece. "Wade, these are beautiful." She sent him a curious glance. "What…why—?"

"Because I noticed you didn't have gloves when you were at the ranch the other day. You may not need gloves in LA, but you certainly will in Owl Creek."

Warmth spread through her. This was the sort of thoughtfulness that had first endeared her to Wade. But now, all these years later, she couldn't afford to fall for him again. He'd made his choice after high school, made clear she wasn't what he wanted. She'd be a fool to forget that and leave herself open to the kind of pain he'd inflicted when he'd left for his military career.

She pushed them back toward him. "Thank you, but... I can't accept them."

He folded her hands around them, encapsulating her fingers with his. "Yes, you can. They come with no strings attached."

She met his gaze and opened her mouth to refuse again, but something pained and pleading, as if this were a test of where they stood, a gesture of apology, the offer of a truce, filled his face. He also bore a faint ripple of scars on his cheek that she hadn't noticed in the dimmer light of the stable yesterday. As much as she wanted to ask about whatever obviously serious incident had caused the injuries and ended his military career, she swallowed the questions. If and when he wanted to tell her, he would.

She gave him a crooked smile. "All right. I accept. Thank you." Without pausing to reconsider, she rose on her toes to kiss his cheek. "I love them."

Dang...he smells good—crisp and fresh like the outdoors.

He peeled off his ranch coat, and she hung it on the hooks by the door, next to hers. Squatting, he held his hand out for Luna to sniff. "I thought your mother was allergic to cats. When did she get this one?"

"She didn't. That's Luna. She's mine."

"She's cute. But why didn't you just have a neighbor feed

her while you were up here?" He angled a curious look up at her while Luna rubbed on his leg.

Because I'm not sure when I'm going back to LA—if I'm going back. She swallowed the honest answer, knowing it would only raise questions she wasn't prepared to answer, and hedged with, "Because I wasn't sure how long I'd be here, and... I didn't want to impose on a neighbor."

She twisted her mouth knowing how lame that answer sounded, mentally tagging on, *and because if the house in LA isn't safe for me, it could have been dangerous for Luna, too.*

Who knew what kind of cruel person her stalker was, and well...she wanted her feline buddy with her, darn it!

After tucking her new gloves in the pocket of her parka, she led Wade to the bedroom where she was sorting clothes. "So this is what I'm into today. I'm putting the outdated or ratty stuff over there to throw out, and the nicer things go over here to be donated."

Wade stopped in the doorway and stared at the pile of women's clothing on the bed. "Seriously? You think I have any notion what is considered out of date in women's clothing? I'm happy to be used for manual labor, but if you're counting on my opinion regarding what to toss..." He angled his head in a way that said, "bad idea."

Harlow looked at the clothes, then back to Wade. "You're right. This will keep. Let's tackle one of the closets. You can help reach the top shelves for me."

Stepping over a box of shoes, Harlow headed for the kitchen. "Can I ask a question?"

He visibly tensed and gave her a guarded look. "I guess."

"If you're helping at the Colton Ranch nowadays, how is it you have time to help me sort through frying pans and thirty-year-old Tupperware?" She opened one of the floor-to-ceiling kitchen cabinets and waved a hand to the clutter with flourish.

Wade's good eye widened in dismay, and he dragged a hand down his cheek. "Wow. That's a lot of frying pans and Tupperware."

"Yeah. It seems my mom did a little hoarding in her later years." She braced her hands on her hips as she considered the job in front of them. "So...are you going to answer my question?"

"I asked Uncle Buck for a few days off. He told me to take all the time I wanted. Winter is usually slower than other months around the ranch." His mouth tightened. "Thing is, I don't think he really needed my help on the ranch from the start. I'm pretty sure he just gave me a job out of...pity."

"Pity? Why would he pity you?" she asked, pulling a stack of mixing bowls from the middle shelf and moving them to the kitchen trestle table. As soon as she created the space on the shelf, Luna jumped up in the cabinet to explore the newly emptied space.

"Really? Isn't that obvious?" His dark brown eyebrows knit in consternation.

"Well, I can assume you mean because you had no job after your discharge from the Marines." She lifted Luna out of cabinet and set her on the floor. "Or maybe even because of the circumstances of your discharge, but I don't like relying on assumptions. It leaves too much room for error and miscommunication."

He grunted and reached for a stack of serving platters of various sizes. Setting them next to the mixing bowls, he sighed. "You're in the ballpark. Let's just say I was in need of something to occupy my time, and he offered a solution I was too—" he hesitated, twisting his mouth and twitching one hand as if choosing the right word "—too desperate to refuse."

Harlow frowned at him. "Desperate? That's an extreme word."

He shrugged.

"Do you mean desperate like…financially? Didn't you get any severance or disability or something from the Marines?"

He chewed his bottom lip for a moment, then said darkly, "Let's just say Buck thought I needed a reason to get out of bed in the morning, and he provided one."

A shimmer of disquiet crept through Harlow. Had Wade gone through a deep depression after his discharge? He wouldn't be the first person to struggle mentally after a life-altering accident that ended their career. She wet her lips and studied his grim expression. "And…did you need a reason to get out of bed?"

He shot her a look, the blue fire in his good eye speaking of an inner disquiet. But his mouth remained tightly clenched. Clearing his throat, he removed a dusty stand mixer from a higher shelf and moved it to the table. "So all of this stuff needs to be emptied from the cabinet?"

Oo-kay. So he didn't want to talk about his discharge, the accident or the days following. She got the message, and she would respect his boundaries.

Probably just as well that she didn't hear his story. She didn't need to get drawn into the strife that Wade had endured or get emotionally tangled in the tragedy that had led him back to Owl Creek. She had her own problems to deal with. A house full of junk, memories and personal treasures to sort. A career that was growing as fast as she could keep up. And, more importantly, a menacing troll, who, though previously blocked, had recently created a new online profile and resumed posting threats to her business Facebook page.

Harlow shuddered and tried to play off her shiver as a response to his query regarding the cluttered cabinet. Averting her gaze from his, she stared at the shelves of kitchen detritus. "Yep. All of it has to go."

She removed the cat from the emptied shelf again, then pulled down another stack of pots and moved them to the table for sorting. Until she found a way to get rid of her stalker, the best she could do was bury herself in cleaning her mother's house—and protect herself from the kind of entanglements with Wade that would break her heart all over again.

HAVING FINISHED THE main kitchen cabinet and deciding to donate all of the pots, pans and small appliances to a charity that helped people in need set up a household, Harlow opted to move next to a hall closet with high shelves. If Wade should decide he'd had enough of the tedious task of cleaning out someone else's home, or if he simply balked for another reason—she couldn't rule out him simply walking away like he had eleven years ago—she wanted to take advantage of his six-foot-one height while she could. Climbing on chairs or ladders was dangerous enough without doing it while alone.

She pulled open the doors of the linen closet, but instead of sheets or towels, her mother had crammed the shelves with boxes of…stuff. Random bits of a life that apparently had no other logical storage place.

A low rumble emanated from Wade's throat when she stood back to show him their next job, and she couldn't help but chuckle. "I know, right? Have I mentioned how much I appreciate your assistance with this?"

"Mmm," he hummed by way of acknowledgment. "Where do you want to start?"

"Top down?" She aimed a finger at the boxes on the highest shelf. "That way, if you decide to run screaming from the house in surrender, at least we'll have gotten the hardest-to-reach part done." She sent him a teasing grin, but his returned scowl reflected no amusement.

"Marines don't run screaming in surrender. From anything."

The blue of his uncovered eye held a bright heat.

"Except their high school girlfriends," she returned before she could bite back the caustic retort.

His chin hiked up, and his mouth firmed. "Harlow…"

She shook her head and waved him off. "No…"

His nostrils flared as he drew a deep breath. "I did ask you to come with me."

Tension coiled in her gut. "And I told you why an unsettled, transient military life was all wrong for me. I needed stability, a home, roots."

He glanced away, his expression stony.

"Tell me something, Wade. How many times did you move, transfer to new bases, not even counting deployment, in the years you served?"

Instead of answering her question, he said, "Are we really going to relitigate this?"

Harlow let her shoulders drop, then, running her fingers through her hair, she sighed in resignation. "No. I'm sorry. My comment was uncalled for. Let's…forget it."

Forget it? She scoffed to herself at the absurdity of her suggestion. First, because there was no way she'd forget anything about Wade or their breakup as long as she lived. And second, what mental health counselor of repute would advise a client to sweep a conflict under the rug to be ignored? Talk about unhealthy...

They were both silent for several taut seconds, avoiding eye contact.

Luna appeared from the kitchen and wove between her legs, meowing for attention.

Wade broke the stalemate. "Seems to me if we're both going to be in Owl Creek, we might need to talk enough to reach some sort of understanding. Leaving things unresolved is a bit like having loose ends of a live wire lying around."

He was right, damn it. And she was supposed to be the one with the cool head, dispensing practical wisdom and hard truths in palatable doses. "Touché. Better to defuse the situation than have it blow up in our faces later. But for the record, I'm not staying in Owl Creek. It's not my home anymore."

When she glanced at him, expecting a nod of consent or understanding, she encountered something far different. His complexion was ashen, his gaze fixed in near space, his square jaw as full of tension as she'd ever seen. She replayed what she'd just said, wondering what he could have been reacting to.

She wasn't staying in Owl Creek. Could that have been such a surprise or disappointment?

"Wade?" She touched his arm lightly, and he flinched, jerked his attention to her, blinking rapidly. "Did you think I was moving back here? All this effort, this cleaning—"

she motioned around her to the boxes she'd been packing and sorting "—is so I can sell this house."

He scrubbed a hand over his face and flexed his hand, shaking tension from it. "Can we just get back to work?"

Turning away from her, he stepped to the open closet and reached for a box on the highest shelf. In his haste, the box tipped, and a cascade of photographs tumbled to the floor. Luna spooked and ran into the back bedroom. Wade grumbled a bad word as he stepped out of the scattered pictures and set the now-half-empty box on the floor a few feet away.

Harlow knelt to begin collecting the photos, taking a moment to glance at the memories captured on paper. Nostalgia washed through her, along with a fresh scrape of grief as she studied the smiling faces of her parents, her grandparents, her favorite aunt. Snapshots of her childhood, the numerous houses where they'd lived, school friends she only vaguely remembered—there'd been so many, each for such a brief time before her family packed up and moved again like circus performers or vagabonds. Fledgling bonds broken, again and again.

She tapped a handful into a neat stack and reached for more as Wade squatted beside her. He scooped up the pictures with efficient swipes, ignoring the images. And why not? He wouldn't feel the pull to linger over her family's captured moments. The faces and places wouldn't stir in his heart the way they did for her. Not his family, not his memories.

That's why when he did pause, lingering over a photo, longer than the others, her curiosity was piqued. "Whatcha got?"

She leaned closer to peer over his shoulder and, seeing

the young couple in the picture he held, she froze. Prom night his senior year. She'd looked resplendent in a garnet dress that matched the red tie and cummerbund he'd worn and the red rose corsage on her wrist. The night they'd stayed out until 5:00 a.m. The night she slept with him the first time. Her body quaked with echoes of the sensual night. He'd made her first experience so wonderful, been so careful, so patient, so thorough as he loved her. He'd awakened feelings, sensations she'd never imagined possible.

She must have made some noise, because he glanced over his shoulder and met her gaze. After a beat, he asked, "Keep or toss out?"

More than the photo, he seemed to be asking if he should hold on to his recollections of that night or discard them on the trash heap of lost dreams.

"Just put all the pictures back in that box. I'll probably have most of them scanned later to save electronically."

He did as she asked, but his movements seemed stiffer to her, jerky. The prom photo had goosed the elephant in the room, adding to the hum of unspoken tension between them.

Sitting back on her heels, she gathered her courage to lance the wound and ease some of the pain between them. She'd like to think she could be friends with Wade going forward, and his presence there helping her seemed to indicate he wanted to put hard feelings behind them.

"It was a good night," she said quietly.

"Hmm?"

"Prom night. I have no regrets about anything that happened that night."

He angled his head toward her, his jaw tightening. "What's your point?"

She gave a startled chuckle. "Just making conversation. And maybe…trying to defuse a little of the tension in the air." A flicker of some sharp emotion flashed over his face when she said this. "What?"

He turned away and continued finger-raking the fallen photos and dumping them into the box.

"I came to work, not talk."

"Is there a reason we can't do both?" Harlow gathered a few pictures around her knees but kept a keen gaze on him.

"There is, if the topic of our conversation is going to be rehashing ancient history. The past is gone, and talking about it does no good. Nothing can change the mistakes we make. We just have to learn to live with the consequences."

He threw the photos in the box with more force than needed, a clear indicator of his agitation. A voice in her head whispered that she should back off, let the issue drop. But something haunted filled his expression that cried out to her, made her heart ache. "We can't change the past, but we can find closure. Forgiveness. Healing."

"So I'm one of your patients now? I don't remember asking for a counseling session." His tone was curt as he shoved himself to his feet and snatched another box from a high shelf.

Harlow sighed and raised a hand in resignation. She didn't want to antagonize him, and pushing someone who wasn't in a frame of mind to listen was counterproductive. "All right. We don't have to talk about anything you don't want to."

Once she'd climbed to her feet, she moved the box of gathered photos to the living room to sort later as she watched television. When she returned to the hall, Wade was dragging down a large box labeled "Harlow college."

She hurried forward, knowing that box would be heavy, and reached for it. "I've got it."

He handed the old cardboard box to her, but as soon as she took it, the side tore, and thick textbooks and a dusty desk lamp crashed to the hardwood floor with a resounding *boom*.

Wade jerked as if shot. Tackled her. His cry of alarm sent a chill to her bones.

He landed on her hard enough to knock the breath from her, and she gasped for air as he pressed her to the floor, his entire body shaking.

"Wade?" she rasped, still struggling to find her voice. "What—?"

She managed to angle her head enough to see the stark terror and bloodless complexion of his face. His unpatched eye stared straight ahead, clearly not seeing what was before him, but some other time and place.

Harlow had studied PTSD in all its forms as she worked toward her counseling degree. But she'd only been in the presence of someone in the throes of a panic attack a handful of times. Wade was having just such a post-trauma panic attack, she was certain.

She wiggled a hand free and stroked his back lightly. "Wade, it's okay. You're safe."

After calling his name a couple more times, her voice finally cut through whatever had terrorized him. His gaze locked on hers before blinking as if trying to recall where he was.

At which point *she* became all the more aware of where he was. Namely, on top of her. The weight of his body, pressing her against the hard floor, conjured images all too recently dusted off. Prom night. Wade's nakedness entwined with hers.

An unbidden wave of desire shimmied through her. Her heart thumped louder in her ears, and her breath caught. "Wade—"

He lurched to his feet, his expression shifting instantly from terror and confusion to something more like horror. Or was it anger? Frustration? His body tensing, he staggered back a step or two, glaring at her. With a shuddering exhale, he stormed past her and slammed through the front door.

Chapter Six

Wade gritted his teeth and plowed fingers through his hair as he worked to quiet the echoes of the explosion that reverberated in his memory. Bad enough that he was still jumpy as hell, every loud noise taking him back to the day of the accident, but he hated—*hated*—that Harlow had seen him experience a flashback. He stalked across the yard, the frozen grass crunching under his boots, and let the icy air wash over him and shock him fully back to the present. He stared up at the bare limbs of the nearest tree, intentionally registering it. Something he could see…a dormant white poplar. He exhaled slowly, tuning his ears to the subtle sounds around him. Somewhere down the road an engine, diesel by the sound of it, rumbled. He inhaled again, noting the scents in the air. Something he could smell…pine. And woodsmoke from the neighbor's chimney.

He heard the front door open, interrupting his inventory of his senses, the exercise he'd been given by the Marine psychologist before his discharge to help root him and calm him when the flashbacks happened. He didn't have to turn to know Harlow was walking up behind him. Didn't have to hear her footsteps in the frosty lawn to sense her pres-

ence. Even before his Marine Corps Special Forces training had taught him to be hyperaware of his surroundings,
he'd had a sixth sense when it came to Harlow.

Without looking up, he'd always known when she'd entered a room. He'd been able to read her thoughts, predict
her moods. Anticipate her phone calls. He'd felt her to
his marrow as if she were an extension of himself. Leaving for the Marines without her had felt like an amputation, a missing part of him for which he still experienced
ghost pains.

"I brought your coat," she said now. "I figured you'd be
freezing out here without it."

He glanced over his left shoulder. "I'm fine."

She scoffed. "You're shivering. Take the coat."

He unclenched his fists long enough to take the coat she
held out to him. As he slid his arms into the fleece-lined
sleeves, he gave her a measuring scrutiny. "Are you hurt?
I shouldn't have knocked you down like that."

She shrugged one shoulder. "I'll live. Question is, are
you okay?"

He ground his back teeth together, resenting the question
he'd heard a gazillion times in the last eighteen months.
"I'm fine."

Her dark eyebrow sketched up, and he realized belatedly
how sour his tone had been. He forcibly shoved down his
irritation and shook his head. "Damn it... I'm sorry. I'm
just...sick to death of answering that question. People won't
give me space. Peace..."

"People are worried about you," she said, her voice as
quiet as the icy breeze stirring the lodgepole pines across
the street.

"*People* don't need to be worried. They need to leave me alone. I just need...time."

"Hmm," she hummed, a sound that neither agreed nor contradicted.

He furrowed his brow. "What does *hmm* mean?"

She blinked as the first few flakes of a gentle snowfall landed on her eyelashes. "It means... I'm listening. I want to hear what you have to say."

"There's nothing to say. Especially not to you." He turned away, debating whether to get in his truck and drive away. *Run away, you mean.* Silencing the judgmental voice in his head, he stalked toward the front door, determined to end the discussion of his mental health there. But of course, Harlow pursued him...and the conversation.

"Why especially not me? What does that mean?" She jogged a few steps to keep pace with his long strides.

"That should be obvious." He stomped up the steps to the front door. "We have history. Even if I did want to talk to someone—which I *don't*—why would I open myself up to someone responsible for the greatest pain and regrets in my life?"

She stopped walking, and after opening the door, he glanced back at her.

Shadows filled her face. Her coffee-brown eyes reflected a hurt he'd seen in his own mirror for years. "Regrets? What kind of regrets?"

He sighed. "Harlow, don't. I didn't come over here to talk about me or my accident or our history. I only wanted to offer my help with what you'd said was a big, taxing job. I just wanted to be useful."

He expression shifted. "Do you not feel useful at the Colton Ranch?"

I haven't felt useful in eighteen months, he wanted to say. Instead, he cleared his throat and swallowed the bitter taste of frustration.

Hitching a thumb toward the open door, he gave her a level look. "Do you want my help or don't you?"

HARLOW RETURNED TO the hall closet, following in Wade's stiff-backed wake. She was accustomed to prickly patients, clients who were wary of her peeking behind their mask to see their tender and hurting core.

Wade's panic attack, the visible wounds on his face and throat, only hinted at a greater turmoil roiling beneath the surface. She'd intentionally *not* asked him about the accident that had led to his medical discharge when she'd seen him yesterday at the ranch. If and when he wanted to talk about it, he would, and she would listen. But she wouldn't pry. In truth, she didn't want to open any emotionally fraught doors with Wade that would scrape raw the wounds she kept wrapped and tucked away where the past couldn't hurt her. But neither could she ignore his obvious pain and distress.

Wade was collecting the textbooks that lay strewn across the floor. He read aloud a couple of the titles as he stacked them next to the torn box. "*Introduction to Chemistry. British Literature from Dunne to Burns. Early American History*. These are all yours?"

She recognized his distraction technique. Anything that could pass as conversation and avoid a return to the topic of his breakdown. "All mine and going to the used bookstore tomorrow, so grab anything you want to keep for yourself."

"Pass. I've already got boxes in storage waiting for me to decide my next move," he mumbled, then in a quieter darker tone. "I don't need to add anyone else's clutter to my life."

"A simple no would have sufficed." She crouched to add *Advanced Psychology Theory* to the stack.

"Fine. Then, no."

She studied the stony set of his jaw and caught the subtle tremor that lingered in his hands. "So you're not staying permanently in Owl Creek?"

"What?" He angled a curious look at her.

"You said you have things in storage until you decide your next move. That kinda implies you are thinking you'll move out of town at some point."

He frowned. "No, it means I don't know what is next, and the cottage I'm renting by the lake is small, came furnished, and doesn't have room for all my stuff."

"Oh. All right. How long do you think you'll stay in Owl Creek before you make a choice about your future?" She collected the desk lamp from the floor, noticing the light bulb had broken when the box fell. She stood to find a broom to sweep up the broken glass.

He slapped a hand down hard on the stack of books, growling, *"I don't know!"*

"Whoa," she said, lifting a hand in concession. "Forget I asked. I didn't mean to upset you."

"Look," he said, his lip pulling in a sneer, "I know you fancy yourself some kind of miracle-working, celebrity counselor—"

"What!" she said, stunned by his bitter tone and condescension.

He raised a hand to forestall her argument. "I've heard

your show. I even heard *the* show that launched your celebrity status, but I'm not in the market for a talk show therapist."

She chuffed a humorless laugh. "Wow." She shook her head, not sure what to address first. His bitterness? The fact that he'd listened to her show? His obvious attempts to push her away with his hurtful comments?

Finally, taking a slow breath to recover her composure, she said, "How about a friend? Are you in the market for a friend? I kinda thought you were, seeing as how you were kind enough to come help me today. And the gloves..."

Wade's face scrunched as if he were in physical pain. "Harlow... I—" He hesitated, then, huffing out a sigh, he said, "Since my accident, everybody I know has had advice for me. My family. My friends. The doctors. Get some rest. Stay busy. Give it time. See a shrink. Talk it out. Put it behind you." His hand clenched into a fist. "I'm just so sick of it all. I want..."

When he didn't finish the thought, she prompted softly, "What do you want, Wade?"

He gave her a forlorn look, then pushed to his feet and headed for the door. He paused at the end of the hall. "I wish I knew."

The front door closed quietly behind him, and Harlow's heart squeezed in his absence.

HARLOW WAS STILL eating breakfast when she heard a knock at her front door the next morning. Pulse jumping, she rose to answer the summons and, finding Wade on the porch, gave him a wary look.

He spread his hands, and his expression filled with regret. "Shall we give this another shot, if I promise not to be such a jerk today?"

She chuckled. "So you admit you acted like a jerk?"

"I've been guilty of that a lot lately, I'm afraid."

She opened her mouth to asked, *And why is that?* But Wade didn't want her to be his counselor, didn't need more probing questions. So she swallowed the query and said, "If that's supposed to be an apology, it needs work. Saying *I'm sorry* is simpler and to the point." She flashed a teasing grin and earned a twitch of his mouth and eye roll in return.

"I'm sorry." He stepped inside, out of the blustery weather, and unbuttoned his coat. "Can we agree not to mention our past or my future plans, though?"

"No past, no future." She pulled her lips into a moue as she pretended to be considering his request. "So…only the present?"

He snorted his amusement. "Something like that."

She waved him into the kitchen. "Care for some coffee? I was just finishing breakfast."

He accepted and pulled out one of the kitchen chairs. "I apologize for my comment yesterday about your internet show. I did listen and…you are good. You were…amazing with the suicidal woman."

She smiled at him and nodded her thanks. "Honestly? I was scared stiff. So afraid of screwing up and losing her." She shuddered, then lifted the coffee carafe from the machine. "But when you help someone get through a crisis, it is so fulfilling. So…worth it."

He wrapped his hands around the mug she gave him, steadying the cup as she poured. "And now your show's popularity has skyrocketed. Congratulations. Would it sound condescending if I said I'm proud of you?"

Startled by his praise, she sloshed some of the hot brew

onto his scarred hand. She gasped and grabbed for paper towels. "I'm so sorry. Did I burn you? Do you want ice?"

He lifted his hand to his mouth and sucked the coffee drips off with a sound a lot like a kiss. Her gaze lingered on his mouth, the pucker of his lips and sweep of his tongue as he licked the brew from his fingers. He took the paper towels from her and wiped his hand dry. "I'm good. I've survived worse." Then, as if realizing what he'd said, he lifted his gaze to hers, adding, "Obviously."

She bit the inside of her cheek, swallowing the reply on her tongue. He didn't want her questions...or her sympathy. So she gave a nod and let it pass. *Patience.*

"I planned to clean out the bathrooms today," she said as she returned the coffeepot to the brewer. "How are you with a mop and scrub brush?"

He lifted one eyebrow, and she laughed.

"All right, all right." She waved a hand of surrender. "We'll tackle the attic instead. Mothballs here we come!"

Several hours later, Harlow straightened from the box she'd been hunched over and stretched the kinks in her back. "I'm ready for a break. Can I interest you in a sandwich or reheated casserole for lunch?"

Wade stood from the plastic crate he'd been using as a stool, and when he straightened to his full height, he bumped his head on one of the slanted ceiling beams. Rubbing his skull, he mumbled, "Ouch," then, "Is it lunchtime already?"

She lifted her cell phone to check the time. "It's past lunchtime. It's almost two."

Harlow noticed she had a new text waiting and automatically swiped to open it. A pit of cold filled her belly when she read the message.

I will make you suffer like I have.

She gasped and dropped the phone as if it had scalded her. She raised a shaky hand to her thundering heart and sat down on the closest box.

"Harlow? What's wrong?" Stooping slightly to avoid knocking his head again, Wade approached her. He squatted to pick up her phone and glanced at the screen. Frowned. "What's this? Who sent that?"

She shook her head. "I don't know."

He knelt in front of her and narrowed a keen gaze on her. "You don't know or you don't want to tell me?"

She raised her head and swallowed the sour taste at the back of her throat. "I don't know who he is. He uses the screen name Chris72584."

"You've had threats like this before, from this same man?"

She nodded stiffly.

His jaw tightened, and a shadow filled his good eye. "Why didn't you say something before now? How often does he send threats like this?"

She wrenched her phone from his hand and sighed. "I didn't want to worry anyone. I've reported him to the LAPD already. And I blocked his number, but he finds ways to get around the blocks and—" She furrowed her brow.

The hard set of his mouth said he didn't like that response, and he repeated in a firmer tone, "How often does he send threats like this?"

"One or two a day for the last couple weeks. Always with new numbers. It's like playing whack-a-mole. Block one number and he gets another."

Wade bit out a curse word. "Why is he threatening you? What's his beef?"

She pushed past him, headed for the attic steps. "I can handle it, Wade. You don't need to get involved."

He followed her down the narrow stairs from the attic and into the kitchen. "I'm just worried for your safety."

Her shoulders drooped. "Yeah, well…me, too. That's… kinda why I came to Owl Creek this week. I wanted to put some distance between myself and LA."

"So this guy lives in LA?" Wade maneuvered himself in front of her, his positioning demanding her attention and answers.

Harlow rubbed her eyes. "I don't know that. But he knew where I lived and implied he was coming after me. I…panicked and fled town that night." She glanced up at him, frowning. "I know. I'm a coward. But I live alone, and the cops couldn't promise more than extra drive-bys on my street."

"You're not a coward. You're smart to get away."

He brushed the back of his hand along her cheek, and the shivers that chased down her back had nothing to do with fear.

"Can I do anything?" he asked, his voice warm.

Hold me, she wanted to say, but instead she shook her head. "I'm here now, essentially in hiding until the police track him down. I think I'm safe here. I mean… Owl Creek is about as off the beaten path as you can get, right?" She forced a laugh. "But once my mother's house is ready for market, I'll be moving on. I might not go back to LA, but I'll find somewhere else to lie low until the stalker is found."

Wade lifted a corner of his mouth, but his stare remained

direct and concerned. "If you need anything, if you get even a hint of anything unusual, I'm a phone call away."

"Thank you, but… I'll be fine." She exhaled a cleansing breath, determined to put the stalker out of her mind. "Now…about lunch…"

Wade shook his head. "Can't. I'm afraid I have to go. My family has a meeting with our lawyer to discuss my father's will with our newly found half siblings."

"Nate and Sarah," Harlow said, and he sent her a startled look.

"How'd you know?"

"Vivian told me. She's dating Nate. They're pretty serious, too. Like really serious. In love."

Wade's nostrils flared, and he grunted. "Good for them."

She chortled. "Really, Wade? You may be down on love, but can't you be happy for Vivian and Nate? Or is it that you have bad feelings toward the half brother you just learned about?"

He raised a palm in self-defense. "I'm not down on love at all! Most of my siblings have found themselves in new relationships in the past several months. I'm happy for them. And as far as Nate goes…" Wade shrugged a shoulder. "I hold no ill will toward him or Sarah. What our father did, the circumstances of their conception, is not their fault. I have no reason to hold a grudge. In fact, that's kinda what this meeting is about." He checked his phone. "Which I'm going to be late for if I don't go now."

Harlow followed him toward the front door, a shiver chasing down her spine at the thought of being alone in the big quiet house.

You can run but you can't hide.

I will make you suffer like I have.

"Hang on a sec." She pulled out her own phone and called Vivian. After a brief discussion, she faced Wade. "Vivian is going to come with Nate to the meeting at the lawyer's office, and we are going to huddle up somewhere and discuss *Harlow Helps* while your family does your thing. Mind if I ride with you?"

The eyebrow over his good cerulean eye lifted. His expression said he understood, even agreed with, her reason for not wanting to stay home alone, but he had the good grace not to make an issue of it. "Sure. Let me move a few things off my front seat."

They grabbed their coats by the front door, and Harlow locked up the house. She stood by the passenger door of his truck while he shifted fast-food trash, a pair of work gloves and a coil of rope behind the seats. After brushing off some crumbs, he waved a hand to the empty seat. "All yours."

She eyed his trash and shook her head. "I thought Marines were supposed to be neat and tidy."

He glowered as he slid behind the steering wheel. "I'm not a Marine anymore."

"What! What happened to 'once a Marine, always a Marine'?"

He stared vacantly out the windshield for a moment before cranking the engine. "There are parts of my military experience I'm trying to put behind me. Deep down, I'm still a Marine, I guess. But…" He didn't finish his sentence, and she could see the warring emotions on his face. As he backed from her parents' driveway, he added, "I made my bed this morning, all tucked tight and smooth as glass. Does that count?"

She pictured Wade smoothing the wrinkles from his sheets and plumping his pillow, which led to a much different image of him rumpling his sheets...with her. A swirl of something warm and gooey puddled in her belly like a sweet dessert. Mercy! She didn't need to go down that mental path. Where your thoughts go, actions follow, and she would not, could not tangle herself up with Wade. Literally or figuratively.

"That counts," she replied finally, hearing the unwanted husky quality in her voice.

The look he gave her said he did as well.

TWENTY MINUTES LATER, Wade and his siblings gathered around the conference table in Henry Deacon's downtown office, copies of their father's will before each of them. Along with drafts of the proposal they were making to change the distribution of Robert Colton's estate.

"And you're sure this is legal? I really don't want to find myself in court over this," Wade's younger sister Hannah asked.

Deacon, the family's lawyer, spread his hands. "Your father's will is valid and will be executed as is. Equal shares of his estate will go to each of his six children with his legal wife, Jenny Colton. What each of you choose to do with your share of the inheritance is strictly your business and separate from the execution of Robert's will. These papers I drew up—" he tapped the new document, of which Wade and each of his siblings had a copy "—simply spells out the terms of the private arrangement Chase discussed with me. If it meets your approval, we'll ask Nate and Sarah to join us, and we'll go over the terms together."

Wade squinted at the document, unwilling to tell anyone he had trouble at times with his "good" eye. He needed to see an optometrist for glasses or a contact for his left eye, he knew, but kept putting it off. He was sick to death of doctors and doctors' offices and dealing with the lingering effects of the explosion. How was he supposed to move on when he saw the physical reminders every time he looked in the mirror?

But Chase must have seen his struggle, because he leaned over to whisper, "Do you want me to ask Deacon to print a new copy in a bigger font for you? Or I could—"

"I'm fine," Wade said tightly. "But if I did need a special copy, I can ask for it myself."

Chase raised a hand in concession. "Okay, just checking."

With effort, Wade made out the important lines of the document, all the more determined to make do with the fine print in light of Chase's deference.

Everything seemed in line with what he and his siblings had discussed prior to the meeting, so he said, "It all looks good to me. I say bring them in."

"I agree with Wade," Ruby said. "It's perfect. It's fair. Let's do this."

Henry Deacon hit the intercom button on the phone at his end of the conference table. "Ms. Shaw, will you please bring Nate and Sarah Colton up to the conference room? We're ready for them."

Chapter Seven

Harlow looked up when the receptionist's phone buzzed. She'd had her head bowed over the printout of media data Vivian had brought her, studying the rising numbers that reflected her show's viral popularity. She wished she could feel good about the growing audience, but the swimming numbers before her reminded her of the dark side of celebrity. Specifically, her stalker.

The text she'd received this morning shook her to her core. How had the guy gotten her private cell phone number?

She watched as the receptionist rose from her desk and motioned to Nate and his sister. "They're ready for you."

Nate bent at the waist to drop a kiss on Vivian's lips. "Wish us luck."

"You don't need luck," Vivian returned, smiling.

Sarah hooked her arm through her brother's. "Come on. Don't make me walk in alone."

When the brother and sister had disappeared down the corridor with the lawyer's receptionist, Harlow returned her attention to the data sheets. "So you think Facebook ads targeting the Southwest region will boost our audience there?"

"That and a few appearances on local news shows. I've had requests for interviews from Phoenix and Dallas TV stations and have a call out to a radio station in Santa Fe."

"Will I have to go in person or can I call in? Do the interviews remotely?" Harlow asked.

Vivian blinked. "Well, in person is best. You saw how your listenership spiked in the Boston market after your live appearance at the public health fair."

Harlow nodded and pressed a hand to the seesawing in her gut. In-person appearance was best for her ratings, but what about her safety? Even tucked away in Owl Creek, she felt as if the stalker was breathing down her neck.

Vivian cocked her head to one side and narrowed her eyes. "What's going on, Harlow? You were fine with the media tour and interviews before. Why do they bother you now?"

Harlow exhaled through her lips, making an exasperated sound with her lips. "I didn't say anything before, because I didn't want to worry anyone, but…well, Wade saw one of the texts this morning, so I guess the cat's out of the bag."

Vivian's expression darkened. "What cat?"

WADE STUDIED THE brother and sister sitting across the table from him and realized he was looking for signs of his father's genes in them. Did Sarah have his green eyes? Nate, their father's chin? Was that lift of his brow a gesture Nate had learned from Robert?

"As you are both aware," Mr. Deacon was saying, "Robert's will divided his estate and holdings among his six—"

"Sir, if I may interrupt," Sarah said, and squared her shoulders. "I think I…*we*," she amended with a glance to her brother, "can cut through a lot of unnecessary business.

We're aware our father didn't leave us anything. And we're fine with that. We don't need a payday, and the last thing we want to do is cause a problem in the family. Having been kept in the dark about our father's other children, we consider the discovery of our six half siblings to be a windfall."

"Ten half siblings, when you count our mother's children with Buck Colton," Nate said.

Hannah smiled warmly. "We feel the same way. Which is why we've asked you here."

Chase cleared his throat. "We've discussed the terms of our father's will amongst ourselves—" he motioned to his five full siblings "—and we are in agreement that it isn't fair."

"I can't imagine why Dad would have left you out! That's just…cruel!" Ruby added.

"Regardless," Nate said, raising a hand to halt the murmurs of agreement from Fletcher, Wade and Hannah. "That was his choice, and what's done is done. We don't blame you or hold any grudges. We don't want to start our new relationship with you by bickering over money."

"Good," Chase said, and tapped the document in front of him with his index finger. "That makes it easy. All you need to do is sign off on this new division of property we six have agreed on, and we can move on in harmony."

Sarah's frown voiced her skepticism. "New division of property?"

Nate picked up the paper Wade slid across the table to him. "The pertinent lines are about halfway down the page. Start reading where it says that the entirety of Robert Colton's estate will be equally divided and distributed to his *eight* offspring."

Sarah gasped. "Eight?"

Ruby beamed as she squeezed Sarah's arm. "That's right. We want the two of you to receive your fair share. We want all of Robert's children to get a share of his holdings and inheritance."

Hannah spread her hands as if stating something obvious. "It's the right thing to do."

"But we didn't ask you to—" Nate's voice cracked, and he tried again, "We'd never presume to—"

"We know." Wade waved off Nate's obvious doubts. "Which makes it all the easier to know we made the right choice."

"Your concern for putting family relationships ahead of the money," Ruby said, "demonstrates to us that our trust and choices are well-placed."

Sarah covered her mouth with a trembling hand. "I—I don't know what to say!"

Nate barked a laugh. "I do! Thank you. This is…incredible!"

Surging from her seat, Sarah wrapped her arms around Ruby, laughing though her tears. Then she came to stand beside Wade and opened her arms. "Can I hug you, big brother?"

Wade blinked and rose from his chair slowly. He couldn't remember the last time a member of his family had hugged him. *Really* hugged him. When he'd come home from the hospital, his burns and raw wounds made hugging painful for him, and his family had avoided the gesture. In the months since, his siblings—even his mother—had treated him like fragile glass. Gentle touches, soft pats, a handshake. But no firm hugs like the one Sarah wrapped him in now. He released a shuddering sigh, privately thanking her for the gift of the embrace. He'd never voice the truth, not wanting to show even a hint of neediness, but he'd missed human touch and connection.

If only Harlow were the one to hug him, hold him, touch him…

The huskiness in her voice this morning hinted that she still thought about the physical relationship, the passion they'd once had.

He released Sarah and stepped back, shoving thoughts of Harlow aside. She'd been clear enough that she wasn't staying in Owl Creek, hadn't forgotten how he hurt her and wanted nothing to do with him. Like the accident had closed the door on his military career, his past actions had closed the door with Harlow, and that was a burden he'd have to learn to live with.

"WHAT AREN'T YOU telling me?" Vivian asked, meeting Harlow's eyes squarely.

Wiping the sudden anxious perspiration from her palms on the legs of her jeans, Harlow said, "A listener has taken exception to the advice I gave in one of my shows. I don't know who it is or what he found offensive, but he's been persistent in letting me know he's upset. I only know him by his username, Chris72584."

Vivian covered Harlow's hand with her own. "When you say he took exception…?"

Harlow shivered, and Vivian squeezed her fingers tighter.

"He's sending me threatening messages. He's managed to get my cell phone number and…based on recent Facebook messages, he's been to my house in LA. He's sending threats about making me pay for something, and I'm afraid he's tracking me. He might even know I left Los Angeles."

"In other words, he's stalking you!" Vivian said, her tone sharp with a cocktail of dismay, anger and concern.

Harlow nodded. "I don't want to cower or let him hold my life hostage, but until I know more, until I feel like this Chris person isn't a threat, I can't see myself traveling to any in-person interviews or presentations. I'm sorry."

"Don't apologize! Your safety is what matters. Have you reported him to Facebook? You can block him, you know."

"Yes, and I have. But then he gets a new account, and it starts over."

Shadows crossed Vivian's face as she mulled this news. "I hate to say it, but it might be best to shut down your social media accounts until this guy is caught."

Harlow shook her head. "That's the platform I use for my show! Besides, if I change platforms, he'd just follow me to the new one. But how many of my current listeners would follow me?"

"I see your point, but if this guy is dangerous…" Vivian sighed, chewed her bottom lip. "I did tell you Nate is a detective with the Boise police, didn't I? I can talk to him, see what connections he has in LA and here in Owl Creek to set up protection for you and—"

The banging of the office's front door yanked them both from their conversation with a jolt. Harlow clapped a hand over her racing heart. "Geez. This whole business has left me jumpy as heck."

"Understandably," Vivian said as they both turned to see a woman with chin-length, pale blond hair storm up to the receptionist's desk.

"Where are they?" the blonde demanded.

"Pardon me?" Deacon's receptionist asked.

The woman, who visibly vibrated with rage, aimed a

finger of her frail hand at the receptionist. "Don't play stupid. You know who I mean! Where are Robert Colton's children?"

Vivian and Harlow exchanged a startled and wary glance. The woman seemed vaguely familiar to Harlow, and she struggled to place the woman's attractive, if sourly pinched, face.

"I'm sorry, ma'am, but Mr. Deacon and the Coltons are in a private meeting."

"Not without me, they're not!" The woman spun from the front desk and whisked past Vivian and Harlow in a cloud of hostility and cloying perfume.

Though the woman's appearance had changed in the last eleven years, her identity came to Harlow just a fraction of a second before Vivian gasped, "Oh my God! I think that's Nate's mother!"

Harlow swallowed hard as she bobbed a nod of agreement. "And Wade's aunt, Jessie."

Chapter Eight

Wade stuck his hand out for Nate to shake. "I hope this can be the beginning of a good relationship going forward. There's no reason we shouldn't all get along, stay in touch."

"I agree. And thank you again for including us in our dad's inheritance. That's—"

The door to the conference room was flung open so hard, it crashed against the wall.

Wade jerked his head toward the sudden bang, his nerves jumping.

His aunt Jessie strode into the room and took in the gathering with narrowed eyes and a black scowl. In a shrill voice, she shouted, "What's going on here? Why was I not included in this meeting?"

Nate faced his mother. "Because it doesn't involve you."

"Doesn't involve me?" she shrieked. Jessie cast her gaze around the room, from face to face. "This is about Robert's will, isn't it?"

"I'm sorry, sir," Deacon's breathless receptionist said, trotting into the room behind Jessie. "I tried to stop her."

"It's all right. I'll handle this." The lawyer moved around the long table toward Jessie. "Mrs. Colton, I have to ask you to leave now."

When Mr. Deacon reached for Jessie's arm, she snatched it away. "Don't touch me! I'm not going anywhere. I demand to know what this meeting is about! If it concerns Robert's will, then it concerns me."

"I don't see how," Deacon said. "You were not named in his will."

Jessie's face grew red. "That has to be a mistake! I know he wouldn't cut me out that way! I deserve my share!"

Sarah approached Jessie, raising a conciliatory hand. "Mom, please don't make a scene. Father had every right—"

"Don't make a scene? Young lady, I have not even begun to make the scene I intend, if I don't get what I deserve!"

"What you deserve?" Wade asked, stunned by his aunt's hubris.

When she turned to face him, she flinched, actually wincing when she saw his scarred face. The reaction shouldn't have hurt, but somehow it did. Her cringe was a reminder of how people saw him now—someone damaged, someone difficult to look at. He gritted his back teeth and held her glare, determined not show anyone how her reaction to him stung.

"Well…" Jessie said, "I'd heard you were caught in an explosion. Left the Marines."

"What of it?" he asked.

She gave a dismissive sniff. "Nothing. Just a bit surprised to see you here. I'd heard you were living as a virtual hermit by the lake."

"Mom!" Sarah said in a low warning tone. "Stop it. You need to leave."

Facing the rest of the room again, Jessie lifted her chin and beneath her heavy winter coat, she drew her shoulders back. "No. I'm not going anywhere until I get what I came for. Either the lot of you cough up my share of the inheritance, or I will see you in court!"

"Court?" Wade's youngest sister, Frannie, cried in dismay. "Why?"

"Because I will contest the abomination that left me out in the cold. I should have inherited *at least* half of his estate! I bore that man two children. I kept his bed warm and kept his dirty secret, his second family, under wraps for years! It is a disgrace that I was excluded from his will." She waved a frail finger at Deacon. "A disgrace and an injustice!"

Henry Deacon, keeping his composure, moved to stand directly in front of Jessie. "Regardless of your beliefs about what you feel owed, the fact is Robert's will was legal and has been executed. According to the terms of that last will and testament, you do not receive anything and therefore have no business here. I must ask again that you leave peacefully."

"And if I don't?"

Fletcher stepped forward. "Then in my authority with the Owl Creek police I will escort you off the premises. Your cooperation or lack thereof will determine whether I take you out to the sidewalk or to the police station."

"Are you threatening me, Fletcher?" Jessie asked with a pinched mouth.

"I'm advising you of your choices," Fletcher replied calmly.

Her mouth pressed in a line of fury, Jessie glared at Fletcher, then at the rest of the family gathered around the conference table. "I will have Robert's money. I deserve my share, and I will get it." Her tone grew darker and trembled with what seemed to Wade to be an almost rabid passion and disturbing intensity. "I have special weapons available to me that I *will* use to get what I have coming." She aimed a finger at the ceiling. "God himself is on my side. I do his work and have his army behind me. Beside me. I will bring down you high-and-mighty Coltons, and I will get my just share! I swear it."

With that, Jessie turned on her heel and stamped out.

Wade and his siblings sat in stunned silence for several seconds before Wade said, "What in the hell was that all about? God is on her side? Special weapons available?"

"Is she talking about the Ever After Church?" Sarah asked.

"You know about her involvement with those crackpots then?" Fletcher asked.

Nate nodded. "Yeah. She's in deep."

"Off the deep end, more like," Frannie said. "She's completely under Markus Acker's sway. And Mom has said for some time she doesn't believe Jessie's involvement with the Ever After Church has anything to do with real religious conversion. It's a money grab. This—" she waved a hand to where Jessie had been standing "—whatever it was she just spewed kinda supports that theory."

Ruby chewed her bottom lip then, dividing a look between Jessie's children and Fletcher, she asked, "Do you think she's dangerous? Could she really cause us trouble?"

"Legally she hasn't a leg to stand on," Deacon said. "The will and your agreement signed today are airtight. Your father's final wishes were clear and aboveboard, and your arrangement with Nate and Sarah has been signed and will be filed by the time the courthouse closes today."

"Seems to me the people at Ever After have done a number on her," Wade said.

Nate nodded. "She's clearly not in her right mind. I'd seen changes in her before this, but I've never seen her quite so riled up and talking nonsense."

"Whether we consider her comments today real threats or not, I'd say it's worth keeping a close eye on her and her dealings with the Ever After Church," Hannah said.

"Agreed." Chase rose from his seat and cast a gaze around the table at his siblings. "We should stay in close contact with each other, especially concerning anything that seem fishy in the coming weeks. We already have far too many reasons to be wary of Acker and his so-called church. If he has his hooks in Jessie, we need to add her to our watch list."

Wade nodded his agreement. "Will do."

A soft knock sounded on the conference room door, and Vivian poked her head in. "Everything okay in here?"

Wade's attention shifted to spot Harlow entering behind her PR rep and scanning the room until her gaze locked with his.

Nate crossed the room to enfold Vivian in his arms. "Besides my angry mother dropping in unexpectedly to make ludicrous demands and threats?" He kissed Vivian's forehead. "Everything is great. My newly discovered family has made a most generous gesture."

"Not the least of which being welcoming us into their fold," Sarah said, smiling warmly at Ruby and Hannah. The women hugged, and Fletcher and Chase added their welcomes and shook Nate's hand.

"Are you finished with your business then?" Harlow asked, motioning to the buzz of activity. "We didn't mean to break up your meeting. We only came to say we were headed out for coffee."

"I'm finished. Can I take you for that cup of coffee? I have something I want to discuss with you. Frannie's bookstore is just down the street, and she serves the best coffee in Owl Creek."

Hearing her name, Frannie glanced over and beamed. "Why thank you, Wade. But if you're angling for free food, I'll have to have a word with the owner."

"I'm not angling for any special treatment," Wade said, an edge to his voice even though he knew his sister was teasing. Frannie's jest cut too close to the irritating habit his family had of tiptoeing around him and treating him with kid gloves.

Harlow gave him a puzzled look. "Uh...sure. That sounds good. But..."

He saw where she was going and added quickly, "Not a date. I've asked Chase and his fiancée Sloan to join us. Sloan has a company called SecuritKey that might be able to help us track down the guy who's been stalking you."

"Help *us* track him down?" Harlow said, her head tipping to one side. "Wade, I appreciate your concern—and I'm definitely interested in talking to Sloan and Chase— but my stalker is my problem. Not yours."

He stiffened, scowling at her. "So I'm not allowed to help? Did you really think I could learn someone is threatening a friend of mine, and I'd turn my back on the situation?" He firmed his mouth as a new thought occurred to him. "Or is it you don't think I'm capable of helping any longer?" He held out his scarred right hand and turned it for her to see, as if showing exhibit A in a courtroom.

Harlow sighed. "Don't put words in my mouth. I haven't given you any reason to believe I think any less of your abilities since your accident."

Chase stepped up and divided a look between them. "I don't want to interrupt, but Sloan says she's at Book Mark It and has snagged us a corner table. Shall we go?"

Harlow nodded. "Yes. I'm ready." She turned and left the conference room with Chase, while Wade let her words soak in.

As he trailed after them, headed out of the office, he reflected on the past couple of days—from his first un-expected meeting with Harlow at the stable through their conversations while packing her mother's house. She was right. While she hadn't pretended he hadn't been injured—which honestly was just as annoying as his family's kid-glove act—neither had she treated him as if his scars or his eye patch made any difference in who he was or how she viewed him. He'd even caught her looking at him with the sort of heat in her gaze that she had in high school. The lingering, hungry stares that had distracted him in physics class and sparked numerous afternoon make-out sessions on the banks of Owl Creek.

He followed Harlow and his brother outside and clutched the lapels of his ranch coat closed against the icy January wind as they all trooped out of the lawyer's office build-ing. He took a couple of quick, long strides to catch up with Harlow and Chase and focused on what his oldest brother was saying.

"Well, the town hasn't changed that much since you left. Small business owners have managed to keep corporate America from storming in and taking over, but some of the shops in the downtown area have changed hands. Book Mark It, Frannie's shop, is in the building where Fincher's Farming Supply used to be."

"That wine shop is new." She pointed across the street

to the shop called the Cellar and slowed her pace. "Weekly tastings?" she said reading the sign in the front window. "Intriguing."

"Yeah. Sloan and I went a couple weeks ago, and she loved it." Chase waved a finger toward Wade. "You should have this guy take you before you leave town again."

"Oh, uh, yeah," Harlow hedged, casting an awkward look toward Wade. "Maybe."

Without commenting on his brother's matchmaking, Wade hustled to the front door of Book Mark It and held it for Harlow. The mellow aroma of books and coffee flowed from the store, and Harlow stopped to inhale deeply. "Oh, Lordy, if there's a better smell in the world, I don't know what it is."

I do, Wade thought as he nearly collided with Harlow. *You.* When he inhaled, his focus was on the notes of something floral that wafted around Harlow as she peeled off her coat and hat, then shook her hair into place. Wade gritted his back teeth, shoving down the surge of desire that poured through him. If he wanted to keep Harlow safe from her stalker, he'd have to spend more time with her. And if he wanted to stay sane while protecting her, he had to find a way to tamp his still-powerful hunger for her.

Yeah, good luck with that.

CHASE ESCORTED THEM to the corner table, where a woman with long dark hair that curled around her face in soft clouds rose to give Chase a kiss. "Sloan, this is Wade's former girlfriend, Harlow Jones. Harlow, my fiancée, Sloan."

Harlow shook the other woman's hand, and Sloan's face lit with recognition. "Hang on. Are you the same Harlow

Jones that has the internet advice show?" She snapped her fingers as she fumbled, then blurted, "*Harlow Helps*!"

Harlow grinned. "Guilty. In fact, the show is indirectly related to what Wade thought you might advise me on."

"Now I'm even more intrigued," Sloan said with a charming smile that put Harlow instantly at ease.

"Before we start," Wade said, peeling off his coat and tossing it on a spare chair, "can I get you a coffee, Harlow?"

She nodded, the chill of the walk over still burrowed to her bones. "Definitely. I've been told it's the best around."

Wade tugged up a corner of his mouth. "Three creamers and a hint of sugar?"

She gave him a wide-eyed look. "You remember?"

He dismissed the knowledge with a shrug. "We drank enough coffee together in high school to float a boat. I'd have to be pretty lame to forget your order."

He could be nonchalant about it if he wanted, but Harlow found it moving that Wade had remembered a detail about her others might consider too trivial to hold on to. She shucked off her gloves—the ones he had given her earlier that week—and watched him stride up to the counter. What did it say that she remembered his regular order was black coffee with a sprinkle of cinnamon?

Chase met Sloan's gaze. "Your usual?"

"Please." The affection in Sloan's eyes as she looked up at Chase tugged at Harlow's heart. Seeing how many of Wade's siblings and cousins had found loving relationships in recent months was heartening. After all the shared high school classes, lazy days at Blackbird Lake, family barbecues at Colton Ranch, Harlow was happy to know her friends, members of Wade's family, were finding happiness.

A warm sense of comfort and familiarity washed through

her, chasing away the lingering chill of the January day. Harlow sighed as she settled back in her chair and glanced around at the cozy bookstore Frannie ran. A half circle of comfy chairs created a homey reading spot in front of a stone fireplace, and a handwritten chalk notice on a blackboard over the coffee bar advertised a weekly story time for children. Harlow loved every book, mug and wicker basket in the store. The bookstore, the renewed businesses of Owl Creek, the warmth of her old friends and new acquaintances, tugged at her soul. She could all too easily fall back into her old routines, the patterns and people of her life in Owl Creek.

Including Wade.

A different sort of heat rippled through her as she studied his profile in the light from the front window. He wore a thick layer of stubble on his cheeks, which only added to his roguish appeal. She was clearly still attracted to him and his thoughtfulness. The easy way he seemed to plug back into her life as if nothing had happened eleven years ago—

But something did happen eleven years ago. Something painful and harsh and devastating to her young heart. She needed to not forget that. Forgive, maybe. But forgetting would be setting herself up for another heartache.

"Harlow?"

She shook out of her wayward thoughts and blinked as she turned to Sloan. "I'm sorry. What were you saying?"

"I asked how long you were going to be in Owl Creek," Sloan said chuckling. "Where were you just now?" Sloan's attention shifted to the coffee counter where Chase and Wade were talking in low voices as they waited for the barista to finish the drinks. "Hmm. Never mind. I can guess."

Harlow opened her mouth to deny Sloan's implication,

then closed it again with a soft click of her teeth. "It just feels strange being back in Owl Creek. It's almost like picking up where things left off after high school. Except… things *have* changed."

The men returned with the coffees, and as he took his seat, Wade opened the discussion. "So I called you—" he divided a glance between his brother and Sloan "—because Harlow has acquired a stalker."

Chapter Nine

Chase and Sloan both sent Harlow wide-eyed looks of alarm.

"I thought you might be able to help," Wade said, "both with some levels of added security and also some computer knowledge. It'd be great if we could track down this guy through his server or IP address. Maybe his cell phone?"

Sloan wrapped both of her hands around her mug and frowned. "Back up a bit. Fill me in on when this all started, how this creep has contacted you, what he's said and so forth."

With a nod, Harlow explained how Chris72584 had first contacted her through the comments on her Facebook Live post, then directly messaged her, progressing from irritation and displeasure with the advice she'd given to implied threats.

"When he messaged me a picture of my own house he seems to have lifted from Google Earth, I got spooked and decided to leave town." She shuddered as the sense of violation tripped through her again.

"Have you reported all this to the police?" Sloan asked, scribbling notes on a small notepad.

Harlow nodded. "I did. In LA, after the picture of my house was sent to me. They took my statement, but the officer who responded to my call didn't sound especially optimistic about finding the guy. He said they get hundreds, even thousands, of online bullying and stalking reports every year and have far too few people to work all the cases."

Wade grunted in a way that said he was displeased with the LAPD's response. "Well, you're not in LA now. We'll talk to Fletcher and get the local guys on it. The department may be small, but Fletcher and his fellow officers will take your case, your safety, seriously."

Chase nodded his agreement.

"If I'm honest, I came to Owl Creek not just to close out my parents' house and get it ready to sell, but because I thought I'd be safer here until this creep either gives up and leaves me alone or the California police find him."

"Not a bad idea. When was the last time you heard from the guy?" Sloan asked.

"Today... Maybe."

Chased pulled a frown. "Maybe?"

When Harlow hesitated, an anxious stir in her gut, Wade said, "This morning she got a disturbing text from an unknown number. While we have no proof it is the same guy, the message read much like the online threats from this Chris72—whatever—person."

Sloan raised both of her delicate eyebrows and tipped her head as she looked at Harlow. "He texted your private phone?"

Harlow exhaled through pursed lips. "Yeah."

Extending her hand, Sloan asked, "May I see it?"

Harlow fished in her handbag until she found her cell phone and handed it to Sloan. Bending her head over the device, Sloan swiped and tapped through a number of screens, studied the text, then groaned. "Yeah. Not good."

Harlow reached for her phone, but Sloan drew the cell away. "Harlow, do you want my best advice? My help keeping you safe?"

"That's why we're here," Wade said, his expression all business.

Sloan waited for Harlow's nod, then reached in her own handbag and took out a small tool kit. She set to work, prying the back cover off Harlow's phone and removing both the battery and a small piece of plastic. "Your SD card. Chase, honey, will you ask at the counter if they have a small plastic ziplock bag?"

Harlow gaped at her dismantled phone. "But... I need my phone."

Sloan shot her a commiserating look. "I understand. Really. And I'm not suggesting you destroy any of the parts just yet. But I do suggest you buy a burner and be very selective who you give the new number to."

"A burner? Where do I get one of those?"

"Not in Owl Creek," Chase said, returning with a small bag that he offered Sloan for the parts of Harlow's phone. "Closest store likely to sell burner phones would be in Conners."

"That presents a small problem, then. I don't have a car. I flew here from LA and Vivian picked me up at the Boise airport." She split a questioning look between Chase and Wade. "Does anyone in Owl Creek drive for Uber or Lyft?"

Wade's brow dipped in consternation. "You don't need Uber, Harlow. I'll take you to Conners. We can go this afternoon."

Her pulse jumped at the thought of an afternoon expedition with Wade.

"Um," Chase interrupted, "I thought the doctor had restricted your driving until your left eye heals completely."

Harlow choked on the sip of coffee she was drinking. "What?" She sent Wade a sharp look. "But...you drove us into town today! And you've been driving over to my mom's house!"

Chase scowled. "Wade? Is that true?"

Wade's jaw flexed and tightened, a sure sign he was grinding his back teeth. "That was months ago. My eye has healed considerably since then."

"How much is considerably? Has the doctor signed off on your driving?" Chase asked.

Wade didn't answer, turned his head. Which was answer enough.

Chase growled. "Wade..."

Wade's jaw tightened. "I'm doing well enough. I don't need a doctor to tell me when I can or can't drive. Besides, I know the roads in town like the back of my hand."

His brother grunted. "Don't be stubborn, Wade. You want to kill someone driving with impaired vision?"

Harlow saw the color drain from Wade's face, the tension that turned his countenance to stone. The pain that flashed in Wade's unpatched eye sent a clawing reciprocal ache through her.

Harlow shifted her attention to Chase. Did Wade's brother see what she saw?

Extending an upturned palm, Chase gave Wade a sympathetic gaze. "Give me your keys, bro. Just like I won't let anyone I love drive drunk, I can't in good conscience let you behind the wheel until your eye's healed or I know you're wearing a contact."

Wade's breath came quick and shallow, his nostrils

flared, and a combination of hurt and anger simmered from him like steam.

Harlow cleared her throat and suggested in a gentle tone, "Wade, what if I drove us to Conners in your truck?"

Wade's head, his attention, turned toward Harlow, and after a beat, she saw his jaw relax a little, his hard-edged glare soften. His breathing slowed enough for him to take a deep lungful of air and release it with a sigh of resignation. He leaned on his hip enough to dig his keys out of his jeans pocket and drop them on the table by Harlow's hand. "Looks like you're Uber now."

Clearing her throat, Sloan took a laptop from a satchel on the floor beside her. She scooted her coffee aside and opened the computer on the table. "Tell me more about your stalker's communication with you through Facebook. Did you delete his comments? Block him from posting?"

"Yes and yes. Blocking him only angered him, and he set up a new account and came at me again."

"You're sure it's the same guy with a new account?" Sloan asked.

"He made sure I knew it was him. And don't suggest I get off Facebook because that is how I make my living, how I reach my audience. Even if I shift to another platform, I'd have to tell my Facebook followers where to find me, so I don't lose my current audience."

"Which would mean the creep would know where to find your show, too," Wade said with a defeated sounding sigh.

"Exactly." Harlow took a sip of her coffee as she mulled over the situation. "I've already put the show on a brief hiatus, presetting show reruns to air for the next couple weeks while I'm here. I don't want to lose listeners over this."

Sloan pulled her hair back from her face with both hands

and secured the unruly curls with a stretchy cloth band. Then unfolding a stylish pair of glasses that she slipped onto her nose, she started swiping and typing on her laptop. "My security company can definitely dig into this for you. We'll need your written permission to access some of your account information, passwords and so forth, but we may be able to track down at least the location of the stalker's computer through his IP address."

"That's a start, but what about her personal safety while she's here in Idaho?" Wade asked.

Harlow sent Wade a startled look. "You think he's tracked me here? That he'd actually travel here to hurt me?"

"You really want to trust that he won't?" Wade replied.

"It's a possibility we need to consider." Sloan looked at Harlow over the top of her glasses. "Does your parents' house have a security system? Cameras outside?"

Harlow shook her head. "This is Owl Creek. When I was in high school, my parents didn't even lock their doors on the nights I went out. I never had to carry a house key."

"Times have changed, even in Owl Creek," Wade said, his gaze full of concern.

"We've had a spate of crime around here lately. Violent attacks, break-ins and murders."

"Fletcher has been busy working cases of all sorts lately," Chase said. "Our cousin Lizzy was even kidnapped."

Harlow gaped, her stomach performing flip-flops. "Lizzy? My goodness. I had lunch with her this week and she never mentioned it."

"She's not the only one in the family who's had a run-in with a dangerous element lately, either," Chase said.

"Good grief! Vivian told me about what happened to her, but I had no idea it was part of a crime spree."

"There's a new church just outside of town," Sloan said, "and we have reason to believe they are involved with all sorts of illegal stuff."

"The Ever After Church I've been hearing about? The one Jessie is tangled up with?" she asked.

"Cult is a better descriptor," Chase said, "and yes. That's the one. We even think the cult could be behind our father's murder."

Harlow jolted. "What? You think Robert was *murdered*?"

Wade nodded. "We have reason to believe so. Yes."

"But *why*? Who would want to kill your father?" She goggled at the notion, remembering Wade's father as a kind and gracious man—secret family aside.

"Good question. Right now, our lead suspect is Marcus Acker, the founder and leader of Ever After."

"Um…" Harlow blinked hard and fumbled to process the onslaught of tragic and disturbing things she was learning. "What… I mean, that's—"

"A conversation for another time," Wade said.

Harlow snorted derisively. "Not much of a selling point for my parents' house. I can see the listing now. *High crime rate in neighborhood.* That'll drive the selling price up. Not."

"What *will* be a selling point is a good security system," Sloan said with a crooked grin. "And SecuritKey can fix you up. I can get someone out there tomorrow if that works for you."

Harlow's head spun as she processed what she was hearing. "I, uh…" She'd always felt so safe in her parents' home, in Owl Creek, but on the heels of the stalker's text on her private phone this morning, the revelations of local crimes rattled her. She imagined herself sleeping in the dark house tonight, only a cat for company, and a shiver raced down her spine. She didn't consider herself the sort to scare easily, seeing danger lurking around every corner. But neither was she foolish enough to take unnecessary risks. "I suppose it would be prudent."

"Good," Sloan said, tapping her laptop keys as she said, "I'm clearing my schedule, so we can take care of that first thing in the morning."

Harlow glanced at Wade, who bobbed his chin in approval. "I can be there to help."

"I don't need—" Harlow started, but when determination fired in Wade's gaze, she dropped her protest. She might not believe she needed his help, but what did it really hurt to humor him? If it gave him a sense of purpose, eased his mind, satisfied a need he had to be useful, so be it.

"Meanwhile, this afternoon, I will call the LAPD and see what progress they have made and get with Fletcher to see what the local police might be able to do for extra protection for you," Sloan said.

Harlow nodded. "Thanks."

"And I'll get my best hackers to track down anything they can find online about—" she consulted the handwritten notes she'd made earlier "—Chris72584. Those numbers after his name could be a birth date or anniversary or part of an address. Most people are not especially creative when creating usernames or passwords. In order to help them remember account information, most people use something personal…which helps my hackers fill in a lot of blanks and track the right information."

Harlow thought about her own passwords and cringed internally. She was as guilty as the next guy of taking such shortcuts.

Sloan closed her laptop and gave Harlow a reassuring smile. "Don't worry. My team is good. I have every confidence we'll root this guy out and get rid of him for you." She finished her coffee and stuffed her dirty napkin inside the cup. "If there's nothing else, I'll get started on this and have my security people at your house at…is 8:00 a.m. too early?"

Harlow rose from the table, collecting her own trash. "Eight is fine. Thank you for your help." She included Chase in her glance. "Truly." Facing Wade, she said, "I guess if we're going to Conners for a burner phone, now's as good a time as any."

Wade nodded, collected both of their empty cups and returned them to the dirty dish rack by the coffee bar. Harlow slid into her coat, and after thanking Chase and Sloan again, pulled Wade's keys from her pocket and accompanied him to his truck.

Despite the bare trees and gray tones of winter, the drive to Conners was beautiful to Harlow. The majesty of the snow-capped mountains and crystal beauty of the lake and streams along the route spoke to Harlow's soul. Like a siren's song calling her home, the natural landscape reminded her of hours spent on Blackbird Lake in the summer and hiking the mountain trails amid the rich fall colors. In a few months, the green shoots of spring would pop up and wildflowers in a rainbow of hues would brighten the fields. Many things in Owl Creek had changed, but the ageless rhythms of the river and hills offered a constant that she craved while so much in her life now was uncertain.

"I missed this," she said, gesturing to the scenery out the truck's windshield. "Having lived so many places grow-

ing up, I can say without question that Idaho is my favorite place on earth."

Wade was silent for a moment, his expression contem-
plative, before he said, "Mine, too."

"That's saying something. I'm guessing you got to see
a lot of the world during your time in the Marines." She
cast him a side glance in time to see him frown. "What?"

"Can we talk about something else?"

"Something besides your travels with the Marines?"

"Something besides the Marines."

"Oh." She focused her attention on the road. "Sure." She
fished for something to break the silence. "Sloan seems
nice. How did Chase meet her? I mean, last I'd heard Chase
was married."

Wade grunted and shook his head. "He's divorced now.
Obviously." He waved a hand in dismissal. "Long story.
Sloan's from... Chicago, I think. That's where Securit-
Key has its main office. But a few months ago, Chase no-
ticed some funny business with Colton Properties and hired
Sloan to help him root out the problem. To put it in a nut-
shell, she came to Owl Creek, they hit it off, and now they
are planning a future together."

"And did they find the problem at Colton Properties?"

Wade grimaced. "Yeah, an employee was embezzling
money. But after Sloan figured that out, she started digging
into the Ever After Church and Markus Acker. It looks like
there are a lot of shady things going on with that church."

Harlow gaped at him. "Good grief! This Acker guy is
everywhere and into everything!"

"We've noticed," Wade said dryly.

"If they can connect Acker to so many crimes, why isn't

he behind bars? Why is the church still operating outside town? Can't they be closed down or...or...*something*?"

"Believe me, Fletcher is working with a number of people and other agencies, trying to find the piece of the puzzle that will make something stick. But the guy is slippery. He uses other people to do his dirty work and buries his connections deep, so that there are multiple layers of deniability between him and the chaos he's causing."

Harlow shivered. "Geez, what happened to the safe and quiet little town Owl Creek used to be?" She gripped the steering wheel tighter and knit her brow. "Maybe I was wrong thinking I'd be safe here until my stalker is caught."

Wade shifted on the seat, angling his body toward her. "Are you saying you want to leave Owl Creek?"

"No, I—" She sighed. "I mean I still have to get my parents' home ready for market. But honestly, I could do that anytime. The dead of winter wouldn't have been my first pick of times to be back in Idaho, but..."

"But?"

She turned up a palm. "But... I don't know. The text this morning, this news about a dangerous man stirring up problems in town...it's all got me spooked. I thought if I lay low up here that I'd be safer—"

"You are safer," he interrupted, his blue eye focused on her with an intensity that penetrated to her marrow, "because I will keep you safe."

"Wade, you don't have to be—"

"And toward that end..." He squared his shoulders and hardened his expression in a way that said he'd hear no arguments from her. "Let's go over what we know about your stalker, your shows and see what we can figure out."

She angled a withering look at him. "Don't you think I've done that?"

"Not with me. Maybe I'll think of something you took for granted."

"Wade…"

"Humor me. We have another half hour in the car."

Harlow groaned but nodded. She pinched the bridge of her nose as she conjured the events of the past couple months to review again with Wade. "I've told all this to the police in LA."

"But I have a vested interest and all day to work on it. Go." He waggled a finger, urging her to start talking.

"Fine." She rolled her head side to side to stretch her neck as she explained, "I got the first message from him in the comment section of one of my Facebook Live broadcasts."

"Which one? Do you still have the broadcast and comments archived where I can look at them later?"

"Uh, yeah. Well. Not the original comment from him. I deleted it after I reported him to Facebook."

She heard his sigh and said, "Yeah, I know. Not the best move, but I just hated having his vitriol polluting my mental health page."

He grunted and waved a hand for her to continue. "But then more comments came in, and I left them for the police to see and trace. After I blocked him from commenting on the show's posts, he started direct messaging me on my personal account."

"And what was the topic of the show he commented on? What was his beef?"

"That particular show was about the need for caregivers to take care of themselves, how mental and physical exhaustion can affect the people responsible for caring for elderly parents or sick family members or small children."

"Huh." Wade's brow furrowed as he considered the information.

"Right? I mean, what is offensive about wanting people to give themselves rest and seek support from others when they feel overwhelmed?"

"And the comment said…?"

Harlow's gut clenched remembering the cruel words. "It said, 'Your *expletive* advice is a crock of…*another expletive*.'" She cut a side glance at Wade. "'It's all your fault. Her blood is on your hands. I'll see you in hell.'"

The creases of concern lining his face deepened. "Whose blood is on your hands? Any indication of the guy's relationship to the 'her' that presumably died if you have blood on your hands?"

She lifted a shoulder. "Your guess is as good as mine. He never said. Because of the content of that show, I was working on the assumption of a loved one, maybe a sick child or elderly parent. Maybe that child or parent was left in someone else's care while the primary caregiver took the respite I recommended, and maybe something tragic happened while the primary caregiver was gone. Maybe the stalker is the caregiver, and maybe he needs to find someone to blame or—"

Wade snorted. "That's a lot of maybes."

She scowled. "Maybes are all I have, Wade!"

He raised a hand conceding the point. "Your scenario is possible, but—" he twisted his mouth as he thought "—if a third party were involved—the babysitter or hired nurse or neighbor who stepped in to help but allowed the child or patient or whomever to die—why not make that person the focus of his rage and blame?"

She shrugged again. "I got nothin'." After a beat, she added, "The thing is, I have people call in to the show who are suicidal, people who are dealing with abusive relationships, people fighting addictions of all kinds, people who are struggling with fears and anxieties and...gosh. So many of life's hardest problems. Any one of the callers' cases could have taken a bad turn, whether they took my advice or not. This Chris guy who's taken exception to something I did or said could be anyone. The father of a teen who died of an overdose. The husband of a woman suffering from crippling anxiety who killed herself. I just—" She heard the pitch of her voice rising and stopped, took a slow breath and exhaled slowly. She braked as they arrived at a crossroad, and she waited for the traffic to clear. In a calmer tone, she said, "I just don't know, Wade. It could be anyone."

He reached for her hand, lifting it from the steering wheel and pressing it between his. She could feel the light ripple of scarring, the rough scrape of ranching calluses and the warmth of affection as he held her hand sandwiched between his. His touch soothed her, steadied her.

"We'll figure it out, Harlow. I promise. We'll figure it out together. Until this creep is caught, I'm all in."

Chapter Ten

All in...

A shudder rolled through Harlow as conflicting emotions swirled inside her. She was both relieved and comforted by the idea of having Wade's support, but also a tad resentful that it took her being in personal danger to hear those words from him. Where had his *all in* been after high school when her world had centered on him? When her heart had been invested, he'd ignored her needs, turned his back on all they had and cut her from his life like a cancer.

When the car behind them honked with impatience, he released her hand, and she shoved down the ache of lost love. Again. How many times would she have to battle back the painful memories before losing Wade no longer hurt so much?

She pulled out on the crossroad to Conners and swallowed against the lump in her throat. As long as she was in Owl Creek and regularly crossing paths with Wade, the past would be hovering, following her like a shadow she couldn't outrun. All the more reason to work quickly on her parents' house and move on to...wherever she decided her next refuge would be. Seattle? Portland? Heck, maybe she'd flee across the country to Boston. Or visit Sydney. It was summer in Australia now, after all. She could escape the winter cold, her stalker and Wade all at once.

Escape. The word roiled in her gut. Wasn't that just a nice way of saying she was running from her troubles? How many times had she told clients that strategy never worked? Problems, conflicts and hard truths needed to be faced and addressed before real healing could take place.

"Let's try this place," Wade said, drawing her out of her ruminations. He pointed out the passenger window to a large supercenter department store.

Within an hour they'd purchased and activated the burner phone for Harlow and had bought a few groceries they each needed.

They were almost back to Owl Creek when Wade said, "How do I access your archived shows? I think I'll do a marathon listen tonight and see if anything pops out for me."

"I can send you a link, but… I've been through them all twice and sent them to the LA police."

"With all due respect, you're too close to the show. I may be able to pick up on something you missed. And the cops?" He shook his head with a twist of his lips. "They're swamped. I can't imagine the backlog of cases the LAPD has."

She cast a glance to him from the driver's seat. "Fine. If that's really how you want to spend your evening…"

"Can't think of a better use of my time than making sure you're safe."

"Then I'll send you what you need once I get home and can boot up my laptop."

"Good." He paused, a worried look crossing his face. "Except…use your new phone to send info, okay?"

"But it's saved on my laptop."

The muscle in his chiseled jaw tightened. "And you've used your laptop since arriving in Owl Creek?"

A chill raced through her as it clicked. "You think my stalker might be able to track me because I used my laptop since coming to Owl Creek?"

He dragged a hand over his jaw as he exhaled. "I guess that depends on how tech-savvy the guy is. He's already found a way to skirt your blocks on Facebook, so he's no dummy. And in the same way the police department and Sloan's computer experts are trying to track your stalker's individual computer fingerprint and IP address, your stalker could be tracking you. Even if you go to an internet café, if you're using your laptop, you're leaving a data trail that can be followed."

Harlow's heart sank. "So I have to get a new laptop, too? I mean, I will if that's what I have to do to shake this guy but…geez!"

Wade shook his head. "You can probably hold off on that for now. Just don't get online, turn off your Wi-Fi connection, and…well, you can come to my place and use my computer any time. And we'll download the files of your show onto a thumb drive for me to take home."

She nodded. Groaned. Then turning to Wade, she said, "If I haven't said it before now…thank you. I appreciate all your help."

LATER THAT NIGHT, after stopping by Harlow's to drop her off and download her program files, Wade plugged the flash drive into his desktop and called up the files on his desktop. While the files loaded, he grabbed a beer from the fridge and a box of crackers from the pantry. He leaned over the computer and opened the first file. Harlow's sultry voice filled the air from his speakers, and he carried his snack and drink to his recliner and settled in.

"Hello, my friends! This is Harlow Jones back with a new episode of *Harlow Helps*."

Wade took a pull of his beer and dug his hand in the box of cheesy crackers.

"I'm a licensed mental health counselor, and I'm here to heal the world and promote mental wellness, one person at a time."

Wade arched an eyebrow. *Speaking of cheesy...*

"But Harlow, you may be saying, there are billions of people in the world. If you reach just one person at a time, you'll never finish in one lifetime!" Harlow's melodic laughter flowed from his computer and tripped down Wade's spine. "You'd be right. But one life can touch another one, then another, in a chain of healing and love that spreads like ripples on the water."

Wade snorted. Harlow was being rather trite and sappy, but he wasn't listening to grade the presentation or her showmanship. His only interest was content. His job was to focus on who may have called in or what Harlow might have said to enrage Chris72584.

The first episode played out without him finding anything of note. The focus of her advice centered on helping a woman deal with her anxiety and trouble sleeping. Next was a woman with a shopping addiction. The next episode turned to grief, a woman who had lost both her spouse and cherished pet within a month and was struggling.

"Grief has no timetable and no set prescription for dealing with it, Helen," Harlow told the woman in a gentle tone. "Don't let society or friends or media tell you how you should react. Your emotions are genuine and important, and no one can tell you how you *should* feel. Don't be afraid to grieve, either. Allow yourself to walk through the emotions, because suppressed feelings only fester and become a bigger problem down the road."

Wade's hand tightened on his bottle of beer. Harlow's advice, meant for the caller, struck a nerve. Were his nightmares, his lingering trouble dealing with the munitions accident a symptom of him suppressing his grief and guilt? His doctors at the military hospital had tried to talk to him about the explosion, but he'd refused. How could he open up about something so raw and painful? The horror of that day was hard enough to get through when it happened without reliving it—with an audience to witness his most private battle, no less.

The next episode tracked along a similar vein. Harlow guided a man with depression and thoughts of suicide over a broken relationship through an emotional exchange in which Harlow acknowledged the man's pain without making any judgments. She listened to the man's story and gave him sympathy and support without sounding condescending. By the end of the show, she'd convinced the man to talk to a professional counselor with whom Harlow had promised to put the caller in touch.

The next episode was from a woman whose husband became violent when he drank. Wade cringed internally at the all-too-common story of violence against women by men who'd sworn to love and protect them. Guys like this woman's husband made Wade's blood boil.

As his fury and dismay on behalf of the caller grew, Wade rose from his chair and hurried to the computer desk. He took out a notepad and pen, and after consulting his monitor, he jotted down the episode number for future reference before starting that episode over. He also wrote down the woman's name, Susan, even though she said it wasn't her real name. But perhaps there was a kernel of truth in the pseudonym. A mother, a sibling, a middle name.

With keenly focused attention, he listened for clues about the woman as she described the abuse she lived with. Knowing Harlow as well as he did, he could hear the tremble in her voice that betrayed her own alarm for the woman's safety and the pressure she put on herself to get this case right. The yearning to reach through the internet and snatch the woman from the dangerous situation and tuck her safely away from harm. He recognized it, too, because he felt the same way. But even with the slight tremor, Harlow still projected a compassion and assurance, authority and urgency.

"I know the idea of leaving him is scary," Harlow said. "I know he's tried to convince you that you could never make it without him. Maybe he's threatened to do more harm if you leave. All of that is terrifying. I agree. But I also know you cannot change him. You must protect yourself, or he will continue to hurt you and control you."

Wade battled his frustration as the woman hedged, expressing her doubts and reluctance, all of which Harlow countered ably with patience, grace, strength and encouragement.

"Susan, you trusted me enough to call tonight and tell me your story. That took tremendous courage. Will you trust me enough when we get offline to give me your real name and location? Will you allow me to contact people who can help you?"

"I—I—" Susan sighed and in a tiny voice said, "Okay."

Wade exhaled for the first time in several long tense seconds. The episode ended, and Wade returned to his recliner, feeling emotionally drained, and took another swallow of beer.

She's good, Wade thought as he realized the tightrope Harlow had walked so skillfully.

In the next episode, she spoke to a woman having ongoing arguments with her boyfriend over finances. He was all the more attuned now to how Harlow dealt with each caller, her comments and questions, her compassion and tactful honesty, all pointing to just how well Harlow was listening, how much she truly cared.

But then she'd been a good listener in high school. They'd talked for hours when they had dated, parked in his car by the shore of Blackbird Lake or sitting on her bedroom floor. His family issues, her teenage squabbles with her mother, high school angst and jealousies and rivalries were all hashed out between them, openly, honestly. And he'd shared his dreams of serving in the Marines, a goal he'd shared with his best friend, Sebastian Cross. That memory caused irritation to chew at his gut. Harlow had heard Wade say how much the Marines meant to him, knew how long the dream had shaped him. How could she not understand his reasons for leaving Owl Creek when he did? And why couldn't she have supported him in that dream?

Wade huffed his frustration. Why was he rehashing their breakup *again* after all these years? He finished his beer and lunged out of the recliner, tossing the bottle in the recycling bin with a bit too much gusto. The bottle broke with a jarring clatter. He gripped the edge of the kitchen counter, letting the mild zap of adrenaline and edginess settle.

From his computer, Harlow's voice continued. "Sometimes it's hard to see your own part in disagreements. Relationships take compromise and a willingness to admit mistakes. Listening goes both ways. If you want your boyfriend to hear you express your needs and unhappiness, then be ready to truly hear what he is saying as well."

Wade stared hard at the countertop, letting Harlow's words wash over him. Had he listened to Harlow when they'd argued that fateful night after her graduation? What had she said about Owl Creek being her home? About not wanting to give up what she'd finally found?

The current *Harlow Helps* episode ended, and another started with her chipper, cheesy introduction. A parent looking for help with a rebellious teen. Wade scrubbed a hand on his cheek. He was supposed to be listening for clues that might identify or point toward Harlow's stalker, not wallowing in his own issues and memories of the past.

He took out another beer, paused, then returned it to the refrigerator. Tonight, he wouldn't use alcohol to anesthetize his pain and help put him to sleep. Tonight, he'd keep his mind sharp, analyzing Harlow's broadcasts, using his focus to help him keep his promise to Harlow.

He would do what it took to keep her safe, and that included putting her need for answers above his own problems. Taking out a can of soda instead, he popped the top and returned to the recliner to continue his listening marathon. Somewhere, hidden in the hours of Harlow's sage and caring advice and her callers' issues with dysfunction, heartache and pain, lay the seed of discontent that had taken root for her stalker. Somehow Wade had to find that seed before Harlow's stalker found her.

Chapter Eleven

As Sloan had promised they would, an installation team from SecuritKey arrived early the next morning. By the time Wade showed up, looking rather drowsy and rumpled, Harlow had shown the installation team where the circuit breakers were and been briefed on the schematic showing where all the cameras and alarms would be placed throughout the house and yard.

"Coffee," was all Wade said as she held the front door for him to come in from the icy cold. "Now."

Harlow closed the door and gave him the stink eye. "And good morning to you, too, Mr. Sunshine."

Looking chastened, he inhaled deeply and said, "Coffee, now...please?"

Harlow chuckled and headed to the kitchen. "Better, but keep working on it."

"I promise to give you all the sugary greetings you want after I have caffeine coursing through my veins." He walked straight to the cabinet where her mugs were kept and helped himself to one. Harlow filled his cup, and he groaned his pleasure as he drank deeply.

The sexy rumble from his throat reminded her all too clearly of the sultry sighs and impassioned moans they'd both made during their sexual encounters in high school. Grabbing the back of a kitchen chair when her knees buckled, she forced the erotic thoughts aside and cleared her throat. "Couldn't sleep last night?"

"Oh, I slept at some point, given that I woke up in my living room chair about ten minutes ago." He drank again, then refilled his cup. "I stayed up listening to your program recordings."

She barked a laugh. "And they put you to sleep? Thanks a lot!"

His good eye glared at her over the rim of his mug. "I didn't say that. The show is good. You're good. But you gave me fortysomething hours of broadcasts to listen to."

He liked her show? Thought she was good? A giddy thrill spun through her. Wade's offhand compliment meant more to her than all the gushing of strangers who followed her Facebook page or her viral status on social media. Wade's approval had always meant more to her than anyone else's. She didn't stop to dwell on that truth.

"And?" she asked, pulling out the chair she'd clutched and sitting in it. "Did you figure anything out?"

"You mean besides the fact that there are a lot of people with problems in this world, and at the end of the day, I wouldn't swap problems with any of them?" He dropped into the chair opposite her and cradled the mug between his hands.

"I think most people would agree with that." She couldn't help but wonder if and when he might share some of his problems, the demons that clearly haunted him. *Don't push. He'll open up when he's ready.* "But did anything jump out at you that might help us identify my stalker?"

"Jump? No. But a thing or two did have me doing a double take. Relationship issues mean there's another person involved, and it was typically the woman that called in. The man in the relationship could have felt you were taking the woman's side and formed a grudge."

Harlow considered that. "But I try so hard not to take sides. I specifically say relationships are the responsibility of *both* partners."

He flipped up his palm. "I'm just saying, a partner who took umbrage at something you told their spouse could hold a grudge." He drew a notepad from his pocket and folded back the top page as his gaze darkened. "Speaking of bad relationships, this lady—" he tapped the notebook "—from episode twelve, called herself Susan—"

Harlow's gut flipped. She knew exactly the episode he meant. Even if the case hadn't burned itself in her memory the night Susan had called, Harlow had been grimly reminded when she got reports back from her contacts in Houston whom she'd called to get the woman to safety.

She nodded, choking back the surge of bile in her throat, even as Wade said, "A domestic abuse situation."

"I remember her." Harlow took a cleansing breath as she met Wade's gaze. "It's not her husband, if that's what you're thinking."

"How can you know that?" he asked, then shifting on his chair his expression grew wary. "What happened with Susan?"

"She left him—her husband, I mean—and went to the safe house the women's shelter offered." She took a moment to gather herself before adding, "But a few weeks later, she went back to him."

Wade sucked in a sharp breath of dismay, mumbled a bad word under his breath. "You're sure?"

She nodded. "The contact I made in Houston let me know when I called to check on Sh—um, Susan."

Wade lifted his hand from his mug, dismissing her slip. "She used an alias. I figured as much. So what happened when she went back?"

"An argument. A neighbor called the police. There was a standoff with her husband, and when he appeared at the door wielding a weapon, threatening both Susan and the police officers, he was shot and died at the hospital."

Wade's jaw hardened, and dread filled his face. "And Susan?"

Harlow's brow crumpled with sadness. "She blamed herself and overdosed on drugs a week later." She swallowed hard, forcing down the knot of regret and disappointment that strangled her. "So it's not Susan's husband. He's... dead."

Wade was silent, his good eye full of pain and shock and frustration. She got up and took the coffee carafe from the brewer, refilled his mug and her own, then stared out the back window where the installation team was surveying the eaves around the back porch.

"How do you do it?" Wade finally said, his voice hoarse.

"Pardon?" She faced him, taking in his haggard expression.

"How do you stay sane when you hear one horror story after another from your clients? How do you get up each morning knowing your day is going to be filled with listening to people complain and hearing life stories full of pain and tragedy and cruelty? How does it not break you?"

This was far from what she'd expected to hear from Wade, and Harlow took a moment to not only absorb her shock, but also formulate an answer that wasn't glib or untrue. She valued honesty in others and would only give Wade the same. "Some days, I wonder the same thing. There is a great deal of stress involved in counseling, but I do it, because I want to help my clients. I keep at it, because I feel I'm making a difference. To say I love what I do isn't quite the truth. It's fulfilling, and I treasure the moments when I share a breakthrough with a client or see the transformation of a hurting soul."

Wade nodded, his expression pensive. "It just seems like you'd get overwhelmed after a while. I mean I just listened to your shows for a few hours last night and my head's reeling."

Harlow sipped her coffee, then said, "There is definitely a lot of self-care required. I have to de-stress at the end of the day and find ways to compartmentalize my work and my private life. Counselors, in general, do suffer a high rate of burnout, just like other professionals with intensely emotional or stressful jobs."

He seemed to be considering her answer. "And how do you de-stress? How do you handle the job so you don't go bonkers?"

She met his gaze, noted the twitch of muscles in his tight jaw and sensed he was asking for advice as much as for interest in her life. "I watch cheesy sitcoms in the evening. Laughter is as good a medicine as the cliché claims. Or I might take a walk at the beach. Or have a hot bath, read escapist fiction or occasionally drink a glass of wine." She paused, feeling compelled as a professional to add, "Not that alcohol should be considered an answer to problems or a way to medicate personal pain. Everything in moderation, right?"

He angled his head, his mouth twitching wryly at the corner. "Of course."

"I start every morning with prayer and meditation," she continued, "and I make time in my schedule every week to hang out with my friends. Social connections are key to good mental health."

His brow lowered now, and the tension returned to his jaw.

"Talking about things," she said, determined to make her point, "even just mundane life stuff, helps me feel supported, connected, loved."

She watched his reaction, knowing from his sisters that Wade had been far too disconnected since leaving the Marines. Though he said nothing in reply, his averted gaze, grim set to his mouth and furrowed brow spoke volumes.

He led a loner lifestyle, even when working at the ranch, preferring time in the pastures checking fences or rounding up strays to sharing duties with other hands. For someone who had been so outgoing and full of life in high school, always ready with a joke and surrounded by friends and family, this change in Wade's routine and persona were troubling to Harlow.

"You've been talking to my family, haven't you?" he said, his attention fixed on a spot across the room.

She didn't pretend not to know what he meant. "They're worried about you. The changes in your personality. They love you, Wade, and just want to help."

"Can they change the past?"

"Of course not. But they—"

"Then there's nothing they can do for me." He stood abruptly and carried his mug to the coffeepot, where he dumped more of the hot liquid in so fast it sloshed over the rim. He cursed under his breath and sucked coffee from his fingers.

"Wade," she said quietly after a moment in which the silence seemed to vibrate with emotion. "I know that it's hard to talk about things that are painful and—"

"Don't," he interrupted, his gaze fixed out the window over the sink.

"You can talk to me." She had to say it, had to at least try to reach him.

He turned, his unpatched blue eye blazing. "Don't patronize me."

She blinked and shook her head. "I'm not! I care about you, Wade. I want to help, if you'll let me. I can see the pain you're carrying and, like your family, I hate seeing you hurt."

"I'm fine," he said tersely, the balling of his hands and clenching of his teeth contradicting his assertion. "I didn't come here today to get psychoanalyzed. I came to help *you* find the creep who's threatening you. To protect you."

She lifted her chin. "Why? Why would you do that for me?"

Her question clearly startled him. "What do you mean, why? You've been threatened by a stalker. I'm not going to stand by and let some guy with an unreasonable grudge hurt you."

Keeping her face placid, she repeated, "Why do you want to do that?"

He clearly caught her drift and gave her a disgruntled sigh. "It's not the same thing. Your life is in danger, and I'm trained with weapons and defense skills that can keep you safe."

"And your mental health is in danger, and I'm trained with the tools and skills to keep you safe."

He snorted and drained the contents of his mug rather than answer her. After thunking the coffee cup in the sink, he strode to the kitchen door, pausing only long enough to say, "I'm going to check on the progress of the camera installation."

Harlow sighed. She was used to having to break down walls of resistance. The first step, admitting one had problems, meant making yourself vulnerable. Asking for help was often the hardest step for her clients. Wade had had eighteen months to build and strengthen the walls he'd erected, believing the fortifications would shut out his pain rather than trap him alone with it. Breaking down those walls would take time. Patience. Determination. For the sake of the man she'd once loved with her whole heart, she would not give up on Wade.

Chapter Twelve

Harlow and Wade spent the day working on her parents' house, and he quizzed her further on the *Harlow Helps* episodes he'd listened to. Had she followed up on Joey? Had she heard anything out of the ordinary in Victor's call? What happened when she talked offline to Sharon? Harlow answered all of his questions, but still no one stood out.

What had been obvious was that Harlow still made his body hum and stirred a restless need in him. He hadn't been with a woman in a couple years, and being around Harlow was feeding the sexual tension coiled inside him. Watching her bend over or reach for upper shelves, inhaling her scent, brushing against her as they collaborated on cleaning and sorting, was a slow torture. He wanted her so badly, but how could he make a move when he had nothing to offer her but a tumble in the sheets?

By 6:00 p.m., the cameras and the door and window alarms had been installed, and Sloan had trained Harlow on their use. Sloan checked with her tech people, but they had no good leads on the stalker either.

Wade should have felt better about Harlow's safety, but the idea that some unknown *someone*, some unknown *somewhere* was gunning for Harlow left him off-balance in a way even his accident hadn't.

At least with the explosion, his injury and his guilt over Sanders's death, he knew who the enemy was. He had a specific something where he could direct his anger, focus his attention and start putting broken pieces back together. He had none of that with Harlow's stalker. The obscurity left him with a sense of helplessness that gnawed at his gut. He was a Marine, damn it! He didn't do helpless. He had to find a way to protect Harlow regardless of the circumstances.

Wade watched from the front window as Sloan's taillights disappeared down the neighborhood street. After the shrill sound of drills and rumble of workmen's voices filling the air all day, the Joneses' house seemed oddly quiet now. He listened for the snick of the front door lock as Harlow returned from seeing Sloan off, and when her feet tapped on the foyer floor, he turned to meet her gaze as she entered the living room.

"It's getting late. I don't want to keep you if—"

"No." He lifted one shoulder. "I'm in no rush. Nothing waiting at home for me other than canned soup and whatever's airing on ESPN."

She crossed the floor to him and angled her head as she eyed him, grinning wryly. "If you're trying to wrangle a dinner invitation with that canned soup line…"

He chuckled lightly. "No wrangling. Just speaking the truth."

"Hmm. Still, I do have the rest of that lasagna Mrs. Norris brought over."

"True."

"And most of Mrs. Vanderbilt's lemon pound cake…which will do my thighs no favors if I eat the whole thing myself."

"I'd be remiss if I let any harm come to your thighs," he quipped back, but growing more serious he added, "Or any other part of you."

Her head came up, and she gave him a skeptical look.

He shoved aside the niggle of doubt and said, "I should stay here tonight."

She chortled as she squared her shoulders. "Oh really? I invited you for dinner, not a sleepover."

"Just the same, security system or not, I don't feel right about you being here alone tonight. Not while that guy is still out there, still a threat."

She took a beat, a breath, shifted her weight. "Wade, this is why I didn't say anything about the stalker earlier. I don't want to be a burden, to inconvenience anyone or cause undue worry. If you hadn't seen that text, I might never have told you."

"Then I'm glad I saw it. You need someone watching your back."

"And you're volunteering?"

He flipped up a hand as if that should be obvious. "I am."

She sent him a dubious frown. "Do you really think you're the best person for that job?"

He stiffened at the unspoken reasons behind her doubts. His voice tight, he said, "Despite appearances, I'm perfectly capable of defending you from an assailant."

"I didn't mean—"

"My vision isn't as bad as Chase implied yesterday," he continued over her, "and my body has healed enough that I'm physically capable of anything I could do before." Feeling peevish and still jittery with the sexual energy that had been firing in him all day, he took fiendish pleasure in stepping so close to her their bodies touched. In a husky tone, he added, "Anything."

He heard the sexy catch in her breath, telling him she got the message loud and clear. But what would she do with the information?

As if in answer to his private question, she took a measured step back from him. "Not a good idea, Wade."

He battled down the stab of hurt her refusal caused but kept his tone even as he replied, "What's not a good idea? My spending the night or what might happen between us if I did?"

She raised a shaky hand to push her hair behind her ear, and she sounded flustered when she said, "Either. Both. I— Wade, I'd be lying if I said I wasn't still attracted to you, but…" She turned and put more distance between them. "Surely you can understand why anything physical between us could only open old wounds."

Before he could acknowledge or deny her assertion, she forged on. "And for similar reasons, I have to believe that you becoming any further involved in my problem with the stalker is unwise. We don't need to be getting entangled again. It can only end badly. My safety is not your problem."

For several moments, he only stared at her, digesting her determination to push him away. Since returning to Owl Creek after the munitions accident, he'd been the one keeping his distance from people. He'd sworn to others and himself that he wanted to be left alone, to brood, to think, to sort out the turmoil in his life, in his mind. The irony didn't escape him that when he found someone he wanted close, she kept him at arm's length. Not that he blamed her.

He couldn't give her the kind of soul-to-soul intimacy she'd want from a sexual relationship. They'd already tried that, and it had failed painfully.

Despite her assertion that the creep who kept sending increasingly dark messages and harassing her wasn't his problem, wasn't his battle to fight, he wouldn't—*couldn't*—let this situation go. He already had Sanders's blood on his hands. He refused to add Harlow's due to negligence or dereliction.

Finally, he cleared his throat and firmed his jaw. "I'm making it my problem, because I believe the situation with this stalker is more serious than you're willing to admit." She flinched, and he raised a hand to calm her. "I'm not saying that to scare you or weasel my way into your life. But to my mind, anyone sick enough, determined enough to find ways around all the roadblocks you've already thrown up, is someone dangerous enough to follow through with hurting you. I choose not to stand aside and let this creep have that chance."

THE NEXT MORNING, Harlow stumbled out of her bedroom and found Wade already awake and doing some kind of stretching or strengthening exercises on her living room floor. "Morning, early bird."

He glanced up, pausing from his regimen long enough to acknowledge her with a nod and quirk of his lips that might be called a grin if she was loose with the definition. "Morning." He continued his workout. "I just have a little more stretching to do. I had to stretch to keep the scars from contracting as they healed, and I've kept up the routine just because…"

"I see. Can I fix you some breakfast? Or coffee?"

"Already had coffee. Hannah woke me at the butt-crack of dawn, calling and wondering where I was."

"Why would she think you were anywhere other than at home?"

He shoved to his feet, still stretching his arms and shoulders. Harlow caught her breath, savoring the sight of all those glorious muscles rippling and flexing. Clearly his ranch work had kept him in good shape since coming home.

"Because she went by my place last night kinda late, and I wasn't home," he said, dragging her attention away from her lusting, "which for me was unusual. And while she didn't panic last night, when I still didn't answer her knock early this morning, she got worried."

"How early?" Harlow said, pulling her new phone out of her pocket to check the time. "I didn't sleep that late, did I?" The screen read 7:32. Luna rubbed against her calf and meowed that it was well past breakfast time.

"She had a morning catering job. Breakfast for a business conference somewhere out of town. I didn't catch the details." He grunted as he shook his head. "If I'd known my family was going to be checking up on me, I'd have told someone I was staying with you. I swear, they've been like helicopter parents hovering over me since I got back last year. I can't even sneeze without someone in my family assuming I need around-the-clock care and monitoring."

"Had you sneezed around Hannah?" Harlow asked with a lopsided grin. "Is that why she was stopping by your house so early?"

"No, she wanted me to know Lucy had lost a tooth and was eager to show me. When I didn't answer the door, she thought Jessie had done something to hurt me, or Acker had come after me for some reason."

Now a warmth filled his face. "Anyway, Lucy wants me to help her price her tooth, so she can leave a bill for the tooth fairy." He gave a soft grunt that might have been a chuckle. "God that little girl's something else. Already quite the negotiator."

Harlow smiled and bent to lift Luna into her arms. "Can't wait to meet this aspiring businesswoman."

"So come with me this afternoon. We're meeting at Book Mark It at four. Hannah is taking Lucy to the story time and cocoa hour after school." Wade strolled closer, stopping to scratch Luna's head.

This close to him, she could smell the crisp scent of soap and see the dampness in his hair that indicated he'd already showered. She *had* been sacked out if she hadn't heard the shower running.

She was usually a light sleeper. But then, lack of sleep while worrying about her stalker had been building. Between accumulated fatigue and the assurance and security she'd felt knowing Wade was close, Harlow had gotten the comfortable night's rest she needed.

Wade made her feel safe. A tangle of relief and regret swelled inside her as she acknowledged the truth.

"Surely you can take a short break from working on the house to get coffee with Hannah and me," Wade said, before heading into the kitchen.

Luna jumped from Harlow's arms and followed Wade, her meow insisting she be fed.

Harlow shook herself out of her distracted thoughts and padded into the next room. "I'd love to meet Lucy and have another chance to visit with Hannah." Harlow pulled the used coffee filter out of the machine and carried it to the trash. "If you'll start a fresh pot of joe, I'll get Miss

Meow her breakfast. You sure I wouldn't be intruding if I go this afternoon?"

He nodded, and as he filled the carafe at the sink, he said, "You're more than welcome. In fact, I'd prefer you come instead of me leaving you here alone."

She rolled her eyes. "I'm sure I'd be fine. Isn't that what the new security system is about?"

"Just the same..."

"Just the same... I'd appreciate the chance to go. All too soon, I'll be done cleaning out the house and moving on. I want to spend as much time with old friends as I can before then." From the corner of her eye, she saw Wade pause, his hands stilling as he measured coffee into the filter. His jaw tightened, and his brow furrowed before he exhaled and continued his task. "You okay?"

He sent her a flat look and grumbled, "Why wouldn't I be?"

She shrugged and let the matter drop. Somehow she'd poked a bear. But how specifically? She could imagine he got tired of people asking if he was okay. His sensitivity to his siblings' delicate treatment of him was obvious. Rather than press the matter, she changed the subject. "I thought I'd tackle the basement today." Harlow filled Luna's bowl with dry food and refreshed her water. "My dad had a lot of fishing equipment and baseball memorabilia stored down there. Feel free to claim anything you want for yourself. The rest of it is getting donated to charity or getting trashed."

He jerked a nod as he turned the coffee maker back on, and it hissed as it heated up. As he opened the cabinet to the right and took down a box of cereal, Harlow was struck by a powerful sense of déjà vu, which was crazy because she'd certainly never woken up with Wade in her house and made breakfast with him.

Yet in high school, she'd pictured this sort of scene—an average day, a life with Wade, mornings as his wife—so often. Perhaps all she was feeling was a longing. The circumstances of her life were not what she'd ever dreamed for them, but had her private fantasies been enough to manifest this moment? She knew plenty of practitioners who believed in visualization as a tool for achieving change.

Wade nudged her, and he gave her a funny look. "Hey, I need to get the milk."

Harlow's cheeks heated as she stepped back from blocking the refrigerator door. He'd caught her daydreaming again, lost in bittersweet memories and heartbreaking wishes that could never be.

"I've been thinking about your shows and what might have triggered the stalker," he said as he sat down with the cereal and milk.

Harlow moaned. "Could we, just for today, not talk about that?"

"But we need to find the guy."

Her shoulders drooped. "I know that better than anyone, but Sloan is working on it, Fletcher is aware of him, and the LAPD has a report. Just for a day or two, I don't want to dwell on the stalker. I finally got a good night's sleep last night, and I want to savor the semi-calm in my soul."

He twisted his mouth. Nodded. "Okay. But I'm still going to call Sloan later and run ideas by her, see what she's found."

Harlow chuckled. "It's been less than two days. Give her time to work!"

He put his spoon down and reached for her hand. "I

admit I'm impatient. But every minute the cops don't come up with anything is a minute you're still in danger. That's not something I can ignore."

"Your being with me is plenty. I got my first good night's sleep in weeks because I knew you were close and looking out for my protection. You don't have to solve the case for the police, too."

"But I want—"

"I know. And I thank you. But the best thing you can do today for my peace of mind is distract me."

He exhaled and squeezed her hand. "Okay. But tonight, I'll be listening to more of your broadcasts. I won't rest until I know you are safe."

A warmth spread through her as she squeezed his fingers back, a sense that went deeper than gratitude and momentary relief from the constant buzz of anxiety over the disturbing texts.

That odd sense, what Harlow could only call *rightness*, stayed with her throughout the morning as they worked side by side. Sharing the tedious sorting together felt good. Making lunch together felt natural. The easy patter of their conversation felt familiar. What's more, she sensed that Wade was growing more comfortable around her. He seemed...happier. Less guarded. His body language was more relaxed. And while the old and easy rapport between them seemed to be returning, the familiarity was also increasingly poignant for Harlow. The more she and Wade got along and found their old pattern and chemistry, the harder it would be when she had to leave town. The house would be cleaned out in a few more days, and she'd have no good excuse to stay put. For her safety's sake, she felt compelled to keep moving, change cities, stay a step or two ahead of her stalker.

At three forty-five, the alarm Wade had set on his phone buzzed, and he shoved the box he'd been sorting out of the way. "We need to head out if we're going to meet up with Hannah and Goose."

"Goose?"

He shrugged. "That's what I call Lucy. Lucy Goose."

Just the fact that the tough Marine had a sweet nickname for his young niece gave Harlow a warm feeling in her belly. Wade would have been such a good father. No, not past tense. He would still be a great father. Knowing they wouldn't be her children sent a sharp pain slicing through her. The ache was an all-too-clear reminder why she'd avoided Owl Creek in recent years, why spending so much time with Wade was dangerous to her heart. She pasted on a fake smile for Wade and said, "Let me get my purse, and I'll be ready to go."

WADE GLANCED ACROSS the front seat of his truck to Harlow, realizing she had dust on her cheek from one of the old boxes they'd sorted that morning. Something warm and tender tugged in his chest.

All too soon, I'll be done cleaning out the house and moving on.

Her comment that morning, tossed out so casually, had rocked something deep in his core. The irony. The truth he'd hated accepting. Harlow was not staying in town. Before, he'd been the one bailing on Harlow and Owl Creek. And now the tables were turned.

She was just passing through his life, a flash of nostalgia that hurt too much to examine closely. Maybe this time with her was supposed to be about closure. Forgiveness. Finally shutting the door on what they'd had together.

He might pretend to the world that he'd moved on after making the hard call to end his relationship with Harlow years ago, but he hadn't been able to erase her from his heart. For the first time in far too long, he'd been hopeful he could repair some of the damage he'd done at age nineteen. He could admit now that he'd made mistakes back then. But when she'd been so opposed to the idea of a life in the military with him, had begged him to follow a different route, he'd believed he was making the right choice.

Wasn't it better, kinder to make a clean break than string her along through murky years of a dying long-distance relationship? Hadn't he, in helping on the ranch with wounded animals, always heard a clean cut, even an amputation, healed faster and was more humane than a wound left to fester?

Apparently, his heart had not gotten that message. Harlow had never left his thoughts, his desires, his dreams of the future. And now, knowing some creep was threatening her made him see red.

After they parked, a couple blocks down from the bookstore, he and Harlow walked down the sidewalk, side by side, and yet, in so many ways, miles apart. They stopped now and again for Harlow to stare in a storefront window at the shop's wares or take in the structural changes to renovated buildings she remembered as other things during high school. "I can't get over how much has changed, how much the town has grown and updated since I left."

"You never came back for holidays with your parents or summer visits?" Hannah had told him as much, but he found it hard to believe. If she'd loved Owl Creek, had called it her home, why...?

"Not really. They came to see me in LA mostly, or we went to Lake Tahoe together for vacation, or if I did need to come to town for some reason, like Dad's funeral and later Mom's, I stayed close to home and was in and out pretty quickly." She angled her gaze up at him. "Too many ghosts, you know?"

His heart kicked. Yeah, he knew. Considering he had avoided Owl Creek and kept to Colton Ranch or his parents' house when he came home from the Marines, he had little room to judge her. Yet considering her vehemence on the night they broke up that she couldn't give up the home she'd found in Owl Creek to follow him in a military career, the news surprised him.

When they reached Book Mark It, he held the door for Harlow and another woman, who gave him the side-eye as they entered. Trying to ignore the woman's curious look, he inhaled the inviting aromas of fresh coffee, woodsmoke and new books as the door swung shut behind him.

Just inside the door, the stout woman stopped to glance around the shop, scowling, then quipped to Harlow, "A fireplace in a store full of paperback books? Bold choice or asking for disaster?"

Wade tried to place the grumpy lady, wondering if her curious look was because she remembered him, remembered how he *used* to look, but he didn't recognize her. However, his family had said many out-of-towners now populated the area, thanks to the growing tourism for the winter skiing in the mountains and summer water sports on Blackbird Lake.

"I think the fireplace is charming and cozy," Harlow

said, wiggling out of her coat. "Perfect for story time on a cold afternoon."

The woman gave Harlow a condescending look, then headed to the counter to order.

Wade took Harlow's coat from her. "I'll hang that up."

"Uncle Wade!" Lucy shouted as she and Hannah entered, letting another cold blast of air inside. "You made it!"

"Of course I made it. I understand you lost a tooth and need some advice from me?" He bent to pull his niece into a hug that lifted the girl's feet from the floor. "Show me this new hole in your mouth."

Lucy opened wide, sticking a finger in her mouth to point. "Wight hehw."

Hannah had met Harlow halfway across the floor and folded her in a hug. "Let's get a table over there, near the story time circle."

Wade carried Lucy with him as he moved to the table where the ladies had seated themselves, telling Lucy, "So here's what I think," he said, loud enough for Hannah to hear. "Each time you lose a tooth, it becomes more and more valuable to the tooth fairy, because it means you have fewer left to lose. It's the scarcity principle in economics."

Lucy's eyes widened. "Huh?"

"It means, your tooth should get…hmm, ten bucks from the tooth fairy, minimum."

Hannah made a choked noise and raised a glare to her brother.

"Ten dollars?" Lucy said with an excited squeal. She wiggled down from his arms and rushed to her mother. "Did you hear that? Uncle Wade say I should ask the tooth fairy for ten dollars! That's enough to get a Junie B. Jones book!"

Hannah gave her daughter a forced smile. "Yes. It is."

Then with a glance to the rug in front of the fireplace, she added, "Looks like story time is starting. Better grab a seat."

Wade reached in his pocket as he claimed a chair next to Harlow and slipped his sister a ten-dollar bill. "Don't worry. I've got you covered."

Hannah shook her head, trying to push the money back. "I can cover my daughter's tooth fairy expenses," she said in a low voice, "but we really need to talk about how this family spoils her."

Wade shoved the cash toward Hannah again. "If she's spending it on books, I don't consider her spoiled. Just smart."

"I agree," Harlow said.

Hannah rolled her eyes as she accepted the money and turned to slip it in her purse.

A sense of satisfaction filled Wade as he sat back in his chair, but the contentedness was short-lived. The prickly feeling of being watched, one he was all too familiar with since his accident, rippled through him. One of the many reasons he chose to stay close to home was the awkward sense of being on display because of his injuries. He felt awkward in public with his eye patch and the pink scars on his hand and the side of his face. He clenched his back teeth and scanned the room.

The woman who'd come into the store with them stared openly. He shifted uncomfortably and scowled. Rather than glance away, he met the woman's stare boldly with his own glare. He didn't care if his actions were rude. He was sick of people staring, sick of being made to feel like a freak because of his injuries. Finally, the woman looked away, took her coffee and left the store.

"Wade? What is it?" Harlow asked, touching his arm.

He shook his head, dismissing the incident. The last thing he wanted to do was bring any more attention to his injuries and the issues he now dealt with all too often. "Nothing."

Harlow's gaze lingered a moment, then turned back to Hannah, who continued with the story she was telling.

"Anyway, I think the lock must be frozen or something," Hannah said, "because I can't get the door open. I called both Fletcher and Chase to see if they can fix it, but neither of them has come by yet. So I had to work with only a fraction of my usual chafing dishes."

"What's stuck?" he asked. "Is it something I can help with?"

Hannah twisted her mouth and wrinkled her nose. "I didn't want to bother you. Chase will probably get to it tomorrow."

Wade sighed. "Get to what?"

His sister licked her lips and hesitated. "The door on the storage shed behind my house is jammed. I can't get inside the shed, and that's where I keep a lot of my extra equipment for catering jobs. I have a big job next weekend and need what's in there. I already had to get creative at my job this morning."

"Why not call me? I'm a lot closer than Chase or Fletcher and have more free time these days."

"I…didn't want to bother you," she said, her grimace saying she knew the excuse was thin.

Shoving down his irritation, he met Hannah's gaze evenly. "I'll have it open by dark tonight."

Hannah opened her mouth, her expression reluctant,

when Harlow cut in. "Great! Problem solved! You know, he's been a big help to me packing my parents' house."

His sister blinked. "He has? Oh...good. I didn't know you'd taken leave from the ranch."

He shrugged. "Things were slow because of winter, so I asked for a few days to help Harlow out."

Hannah divided a look between Harlow and Wade. "I see."

"Don't read anything into it. I just needed someone tall and strong to do some reaching and lifting. And, of course, the free labor for all the stuff in between." Harlow gave him a smile and a wink. "So...what's this big catering job you have? And when do I get to try your wares?"

The conversation shifted away from him, and he mentally thanked Harlow for coming to his defense. Like she had so many times in high school, her verbal rescue now showed she still had his back, could sense what he needed and had been there for him. When he caught her gaze a moment later, he mouthed, *thank you*. And she smiled.

THE NEXT DAY, Harlow turned her attention to the rest of the boxes she and Wade had dragged up from the cold, damp basement the previous morning. As they worked, they continued listening to the recorded episodes of *Harlow Helps*, trying to single out the caller who might have been triggered by her advice...and growing more concerned that the answer wasn't in the recorded episodes. Anyone who'd listened could have taken umbrage to what she'd said. Or the stalker could be a random individual who got his kicks terrorizing women. But reviewing the broadcasts seemed to give Wade a sense of purpose and usefulness, so they persisted.

As they sorted the boxes, Harlow was surprised at how much her parents had kept, considering they'd moved time and again with her father's changing military assignments. Boxes full of her childhood toys and books, knickknacks acquired from vacations all over the globe, tools for her father, outdated home decor her mother had kept, more pillows and quilts than they'd ever use, and sports equipment that reflected the variety of locales they'd called home. Boogie boards from their years in Florida, skis from their time in Colorado, the pink basket and bell she'd had on her first bicycle when they lived in Texas, snowshoes from their years in Germany.

She found herself lingering over the memorabilia, letting her mind recall the houses, the schools, the friends, the unique traditions of the far-flung locations. "As much as I hated the transient lifestyle," she said, and Wade glanced up from the stack of magazines he was tying up for recycling, "I certainly got a broad education and exposure to so many cultures."

"Join the Navy and see the world. Wasn't that the recruiting mantra of old?" Wade asked.

"I think I've heard that before. But my dad was in the Army."

Wade lifted a shoulder. "And I was a Marine, but I still got stationed in the Middle East and a brief assignment in Japan."

Harlow chewed her lower lip. "It's just that when you're a kid, trying to make friends, trying to figure out who you are, wanting stability in your life, the constant movement and changing scenery gets old. All I wanted for so many years was just to feel like my family had a place to put down roots. I wanted to keep the same friends for more than two years, wake up in a room that felt familiar and safe, and finally be able to call a place 'home' and know it would stick."

Wade grunted as he sat back on his heels. "And after living in this small, remote town my whole life, I was champing at the bit to get the hell out of Owl Creek."

"Yeah," Harlow said, her tone sad. "The key difference and great divide we hadn't seen coming until too late."

Wade's jaw tightened, and he shoved to his feet, grabbing a few stacks of bundled magazines. "I'll put these in the back room until we're ready to take a load to the recycling drop-off this weekend."

Harlow rose from the living room floor as well and stretched the kinks from her back and shoulders. She glanced around at the sorted piles stacked in all four corners of the room. They'd made significant progress but still had more to do. Would she be here another week?

She laughed at herself for having thought she could do the job over a long weekend. Her parents' whole lives were stored in this house, forty-five years of marriage and numerous moves and rearing Harlow together. She rubbed the spot in her chest where a hollow pang settled, the sting of grief for her parents and the memories she was packing away.

Hearing the rumble of an engine, Harlow glanced up. Situated at the end of a cul-de-sac, her parents' house had little drive-by traffic. Was another neighbor bringing a meal?

A dark blue pickup truck with a US Mail decal on the door was at the mailbox at the street curb. She reached the window in time to see the arm poking from the driver's window close the mailbox and the truck drive away. She furrowed her brow in confusion. She'd notified the post office that her mother was deceased and the house was vacant. All deliveries should have stopped.

"Hey, Wade, I'm running down to the mailbox," she called as she moved to the foyer to put on her coat. "Be back in a second."

Wade appeared from the hall, folding the sleeves of his shirt up his forearms. "What'd you say?"

She aimed a thumb toward the door. "Mailman just put something in my box. I'm going to see what it is."

His dark brow dipped, his face expressing skepticism. "You're sure it was the mailman? Seems kinda late in the day for deliveries."

"That's what the truck door said. I'll be right back."

Wade's mouth opened as if he were going to say something else about her errand, but she slipped out the door and hurried down the front steps. She walked carefully down the driveway, spotting patches of ice, and shivered as a stiff wind buffeted her.

At the bottom of the driveway, she cast a glance down the street, but the delivery truck was long gone. Moving over to the mailbox, she opened the box and made a mental note that for street appeal, she might need to repaint the—

From the inside the dark mailbox, she heard an angry hiss. And a large snake launched out at her.

Chapter Thirteen

Harlow screamed and jumped back several steps, stumbling and slipping on a patch of ice. She fell on her backside as the snake landed on the pavement, writhing inches from her. Recognizing the snake as a rattler, she screamed again and scuttled crab-style until she could roll to her feet. Turning to look for the viper, she saw the creature slither quickly across the road and into the woods opposite her parents' house. Casting a wary eye back on the mailbox, she found the open end of a plain white pillowcase hanging out of the box, no doubt how the snake had been transported.

She trembled from the inside out, and nausea sawed in her gut.

The pounding of running feet sounded behind her, and she spun to fall into Wade's arms as he rushed to her.

"What happened? Harlow, are you all right?" Wade lifted her hands, which bled from being skinned on the street when she fell.

She shuddered, replaying the blur of motion as the serpent shot out from the mailbox, fangs bared. "S-snake... rattles-s-snake!"

Beneath her embrace, his body tensed. "What?"

Clutching at his shirt, she pointed toward the woods

where the rattler had disappeared. "It slithered off th-that way!"

He shoved her to arm's length so he could examine her. "Did it bite you?"

Shock had so numbed her, she hadn't even considered that. As he gave her an up-and-down appraisal, she took inventory as well. Her hands stung and bled, and her bottom ached from dropping so hard on the pavement. She'd bitten her tongue and tasted the coppery tang of blood in her mouth, but she didn't—

Wade's expression darkened as he focused his attention on her puffy coat. He fingered the fabric next to two small, neat holes, spaced an inch apart near her shoulder. "It got you. Or your coat anyway. Without that puffy coat, we could've been making a trip to the ER."

Knowing how close the strike came to her face, Harlow gasped. "Ohmygod." Casting a wary eye to the woods, she asked, "What do we do? It…it went that way." She pointed across the street, her hand trembling.

"Nothing about the snake," Wade said, drawing her close again and buffing her back with soothing strokes.

Her chin shot up as she angled her gaze to meet his. "Nothing?" She heard the note of near-hysteria in her tone. "I don't want that thing hanging out around the house, waiting to jump at me again when I take out the trash or—"

The low chuckle rumbled from his throat. "Trust me, sweetheart. As little as you want to do with the snake, he wants even less to do with humans. I'm sure that, one, he's long gone, and, two, his first priority right now is finding someplace he can burrow in, curl up and hibernate. Snakes are cold-blooded, and whoever put him in the box clearly woke the poor thing from his winter nap. No wonder it was pissed off."

She stepped closer to his warmth, unable to banish the chill that had seeped to her bones, a cold that had nothing to do with the January weather. She swallowed hard as she considered the truth of his reply. "I guess you're right."

He grunted, clutching her close. "The bigger question is who put it in there. This was clearly a malicious act."

Her mouth dried as the most likely scenario finally dawned on her. "It was…him. He found me."

WADE GUIDED HARLOW back inside the house and had her sit at the kitchen table while he fixed her a hot drink and called Fletcher. Harlow's assertion replayed in his head like a bad earworm. *He found me.* He had to agree with her. He could see no other reasonable explanation for someone to put a poisonous snake in her deceased parents' mailbox.

Once he'd summoned his brother so Harlow could file a report and get the local cops started on the case, Wade took his own mug of coffee and sat in the chair beside her.

She stared at the walnut table, her face a mask of horror and tension, her drink cradled between her hands but obviously forgotten. When he gave her shoulder a comforting rub, she twitched as she snapped out of her daze, sloshing the hot tea and angling her gaze up to his.

With a heavy exhale, she gave her head a slight shake and reached for a napkin to mop up the spilled tea. "I'm sorry. Geez, I'm a ball of nerves."

"Don't apologize. More than most people, I can understand being jittery after a scare." He wrapped both hands around his mug, wondering why he'd admitted such a telling detail. But then she'd already witnessed one of his episodes. His aversion to sudden loud noises was no secret to her.

He took a sip of his coffee, and when he cut a side glance at her, he met her searching brown eyes. She covered his wrist with her hand and squeezed. "I suppose so. Any chance you'd tell me the story behind your scare the other day?"

He was spared from answering when the doorbell rang. Harlow stood to answer it, and he pushed his chair back. "Let me go. Just...in case."

Her eyes widened, clearly alarmed by the notion that her stalker could be at her door, as unlikely as it was that the creep would bother to ring the bell. Wade found Fletcher and one of the other patrolmen from the city police department on Harlow's porch, and he let them in.

"She's back here." Wade led them into the kitchen and ignored the obvious question in his brother's gaze about what he was doing at Harlow's house to begin with.

Harlow stood as Fletcher and the uniformed officer, who introduced himself as Brad Kline, entered the kitchen. Fletcher gave Harlow his full attention, becoming all business as Harlow explained what happened, detailed the snake's escape and told him about the empty pillowcase.

Fletcher asked for further description of the dark colored truck with the USPS insignia on the door, but Harlow couldn't remember any more detail. "While it was curious to me that I was getting a delivery, I didn't see it as a threat...at the time. And I only caught a glimpse of the truck as it hurried off, so I didn't get a plate number. I assumed the delivery was real because of the logo on the truck."

Officer Kline rested his hands on his gun belt. "The

insignia on the door would be easy enough to obtain. A number of mail carriers in the rural areas around here use their personal vehicles with a magnetized postal logo on the door. The person who left the snake could have stolen the decal from a legit delivery person."

"I'll check with the local post office and see if any of their delivery people drive a dark blue pickup or have reported their car decal missing," Fletcher said. "I know you had a security system installed earlier this week. Do any of your cameras face the street? Would you have any images of the truck that might help?"

Harlow glanced at Wade, then shook her head. "The cameras just monitor the perimeter of the house, the doors and windows."

Fletcher pressed his mouth in a hard line of frustration. "Well, we'll do our best, of course. As we leave, we'll collect the pillowcase as evidence, and I'll have forensics out shortly to dust the mailbox for prints. Beyond that… I can ask the chief to assign extra drive-by patrols for the neighborhood. And I'm always just a phone call away. Wade has my number."

She nodded and a strained smile touched her lips. "Thanks, Fletcher."

Wade's brother turned to him, adding, "Security system or not, it might be wise for you to stay with her tonight, in case the guy comes back."

"Way ahead of you, brother." Wade sent Harlow a level look as she sipped from her mug. "In fact, I plan to have her move to my cabin until this guy is caught."

Chapter Fourteen

Harlow sputtered and choked on her tea. Setting her drink down with a clunk and wiping her mouth with her fingers, she wheezed, "Excuse me?"

"You heard me. Your stalker has shown he's far too determined to track you down and menace you. If he does come back, I don't want you here, security cameras or not. Better that you move to a new location. My cabin is off the beaten path, and I can keep an eye on you."

Harlow blinked and coughed again before she shook her head. "Wade, I appreciate the offer—"

"It's not an offer. It's a fact. You need to relocate." His jaw set with mulish decisiveness.

Fletcher gave a soft chuckle under his breath. "Buddy, you have a lot to learn about relationships with women. No wonder you're still single."

Wade lifted the eyebrow over his good eye. "You disagree with my assessment?"

"No. She'd definitely be safer at your place. But your delivery needs work." With a glance to Officer Kline, Fletcher hitched his head toward the door and started for the foyer. "Come on, Brad. Let's let the lovebirds hash this out for themselves."

"We're not—" Harlow said at the same time Wade said, "It's not like that."

They exchanged an awkward glance, and Harlow rose from the table to see Fletcher to the door. She thanked him again as they left, then returned to the kitchen where Wade was waiting, his expression brooding.

"I don't think we should—" His stern look stopped her before she finished.

She understood that he could keep her safer if she relocated, so she didn't bother finishing her protest. The dangerous intimacy they'd face with her living under his roof was of far less concern in the big picture than the man threatening her with poisonous snakes.

His expression softening, he gripped her shoulders and met her gaze with a gentle look. "Your opinion counts, of course, but I know how fiercely independent and stubborn you can be. I didn't want to haggle over what is obviously the right choice. You heard Fletcher. You'll be safer with me at my cabin."

"Me, stubborn? You're the one who—" She chuckled and bit off her words again. She didn't want to debate with him. Especially when she still had adrenaline coursing through her after the near miss with the rattlesnake. Instead, she stepped closer to him and let him enfold her in his arms. He rested his chin on the top of her head, and she simply let herself inhale the clean scent of him, wishing she could shut down the anxious thoughts parading through her head.

Her stalker had found her. In Owl Creek. At her parents' house. This was no passive, angry listener who just wanted to rant and spook her. He'd researched her, tracked her, found her when she fled Los Angeles. He meant business, and she knew in her bones she hadn't heard the last of the creep.

"What about Luna?" she asked.

He tipped his head as he frowned down at her. "What do you mean?"

"I'm not leaving my cat here alone. Is Luna allowed at your house?"

His mouth opened and shut. He blinked. Clearly he'd never pictured himself with a feline roaming the halls of his bachelor pad. "Uh, sure. Of course. Bring Luna."

With a sigh, she nodded. "All right then. I'll go pack a bag."

AN HOUR LATER, Harlow had Luna's litter box set up in Wade's utility room, her food and water bowls by the kitchen counter, and her own suitcase and toiletries unpacked in his guest room. With those jobs accomplished, she had no further excuses not to join Wade in his living room, no matter how oddly intimate it felt. She fixed herself a cup of hot tea, then took a seat on the faux leather couch and cast her gaze around the surprisingly stylish decor, which leaned heavily on shades of navy and hunter green and featured a woodsy theme appropriate for a lakeside cabin.

"I like what you've done with the place." She picked up the carved wooden bear tchotchke from the end table next to her and studied it. The bear held a sign that said Welcome to the my den.

Wade grunted. "Thanks, but I rented the place already furnished. Very little of this is mine."

She set the bear down. "Oh. I didn't think the bear was your style. So where are your things?"

"In storage, until I decide my next move." He pressed his mouth in a grim, taut line.

"As in...until your find a house here in Owl Creek or...?" She flipped her hand, inviting him to fill in the blank.

"As in... I don't know what I'm supposed to do next." He sighed heavily, his hands balled, and glanced away. "I never had any other plan besides the Marines. But the explosion changed all that."

His statement was so close to the argument they'd had years ago when they broke up that an unexpected pain slashed through her. She worked to hide her reaction, lifting her mug to sip her tea, not wanting to interrupt Wade when he was finally opening up to her, if only a crack.

When he glanced at her, she met his gaze with an open, encouraging look that asked silently, *Will you tell me about it?*

WADE CLAMPED HIS back teeth tighter, doggedly fighting the quiver of ill ease that stirred at his core. If he gave his nightmare an inch, he feared he'd never get the beast back under control. He'd spent the past several months reining in the images and sounds of fire and screams and earth-shaking blasts. Blocking out the phantom scent of burned flesh and acrid smoke and choking down the bitter taste of bile and fear. "I know I should talk about it. But... I don't know how."

Harlow turned to face him and angled her head. "I am a professional counselor. I could help."

He frowned. "Is that what I am to you? A case to be analyzed?"

Her brow furrowed, and her tone was firm as she said, "No. You are far more to me than a client or a PTSD case to be studied." She reached over and squeezed his wrist. "You're…my friend."

Friend. He let the word sit for a moment, a measure of disappointment settling inside him. "Your friend."

"Well, yeah. Isn't that why I'm here at your house? I wouldn't have thought you'd be concerned about my safety if I weren't your friend."

"But…is that all? I kinda thought the last several days had changed things. Am I wrong that you still feel the chemistry between us?"

Her forehead wrinkled, and she drew her hand back as she sighed. "You're not wrong. But… I can't afford to act on that attraction."

Frustration gnawed at him, but he'd be damned if he'd let her know how her rejection stung. He tore his gaze from her to stare across the room at the stuffed trout mounted on his wall. He'd have been better off not having run into her again, not having fanned that hope of rekindling the passion and connection they'd once had.

After a moment of silence, she added, "That doesn't mean I don't care about you or your happiness. And based on what I've seen in the last week, you aren't happy. You only truly smile when you're with Lucy."

"Because she doesn't judge me or treat me like I'm less of who I was before—" He gritted his back teeth, hating the topic of his accident and how his family still treated him.

"No one thinks you're less of who you were."

He frowned skeptically. "Really? Have you not seen the way they hover and defer and look at me with pity?"

"Not pity, Wade. Concern. They love you, and you have not acted like your old self since you returned. How can you expect them to believe you're okay when you keep to yourself and don't laugh and don't have the same joy for life that you had before?"

He scoffed. "So I'm supposed to pretend a man didn't die on my watch?" Wade heard the sharpness of his tone and immediately regretted it.

She placed a hand on his arm again, and the warmth of the gesture burrowed deep inside him. "No one is asking you to pretend anything, Wade. Pretense is unhealthy and counterproductive. Suppressing genuine hurt and trauma is never the answer."

He fisted his hands and tensed his mouth, knowing she was right but not knowing how to answer. His head throbbed as tension built at his temples.

"When I found that snake in the mailbox and I was shaken and scared, what did you feel? How did you respond?"

Now he jerked his head toward her and scowled. "What? That's—I'd think that was obvious."

His heart raced like it had that afternoon as a fresh wave of panic and cold dread rolled through him.

"Humor me," she pressed. "Why am I here?"

Because I love you, and I'm genuinely scared your stalker will take you from me again.

But all he said was, "Because I was shaken, too, and wanted to help you." And once he'd known she was unharmed, he'd wanted to find the man responsible for trying to hurt her and wreak his vengeance in a most barbaric way.

"So think about how your family felt," she said, her gentle tone in stark contrast to the roil in his gut, "when you were so severely injured in the explosion. Can you imagine how it scared them?"

He didn't have to imagine, because too many times in

the past several months, he'd been terrified when murder, kidnapping and other danger had threatened his family. Just thinking now of his father's death, his brother tangling with a serial killer, or his sister being held hostage by a cult member was enough to fill him with an icy horror. He shuddered and struggled for a breath, shoving the bad memories aside.

"And while you're healing physically," Harlow was saying, "you haven't given them a lot of reason to believe you're healing inside." She tapped her chest at her heart. "Cut them some slack for loving you and wanting to help with your PTSD, huh?"

Wade took a beat, needing a moment calm his spinning thoughts and racing pulse before he could respond. Her request wasn't unreasonable. If he was honest, he didn't like the version of himself that had groused and kept his family at bay.

Had he kept Harlow at bay the same way? Was he scared to open himself to her, show her the true depth of his regrets and doubts? Probably.

His only excuse was that Harlow, even before she'd become a mental health counselor, had known him better than anyone. Even better than his own family. She was the one person most likely to see through any pretense he put up, to call his bluff on his attempts to convince his family and friends that he'd moved on from the explosion, that he didn't still wake at night in a cold sweat and shaking from bad dreams and suffocating from guilt and grief.

Realizing he'd still not answered her question, he muttered, "Of course. I know I've been…difficult. I don't mean to be an ass, I just—" He turned up a palm and left the thought unfinished.

With a nod and a half smile, she withdrew her hand and sipped her tea. "Good."

They sat in silence for another moment before he said, "PTSD, huh?" And there it was, the name he'd been trying to ignore but could no longer deny.

"How can you say I have PTSD without even hearing my whole story?" Wade asked.

Harlow lifted a shoulder and flashed a smile. "I know enough. You were in a bad accident. Loud noises rattle you. Your family says you've been withdrawn, moody, hard to reach."

He gave her a startled look. "Who have you talked to?"

"Hannah and Lizzy directly. All of your siblings indirectly. It's in their eyes when they look at you. I saw it in Chase's expression at the bookstore when we met with him and Sloan. And... I see the changes in you for myself."

A moment passed before he said, "Of course I've changed. My whole world's been flipped on its end. After the explosion, I couldn't work—*anywhere*—and in the last few months..." He scrubbed a hand over his short, cropped hair, and the muscles in his jaw flexed as he gritted his back teeth.

When he spoke again, tension darkened his tone. "I've... procrastinated making any decisions. Ranching is okay, but it's not what I want to do with the rest of my life."

Luna, having finished her exploration of her new digs, strolled into the den and paused by Wade's chair, looking up at him with her whiskers twitching. Wade stuck a hand down for the cat to sniff, and when she bumped his fingers, asking for pats, he lifted the cat onto his lap and stroked Luna's fur. The gesture surprised Harlow, though she couldn't say why. She'd seen Wade's gentle interaction with all kinds of animals throughout high school. Ranch dogs, cattle, horses, chickens, and, yes, the barn cats whose job it was to keep the mouse population under control.

As she watched him run his hand down Luna's back again and again, heard her feline companion's rumbling purr, she imagined a tingle on her own skin, remembered the heady feeling of Wade's hands on her when they'd made out in high school. To an inexperienced teenager, her intimacies with Wade had seemed like the most erotic and exciting thing on earth. And having shared only a couple sexual liaisons since then, both sadly disappointing, he was still her high-water mark of sensual experience.

As a quiver raced through her, she wrapped her arms around herself and averted her gaze. She was *not* jealous of her cat! she told herself, though not convincingly.

"What do you want to do with your life?" she asked, forcing her attention back to the conversation, though she kept her eyes on the dark window across the room.

"If I knew that, I wouldn't still be herding cattle, fixing fences and vaccinating calves for my uncle."

She nodded once. "Touché."

"It's hard to see myself in any other role than the one I dreamed of, trained for, spent a third of my life doing."

The sadness in his voice broke her heart and drew her gaze back to him. Luna hopped down from his lap, and he dusted cat hair from his hands. Despite his glum admission seconds before, Wade seemed...*different* as she studied him now. She bit her bottom lip as she tried to figure out what she was sensing.

"You were always a good student. You had good grades in everything, especially math and physics. Do either of those fields interest you?" she asked, as she began piecing together the subtle change she'd noted. His hands had unclenched. His jaw was more relaxed. His shoulders less tense.

Petting Luna had relaxed him.

A tickle of an idea started but danced just out of reach.

"Hmm. Maybe. I just don't want to commit to anything while I'm still—" His fingers bounced restlessly on the arm of the recliner where he sat. As if noticing his anxious fidgeting, he grabbed one hand with the other, then stared down at the scar tissue on the back of his right hand.

"Wade," Harlow said softly, "will you tell me about the accident? What happened? What is it about that day that still haunts you the most?"

His brow dipped, but he didn't look at her. He remained silent so long, she began wondering if he hadn't heard her question or was refusing to answer.

But finally, he spoke, his voice a whisper at first, hoarse and choked with emotion. "I was responsible for my men. It's on me. Sanders…" He took a shuddering breath. "Sanders died. Just like that. We were joking together just that morning at breakfast. Then at training, I had him go first, setting the charge. I knew he was inexperienced. Nervous. But I turned my back. Just for just a few minutes. To talk to Sergeant Major Briggs. Next thing I knew…" Wade squeezed his good eye shut, grimacing. Shaking.

Harlow launched from the couch to kneel in front of him and take his hands in hers. "It's okay, Wade. You're safe. I'm here."

"I can still hear the blast… Feel the shock wave that knocked me back. The flames that—" Instead of finishing the sentence, he loosed a half growl of frustration, half wail of despair.

She rubbed his arms, leaned in to hug him as he rocked back and forth in agitation. Luna, roused by Wade's anguished cry, trotted over as if to ask what was wrong.

And it clicked. The idea that had niggled earlier jelled.

At lunch a few days earlier, Ruby had talked about the dogs she and Sebastian raised at Crosswinds. Most of the dogs were trained for search-and-rescue, but she'd mentioned PTSD companion dogs as well. Luna had calmed Wade earlier. How much more so would a dog trained to recognize PTSD, taught to ease an owner's stress and quiet their fears? She definitely needed to look into this idea and discuss arrangements with Ruby and Sebastian.

When Harlow's awkward angle, hugging Wade while still kneeling by the large chair, made her back hurt, she pulled away, only to have him grip more tightly on her arms. "Harlow…" he rasped.

Wedging herself into the chair with him, she draped her legs over his and looped her arms around his neck. He pressed his face into the curve of her shoulder and released a trembling sigh. As she held him, feeling his tremors ease, he whispered, "Sanders's death on my watch is the second-worst event of my life. My biggest regret is letting you go."

Chapter Fifteen

Harlow stiffened in his arms, and Wade stopped breathing. Why had he said that aloud? He should have pushed it back down, tucked it away under all the other unspoken things, the rest of the black memories and parts of his life too ugly to look at.

Except now he'd not only shared his guilt over Sanders's death, but he'd shared his sorrow over losing her. *Damn it.* He'd not only exposed the source of his nightmares, he'd admitted a truth that left his heart more vulnerable than it had been in a decade. He hadn't dated anyone while in the Marines. Not seriously, anyhow. Dates, sure. Most of them fix-ups by mutual friends. But how could he get involved with any other woman when his soul still belonged to Harlow?

With his jaw clenched and his eye squeezed shut, he wished he could reel the words back in, erase them from her memory as easily as deleting a computer file. He startled a bit—damn his adrenaline-drenched blood—when she stroked a hand along his cheek. Her sigh escaped as a wisp of breath that bathed his face and teased his senses.

"Wade, look at me. Please."

He didn't want to. Hellfire, he didn't want to see pity

or disgust or censure in her eyes. He considered getting up from his chair and closing himself off in his bedroom. Walking away from this conversation before he dug the pit of shame any deeper. But Harlow was on his lap, and when he nudged her, letting her know she should get up, she stayed.

"Wade," she repeated, her grip on his scarred chin firm.

Man, her touch felt good. He hadn't had gentle hands touching him, loving him, in so long. His body thrummed in response as his turmoil faded and a keen awareness of her bottom snuggled in his lap crackled through him. Harlow was on his lap, in his arms, touching him. He'd longed for this, dreamed of this, ached for this for so long. How could he squander this moment? This chance?

"Talk to me. Don't shut me out. Not now."

If talking to her, opening up about the accident, confessing his culpability in Sanders's death, meant he could hold Harlow close for a few more minutes…

He dipped his chin to press his forehead against hers and whispered, "Sanders died because of my distraction, my dereliction. His blood is on my hands."

In his embrace, Harlow stiffened. She lifted her head and said with a groan, "No. Wade, don't put that on yourself."

"I was his commanding officer, in charge of the exercise that day. I knew he was nervous, that he needed extra coaching and encouragement and careful observation, and I…turned my back. I walked away to talk to another officer and—" He paused as another dark thought occurred to him. "Someone had given us live ammunition instead of inert materials to practice with. I had double-checked the paperwork the night before to be sure I had everything right before the drill that day. But that day I hadn't noticed the screwup. I—"

Fresh waves of well-rehearsed recriminations and shame poured through him, scalding him hotter than the flames that had seared his skin that terrible day.

"No," Harlow said, her tone as hard and unyielding as he'd ever heard it. "Wade, just…stop right now. Stop lashing yourself with these bitter self-indictments."

Her hands framed his face, and she gave him a small shake, saying, "Look. At. Me."

His chest tight, his breath stuck in his throat, he peeked at her, reluctantly. When her thumbs tipped his chin up higher so she could stare more fully into his good eye, his gut flip-flopped. Her dark brown eyes sparked with a passion, a determination and conviction that shook him.

"You did not kill Sanders."

"Maybe I didn't light the fuse, but I was responsible—"

Her grip tightened. "You are *not* to blame for Sanders's death."

He had to swallow several times against the rising bile in his throat before he could counter, "You weren't there. I know you're trying to make me feel better but—"

"Screw feeling better! This isn't about giving you some emotional salve you can spread on when you're feeling guilty."

Her unexpected reply stunned him, silenced him. For a fraction of a second, he allowed himself to feel hurt by her harsh stance.

"I don't want to simply soothe your wounds by applying a comforting balm. I want to help you root out the source of the infection and heal from the inside out. I want you to be healthy going forward, not just stuck in a routine of applying medicines to ease the pain."

Her eyes, locked on his, penetrated to his soul, and something inside shifted.

Not a balm. Real healing.

He thought of all the times people had said how sorry they were for his accident, how often his well-meaning family had offered to do things for him to make his life easier, had pasted on smiles around him and avoided talking about hard topics they thought would trigger bad memories for him. And he'd cringed internally at the pity and deference and soft treatment. And he'd grown more and more isolated to avoid the pitying, worried looks and kindness that only reminded him how far he'd fallen, how different he was now in their eyes, how much he hated the pretense he put up to alleviate their concerns, as well. They were all playacting, tiptoeing around each other.

And he hated all of it.

But Harlow had stormed into town and hadn't shied from confronting him, wanting answers, offering solutions.

He drew a tremulous breath. "How?" Hearing the rasp in his voice, he cleared his throat. "How do I heal?"

A gentle warmth and compassion filled her face. "You have to let the poison out. Lance the wound and drain the stuff you've been letting fester."

He groaned. "You want me to see a shrink, don't you?"

"Not necessarily."

Again, her answer startled him. But then Harlow's unpredictability had been part of her appeal when they dated. Spontaneous trips, taking picnics on hikes after school, making love in a dressing room at the Boise mall, gifts of no real cash value but huge sentimental significance for no reason except she'd thought he'd like it. Choosing Thai food in Conners instead of their social group's regular pizza after a football game…and her refusal to marry him when he left for the Marines.

That had been the biggest surprise of all. She'd wanted to go to college. Understandable, he supposed. She'd thought they were too young. Maybe, but they could have made it work. And she'd wanted to stay rooted in Owl Creek. Unfathomable. All he'd talked about for months was how he couldn't wait to leave the small town in the dust, see the world, serve his country, pursue bigger, better things for their future together. How could she not support him in that dream?

He noted, now, that she had yet to comment on his admission of his regrets concerning their breakup. He knew she'd heard him. He's seen the color wash from her face, felt the shudder that raced through her. Shoving aside memories of her perfidy on that painful night that they split, he eyed her skeptically. "What do you mean? How else am I supposed to *let the poison out*?"

"There are support groups for veterans with PTSD." When he frowned and opened his mouth to reject the idea, she rushed on to say, "*Or*…you could talk to Sebastian. I think he'd understand most anything you're feeling. And he's your best friend."

Wade clenched his back teeth. Admit all his failures and fears to his best friend? Maybe. He knew he could trust Sebastian's confidentiality, but…

"Or me," she said, and he blinked as he returned his attention to Harlow. "You've made a good start tonight. And I will listen whenever you need to talk to someone." She stroked his face tenderly. "We may not be together anymore, but I still care deeply about you. About your happiness."

A bubble of something tenuous swelled in his chest—and then popped as soon as her earlier assertion replayed in his head.

I can't afford to act on that attraction.

He reined his hope, doused the flicker of emotion that sparked whenever he sensed a growing connection with Harlow. She was leaving Owl Creek again. Soon. And she'd told him in so many ways she wouldn't give him her heart again. He'd squandered his chance with her eleven years ago.

"And…" she continued, calling his focus back to what she was saying. Her expression said she was about to drop a radical idea on him. "What would you think about getting a support animal? One of the dogs that Sebastian is training out at Crosswinds?"

He arched one eyebrow. "Most of those dogs are for search-and-rescue."

"True, but not all of them. I hear that Sebastian has started branching out a bit in other specialties."

Sebastian had suggested he get a PTSD-trained companion dog before, but Wade shut him down quickly, not wanting to admit he needed help of any sort. His best friend had offered other kinds of assistance and advice in the past, too. Wade exhaled harshly and scrubbed a hand over his face. Going to Sebastian now with any sort of ask would be…hard. Humbling. Humiliating.

As if reading his mind, Harlow said, "You have to know anything you ask from your family and friends will be greeted with compassion and readiness to help. I'm sure Sebastian and Ruby would move mountains to get you the perfect dog if you'd agree. Your sister and best friend love you as much as—" she stopped short, her mouth open, before finishing awkwardly "—as much as the rest of your family does. They all want what's best for you. Surely you know that?"

He tried not to dwell on the fact that she'd refused to say she loved him—because he sensed that's what had been on her tongue. Instead, he considered her suggestion of getting a companion dog.

"Earlier, when you were talking about your future, your memories of the explosion, you seemed to find some comfort when Luna got on your lap. Animals are well known to be therapeutic, and if you got one trained to help with PTSD…" She turned over a hand as if to let him fill in the blank.

"I don't know." He chewed the inside of his cheek, and her idea tickled his brain, growing more palatable the longer he considered it. "Maybe."

"Do you have a good reason *not* to?" she asked, then fell silent while he stewed, debated, warmed to the idea.

Finally, he threw up his hands and gave a defeated chuckle. "Okay, okay, I'll get a dog!"

Harlow beamed at him for his decision. Her eyes sparkled with joy and pride and relief.

If he weren't already beginning to believe a companion dog would at least be—well, a good companion, he'd have been satisfied with his choice simply to know, this once, he'd made Harlow happy.

After devastating her with the cruel words he'd tossed at her to make their breakup cleaner, anything he could do to make her smile, any effort it took to give her a moment of happiness, was a small price.

"I'll go call Ruby now," she chirped as she started to wriggle off his lap to retrieve her burner phone.

He stopped her with a hand around her wrist. "No need. If I'm going to do this, then I should take complete ownership. I can call Sebastian myself."

"Absolutely." Harlow gave a firm nod. "You are right." Before turning away to climb off his lap, she leaned in and kissed his cheek, catching the corner of his mouth. A quick kiss. A kiss not unlike ones he'd seen her give other friends' cheeks. But the small peck set his blood ablaze and roused memories of greater intimacies he'd shared with Harlow in the past. Rather than release her wrist, his grip tightened, drawing her up short.

Harlow gave him a querying look, and his heart thumped harder against his ribs. Was he bold enough to act on his impulse? He wanted to taste her lips again, wanted to explore the velvet recesses of her mouth and feel her shimmy with pleasure as she had when they were younger. She must have read his intent in his gaze because her breath caught. When he tugged her closer, her pupils dilated and her fingers curled against his chest. He could hear her breath grow shallow and quick…or was that his own?

As he seized his chance, ducking his head to slant his mouth across hers, he whispered, "My God, I have missed you."

Chapter Sixteen

Harlow greeted his kiss with her own, parting her lips to draw fully, deeply on his.

Sliding his hand into her hair, he cradled the back of her head, massaged the tendons of her neck as he slaked years of longing in their kiss. But all too soon, she pushed against his chest and averted her head.

Harlow sighed sadly as she ducked her chin. "Wade, stop. I'm not—we can't—"

When she wiggled to get up this time, he released her, and she scrambled to her feet, crossed the room. Reaching the kitchen door, she paused, not looking at him. "I've spent the last eleven years trying to get over you, trying to put the pain of our breakup behind me."

He swallowed hard as bitter guilt rose in his throat. "I know I hurt you. I said the harsh things I did thinking it would make it easier for you to hate me, to move on."

She spun now to face him. "Hate you? After what we meant to each other, shared together, how could I ever hate you? I hurt *for* you, because I knew I'd let you down. I was selfish. I wouldn't give up the home I'd found in Owl Creek to make a home with you. You were understandably angry with me. I hurt because I knew I'd lost you, because I knew I'd hurt you."

Wade scoffed wryly. "God, Harlow, I never blamed you. I'm the one who left, who joined the Marines and told you I'd never loved you."

His mind whirled. If she blamed herself, if they both were clearly still attracted to each other, was it possible they could rebuild what they'd thrown away? He scooted to the edge of his recliner, narrowing his gaze on her. "Harlow, if we both have regrets over what happened, if we both have blamed ourselves all these years, do you think we could ever—"

Her hand shot up to silence him. "Wade, no. I know where you're going, but I've told you, I'm not back in Owl Creek to stay. My life has changed. We've both changed." She paused, shaking her head and biting her bottom lip. Then with a deep breath, she said, "When we were together before, we had so many things working for us. We had passion and a foundation of friendship and interests in common, but we still failed to make it work when life happened."

We failed...

Wade gritted his back teeth to bite back the growl of frustration her words stirred in him. She meant *he'd* failed. He'd failed to fight for her, failed to prove his love for her, failed to do everything he should have to make her happy.

"How are we supposed to build something that will work now at a time when your life and mine are both in a state of limbo? With so many factors still unresolved, trying to put the pieces of a broken relationship together now is... not a good idea."

And there it was. Her doubt, her lack of faith in him. Not

that he blamed her. He couldn't even see a path forward in his own life. How was she supposed to believe she could depend on him, trust him with her future, when he couldn't even sort out his past?

When he didn't answer her, Harlow glanced away, then headed for the back bedroom. She hesitated only long enough to say, "Thank you for sharing your story with me. I know it was difficult." She cast a quick glance over her shoulder. "But it's an important first step toward rebuilding your life and being happy again."

Bracing his forearms on his thighs, Wade bent his head and thought, *No. You are.*

HARLOW STARED AT the ceiling in Wade's guest bedroom. Her mind was too keyed up, too full of the day's hideous twists, tantalizing moments and heartbreaking revelations to simply turn her thoughts off and find much-needed rest. When she closed her eyes, she saw the fangs of the rattlesnake lunging at her, fiery explosions, Wade lying burned and suffering in a hospital, taunting text messages, and the bleak expression on Wade's face when he'd told her how much he regretted breaking up with her after high school. As much as the physical threat of the snake had shaken her, hearing Wade speak of his grief over losing her, his wish to reunite, was what had left her the most unsettled. And the kiss...

Heaven help her, the kiss had been a mistake. While she was actively trying to quell her misguided longing for Wade, when she'd just finished telling him she couldn't see a way forward for them, why had she let herself be tempted into kissing him back? The last thing she wanted to do was send him mixed messages. He was already tortured by his past and confused about his path forward. Any confusion over her feelings for him could only be unhelpful.

She could have pulled away, told him no. Wade had always honored her choices, respected her no without coercion or guilt. So she could have walked away from the allure of his lips, the heat that had sparked between them. So why hadn't she? And, damn it, now that she knew how strong the pull between them still was, had experienced again the crackle of the electricity that still sizzled with Wade, what did she do with the fire in her blood, the yearning in her soul?

He hadn't pushed when she rebuffed his suggestion that they give their relationship another shot. Wasn't that proof he wasn't fully committed to a reunion? Their life choices were what had pulled them apart before, so how could she risk her heart when he was still uncertain what he wanted for his life going forward?

Had he not pushed back because he saw the truth of her argument? And why was she disappointed he *hadn't* challenged her position? Didn't the past prove that without certainty and a shared commitment, anything else was a recipe for heartache? She knew better than to repeat old mistakes.

She rolled onto her side and punched the pillow, sighing her frustration and choking back the tears that clogged her throat. Luna, who'd been trying to sleep curled at her feet, stood and stretched, casting a baleful glare at Harlow and hopping off the bed.

"I'm sorry, Luna," she whispered, snapping her fingers and clicking her tongue to try to call the feline back to her. She patted the top quilt. "Come on, girl. I promise I—"

She fell silent, hearing an agonized cry from the next room. Tossing back the covers, she padded in her bare feet to the door of Wade's room. A slice of light from the moon and the outside security light spilled across Wade's face. He scowled, and sweat had beaded on his forehead. His body writhed as if in pain, and he moaned again in his sleep.

She blamed herself for his nightmare. She'd encouraged him to relive his accident, to open the wounds he'd swathed in layers of gauzy denial and distance. She hovered there on the threshold, debating whether to wake him or not. It seemed cruel to let him continue the bad dream. But how would he react to being woken? She couldn't imagine he'd enjoy having his nighttime torture set out before her like exhibit A in an examination of his hurting soul.

She stood watching him, debating and hurting for him long enough that after a few moments, his twisting limbs stilled and his grimace relaxed. Releasing a deep breath, she backed from his door and climbed back in her own bed. Luna followed her and curled on the second pillow of the double bed. Stretching out her hand, she sank her fingers in Luna's warm fur and listened to the mesmerizing sound of her cat's purr.

At some point, she finally drifted to sleep, because the next thing she knew, watery light peeked through the curtains and the scent of fresh coffee brewing greeted her. Luna was nowhere around, but she suspected she knew where her cat had gone. The fuzzface was a sucker for an early breakfast.

Sure enough, when Harlow scuffed in her slippers down the short hall to Wade's kitchen, she found Luna rubbing against Wade's legs and meowing insistently.

"Give me a sec, cat. I have to get a plate or something. You know, the barn cats at Colton Ranch get their own breakfast. Ever thought about hunting mice, Luna?" He popped open a can of cat food and dumped it all on a small plate. Moving to a corner of the kitchen, he placed the dish of the floor and tossed the can in the trash. "Bon appetit."

Turning back toward the counter, Wade finally noticed Harlow. The instant joy that crossed his face when he spotted her warmed her heart. But in the next second, he schooled his expression, sobering to a more sedate smile and nod. "Morning."

"Morning. Thanks for feeding the beast. I know she can be a pest about breakfast."

He shrugged. "No big deal. Getting up early and feeding animals is the story of my life these days. I don't mind." He gave his attention to a bowl of beaten eggs waiting to be cooked. "Hungry?"

She chuckled. "Am I another animal to be fed?"

He shook his head. "I'm not going to answer that."

She squeezed his shoulder. "You always were a smart man."

He twitched a grin. "How'd you sleep?"

"Honestly, I…didn't sleep too much. A lot of tossing and turning until the wee smalls." She cast him a tentative glance. "And you?"

"Good enough, I guess."

No mention of his nightmare, so she let it go. Instead, she moved to the front window to gaze out at the thin layer of snow that had fallen overnight. She relished the sight, having not seen snow since moving to LA. She was surprised to realize she'd missed it.

"I called Sebastian a few minutes ago," he said as he dumped the eggs in a hot pan.

"Oh?" Harlow turned from the window and into the kitchen.

"He has a husky mix that he's been training as a PTSD service dog."

Harlow looked up from the mug she was prepping for her coffee. "Perfect!"

He raised a hand toward her. "But…she's young and still needs more training."

Disappointment plucked at her. Wade needed help now, not months from now. "How long?"

He shrugged. "He wasn't sure. Depends on the dog. And the owner." He exhaled. "I'm going to need to spend time at Crosswinds learning how to work with the dog." He stared into the frying pan as he stirred the eggs. "But I can bring her home today, let her start learning her new environment."

Harlow beamed. "Excellent!"

HARLOW HELPED WADE shop for dog accessories that morning, loading the back of his truck with food, a kennel and a dog bed. Once equipped for his new roommate, she and Wade arrived at Crosswinds after lunch. Sebastian met them just outside the kennel where the dogs currently in training were kept. The place was surprisingly quiet, and Harlow cast her gaze around looking for the dogs. "Where is everyone? And by everyone, I mean all the dogs."

"In class," Sebastian said, guiding her around the corner of the kennel building so she could view a large field where several dogs of various breeds were practicing skills for search-and-rescue. Some were adult dogs, while a few puppies seemed to be receiving basic obedience training. Harlow grinned watching the wiggly and enthusiastic puppies.

"So—" Sebastian shook Wade's hand in greeting "—what made you change your mind about getting a dog?"

"Harlow did," Wade said simply, his expression still skeptical.

Harlow tipped her head as she turned toward Wade. "Changed your mind?"

"Yeah. Sebastian's been nagging me about getting a dog for months," Wade admitted.

Sebastian grunted. "Nagging makes me sound like an old lady. I've been helpfully suggesting that a dog would do you a world of good." He shifted his attention to Harlow. "And stubborn mule that he is, he's refused to hear anything I had to say."

Wade growled under his breath, shoving his hands in his jeans pockets.

"Well, my idea might not have been original, but at least I got him to listen. So where is the dog you picked out for him?" Harlow raised her hands in query.

"Inside." Sebastian hitched his head toward the door of the kennel. "Ruby's just giving her a bath and a last minute once-over to make sure she's shipshape."

Harlow and Wade followed Sebastian inside the kennel building and down the long row of pens to a back room where Ruby was brushing out a white husky.

Hearing them approach, Ruby looked up and smiled brightly. "Look, Betty Jane, it's your new dad."

Betty Jane, who'd been sitting obediently while Ruby groomed her, rose to all four feet and wagged her tail seeing the trio arrive. Sebastian rubbed Betty Jane's head and received an affectionate nuzzle in return. "Good girl." Glancing to Wade, he motioned him forward. "Come meet her. Let her smell your hand."

Harlow wanted to move closer to ruffle the beautiful dog's thick fur but checked herself. This introduction was about Wade and Betty Jane. She was just along for the ride.

Wade moved toward Betty Jane and let the husky sniff his hand before scratching the dog's cheek and ear. "Hi, Betty Jane." After a few moments of petting the husky's head and looking into Betty Jane's different-colored eyes, Wade quirked a lopsided smile and asked, "So, girl, you wanna go home with me?"

Betty Jane wagged her tail and lifted a paw to Wade's arm.

"I think that's a yes," Harlow said. She waited until Wade had had a minute or two more to greet Betty Jane before she stepped closer and stroked a hand down the dog's soft fur. Betty Jane turned to sniff Harlow, and she held her hand out for the dog's inspection.

"Okay, what do I need to know? How does this service dog thing work?" Wade asked.

"Well, like I told you earlier, Betty Jane is still pretty young and needs a bit more training. She can live with you, but you'll need to bring her in daily for a few hours to work with Della. Best case would be if you were involved in the training. You two need to learn each other." Sebastian wagged a finger from Betty Jane to Wade and back. "Like a squad in the military, you two are a team now, and you have to get to know each other to be able to work seamlessly together, depend on each other, support each other."

Harlow caught Wade's almost imperceptible wince and wondered what part of Sebastian's instructions had landed the sour note.

"I still have to work at the ranch, earn a living. What do I do with her during the day?" Wade asked.

"She'll go with you."

"What?"

"Betty Jane will become your shadow. She'll go everywhere you go." When Wade's expression reflected his surprise at this information, Sebastian chuckled, adding, "What good is a service animal that's not with you when you need their service?"

"I, uh…just…" Wade scratched his cheek, his brow furrowed. "You don't think she'll be in the way at the ranch?"

"Why should she be?" Ruby asked. "The other ranch dogs aren't in the way."

"But…" Sebastian said, and paused to chew his bottom lip as he mulled something. "We should probably take her to the ranch and do some training there as well, so she can get used to the cattle and horses, the smells and general activity of a working ranch. The idea is for her to learn not to be distracted by the kind of things that rile up other dogs. To focus on you."

Betty Jane nudged Wade's hand again with her nose, and Wade gave the husky a good scratching behind the ear. "Partners, huh?" he said, obviously directing the comment to Betty Jane. "I'm in if you are, girl."

Betty Jane's plumed tail swished as she licked Wade's face.

In the purse she had tucked under her arm, Harlow's new phone rang. She responded as conditioned, opening her purse to fish it out, when a disturbing thought gripped her, and for a moment, she froze.

She'd changed phones. So who had her new cell number?

Chapter Seventeen

Harlow stared into the pocketbook as if the phone were a growling beast instead of a device. Though she tried to play it down, for Wade's sake, she lived in fear of the stalker getting the new phone number and resuming his reign of terror. When she felt Wade watching her, she took a breath for courage, dug the cell phone out and checked the screen.

Relief whooshed through her, seeing a number she recognized. Still shaking from the spike of adrenaline, she answered the call with what she prayed was a steady and cheerful tone. "Hannah? Hi! How are you?" Had she given Hannah her new number? Texted Hannah from her new phone?

"I'm good. Say, Lucy and I stopped by your parents' house earlier and everything was dark and locked up. Have you finished packing it up already?"

Harlow scoffed a laugh. "Far from it. But I'm taking a break for a while to…work on a different project." She paused a beat then asked, "How…did you get this phone number?"

"You called me from that number yesterday. I saved it to my contacts." Hannah sounded confused and wary, then continued, "So…what kind of project? Something for *Harlow Helps*?" Hannah asked.

"More like something *because* of *Harlow Helps*."

"O-kay," Hannah said, her confusion obvious. "Anything I can do to help?"

"Thanks, but no. Wade's helping me out, and in return, I'm helping him with a new project, as well."

"Wade?" Intrigue filled Hannah's tone. "Do tell!"

"I know what you're probably thinking, and it's nothing like that," she said in a hushed tone, turning her back to the others. "We're at Crosswinds, getting Wade a dog."

"What!" Hannah's shocked reply was so loud, Harlow was sure Wade and the others had heard it. "I have so many questions right now," Hannah said, a chuckle in her voice.

Harlow walked away from Wade, Ruby and Sebastian so she could talk to Wade's sister more privately. Did Hannah know about Wade's PTSD? She didn't want to break Wade's confidence, but the fact that Wade was getting a service dog would be evidence enough to his family that he was dealing with the lasting effects of his trauma. "Apparently, Sebastian had been urging him to get a service dog, and I was finally able to convince him it would be helpful. So we're here to take Betty Jane back to Wade's cabin."

Hannah was silent for a moment, and Harlow could imagine her friend processing the news and all its implications. "That's great! A dog will be good company for Wade. And if Betty Jane serves a greater need as well, then that's even better. I'd been so worried about him. He seemed to be…searching. Alone, despite all our offers to help. Chase and Fletcher said to give him space, but…"

Harlow glanced behind her where Sebastian was fitting Betty Jane with a vest that read Service Animal. "So, we kinda got sidetracked. You must have had a reason you stopped by my folks' house."

"I thought you might like to join Lucy and me for lunch. We were going to give you a break from packing boxes and dusty closets."

"Oh, I'm sorry I missed that. Rain check?" Harlow moved back down the center aisle of the kennel toward Wade, who was taking Betty Jane's leash and shaking Sebastian's hand again.

"Of course. I can't tomorrow. I have a catering job out of town, but maybe Thursday?"

"Sounds good." Harlow caught the nod Wade sent her, and she added, "I better run. I think Wade and Betty Jane are ready to head home."

"Hey, before you go, can I have a word with my brother?" Hannah asked.

"Sure." She held the phone out to Wade. "Hannah wants to talk to you."

Furrowing his brow in query, he took the phone and said, "Yes?"

Harlow squatted to give Betty Jane a scratch behind the ear. "Listen, girl, Wade has a cat visiting him. Luna is pretty laid back, so she won't bother you, but I expect the same from you. Okay?"

"A cat shouldn't be a problem. She's been trained not to let other animals distract her from her watch over her person," Sebastian said. Then, giving Harlow an odd look, he asked, "But why is your cat at Wade's house instead of your parents'?"

"I've moved out of my parents' place, at least for a while. Wade thought I'd be safer staying with him."

Sebastian's frown deepened, and his spine straightened. "Safer from what?"

Harlow hesitated, glancing at Ruby and back to Sebastian. She didn't want to alarm them. The two had a new relationship, a new baby, a new start that she didn't want to cast a pall over. She waved a dismissive hand and kept a light tone as she explained, "A listener from my show has been kind of harassing me. Wade's just being protective."

Ruby arched an eyebrow and cast a glance to Wade, who was in conversation with Hannah, but clearly still listening to what Harlow was saying. "Just protective?"

Harlow stood, dusting dog fur from her hands. "I know everyone wants to play matchmaker. While we've addressed our high school breakup and are friends again, we both agree that a romance is not in the picture. It's not practical for either of us. Neither of us plan to stay in Owl Creek, and starting something now just doesn't make sense."

Even as she said the words, denying she wanted more with Wade, her chest ached and a hollow loneliness pulsed inside her. Despite a successful career and new friends in Los Angeles, had she really felt whole since she and Wade split up years ago? She didn't want to admit that he was the missing piece in her soul. How could she risk putting her heart on the line again when so much about their futures was unknown, likely transient?

Ruby twisted her mouth, and her eyes reflected her disappointment. Her reaction didn't surprise Harlow. She knew Ruby only wanted her brother and friend to have the happiness she'd found, to regain the passion that had been so fulfilling in high school. What did surprise Harlow was Wade's reaction to her answer. His gaze darted to her, and he seemed startled, as if learning this information for the first time.

Letting you go is the biggest regret of my life.

When she studied him closer, he quickly schooled his face …but not before Harlow saw a flicker of melancholy drift over his expression. He turned his back to her as he ended his call with Hannah saying, "Sure. Anytime. Kiss Lucy for me."

Sebastian gave Wade a few more last-minute directions, and they were soon on their way back to Wade's house.

Betty Jane crowded into the front seat with them, seemingly excited by the truck ride and the new adventure.

"Her heterochromia is kinda cool, don't you think?" Harlow asked.

"Her what?"

"Heterochromia. Her different-colored eyes."

Wade nodded. "Sebastian said it's not uncommon in huskies, especially since BJ is a mixed breed."

"Oh, so she's already BJ, huh?"

Wade shrugged. "Maybe."

When they pulled off the state highway and drove up the long driveway to Wade's house, an unfamiliar car was parked in front of his cabin.

Harlow stiffened, her senses going on full alert. As far as she knew, Wade wasn't expecting company. "You know this car?"

"Well, that didn't take long," Wade mumbled. He pointed out toward the shore of the lake just past his house to the two figures silhouetted against the afternoon sun. "Hannah and Lucy. Hannah said she might bring Lucy by to meet Betty Jane, but dang. She beat us here."

Hannah turned, obviously hearing Wade's truck, and as

Harlow climbed out, holding Betty Jane's leash, she heard Hannah call to her daughter.

The small girl turned, spied Wade climbing down from the driver's side and squealed her delight. "Uncle Wade!" Lucy ran full speed, her pigtails flying, straight to her uncle.

Wade crouched so he could scoop the five-year-old into his arms, catching her against his chest with an exaggerated "oof!" when Lucy leaped into his embrace. The child's cheeks and nose were pink from the cold, and her eyes were bright with excitement.

"Hi there, Lucy Goose. I'm so glad you came to see me," Wade said, hugging her.

"Not you," Lucy said frankly, still balanced on his hip but casting her gaze about until she found Betty Jane. "I came to see your dog! Mommy said you got one of Uncle Sebastian's dogs."

Wade chuckled, then pretended to be crestfallen. "What? You didn't come to see your favorite uncle? I'm crushed!"

Leaning back in Wade's arms, Lucy framed Wade's scarred face between her mitten-encased hands and said with grown-up sincerity, "Don't worry. I still love you."

He tipped his head, a grin tugging his lips. "Do you? How much?"

Harlow acknowledged Hannah with a smile as she approached and bent to pat Betty Jane's head, but her focus was all on the interaction between Wade and his niece. The man and small girl entered a verbal contest over who loved who more that echoed books Harlow could remember from her childhood.

"Well, I love you to the sun and back," Lucy announced. "The sun is farther away than the moon."

"Hmm," Wade said, giving the child a thoughtful frown. "You're right. In that case, I love you to the end of the Milky Way!"

Lucy's eyes widened, apparently trying to decide what was bigger than Wade's offering. "Well, I love you this much..." Lucy proceeded to kiss Wade's scarred face, time and again in rapid fire, saying, "Mu-ah. Mu-ah. Mu-ah," with each smacking kiss to his cheeks and chin and forehead.

Beside her, Hannah tensed and called, "Be careful, Lucy."

But the man and child ignored Hannah. Instead, a chortle rumbled from Wade's chest and lit his face, and the joyful sound shook something loose deep in Harlow's core. She realized it was the first time she'd heard Wade really laugh, not just a wry snort, since she'd returned to Owl Creek.

Wade's laugh, his sense of humor and joyful disposition had been a large part of what had made her fall in love with him in high school. Hearing the laughter that had been missing in their earlier interactions only sharpened by contrast how much the interceding years had changed Wade. Or, perhaps more specifically, how the explosion had changed him, left him searching emotionally for a way forward.

Wade pulled Lucy close in a tight hug, saying, "And I love you this much!" He made grunting sounds pretended to be squeezing her as hard as he could in the hug. The embrace was tight, but clearly not enough to hurt Lucy.

"Ack!" Lucy let her head loll and acted like she couldn't breathe, her tongue out as she panted. "Okay, okay, you win!" The girl wiggled. "Now put me down! I wanna pat your new dog."

Wade complied, his face still glowing with love and the reciprocated affection and teasing of his niece.

Because she doesn't judge me or treat me like I'm less of who I was before... Something deep in Harlow's core gave a painful throb.

When Lucy raced over to Betty Jane, who sat patiently on her leash, her nose up, sniffing the new smells of the lakeside terrain, Wade followed. "When you said you might bring Lucy by to meet the dog, I didn't expect you to beat me home."

Hannah shrugged. "What can I say? Lucy heard me say *Wade* and *dog*, and nothing would do but that we come immediately. She's been obsessed with dogs since her school friend got one."

"You must live close," Harlow commented. "We only had a ten-minute drive from Crosswinds."

Hannah chuckled. "You're in Owl Creek, Harlow, not Los Angeles, remember? Everything is close. But for reference, we just live that way along the shoreline about a half mile. You can see our storage hut from here, by the water's edge. If the ice were thicker, we could have walked across the inlet, as the bird flies, and it'd only be half that distance."

"But the ice isn't thick enough yet," Wade warned, "so don't try it."

Hannah gave Wade an I'm-not-stupid look. "Yes, big brother. I know."

Harlow moved closer to the lake and peered across the frozen water. "I see it. The gray building just there? Is that your storage building?"

"That's the one. It looks so innocent from here, but inside

it's so…messy." Hannah sighed. "Well, that's a project for another day when I'm not so busy with single parenting."

"Oh, Uncle Wade, I love your dog! She's so soft!" Lucy hugged Betty Jane's neck, earning tail wags and a face lick in return. The girl laughed and stroked the husky's fur, beaming. "Mommy, look, she has one blue eye and one brown eye!"

"Sebastian said that's because she's a mixed breed. Her father might have been a malamute or German shepherd," Wade said, moving to the tailgate of his truck to unload the large bag of dog food, fleece-lined dog bed, and grocery sack with water bowls, brushes, and other accoutrements that went along with dog ownership, whether service animal or pet. He left the pile of supplies on the frozen ground while he fished in his pocket.

After pulling out his keys, he extended them to Harlow saying, "Here. You and Hannah can get out of the cold while Goose and I get this stuff inside and make sure BJ takes care of any business she needs to before we go in."

"Sure." Harlow offered the leash to Lucy, but the girl continued hugging and getting face licks from Betty Jane.

"Mommy, can we get a dog?"

Hannah bit her bottom lip, looking pained. "No, honey. That's not a good idea."

"I think it's a great idea. I love Betty Jane, and I'd love my dog, too. Pleeeease!"

Harlow could see refusing her daughter was difficult for Hannah, and she sensed there was more to Hannah's answer than simple logistics of dog ownership.

When Wade crouched to lift the large bag of dog food, Lucy flung herself on his back. "Can I have a piggyback ride? My daddy used to give me piggyback rides."

Now Hannah's face paled, and she fussed, "Lucy, no! Get off Wade's back. You'll hurt him!"

But before the little girl could wiggle off, Wade looped his arms under her legs and rose to his full height again, sending his sister a scolding glare. "Why don't you let me decide what I can and can't do." He shifted Lucy so that she bounced and giggled, and Wade cast a glance over his shoulder. "You holding on tight? This bronco's been known to buck!"

He jogged off with Lucy on his back and jostled and bounced his niece while Lucy squealed her delight. Betty Jane tugged on the leash and Harlow dropped it so the dog could scamper after them.

Harlow studied Hannah's frown as Wade trotted off with Lucy on his back. She debated whether she should say something to Hannah about how she and her siblings treated Wade with kid gloves. She didn't want to interfere, but the Coltons needed to understand that their coddling and overbearing caution with him were doing more harm than good.

Hannah sighed and shook her head. "I've told Lucy she has to be careful with Wade, that she can't roughhouse with him the way she does with her other uncles. But she doesn't listen."

"Or maybe she's listening to Wade, where you and the rest of the family aren't?" she said, her tone gentle to offset the chiding.

Hannah refocused her frown on Harlow. "What do you mean?"

"He's chafing under all the overcautious treatment. He wouldn't have offered Lucy a piggyback ride if he didn't feel up to it. I've seen how you act toward him. All of you.

I'm not singling you out. And I see how your walking on eggshells irritates him and makes him feel…belittled."

"But…" Hannah's face creased with pain. "Oh, Harlow, you didn't see him when he got home from the hospital. He was in such bad shape. We're only concerned that he not push too hard, that he heal properly."

"He's had a year and a half to heal since then, though. I know your caution comes from a place of love, but even love can be misused or become smothering."

Hannah seemed truly startled and chastened. "But we never wanted to— You think he resents us?"

"Well, I can hear the frustration in his voice when one of you tries to protect him or holds back somehow out of concern. Don't you think he's a better judge of what he can and can't do? What he needs most is your faith in him and encouragement."

Hannah looked back out on the yard where Wade and Lucy tossed a stick for Betty Jane, and he swung the little girl up over his head to peals of her giggles. "They are having fun. And he doesn't appear to be in pain."

"And he's laughing." A ripple of awareness and affection sluiced through Harlow seeing this hint of the old Wade. "How often does he truly laugh anymore, Hannah? I know he's been awfully somber around me. But with Lucy, he feels happy, safe, not judged or seen through the lens of his accident. He's more like his old self. She takes him at face value and treats him the same as she does her other family, like a whole person, like a beloved uncle."

Harlow shivered, not from the cold, but with a self-conviction. Had she treated him differently? Had she unconsciously measured Wade with a bias?

Hannah wrapped her arms around herself, her expression

bereft. "The last thing I ever wanted was to cause Wade more grief. I just—"

Harlow sidestepped closer to her friend and draped an arm around her shoulders for a side hug. "I know that. And deep down, he knows that. But while he's making his own adjustments to a new normal, a new face in his mirror, new physical limitations from the loss of his eye, what he needs most from his family are support and faith."

Hannah exhaled heavily. "Of course. Absolutely. And I'll talk to everyone else. Mom has been especially worried, because—well, she's a mom. And mothers worry. But if she and I set the tone, I think everyone else will back off." Her friend chewed her bottom lip. "It's just with him keeping himself so isolated, it's hard to gauge where things stand with him."

"So ask him. Engage him like you would have before the accident. Tease him. Include him. Confide in him. Ask him for help fixing something at your house. He needs to feel needed, accepted, wanted...*normal*. Not damaged."

A male shout from near the lakeshore drew their attention back out to Wade and Lucy. Based on the way Wade was wiggling and tugging at his coat, Harlow surmised that Lucy had stuffed a handful of snow down the back of Wade's collar.

Betty Jane whined and poked her nose in the huddle of bodies, apparently agitated by the antics of Lucy and Wade. Did Betty Jane think Lucy was hurting Wade or vice versa?

A moment later, Lucy shifted her attention to Betty Jane, again enveloping the husky in an enthusiastic hug.

"So...that crew," Harlow nodded toward the man, child and dog, "may be a while. Why don't we each grab an armload from the truck and head inside? We can have hot chocolate waiting when they get in."

"Sounds like a good plan." Hannah put a hand on Harlow's arm as she moved away, stopping her. "And thank you for being frank with me. You're a good friend, and I've really missed having you to talk to."

Chapter Eighteen

"So, what were the two of you gossiping about so seriously earlier?" Wade asked Harlow as he washed mud and dog hair from his hands while Harlow filled mugs with steaming cocoa from the stove.

"What makes you think it was gossip?" She gave him a side glance and a smirk.

"Because I remember all too well conversations I overheard between you and my sisters in the past. We grew up in a small town, remember? Gossip is kinda a hobby around here."

Harlow grunted. "I remember."

"Please, Mommy?" he heard Lucy say from the front room where Hannah was getting her daughter out of her wet coat and socks. "Bella's mom let her get a puppy!"

He carried a towel with him, drying his hands as he moved to the door of the kitchen to follow the exchange between his sister and niece. He curled his mouth to the side in a teasing grin, a quip on his tongue for his sister about fighting a losing battle, until he saw Hannah's expression.

"Baby, I'm sorry. We just can't. Not now. I've got too much my plate these days to add a new dog to the mix."

Lucy scowled and stomped her foot churlishly, shouting, "I wish Daddy was here! Daddy would let me have a dog!" Whirling away from her mother, Lucy flounced off to throw herself down on the couch with a pout.

As bad as he felt for his niece, who clearly missed her absentee father, he felt worse for Hannah, who looked like she was fighting not to cry.

"Yeah," Hannah muttered under her breath, "A lot of things would be different if your daddy were here. But he's not, so…"

The pain lacing his sister's tone was so thick and heart-breaking, Wade's own chest ached as if slashed with sharp claws. He stepped over to Hannah and pulled her into a hug. "That bastard you married may have left you fending for yourself, but you are not alone. You have me. You have all of the Coltons. And we're a pretty formidable bunch when it comes to taking care of our own."

Hannah sniffled as she chuckled. "Formidable, huh? Yeah, I guess we are, huh?" She embraced him gingerly and then, as if thinking about it again, she squeezed him tightly, as tightly as Lucy giving one of her bear hugs. As tightly as his mother and sibling used to hug him before he'd come home with significant burns and scar tissue. And he reveled in the firm squeeze, the first peek at normalcy in his family interactions in too many months.

Over Hannah's shoulder, he spotted Harlow watching from the kitchen door, smiling. A niggle of intuition told him he owed this warm hug to the talk Harlow had had with his sister. *Thank you*, he mouthed to her.

She bobbed a nod with a satisfied grin.

OVER THE NEXT few days, Wade divided his time among the ranch, Crosswinds and Harlow's house. Not wanting to leave his uncle in the lurch, he showed up at Colton Ranch early most mornings after dropping Betty Jane off for training with Sebastian and Della. He spent a few hours doing ranch chores, then returned to Crosswinds to get his own training, working with Betty Jane. In the afternoons, he and Betty Jane would arrive at the Joneses' house to wrap china or repaint bathrooms or bag clothes to be donated to charity.

During the hours he wasn't with Harlow, he encouraged Hannah or Vivian or one of his cousins to keep Harlow company and provide another level of security beyond the new cameras and alarm system.

On a Friday in mid-January, he arrived at Harlow's to find his mother and Lucy in the kitchen and the house smelling like fresh-baked gingerbread cookies. He gave his mother's cheek a kiss, then bent to unhook BJ's leash. "How exactly does baking cookies get the house ready to sell?"

"It doesn't," Jenny said, "but who can say no to warm cookies after a long day of work?" She offered a plate of the treats to him, and he helped himself to a few. "Besides," she said in quieter voice, "I'm babysitting for Hannah while she preps for a catering job, and baking cookies kept Lucy out of Harlow's way while she painted the trim in the guest bedroom."

"I see," he said as he shoved a whole cookie in his mouth at once. "Any problems here today?"

Jenny frowned. "Problems? Were you expecting there to be trouble?"

"Not expecting any so much as hoping to avoid it." When his mother gave him a look that demanded further explanation, he said, "Harlow's internet advice show, *Harlow Helps*, has attracted negative attention from a listener."

"Oh, dear," Jenny said, lifting a hand to her throat. "Negative attention as in...?"

Wade glanced over at Lucy, who was draped over BJ, ruffling the dog's thick fur. "As in, that's why I've asked people to help with keeping Harlow company when I'm not here. I don't want her to be alone, just in case..."

"I knew it!" Harlow said from the kitchen door, her expression exasperated. "I was suspicious when I had a different visitor drop by randomly every day this week and stay for hours at a time." She wrinkled her nose, which had blue paint smudged on it.

"Which reminds me," he said, turning to his mother, "I don't have anyone scheduled for tomorrow. So can she come with me to the ranch?"

Jenny blinked and pulled an odd expression. "Well, why are you asking me?"

Wade placed a hand on his mother's shoulder and raised an eyebrow. "When are you going to give up the charade? I know you spend more time at Uncle Buck's than your own house. We're not blind to the looks you give each other."

"Looks?" Jenny's cheeks flushed.

Wade chuckled. "Just admit you have feelings for Buck and...well, make your relationship public. Date him without hiding it. You're not fooling anyone, and we're all happy for you both."

"You've talked about us to your siblings?" His mother looked startled.

"And the cousins." He popped another cookie in his mouth.

Jenny sat down hard in one of the kitchen chairs. "Oh.

Well, I…" She lifted her gaze then to Harlow, who stood at the sink, washing paint from her fingers. "Maybe I will, if you'll admit that the two of you still have feelings for each other."

Wade's cookie went down the wrong pipe. He coughed and met Harlow's wide-eyed look, before shaking his head and in a strangled voice saying, "What?"

"You two aren't fooling anyone either." Jenny stood and patted Wade's back gently as he continued coughing to clear the crumbs from his throat. "You're good for each other, and I haven't seen you this engaged and happy in months."

"Mrs. Colton," Harlow said, taking a towel from the counter to dry her hands, "we're not back together. I'm not staying in Owl Creek. In fact, I think the house will be ready late next week, and I'll officially put it on the market."

His mother's face fell, then lifting her chin and squaring her shoulders, she divided a look between Harlow and Wade. "Well, that's a shame. Anyone can see you two are perfect for each other." She glanced at her granddaughter, who was feeding dog treats to Betty Jane. "Lucy, dear, get your things together. It's time to go."

"Aw! I want to play with Betty Jane!" Lucy whined.

"Betty Jane is a working dog," Jenny said, putting a lid on a Tupperware box of cookies. "She not supposed to play with little girls."

"Even ones as cute as you," Wade added, ruffling Lucy's hair.

Shoulders sagging, Lucy got up from the floor and gave BJ a last pat.

"Now come get this box of cookies to take home. We'll leave the rest for Wade and Harlow," his mother said. "We need to get on the road before the snow gets any worse. I hear we're supposed to get a foot of it by morning!"

Lucy's eyes brightened at the idea of a big snowfall. "Yea!"

"Speaking of tomorrow morning," his mother said, turning to Harlow, "why don't you take a break from the house and come visit with me at the ranch in the morning while Wade works? If what you're looking for is added security, where could you be safer than the ranch with all the extra men close by?"

Harlow shot him a look, then shrugged. "Why not? Sounds like a plan."

As PROMISED, HARLOW accompanied Wade to Colton Ranch first thing the next morning. While he prepared to help his uncle and the other hands deal with the snow and effects of the freezing temperatures on the livestock and equipment, Harlow headed toward the main house to visit with Jenny. This morning, his mother made no secret of the fact that she'd spent the night at Buck's, welcoming them warmly on the front porch, as if Buck's house were hers. Wade sent his mother a knowing look as the women headed to the kitchen for "hot coffee, fresh biscuits and juicy gossip," as his mother put it.

"I don't know what that look was for, Wade Colton," Jenny said, lifting her chin, "but I'll thank you not to track snow into the house." She made a shooing motion, adding, "Buck's waiting for you at the barn."

Wade left the truck keys with Harlow. "If you get tired of waiting for me, you can use the truck, but I'd rather you didn't go anywhere alone."

Jenny cocked her head and scoffed. "For Pete's sake,

Wade. She's a grown woman. She's perfectly capable of going wherever she wants by herself." Turning to Harlow, she asked, "You remember how to drive in snow, don't you?"

"Well, it has been a while, but…" Harlow met Wade's gaze "I'll wait for you. I promise."

Ignoring the curious and hopeful look his mother shot him as he exited the house, Wade walked across the ranch yard, hiking up his coat collar against the frigid wind.

Buck greeted him with smile and an appraising look. "I hear Harlow's been staying with you. What's that about?"

"Long story, and not what you're thinking." Wade walked straight to the corral and got to work with the other hands.

Most of the heaters in the watering troughs had done their job, but Wade helped make checks to see that all the animals were fed extra forage. They also set up windbreaks, made with hay bales and tin sheeting, for the cattle to huddle behind. Next, he saddled Cactus Jack, preparing to ride out to check that the snow hadn't damaged any fences and to break the ice on the ponds where the cattle preferred to drink.

He was busy at one of the ponds late in the morning when he heard a shout from down pasture. He glanced up to see a lone rider headed toward him on Sunflower. He set aside the pickax he'd been chopping ice with and resettled his hat when the wind knocked it askew. When he recognized the coat and knit cap as Harlow's, pleasure spiraled through him, followed quickly by a prick of irritation. He strode toward the scrub tree where he'd tied Cactus Jack and she was now dismounting Sunflower and squared his shoulders.

"Exactly what part of 'don't go anywhere alone' was unclear?" he groused.

She blinked at him, clearly startled by his salvo. "Whoa, cowboy." Narrowing a glare, she said, "And what part of 'you're not the boss of me' was unclear to you?"

He clenched his back teeth for a moment, then started again. "I'm just trying to keep you safe."

"I appreciate that, but we are out in the middle of nowhere after a snowstorm. There are hands back at the stable and scattered throughout the pastures, and Buck and Jenny are at the house. I'd think I was pretty safe."

He sighed. "You probably are, but...what are you doing out here? It's freezing!" He pulled her into his arms to buff warmth into her, but found she was the one warming him. His hands were stiff with the cold despite his gloves, and his face stung from the icy wind.

"Which is why Jenny sent you this." Harlow lifted the flap on a saddlebag and pulled out a large thermos. "Hot soup? You didn't come in for lunch, and we figured you had to be getting hungry."

Just the thought of some hot soup made his stomach growl. Loud enough for Harlow to hear.

She chuckled as she passed the canister to him. "I'll take that as a yes."

"That'd be a yes." He uncapped the thermos and tipped it up to drink, not even bothering with the small lid-slash-cup.

"So clearly your mom took your advice about your uncle Buck."

Wade coughed and had to wipe soup from his chin. "Why do you say that?"

Harlow grinned. "Because they're acting like lovesick teenagers back at the house."

Wade arched an eyebrow. "Really?"

"Yeah," Harlow sighed contentedly. "It's nice to see them so…happy."

When another strong gust of frigid wind buffeted them, Harlow shivered, and Wade put the lid back on the thermos of soup. "Listen, I'm done out here. Let's head in. We'll swing by to get BJ on the way back to your folks' house and get that last wall in the bedroom painted."

She tugged her knit hat lower on her ears. "Sounds good to me."

He gave her a boost up onto Sunflower, untied the reins for both horses and set out for the stable.

"I heard from Sloan this morning," Harlow said as they rode back. "She said her team has tracked the computer used to send the earliest threats from my stalker to the area around San Diego. They've been working with the LAPD, sharing the information SecuritKey tracked down to assist with the police's case."

"Good. Anything new on the cell phone numbers used to text you?"

She shook her head. "Just like I didn't want my traceable, apparently neither did my stalker. The numbers were burner phones apparently. They can track where they were used, where the number pinged on a cell tower, but nothing about who bought the phone."

He narrowed a worried look on her. "And where did the phone ping?"

She exhaled heavily, a large puff of vapor clouding around her. "Here. In Owl Creek. Just as we suspected."

His hand tightened on his reins. "That's it then. I'm not leaving your side until this guy is caught. And Fletcher needs to be updated. His officers need to be looking for strangers in town and checking hotels and rental houses and—"

"Wade, it's ski season. The hotels and rental houses are full of out-of-town travelers," she countered.

He firmed his mouth. "Maybe, but there's got to be something we can do to find him before he—" He couldn't bring himself to finish his sentence. The thought of harm coming to Harlow was too much for him to bear.

She was quiet for a moment, before she said, "Or I could leave. Move on to another town, another state, somewhere with no ties to my past or my friends."

Somewhere without me. His gut clenched. "Let's see what Fletcher says before you do that. I hate to think of you out there somewhere alone. Unprotected."

She cut a glance toward him, then gave a nod.

As they neared the stable, Cactus Jack and Sunflower picked up their pace, clearly ready to get out of the cold and get a snack. Wade turned to Harlow to say something about the eager horses, and he caught a movement, something dark and out of place at the edge of his vision. A prickle raced up his spine, a wariness he'd honed while in the Marines. Before the edginess could take form, before he could give voice to his concern, a loud crack of gunfire shattered the calm.

Chapter Nineteen

A hot flash of adrenaline spun through Wade.

Sunflower reared, and Cactus Jack danced sideways in alarm.

Harlow gasped as her horse bucked, but she managed to stay seated. "What was—?"

Another crack echoed across the snowy landscape, and Wade reacted instinctively. Flinging himself off Cactus Jack's back, he shouted, "Get down!"

Harlow, who was struggling to bring Sunflower under control, shot him a startled look. "Wade?"

"Gunfire!" Reaching up, he grabbed a handful of her coat and yanked hard, dragging her out of the saddle. He caught her as she tumbled down. Cushioning her fall with his own body, he flopped into the snow and rolled with her out of the range of the horses' agitated hooves.

Free of her rider, Sunflower bolted toward the stable. Cactus Jack whinnied as he stamped his hooves.

Another shot rang out, then another. The bullets made dull thuds as they hit the ground around them.

Harlow jerked and gave a soft cry of alarm as each shot whizzed close to their heads.

Wade's heart slammed against his ribs. They had no

protection from the rain of bullets. He shifted, making sure Harlow was completely shielded. If he was hit, so be it. But he couldn't stand the idea of anything happening to Harlow. She was everything to him. She'd always been everything for him. Why hadn't he fought harder for her all those years ago? He'd been too proud, too stubborn, too hurt by her rejection of his career goals...

The sound of gunfire had alerted the ranch hands and family, and Wade could hear distant shouts coming closer. He raised his head, glancing toward the line of trees, the direction from which the shots had come. A figure clad in thick layers of dark outerwear and a ski mask stumbled deeper into the woods, out of sight.

"There!" he shouted to his cousin Greg and Uncle Buck as they arrived, bearing rifles. He pointed to where the intruder had been, and Greg and his uncle were gone in a heartbeat, pursuing the gunman.

"Call Fletcher!" he heard someone else shout.

Only as the reality that the danger had passed sank in did Wade allow himself to acknowledge the buzz of adrenaline in his ears, the tremor in his core and the black spots that danced at the edges of his vision. *No!*

He squeezed his eye shut and battled the rising panic. He gritted his teeth and struggled to draw deep, even breaths. Instead of the snow, he felt the scalding heat of flames and heard a deafening explosion reverberating in his head.

Beneath him, Harlow squirmed, and he used the distraction to jam down the roar of the fire and smoke in his brain. He drew a ragged breath and rolled to a seated position, letting Harlow up. Shaking himself out of his mental slide, he focused on Harlow's wide dark eyes. "Are you hurt?"

She took a few extra beats to answer, as if needing to

gather herself before she could assess her physical condition. "I—I…think so." Her expression shifting from shock to concern, she reached for his cheek. "You're bleeding! Were you hit?"

Wade touched his face and found a spot with sticky warmth. "I don't think this is from the shooter. Cactus Jack may have cuffed me a little. Or a scrape from the ground." He motioned to the ice and rock uncovered as they'd rolled in the snow. He didn't tell her that his facial cut could have been a ricocheting bit of bullet, ice or rock thrown up when one of the sniper's shots hit near their heads.

She sent a lingering scrutiny up and down the length of him, clearly checking for other wounds. "Wade…"

He caught her hands between his. "I'm okay…as long as you are. Honest. My face is so numb with cold right now, I don't even feel the cut."

Slipping her hands from his grip, she threw her arms around his neck and hugged him. Tight. Like one of Lucy's bear hugs that nearly squeezed the breath from you. He squeezed back. The notion that he'd been so close to losing Harlow forever moments earlier terrified him. If the shooter had had better aim, if he hadn't gotten her off Sunflower and on the ground as quickly as he did, if he hadn't been with her…

"Hey, are you guys all right?" Greg called as he hurried up to them—or hurried as much as one could through the calf-deep snow.

"Thankfully, yes." Wade shoved to his feet and offered a hand to help Harlow rise. She dusted caked snow from her coat and jeans before turning her ministrations to the back of his jacket. He turned his gaze toward the woods where the dark-clad figure had disappeared. "What happened with the shooter? Did you catch him?"

Greg shrugged one shoulder. "Don't know yet. Dad, Malcolm and some of the guys went after him. Dad sent me back to check on you. Your mom's called 911. I've texted an SOS to Fletcher."

"A very efficient Colton crisis response," Harlow said with a strained smile. She was shivering. Probably post-adrenaline tremors as much as cold, Wade suspected, drawing her back into his arms.

"I'm afraid the Colton crisis machine has become well-oiled in recent months," Greg said, his tone dark. "Thanks to the bastards in Acker's cult—" Greg glanced at Harlow and twisted his mouth to the side "Pardon my French."

She waved off his apology. "Sometimes French is called for."

"I know Jessie threatened retaliation when you met with your lawyer about Uncle Robert's will, but sending a cult member to shoot up the ranch is just—" Greg clamped his lips in a tight scowl of disgust.

Harlow blinked, then divided a look between Wade and Greg. "So then…do you think that's who it was? Someone from that church Jessie is involved in?"

Wade could see something akin to hope in her expression. Knowing Harlow, knowing personal trauma, knowing his own jumbled feelings about who the shooter might have been, he could guess the source of that hope. If the shooter was from the Ever After "church," then it wasn't her stalker, wasn't personal, wasn't directed at her. And she could better distance herself from the frightening event, better shut it away, more easily move on.

Greg flipped up a gloved hand. "Who else would it be?

Marcus Acker and his lackeys have been behind most of the sh—stuff that's happened to the family this year. We know he wants to take our land, push us out, steal the money from your father's estate."

"*Jessie* wants to steal Dad's money," Wade corrected.

"For Acker!" Greg said. "If she gets any of Robert's money, she'll give it to Acker and his minions in a hot minute. She's deep under his sway."

Wade nodded. His cousin had a point, but he still couldn't sell himself on the idea of the cult's culpability in this instance. He'd be remiss to dismiss the possibility the sniper was Harlow's stalker. They knew he was close by, if not currently in Owl Creek. The cell phone ping and the snake in the mailbox were evidence of that.

"The thing is," Harlow said, her voice shaking, as she backed out of his arms to face Greg, "the shooter may have been after me." She paused and cleared her throat before explaining her situation to Greg.

His cousin divided a concerned look between Wade and Harlow. "Does Fletcher know about this?"

Harlow nodded. "I asked him not to worry the family with it, knowing how much else was on your minds, what with the Acker church—"

"Cult," Greg interrupted. "Calling it a church is a disservice to churches everywhere."

Harlow nodded her agreement. "My point is, it's possible—likely even—that I was the target."

"I hate to hear that. I wish we'd known. When a member of this family is threatened, we rally. This year has taught me that for sure."

Harlow gave a weak half smile. "But I'm not a Colton."

Greg tipped his head, raising an eyebrow. "Aren't you,

though? As good as?" He gave Wade a meaningful look before returning his gaze to Harlow. "Family can include people not related by blood. It's more about love."

The sound of voices and snowmobiles behind them hailed the return of the men who'd chased the shooter. Wade wanted to talk to them about what they'd seen, where the gunman had gone. He saw Fletcher pull up in his squad car, lights flashing, and Wade jerked his chin toward his brother. "Come on. We'll talk to Fletcher, then I'll take you home."

HARLOW SAT NEXT to the roaring fire in Buck's living room but couldn't seem to chase the chill that had settled in her bones from moment the first shot cracked across the ranch yard. She listened with only half attention as Wade, Fletcher, Buck and his male cousins debated the next steps—for finding her stalker, for protecting the family, for resolving unfinished business with Marcus Acker. She'd brought danger to the Colton Ranch, to a family she cherished as much as her own. Why was she still in Owl Creek? As soon as she suspected the stalker had found her, the same day the snake showed up in her mailbox, she should have packed her bags and left town. So what had kept her here? Why had she risked exposing the Coltons, and especially Wade, to the danger her stalker presented?

Wade's mother sat beside her, a calming presence, but the worry knitting her brow only made Harlow feel more guilty for the threat she'd brought to the Coltons.

She glanced across the room where Wade was engaged in deep, serious discussions with Fletcher and the others, and as if he felt her eyes on him, Wade turned his head and met her gaze.

His expression asked, *You okay?*

She flashed a weak smile and gave a nod, which seemed to mollify him for the moment.

"Other than tracks in the snow, we don't have a lot to go on," Buck said to Fletcher. "By the time we reached the road, the guy was gone."

"Can you do anything worthwhile with the boot tracks he left in the snow?" Wade asked.

Fletcher shrugged. "I've sent a guy out there now to see if any of them have a clear tread we can match. We can measure for boot size and stride length. Beyond that, we can get a ballistics report on the bullets, but without a weapon to match them to, ballistics won't go far until an arrest is made."

"I still say we shouldn't rule out a link to Acker," Greg said, his tone vehement. "Is it possible that Harlow's stalker is connected to the Ever After Church and Acker's minions?"

The men glanced to Harlow, and she perked up. "I can't imagine why he would be. This all started before I arrived in Owl Creek."

"But if the shooter knew you were once involved with Wade…" Jenny offered.

Fletcher shook his head. "That's rather a stretch, Mom. I mean, we'll keep all possibilities on the table, but there are more likely scenarios that bear more attention."

Buck folded his arms over his chest, scowling. "The hell of it is, the more things like this shooter crop up, the more your attention is diverted from finding proof that Acker killed Robert and is behind the other crap that has happened this year. We need Acker in custody!"

Greg and Malcolm both nodded their agreement.

"What else can be done to resolve the case against Acker? What can *we* do that we aren't already?" Malcolm asked.

"Be patient. Acker is smart, but he's not bulletproof," Fletcher said, then winced and cast Harlow an apologetic look as if realizing how harshly that phrase might resound for her. "In the meantime, if you want me to move you to a safe house outside town, I can do that."

Harlow swallowed hard, considering another relocation.

"Or you can stay here," Jenny offered, consulting Buck with a glance. "Surrounded by several Coltons and all of the ranch hands, you'd be plenty safe."

Harlow gripped Jenny's hand but shook her head. "Thank you for the offer but... I'm settled at Wade's now and..." She met his gaze again, and a thread of warmth flowed through her, remembering how he'd pulled her off Sunflower, covered her with his own body, held her in the aftermath of the chaos and numbing fear. "I feel safe with him."

Wade's head came up, and his startled look morphed into what she could only call resolve. Gratitude. Relief. Shoulders squared and jaw firmed, he nodded to her.

An hour later, they were back at his rental cabin with Betty Jane and a takeout order of burgers from Tap Out Brewery.

"Thank you for what you said today." Wade dragged a french fry through ketchup and popped it in his mouth. "About feeling safe with me."

Harlow took a small bite of pickle and ignored her burger. Unlike Wade, who'd only had a few sips of soup for lunch after a morning of manual labor, she had no appetite. Getting shot at had a way of doing that. "I do feel safe with you. Your quick response saved my life this afternoon."

He shrugged. "I mean I appreciate you telling my family. They were ready to take over and push me aside today when—"

"Wade." She tipped her head. "They were doing what any self-respecting, worried family would do. Offering help. And since I have no family of my own anymore, I was touched by their concern." She reached for his left hand as he ate another fry. "And I do feel safe with you—as safe as I can feel until Chris-whoever-he-is is caught."

She squeezed his fingers. Abandoning his meal, he turned to meet her gaze. "Nothing is more important to me than keeping you safe."

A smile pulled at the corner of her mouth. "Can I say that is a very sexy thing to hear without surrendering my independent woman card?"

"Oh yeah?" His eyebrow sketched up, and his expression brightened. "How sexy?"

Scooting closer to him, moving to the edge of her chair, she leaned forward. With her palm, she stroked the side of his face, then dragged her fingers over the day's growth of beard. "This sexy."

She touched her lips to his, barely brushing his mouth with hers, but it was if she'd struck a match and dropped it in gasoline. Heat rushed through her blood, and desire blazed at her core.

Wade canted toward her, capturing her lips again with a deeper kiss and cradling the base of her skull to hold her close. He drew on her lips hungrily, his kiss rousing all the feelings she'd worked these past weeks to deny. The yearning she'd shelved years ago in order to survive her life without Wade roared back from the shadows.

Maybe because she'd had a brush with death today,

maybe because her life was still in danger from her stalker, but tonight she wanted to feel fully alive. She wanted to reclaim the earth-shaking experience of being one with this man, of having all of her senses awakened and sharing with Wade the life-confirming and joyful sensations that were as old as time. One look at the passion in his blue gaze told her he needed the same—that he needed to feel deeply human, entirely alive and intimately connected to her.

With her hands framing his face, she simply whispered, "Yes."

Beneath her palms, Harlow felt his tremor in response. He pushed to his feet and scooped her into his arms. With long strides, he carried her to his bedroom and followed her down as he set her on the bed. "There's been no one else for a very long time, Harlow. No one else ever meant what you did, and I quit looking for—"

She silenced him with her lips on his, her legs wrapping around him and her arms circling his neck. She broke the kiss only long enough to rasp, "Same here." And by silent agreement, they knew that was all that had to be said.

They took their time, slowly peeling away each other's clothes, rediscovering each other's bodies, relearning each other's preferences. With her fingers, she traced the scars on his chest and face, then followed the path with her mouth, her tongue. Wade groaned his pleasure, and the rumble quivered in her belly and roused her all the more.

When he tugged her shirt over her head, exposing her midriff and bra, he dipped his head to rub his cheek on her skin. The scrape of his one-day beard sent tingles deep into her womb. "You're so warm, so soft, so precious to me," he murmured, trailing kisses up to her collarbone. He cupped a breast with his hand, and the stroke of his thumb shot such sweet torture through her that she writhed and gasped. "Please, Wade. Now…"

But he took his time, teasing her, working her to the edge of madness before he sheathed himself and made them one. Tears of happiness prickled in her eyes as she held him close, savoring the sensation of being near him, of moving with him in a rhythmic sway and undulation. And she cried his name when her world exploded in a thousand brilliant stars and a vortex of pure pleasure.

They made love several times before fatigue and the pull of slumber overtook them. She dozed briefly before Wade's snore woke her, and she snuggled close, smiling at the memory of their joining.

For the next couple of hours, Harlow lay awake, listening to Wade's heavy, steady breaths, staring into the darkness. After a while, the sweetness of their night together gave way to the bitter fear of the day. The terrifying moments as bullets had whizzed past her replayed in her mind's eye.

If she'd had any morsel of doubt that her stalker meant her harm, the hail of bullets this afternoon had erased all suspicion. The jerk with a violent vendetta against her meant business. Not only had he had managed to track her to Idaho, he'd made not just one but two attempts on her life—because the rattlesnake had clearly been the stalker's handiwork as well.

What frightened her even more was the fact that any of those shots aimed at her today could have wounded Wade…could have *killed* Wade. A muffled whimper escaped her throat before she pressed her lips tight and force-fully shoved gruesome imagined images from her mind.

Beside the bed, Betty Jane lifted her head, her dog tags jingling.

Harlow angled her head to peer over at the husky and whisper, "Good girl," before rolling to her side to try again to fall asleep.

The click of claws on the hardwood floor preceded the touch of a cold nose, the nudge of a warm muzzle. Harlow smiled as she rubbed Betty Jane's ears and neck. "I'm okay, sweet girl."

But Betty Jane hopped onto the bed and settled in the small space between Harlow and Wade, draping a paw on Harlow's leg.

"Really?" Harlow whispered to the dog. "Isn't three a bit crowded for this bed?"

Betty Jane chuffed and put her head down on her out-stretched legs, her mismatched eyes watching Harlow. Sinking her fingers into the dog's warm fur, Harlow inched over to give Betty Jane more room, then, feeling more settled, tried again to find sleep.

She must have dozed eventually because some time later, a groan and the slap of a thrashing arm woke Harlow. She dragged herself awake as more moans and writhing alerted her to Wade's nightmare. Betty Jane shoved her way up from the foot of the bed to Wade's side and lay down across Wade.

Wade's brow was damp, his legs kicked and his face furrowed with anguish.

Harlow felt an answering twist of sympathy in her gut. "Wade, wake up!"

Betty Jane gave a soft bark, licked her owner's face and continued to nudge Wade's chin with her nose. Harlow held her breath, watching the companion dog work until Wade woke with a startled gasp. His gaze darted around the room, his confusion obvious even as Betty Jane gave another quiet chuff and wiggled higher on Wade's chest, pawing his cheek softly and bumping his hands and neck with her nose. Betty Jane's insistent but gentle nuzzling soon earned a pat from Wade. The ragged saw of air he gulped calmed to an even rhythm, and he dug fingers into Betty Jane's fur as if clinging to a life raft.

After a moment, Wade pushed Betty Jane aside, murmuring, "Good girl. I'm okay now."

He fumbled in the drawer of his bedside stand and found a baggie of dog treats. He gave BJ a couple treats, stroking her head and repeating, "Good girl."

"Are you really okay?" Harlow asked.

He swung his gaze toward her as if only then remembering she was there. He frowned as if embarrassed and glanced away. "I wish you hadn't seen that."

"Oh, Wade." She grasped his arm. "Do you really believe I'd think any less of you because you have nightmares? You went through something horrible that no one should ever have to experience. Nightmares are a normal response to a trauma."

"Maybe, but—" he exhaled a choppy breath "—that doesn't mean I want you to witness my struggle."

She looped her arm around his neck and snuggled closer. "If you can't share your struggle with me, then who can you share it with?"

He wrenched free of her embrace, growling, "No one! I can handle this by myself!"

Betty Jane, clearly sensing Wade's continued tension from his tone and body language, moved close to Wade again and pawed his leg until he stroked her head.

Harlow said nothing, giving Wade a moment to compose himself. But after a few deep breaths, he cut a side glance at her and said, "I'd like to be alone for a while. Would you...go back to the other room?"

Pain pierced her heart. Not only was Wade continuing to isolate himself, she'd thought when they'd made love that she'd finally reached him, made the connection she wanted that would warrant changing her life plans to give their relationship another shot.

But here he was holding her at arm's length again. Pushing her away. Closing himself off. That was no way to build a future together. If he couldn't trust her enough to share all of himself with her, how could she open herself to him again?

She gave Betty Jane's head a pat, picked Luna up from the chair where she slept and carried her cat back to the guest room to finish the night alone.

She was fooling herself thinking she had any reason to stay in Owl Creek. Her parents' house was ready to put on the market. Her stalker was clearly in town, lurking, waiting for another chance to hurt her or someone she cared about. And Wade was no closer to sharing his life with her in the open and honest way she needed than he had been eleven years ago.

In the morning, she would pack her things and move on. She would find a new city to take refuge in and put away the false hope of a life with Wade Colton.

Chapter Twenty

Wade spent the final hours of the night tossing and turning, trying to quiet the turmoil in his head and heart. After making love to Harlow, he'd thought they'd finally reconciled and found a way forward. But when Harlow had pressed him to talk about his nightmare, while the haunting shadows and screams were still so vivid in his brain, he snapped at her and pushed her away.

Why couldn't she just let him heal at his own pace? He was doing his best. He had already talked to her more openly about the day of the explosion than he had to anyone else. He'd gotten Betty Jane. He'd made progress with his family.

And it was still not enough for her.

Even as he tried to justify his actions, his conscience pricked him.

You were rude to her. Too harsh when she only wanted to help.

Wade groaned and threw an arm over his eyes. Betty Jane snuggled closer, pushing her nose into his hand. He stroked the husky's head idly and took a few calming breaths. When the first weak rays of sunlight seeped through his window and he felt more in control of himself, he finally got up and went looking for Harlow.

He found her in the guest room, tossing clothes into her suitcase. His heart squeezed. "What are you doing?"

She stilled for a moment before resuming her packing. "Leaving."

Wade's pulse spiked, and he blurted, "Hell no. Not with that lunatic still after you."

She scoffed and spared him a brief side glance full of irritation. "Maybe I'm going *because* of my stalker. If he's here, I should leave."

He shook his head, too gobsmacked by her decision to process it fully. "Wh—where will you go?"

"I haven't decided. Anywhere that is not Owl Creek."

He snorted and smacked the frame of the door with his open palm. "That's rich."

She paused again from her packing and faced him. "Pardon?"

"Eleven years ago, I asked you to marry me, to go with me when I left for the Marines, and you said you couldn't. You said Owl Creek was your home, and you would never live anywhere else." Frustration soured his gut. He moved closer, glaring down at her. "Of course we now know that was a lie, seeing as how you left for college in California and never moved back. That you avoided Owl Creek until a few weeks ago when you had to come to close out your parents' house."

She straightened her back, her face flushing as her mouth tightened. "That is not what happened."

"Really?" Wade folded his arms over his chest knowing his tone was bitter and wanting to reel it back, but somehow not able to stop the poison that spewed from him. "And just what did I get wrong?"

Harlow's shoulders sagged as if reluctant to dive into this argument, but after taking a slow breath, she raised her chin. "First of all, what I said the night we broke up was that for the first time in my life I had a place in Owl Creek that felt like home. You knew I'd spent my childhood moving as an Army brat. I was trying to explain to you that I finally felt like I had some stability and consistency in my life in Owl Creek. I had friends I considered family. Your family! But you were asking me to give up that safety net, the sense of home I cherish for the same transient life I'd grown to hate."

"I was asking you to trust *me* to give you stability and safety. I wanted to be your home, to be your husband!" Hurt welled in him as it had that night long ago. "I wanted to matter enough to you, I wanted to *be* enough for you… but you rejected everything I was trying to offer you. My heart, my life, my future."

Her face fell, and she shook her head slowly. "And yet… that same night you told me you didn't really love me. You broke up with me and pushed me away saying horrible mean things."

Wade grunted and balled his fist. "I didn't mean those things! I was angry and hurt. In the moment, I thought it would make it easier for us both to move on if you hated me."

"I didn't want to move on!" she shouted, her voice thick with tears. "I wanted time for us to figure out a way to compromise, to salvage our relationship as we both worked toward our dreams."

"You never said that!"

"I tried to but—"

"You can't expect me to buy some revisionist version of

what happened and think it excuses everything that happened and that it erases the years of pain and regret."

"No. Nothing will change the past. But we can see the truth with more understanding and forgiveness...if you're willing." Harlow raked both hands through her hair. "God, Wade, we were still kids. Teenagers are notoriously self-involved. We were both selfish and unprepared for the realities of marriage. We both made plenty of mistakes. Obviously, we let our emotions and blind spots push us into defensive corners rather than listen to each other."

Wade gritted his teeth. "Seems as though we still are."

"Well—" she returned to her packing "—since I've been back in Owl Creek, I've tried to reach out to you and have the open and honest conversation we need to repair the past, to find common ground."

"So once again, it's my fault."

Harlow stilled for a moment, then threw the blouse in her hand onto the bed with a growl. "I didn't say that!" She stomped toward the door and pushed past him.

"Where are you going?" He dogged her steps, his insides a knot of pain and confusion and fear. Yet when he should have been showing her that he wanted to change, that he wanted to find a way back to her, his frustration boiled up instead. "Running away from this conversation like you're running away from me and Owl Creek?"

She only slowed down enough to snatch her coat and hat from the peg by the door. "We both need a minute to cool down. I don't want to leave town with angry words between us again."

"Harlow, don't—"

She strode briskly outside, and the door slammed shut behind her.

HARLOW STOMPED THROUGH the snow, seething with hurt and frustration. She didn't stop until she reached the edge of Blackbird Lake, where she stared out over the flat expanse of ice. The empty, frozen lake reminded her a bit of her future. Nothing there. No one in sight. Sure, she still had her show, but a Facebook advice show didn't keep her company at night or share her dreams of children. She'd warned herself that letting Wade back into her heart was dangerous, but she'd been foolish enough to believe—

The crunch of footsteps in icy snow yanked her from her deliberations, and she spun around, half expecting Wade, half fearing her stalker.

Instead, she met the pale blue eyes of a late-middle-aged woman in a black coat and knit hat. She exhaled her relief—until she noticed the pistol in the woman's hand.

Confusion mixed with the shot of nervous energy that rushed through her blood. "What…who are you?"

"I'm your reckoning," the woman said hotly, her eyes narrowing. "Sharon's vengeance."

And it clicked. With a spurt of adrenaline that balled like ice in her gut, she knew. "You're Chris72583?"

"*72584!* Her birthday! July 25, 1984."

"And… Chris?"

"Short for Christina. It's what Sharon called me," the woman said, her voice breaking.

Even with the confirmation, Harlow goggled and fumbled to process—her stalker was a woman? Her mind whirled trying to reassess everything she'd assumed, everything that had happened—

The woman took a step closer, and Harlow shifted all of her focus to the weapon aimed at her, the hatred blazing in the woman's expression. "Wh-what do you want? Why—"

"My baby sister is dead because of *you*, because of your terrible advice," Chris snarled.

Harlow raised a hand, palm out, hoping to signal a truce, a plea for calm. "I'm so sorry for your loss. Truly. Maybe if we talk about—"

"Ha!" Chris barked bitterly. "Your turn for talking is long over, *Harlow*." She gritted her teeth as she grated out Harlow's name like a curse word.

Swallowing hard, Harlow cast a quick glance toward Wade's cabin. From this angle, could he see her out his window? Probably not. And he'd closed the curtains overnight to help conserve heat and block drafts. Should she scream for help? Stay cool and try to talk Chris down? Panicking wouldn't help, but without signaling Wade in some way—

Chris surged forward, grabbing Harlow's arm and jabbing the gun under her chin. "If you make a sound, I'll kill your lover boy, too, just for sport."

Kill Wade, *too*? Harlow gulped. So murder was what Chris had in mind, just as the threats had promised. While her gut swooped with dread, her heart clenched at the notion of doing anything that would put Wade in danger. More danger than she'd already put him in…

"Got it?" Chris asked, shoving her nose close enough to Harlow's that she could smell a hint of coffee on the woman's breath.

Coffee. A flicker of recognition teased Harlow. "You were at the coffee shop… I mean, the bookstore the other afternoon."

"I was. Close enough to kill you, even then…if not for all the other people that would have hampered my getaway. But we're all alone now…aren't we?" Chris hissed, poking the underside of Harlow's chin harder with the muzzle.

Harlow nodded. She had to think of a way to reason with Chris, to find a solution that didn't involve bloodshed—hers or Chris's.

Chris took a moment to glance around, frowning. "I can't do it here in the open. Lover boy will hear and come running."

"You don't have to do it at all," Harlow said gently. "If I could do something to make amends for—"

"You can't! Not unless you can bring my baby sister back from the dead!" Chris choked out the words, then drew a deep breath, composing herself as her gaze landed on something in the distance. Something in the direction of Hannah's house. "Come with me."

"Where…?" As Chris dragged her by the arm, shifting the weapon to the base of Harlow's skull, Harlow angled her head and spotted their likely destination. Hannah's storage building at the end of her friend's short fishing pier.

A new location, hidden from Wade's view. Nothing about that was good. Harlow braced her legs, refusing to walk, but her feet slipped in the icy snow. She went down, dragging Chris off-balance as well. Her captor only stumbled and soon had righted herself, only to lash out at Harlow. She smacked Harlow across the cheek with the butt of the pistol.

Pain ricocheted though Harlow's jaw, and she tasted blood. The cry of anguish slipped from her lips before she could catch it.

"Shut up!" Chris said through clenched teeth, then smacked her again, hitting Harlow in the temple this time.

Harlow's howl this time was as much rage and frustration as pain. "Stop it! Just…stop! I'm sorry your sister died, but blaming me, killing me solves nothing." She took a trembling breath as Chris hauled her to her feet again.

Mustering her courage and her wits, Harlow turned, facing the woman squarely. If she kept her talking, had more information, maybe she could find a way to negotiate with her. "Tell me what happened. How did your sister die? Why do you think I'm to blame?"

"Because she called in to your show." Chris seized her arm again and dragged her forward. "She *told you* how dangerous her husband was, and you told her to leave him. She *told you* how mad he'd be, how he'd come after her and kill her, and you didn't listen!"

Harlow tried to sift through her memories of the calls she and Wade had been replaying, analyzing. Had there been an abused woman named Sharon? She recalled counseling several people, men and women, concerning domestic violence, always counseling safety for the party involved above all else.

Harlow stumbled along with Chris, moving farther away from Wade's cabin and the hope that he'd see her, see Chris and the gun. Her mouth was sore from the woman's blow, dry with fear, numb from cold. She licked her chapped lips and said in the calmest voice she could muster, "If she called about a violent partner, I would have wanted her to remove herself from the situation for her protection. If I told her to leave her husband, it was because I believed she'd be better off—"

"Dead? Better off dead? She *told you* he'd kill her, and you told her to leave anyway." Chris stopped suddenly and whirled to face her, growling, "I raised Sharon after our mother died. She was like a daughter to me! I loved her more than anyone on earth." Fury darkened Chris's face. "My Sharon's blood is on your hands!"

A pang of grief and guilt spun through Harlow. The

absolute worst-case scenario for her was always that her counseling failed and a client was injured or killed. Even if the loss of life came because the client ignored her advice, Harlow felt a sense of failure. While her training taught that she couldn't be blamed for other people's actions, that ultimately every individual must be accountable for themselves, the losses hurt. She wouldn't be in this business if she didn't truly and deeply care about her clients. She couldn't bring Sharon back for Chris, but could she do something, say something to ease the sting of the woman's grief?

"Chris, I understand that you are hurting. Losing a loved one is difficult. Especially—"

"Shut up!" Her captor jerked hard on her arm and shot her a poisonous glare. "You had your chance to—" Chris's step faltered, and an oddly smug look crossed her face. "Fine. You want to talk? Then you will." Planting a hand in Harlow's back, she shoved her forward.

With her arm free of Chris's grip, Harlow recognized her chance to attempt an escape. She *almost* ran. A tingle of energy shot down her legs to her feet that she reined in at the last second. She couldn't outrun a bullet in her back.

Instead, she plodded on through the wooded property between Wade's cabin and Hannah's house. And what about her responsibility to this grieving woman? If she spent a little time with her, could she help Chris find a path through her suffering? Sure, the woman had committed several crimes—not the least of which was threatening her life and Wade's when she shot at them. Chris would have to answer to the justice system for her wrongdoing, but she didn't have to add murder to her rap sheet—not if Harlow could talk her down.

Chris grabbed Harlow's coat at the nape and, shoving her to a faster pace, guided her to the door of the storage house. The latch wasn't locked, and Chris was able to open the door. With a jerk of her head, Chris said, "Inside, Harlow. We have business to take care of."

WADE PACED THE living room floor, debating whether to follow Harlow or give her time to calm down before he tried again to explain himself. As he stalked restlessly back and forth, Betty Jane treaded along by his side. She tried to block his path, tried to get his attention with soft whines and hand nuzzles. He acknowledged Betty Jane, giving her a treat, but walked around her to continue his pacing. He replayed Harlow's parting words and wrestled with his accusation that she was running away. But was he the one who was running away? Not literally, perhaps, but by avoiding hard topics, ignoring difficult truths?

He'd always believed his choices, the way he'd handled everything in their relationship had been about protecting Harlow and giving her the best chance for the kind of life she wanted, even when those decisions and actions cut him to the bone. How could she call that selfish? How could his willingness to sacrifice for her and let her go be rooted in fear?

He shoved the suggestion aside. It was preposterous!

And yet...a strange nagging sensation chewed at his belly. He had been dealing with a lot of unsettled feelings, anxiety and self-imposed isolation since coming back from the Marines. He had to admit he had been more anxious in recent days because of the rising stakes with her stalker, because of the reminders of the relationship they'd lost, because of the incidents that had stirred up his PTSD night-mares and flashbacks.

God, could she be right? The last thing he wanted, as a Marine—because though he'd left the service, he was still always a Marine in his head and heart—was to be labeled frightened. Marines didn't do scared. Marines faced intimidation with their teeth bared and a growl in their throat. *Oorah!*

Huffing out a breath of frustration, Wade dropped onto his recliner and rubbed the heel of a hand into his good eye. His shoulders drooped as he took a hard look at his life, at the changes that the past years had wrought and the way he'd dealt with his injuries and guilt.

Betty Jane propped her chin on his lap and bumped his elbow with her nose until he patted her head. "Good girl," he said, retrieving another dog treat from the drawer of the lamp table beside him. With a soft chuff, he acknowledged that stroking Betty Jane's head and having her warm body snuggled sympathetically close *did* ease the tension wound through his chest.

Sebastian and Harlow had been right about the service dog helping him. On the heels of that admission, he allowed himself to consider what else Harlow had been right about. He leaned his head back on the chair and closed his eye. He sat like that for several moments, taking slow breaths and trying to refocus his thoughts, trying to search his heart and word an apology to Harlow. But then Betty Jane's head jerked up, her tags jangling. She glanced toward the back window and whined.

Wade studied his dog's behavior. "Betty Jane?"

The husky licked his hand but continued to send agitated

glances toward the back window. What could have bothered her? A squirrel? Harlow walking the yard as she fumed?

Sebastian had said the dog's training included teaching Betty Jane not to let other animals, people or noises distract her from her job of guarding and aiding Wade. Wade was about to correct the dog, run through the steps that Sebastian had given him for refocusing the young service dog.

Then he heard it, too. A cry. A panicked shout. Harlow.

He bolted from his seat, nearly tripping over Betty Jane in his haste to get to the door. As he snatched his coat from the wall hook, he shoved BJ away from the door. "Stay!" he told the dog and raced outside.

He visually followed the path of Harlow's footprints, which wound around the side of the house, before he set out, but the next noise he heard, a distant, angry voice, came from the opposite direction. Wade needed no further information. He hurried through the snow and ice, crunching across his yard, tracking the voices, scanning the surroundings as he trotted.

When he found footprints coming from the woods close to the road, he rushed over to them for a closer look. Again, he visually tracked the path of the depressions in the snow toward the edge of Blackbird Lake until he spotted a second trail of footprints joining the first set.

Cold dread settled in Wade's chest. Harlow's stalker? He struggled to keep his panic at bay. Harlow needed him to focus, to think, to act.

At the edge of the lake, the prints became messy, snow scattered as if there'd been a tussle, and his gut roiled with dread. Moving quickly, he tracked the footprints in the direction of his sister's house. Could the second set of prints be Hannah's? Had Hannah recruited help from Harlow because something happened to Lucy?

A fresh wave of concern flowed through him at that notion. But…if Hannah or Lucy were in trouble, they'd have called 911, not come for Harlow. And the second set of prints came from the road, like the shooter had yesterday at the ranch. Hell! He trotted faster, the possibility of slipping and falling on the slick ice his only concession to speed.

Wade skirted the edge of Blackbird Lake as he rushed toward his sister's property. He'd traveled about half the distance when a sobering thought pierced his panic, and he hesitated to take a mental inventory. He was unarmed. He had no backup. He was blind in one eye and headed toward an unknown, likely dangerous situation.

Did he go back to the cabin for his service weapon? He'd run out the door without his phone, too. Damn it! Going back would eat valuable time, and Harlow needed help *now*.

Another loud, distressed cry settled the matter. He didn't have time to equivocate. Picking up his pace, Wade continued following the footprints.

HARLOW HESITATED ON the threshold of the dim building, dreading what would happen, shut away from view. At least outside, there was a chance Hannah would look out her window and call 911. Or Wade would realize how long she'd been gone, step out in his yard and see her with her abductor.

"Go on! Get in there. Hurry!" the woman said, jabbing Harlow's nape with the cold muzzle of her gun.

The inside of Hannah's storage building was dark and musty-smelling. The walls were lined with shelves, loaded with plastic storage bins and dishes, and the center of the floor had four sawhorses supporting two canoes. Harlow shuffled in, dread coiling in her gut.

Behind her, Chris found the light switch and a fluorescent glow blinked on, illuminating the dank space. Harlow faced the woman, trying not to stare at the gun aimed at her. She needed all her confidence and composure to address her volatile captor. "Chris, I know you are hurting. Grief is difficult, and everyone has to grieve in their own way."

Chris's face darkened. "You don't know squat about what I'm feeling! And I didn't ask your opinion." While holding the gun leveled at Harlow with her right hand, she fished a cell phone from her pocket with her left. "You like preaching to people on the internet? Well, we're going to make a little video, right now, that I'm going to blast all over the web."

Harlow stilled, her mind racing. If she complied, could she buy time for Wade to realize she was missing? She thought about the angry words she'd thrown at Wade before she stomped out. Why had she let her temper, her pain, her frustration get the better of her? The wedge that had divided her and Wade for all these years couldn't be wiped away by snapping her fingers. Reconciliation would take commitment, understanding and effort from both of them.

"You're going to tell the world how you were responsible for Sharon's death," Chris said, bringing Harlow's focus back to the problem at hand.

Before she could resolve things with Wade, she had to survive this confrontation with her stalker.

"You're going to tell the world how your horrid advice got my sister killed. How Sharon's death deserves to be punished," Chris said, "And that you're taking your own life because of your guilt."

Alarm streaked through Harlow. "What? No!"

Chris took a long step closer, jamming the gun in her face. "You will! Your screwup cost me everything I love, and you're going to tell the world you were to blame!"

Harlow raised a shaky hand, signaling for calm, for patience. "Chris, please, put the weapon down. Shooting me will not serve any purpose. It's not too late to rethink this situation."

"I've done all the thinking I need to. You got Sharon killed, and for that you deserve to die!"

"I'm sorry Sharon was killed. So deeply sorry. I never wanted that to happen. I only ever want to help my callers and ensure their safety."

"Fat lot of good your sorry is worth now! She's *gone*!" Tears pooled in Chris's eyes. "I have to make you pay for what you did! I have to give my Sharon justice!"

"Chris," Harlow said, infusing her tone with warmth and compassion. "You're not a killer. You don't want to go to prison. Sharon wouldn't want that for you, would she?"

"Shut up! You're not worthy to speak her name!" With the back of her left hand, Chris swiped the tears from her cheeks.

"Chris, Sharon wouldn't—"

"Shut up!" Chris shouted—and fired the pistol.

Chapter Twenty-One

Wade studied the tracks in the snow as he moved stealthily along the frozen shoreline. The two sets of footprints were practically on top of each other rather than side by side now. Whoever was with Harlow was walking behind or in front of her, not beside her. Why—

The sound of a gun firing echoed across the water and ricocheted from the line of trees. Wade skidded to a stop, his heart rising to his throat. Horror choked him. He couldn't be too late. Couldn't! *Please, God, let Harlow be okay!* He set off again at a run, his feet sliding on the icy snow.

As he neared Hannah's property, the storage building at the end of her pier, he heard voices again. Women's voices. He frowned. He'd thought the person with Harlow was her stalker, but—

He grimaced and whispered a curse under his breath. He'd assumed her stalker was a man. Statistically speaking, it wasn't a bad assumption. Except making assumptions was usually a mistake. And his mistake could now cost Harlow her life.

Pressing his back to the outside wall of the storage building, he eased to the corner where he could peer around the edge. The door stood ajar, and he saw shadows shifting inside. Straining to listen, he followed the conversation to get a read on where things stood inside, what he was walking into, who was standing where relative to the door.

"Next time it will be in your brain," the unfamiliar voice said, her tone dripping menace. "Now the only talking you're going to do is for your confession. You'll say exactly what I tell you and nothing else. Understood?"

Confession? Wade frowned. *What the...?*

As he crouched at the corner of the storage building, he heard a noise to his left and glanced to Hannah's back door. His sister had stepped out, clearly concerned by the gunshot, and called to him. Rising to his feet, he signaled her urgently with his hands to stay back and be silent. Then he made a gesture like using a phone and held up his fingers signaling 9-1-1.

Pressing a hand to her mouth, Hannah nodded and disappeared inside. He hoped that Hannah would call Fletcher first, knowing their brother and his men could get here faster with a direct call rather than waiting on 911 to collect information and reroute the call.

Taking a breath, he refocused on the sounds coming from the storage building. He needed to get in there, unseen. If he could move in from behind and take the stalker down, even if he got hurt in the process, it would be worth it to save Harlow. Harlow was what mattered.

And in that instant, he knew that his life, his future happiness depended on having Harlow beside him. Whatever it took, whatever words she needed, whatever changes to his life he had to make, he would do it to keep Harlow close. He'd give anything to have the woman he loved safe, fulfilled and at his side.

From inside the storage building, he heard the other woman say tightly, "I am responsible for the murder of Sharon Wilson. Because of my reckless and unprofessional advice that she leave the marriage, her husband killed her. I am to blame for—"

"No. Chris, Sharon's ex is the only person to blame. I did what I was trained to—"

"Say it, or I swear I will kill you!"

A chill slithered down Wade's spine. He needed to get in there and stop this standoff before the unstable woman did something rash, something deadly.

"Don't you plan to kill me after I make your video? Why would I give you a false confession if you're going to shoot me anyway?"

He heard the woman growl her frustration. "I want to hear you say it! Tell the world what you did to my sister or... or..." There was a pause, and in the silence, Wade could hear his own heartbeat pound in his ears as he eased along the side of the storage hut.

"Say it, or I'll hike back over to that little cabin and kill your boyfriend," the woman said, her tone gloating.

Wade pulled up, startled by...what? Being called her boyfriend, or by having his own life used to bait and influence Harlow?

"I don't have a boyfriend." Harlow's voice trembled, and the fear he heard stabbed Wade's gut. She was trying to protect him, deflect the threat even at the cost of her own safety. He was filled with an odd cocktail of loathing for the woman who'd put Harlow in this position, who even now was threatening her, and a pang of despondency over Harlow's denial of their relationship.

Wade gritted his back teeth and shoved the swirl of emotions aside. He couldn't let his feelings distract him. His distraction eighteen months ago had gotten a soldier in his charge killed. He had to do a better job now. Harlow's life depended on him getting it right. *Stay focused.*

"Mr. Eye Patch?" the woman with Harlow squawked. A chuff of dismissal. "Maybe he's not your boyfriend, but I'm not blind. I've been watching the two of you together."

This bit of news rankled. They'd been *spied on*, and he'd missed it. He'd failed Harlow, damn it.

"You love him," the woman taunted. "And why should you have someone you love when you cost me the person I loved most?"

Wade rounded the corner of the building, stepping slowly to minimize the crunching of the snow under his feet.

"Why do you get to be happy when I've been left in misery because of *you*?"

"Killing me, killing…anyone…is not the answer, Chris."

Back pressed to the front wall, Wade peeked inside the storage room.

Harlow held both hands in front of her, palms out in a *stop* gesture. "If you put the gun down and walk away, I promise not to press charges. I can get you help for your—"

Harlow stopped abruptly as her gaze flickered to him in the door. Wade gave a quick shake of his head and touched a finger to his lips.

"Help? Like you gave Sharon?" The woman cackled derisively. "No, thank you!"

The subtle shift in her expression told him Harlow was making mental calculations in light of his arrival. She was still at the business end of a pistol. She was still negotiating with an irrational and dangerous woman.

"The only thing I want from you is retribution. And a

public admission of fault. I don't want anyone else's baby sister following your horrid advice and dying."

"I don't want anyone to die either, *Chris*."

Wade picked up on the subtle emphasis Harlow put on the name, understanding the message she was sending him. *This is the stalker.* He gave a small nod, then pulled back from the door as he weighed his options. He felt sure that with the element of surprise, his Special Ops training and his size and strength advantage over Chris, that he could overtake and disarm Harlow's stalker. But...

Chris was a panicked finger squeeze away from shooting Harlow. He needed to signal Harlow, warn her of his intentions, instruct her to get down, to ball up and protect her vital organs.

Waving the cell phone in her left hand, Chris grated again. "Say the words! Say you are responsible for my sister dying!"

Wade edged from the outside wall to fill the doorway, praying the stalker didn't notice the shifting shadow as he blocked the outside light. He lifted a hand, waiting for Harlow to glance over again. She was obviously trying not to give him away, trying to ignore his presence. But damn it, he had to get her attention! He gave her a stilted wave, and as soon as her eyes flickered toward him, he pointed at the ground, then clenched his fist.

Please understand what I'm telling you.

He repeated the signal.

Harlow gave the merest of nods as she said, "All right. I'll make the video. I'll apologize."

"Any time," Chris said, "I'm already recording."

With a long stride up behind the woman, Wade swept his arm from high to low, knocking Chris's gun arm down.

As expected, Chris yelped her surprise and fired the gun, even as Wade completed the downward arc of his arm with a hooking twist. The motion brought Chris's arm behind her back, the gun within range of Wade's grasp. He reached for the weapon, but possession of the gun was not so easily won. Chris spun around, following the tug on her arm until she faced Wade. Her alarmed expression quickly morphed to rage, and a battle for possession of the pistol began.

As soon as Wade made his move, Harlow dropped to the floor and curled in a ball, covering her head. She gasped as the gun fired again. Something stung her as it grazed her cheek. She heard the scuffle of feet and angled her head to find Wade and Chris grappling for the pistol.

"Wade!" she cried as she pushed to her knees.

"Stay down!" He backed Chris against the shelving that lined the walls, and dishes rattled as they jostled and jockeyed.

Despite his directive, Harlow hated the idea of staying on the floor, cowering and unhelpful. She moved to a crouch, ready to spring up or drop again as the situation merited. She cast her gaze about for a tool, a makeshift weapon, *something* she could use to defend Wade and swing the momentum in their favor. Spying a kayak paddle propped in the back corner, she rose to her feet but only made it one step before Wade's voice echoed through the small room. "Freeze! Get on the ground!"

And Harlow pivoted toward him, her breath stuck in her lungs.

Wade didn't want to hurt the woman, but if he had to, he would incapacitate her, injure her in a way that would bring the situation under control. The woman's stubborn refusal to release the pistol made the necessity of stronger force more and more likely. Chris grunted and growled her outrage as he pinned her against the shelving unit and forcefully peeled her fingers away from the weapon. If he had to break a finger, so be it. He had to neutralize the threat of the gun. One on one against him, Chris was outsized, outskilled, outmaneuvered. Once unarmed, Harlow's stalker could be taken into custody easily.

But she wasn't going quietly. Chris screamed and bit and thrashed and slapped as he fought to wrench the gun from her. Finally, he managed to pin her scrabbling limbs enough to twist the pistol out of her grip. Howling her frustration, Chris clawed at him and fought to regain possession of the pistol. He held it above his head, out of her reach, until he could break loose of her battling hand and take a determined step back.

She lunged toward him, and in order to stop her—and *only* to keep her in line and exert his control over the situation—he aimed the pistol at Chris and shouted, "Freeze! Get on the ground!"

For a moment, Chris stilled. But in an instant that caught Wade off guard, she reached for a tray on the shelving unit, snatched up a large butcher knife and held it up in front of her.

A curse word flittered through Wade's brain. Why did she have to make this difficult? He could shoot her, end this standoff now, but that wasn't how he wanted things to go. He wanted no part of ending another life. He already had to grapple with his part in Sanders's death. Through clenched teeth he snarled, "Drop the knife, or I *will* drop *you*."

He saw the flicker of fear in the woman's eyes. Recognized the moment her resolve hardened stubbornly. Her mouth firmed. Her eyes blazed.

And with a couple quick, backpedaling steps, she seized Harlow, shoved her in front of her as a human shield, and pressed the knife to Harlow's throat so hard she drew a thin trickle of blood.

Ice shot to Wade's marrow, and adrenaline kicked his pulse into overdrive.

Focus, he reminded himself, even as a roar like fire exploded in his mind. *Don't get distracted.*

"Drop the knife," he repeated, his tone commanding, despite the frantic pulse in his veins.

"Give me back my gun," Chris countered. When he didn't flinch, the stalker added, "I will cut her throat! I swear I will!" Chris's volume was rising even as her patience was clearly eroding.

"Chris," Harlow said, her voice somewhat strangled by the pressure against her windpipe. "Please. This doesn't have to end badly. You can still do the right thing. Sharon wouldn't have wanted this for you."

"Put the gun on the floor and kick it to me." Chris shoved Harlow forward, closing the gap between the women and Wade. "Now!"

Wade stood his ground until it occurred to him that outside, Chris wouldn't have the variety of further makeshift weapons. If, between him and Harlow, they could disarm the irate woman…

Harlow must have been on the same wavelength, because at that moment she threw her head back, hard, smashing the back of her skull into the other woman's nose. The move gave Harlow just enough advantage to wrench her hands up around the knife handle and push the blade away from her throat. Once free of the blade's threat, Harlow stomped on the other woman's instep.

Wade goggled, admiring Harlow's grit as he watched her twist and jab her elbow, employing classic self-defense moves.

Enraged, Chris fought back, and Wade decided his best move with the least bodily harm was disarming the stalker. But first...

"Chris! You want your gun?" he shouted as he walked backward out of the storage building.

Chris paused, lifting her head toward him. Harlow seized the chance to dig her fingernails into her opponent's wrist and pry the knife from Chris's hand. Standing between Harlow, wielding the butcher knife, and Wade, holding the pistol, Chris panted for a breath and glared.

Before she could rearm herself with another knife, Wade knew he had to draw the woman away from Harlow. He set the gun on the ground, just beyond the threshold, and stepped back, his hands up and empty. "Here it is. Come get it."

Chris scowled, staring at him as if trying to work out the trick. Then, giving herself away with a glance toward the pistol, she lunged for the gun. Wade was faster. He stepped forward and kicked the gun from her reach. In the same forward motion, he knocked Chris to the ground. While Chris scrambled to stand on the slick icy snow, he snatched up the pistol again. With a windup and pitch that would have made his Little League coach proud, Wade threw the pistol far out onto the ice-covered lake.

From the frozen ground where she'd landed, Chris's eyes widened and fury pinched her face. "Nooo! You son of a bitch!"

Harlow emerged from the storage shed, her fingers wiping blood from the small cut on her neck, and handed Wade the knife. "You can get rid of this, too. But maybe don't throw it on the lake and lose it permanently. I'm guessing Hannah still wants it."

He bobbed a nod of agreement and turned to fling the large knife toward Hannah's house to be retrieved later.

He'd only just released the knife, watching it hurtle through the air, when snow crunched behind him.

Harlow gasped. "Wade!"

Before he could turn, he was struck, low and hard, as Chris plowed into him, her shoulder lowered. He stumbled forward, his feet slipping on the packed snow, and went down. His breath whooshed from his lungs, and a searing pain shot through his shoulder. He gasped like a fish out of water, unable to move his arm. Before he could regain his breath and warn her away, Harlow rushed forward to assist him, attempting to grab her rage-fueled and vicious stalker.

Harlow grabbed the sleeve of Chris's coat, shouting, "No! Chris, stop this! Now! It's over."

But instead, her stalker spun toward her and grabbed a fist full of Harlow's long hair, winding the tresses tightly around her hand. A thousand pin pricks stung her scalp, and Harlow cried out in pain.

"Nothing is over!" Chris jerked hard on Harlow's hair, towing her toward the edge of the frozen lake.

Tears filled her eyes as Chris tugged brutally, grabbing more and more of Harlow's hair into her fist as she marched briskly across the snow.

"Stop! Ow! What are you doing?" Harlow panted as she stumbled, bent over at the waist, while Chris dragged her to the lake's edge. Harlow battled Chris's hands, but her opponent had wrapped the strands tightly, tangled her fingers in Harlow's hair. "Please stop!"

"I'm getting my gun," Chris said, "and then both you and the pirate are going to die."

When Chris took her first few steps onto the ice at the edge of the lake, a fresh terror swamped Harlow. It hadn't been cold enough, long enough for the lake ice to support the weight of an adult...much less two adults.

"Stop! The ice is too thin!" Despite the pain of her hair pulling, ripping out at the roots, Harlow struggled against Chris's grip. "We can't go out there. The ice will break!"

"Shut up!" Chris growled, yanking harder on Harlow's hair, plodding faster across the ice.

Bent over at the awkward position she was in, Harlow couldn't tell how far out they'd come, but she knew with every step the danger to them grew—the ice would be thinner, the shore would be farther, the water would be deeper.

"Please," she begged, tears of pain and fear filling her eyes, "Please go back! It's too dangerous to be out here!"

"I'm getting my gun!" Chris grated.

And Harlow heard the first pop, the cracking sound that shot cold terror to her bones.

Chapter Twenty-Two

Both winded and with his arm dislocated, Wade was slow getting to his feet. Too slow. By the time he'd struggled to his knees, using only one arm for balance as he rose, Chris had dragged Harlow to the shore of Blackbird Lake. He realized the stalker's intent immediately but couldn't get the air in his lungs to shout a warning.

How far out were Fletcher and his men? An ambulance? Had Hannah reached them and requested backup?

If they weren't here now, they were still too far away.

"Wade!"

He angled his head toward Hannah's house as his sister burst through the back door and ran across her lawn to him. "Are you all right? Who is that woman? I called 911, but—"

"No!" he gasped thinly, waving her off. "Go…inside."

"You're hurt!" Hannah shoved her phone in her pocket and used both hands to help him gain his feet and traction. "Oh my God! Your arm!"

"Get…inside!" He sucked in a thin breath as his lungs finally loosened. "Call… Fletcher and…keep Lucy out of harm's way!" He shoved his sister back toward the house, but she twisted free of his grasp.

"Fletcher is coming." She pulled the phone out of her

pocket and told the person on the line, "My brother's injured. I think his arm is dislocated!"

He pushed Hannah toward the house again. "Get inside, damn it!"

Hannah's gaze flickered to the lake, and she gasped. "Harlow! Oh no, no, no! The ice—"

"I know." He staggered toward the lake, cradling his injured arm, and he called over his shoulder to Hannah. "Tell them we'll need an ambulance!"

He'd only made it a few loping steps, each one jarring his throbbing shoulder, when he heard the loud crack that echoed from the trees across the lake. His heart stilled, and his gaze darted to the two figures on the ice. In the next moment, the ice beneath them shattered, and the freezing water swallowed Harlow and her scream.

THE ICY BLACKNESS closed over Harlow's head. She could feel the thrashing of Chris's limbs as her captor fought to free her hand—now needed to save her own life—from Harlow's hair. The sting of ripping hair paled in comparison to the suffocating bite of the icy water. The lake was so cold it hurt. Instantly and deeply. She could feel the numbing, paralyzing ache of cold sinking quickly to her core.

Air. She needed air.

As much as the freezing water hurt, the ache in her lungs for oxygen seared as harshly. Worse.

She finally broke the surface and gasped in air. Once. Twice. She was hyperventilating, panting from fear and shocking cold. She tried to tread water, but her arms and legs were stiff, slow to move or obey the command of her brain. She managed to use her feet to push off her snow boots, lightening the weight that dragged at her. When with a final rip of hair, Chris pulled free of her, Harlow flailed her arms, groping blindly for the edge of the ice. Chris's weight pulled her down. Her captor's thrashing was breaking more and more of the ice ledge.

No! her brain screamed. She couldn't die like this, not when her last words to Wade had been so cruel. So untrue. Of course she loved him! Of course she wanted a life with him! She had to get out of this water, had to tell him that. If she died today because of her stalker, because of this frozen lake, so be it. But Wade had to know the truth.

THE INSTANT HARLOW disappeared under the ice, Wade sprinted for the lake, his dislocated shoulder all but forgotten. All that mattered was Harlow. He had to get her out of the icy lake before hypothermia took her from him.

"Wade, stop!" Hannah shouted. She was on his heels, grabbing at his jacket. "You can't go out there! You'll fall in, too!"

He stopped at the edge of the ice, pulling off his heavy boots. "I need a rope. A long, strong one." He turned to his terrified sister. Hannah was shaking her head, clearly worried for him. Gritting his teeth, he growled, "I will not let the woman I love die! I have to try!"

Hannah's mouth opened, as if to argue, tears filling her eyes, then she sighed and said, "Rope. What else?"

Wade sorted through his tumbling thoughts, forcibly quashing the panic that would steal his ability to reason and act judiciously. "One of the kayak paddles. A carabiner or two. And blankets and heat packs. Lots of them. Hurry!"

She ran for the storage building, and Wade took a few tentative steps out on the ice. After a few feet, where the ice was thickest, he lay down his stomach, which distrib-

uted his weight over a larger area of the ice. His body pros-
trate, he pulled with his good arm and pushed with his feet,
scooting across the frozen surface. He was approximately
halfway to the hole where the women splashed and struggled when Hannah shouted from shore. "Wade!"

He twisted enough to look back just as she half threw,
half slid the paddle to him with remarkable aim. Hannah
had known to tie one end of the sturdy rope to the paddle,
and Wade sent up silent gratitude for his sister's instincts
and quick response. Scooting the paddle in front of him as
he inched across the ice, he shouted, "Harlow!"

Drawing nearer to the hole, he saw a floundering hand,
a flash of her dark hair as her head bobbed up then sank
again. Hypothermia happened so fast. He couldn't remember the statistic in the moment, but he knew he had a fright-
eningly small window to get her out of the icy water before
her body shut down.

When he'd moved as far out on the ice as he dared, he
paused to tie a lasso at the end of the rope and shove the
loop to the end of the paddle. Extending it toward the hole,
he shouted again, "Harlow, grab the rope! Put the loop
around you, an arm through it."

When her head rose at the edge of the hole and she
dragged her arms to the top of the ice, a small frisson of
relief and hope spun through him. Quick as it came, the
relief died. Harlow was far from safe yet, and her clock
was ticking.

AN ODD CALM settled over Harlow after a couple of minutes. The icy water was still horrifying, still dragging at
her, but the initial gasping panic had passed. The freezing
lake had numbed her skin. Chris, too, had stopped flailing,

and with a side glance Harlow saw the other woman groping methodically for purchase across the growing hole in
the ice. Chris hoisted her body halfway out of the water,
only to have the ice break and send the woman back into
the slushy lake.

"Harlow!"

She lifted her gaze to find Wade, his body low to the
ice as he belly-crawled toward her. A poignant cocktail of
gratitude and dread spun through her mind, her brain too
cold and slow to sort out any reasoning behind her feelings. "W-Wade," she rasped, her voice thready as the cold
stole her breath.

He shouted something to her, and she tried to focus, to
stay conscious as the paralyzing cold made it harder and
harder to concentrate. A kayak paddle poked her hands,
and she saw the rope draped on it.

Grab it! a voice in her head said. Or maybe it was Wade's
voice.

She reached for the rope with trembling hands, her arm
heavy and weak. When she couldn't close her hand around
the rope, she struggled to pull off her sodden and refreezing
mitten. With her fingers freed from the mitten, she curled
her fingers enough to hook around the rope, drag it closer.
She had to rest. She paused and closed her eyes.

So cold…

So stiff…

So tiring to move…

"Harlow!" Wade's voice cut through her drowsy lethargy.
"Don't you dare leave me, damn it! I need you! I love you!"

Love…you…too. The words were there. On her tongue.
But stuck. Frozen.

Something deep within her rallied. She had to stay

alive...had to tell Wade...had to apologize. She seized the flash of determination and pulled the rope closer. Tried to move it over her head. Couldn't. Put an arm through it. Then the paddle lifted from the ice and bonked her head as it wavered and dropped the rope over her head. With small choppy movements, she wiggled the rope down, under her armpit.

"Kick your legs!" Wade shouted. "Get as flat as you can and hold on!"

Kick? She wasn't even sure she could move her legs.

Wade pulled on the rope, and it tightened around her, pulled her higher out of the water. When she tried to push, to lift herself out on the edge of the ice, the shelf crumbled. Frustration flared in her gut, and she tried again. Again, the ice chipped and collapsed under her.

"Kick your legs! Get flat!" Wade repeated.

And somehow through the fog in her brain, she recalled the technique they'd learned in high school that called for distributing one's weight as much as possible over the weak ice. She needed to leave the water as horizontally as possible, not with a vertical push.

Kick your legs...

She focused all her energy, all her concentration on moving her numb legs. Her limbs were heavy. Ached. But with effort, she managed a weak scissor kick. Then another.

Wade tugged harder on the rope and shouted, "Come on, Harlow, kick! Harder. You can do it, love."

Love? The term of endearment pierced the muzziness that swamped her. Her eyes prickled, and his plea prodded her to give more effort.

Kick. Kick. She heard the splash that said her efforts had brought her legs to the surface.

"That's it. Keep kicking!"

She groped with her arms as she slid higher, then slowly across the ice.

"Can you roll, Harlow? Roll to me!" Wade called.

She tried. Got about halfway over. The tug of the rope helped pull her over. Between Wade's pulling her and her sluggish assistance, he slowly dragged her to the edge of the lake. By then her entire body was shivering violently.

"Thank God!" Wade said, his voice choked with emotion as he gave her an awkward embrace. "Harlow, stay with me."

Then Hannah was there, helping him peel off her wet coat and clothes.

Her teeth chattered so hard she thought she might bite her tongue, but she tried to speak. "H-h-h—" Her throat wouldn't let her form the harder consonant she wanted, and she whimpered in pain and cold.

"I'm here, love." Wade bent and kissed her forehead.

She tried again, struggling to get any sound from her throat. "Ch-Chris."

Wade met her eyes, and she knew he understood. "Promise not to leave me?"

She managed a small nod, and after placing another kiss on her lips, Wade headed back out onto the ice.

Chapter Twenty-Three

Wade belly-crawled back out to the hole in the ice, picturing Private Sanders in his mind's eye. No way in hell would he let anyone die on his watch again, not even someone who'd tried to kill Harlow. Let the stalker pay for her crimes in prison, not with her life. Not while he still had a chance to save her.

He looped the rope on the paddle again and shouted toward the hole. "Chris! Can you hear me? Lift a hand or shout if you can."

He got no response. He inched closer, his progress impeded by his throbbing shoulder. No time to dwell on his own injury. He drew on his Special Forces training and used his mental reserves to help him ignore his pain and solve the problem he faced. One step at a time.

"Chris!" he called again as he reached the edge of the hole. He tossed the lasso, and the rope landed, circling her shoulders. "Chris, hook your arm through the rope!"

But the woman was unresponsive, and Wade watched in horror as she slid deeper into the icy water. He shifted, trying to catch her arm, a handful of her coat…something.

Crack!

The heat of adrenaline shot through Wade as he recognized the sound of the ice breaking. Before he could wiggle backward, he plunged into the icy lake. He shuddered with the shock of the freezing lake but kicked hard to get his head above water.

He grabbed the edge of the ice and gathered his wits, even as the cold tried to steal his breath. He panted a few times, sucking in shallow gulps of air, then forced his brain to focus. He turned to find Chris sinking even farther into the lake. Damn it!

"Wade!"

He blinked hard as he moved his gaze to the lakeshore where several figures now stood. Fletcher, Malcolm and Sebastian were among the men helping Hannah with Harlow and making their way, well spaced out, across the ice to him.

Moving hand over hand to pull himself to Chris, he hauled the woman up and fumbled the rope under her arm. Chris was shaking hard now, still unresponsive. But the tremors said she was still alive.

Malcolm, on his belly, reached the frozen rope and paddle first. "Are you tied on?"

Through chattering teeth, he replied, "Th-the woman f-first."

Fletcher, also flat on the ice, positioned himself a few feet down the rope and added his strength to the pulling. Sebastian was on shore with his feet braced as he tugged.

Wade's hold slipped, and he went under briefly, but as he kicked to the surface, he grabbed Chris's leg and shoved it upward. The added horizontal angling of the woman's body allowed their rescuers to haul her out of the lake.

Malcolm removed the rope and tossed it back to Wade. "Your turn, hero."

Wade growled in frustration as he worked the rope over his head and under his dislocated arm. At least the icy water had numbed the shoulder pain. Small favor. Exhaustion dragged at him when he tried to kick again, his legs finally rising to ease his exit as his family pulled him from the lake and across the ice. When he reached thicker ice, Fletcher hooked an arm under Wade's bad shoulder help him sit up. Wade gritted his teeth and growled his pain.

"I know, man. But you're safe now." Fletcher was unzipping Wade's coat and getting him out of his wet clothes.

"H-Harlow—"

"Awake and waiting for you in the back of the ambulance. You've done well, brother. Really well. Now let's get you warmed up."

Chapter Twenty-Four

"And how are my favorite human Popsicles doing?" Fletcher asked as he poked his head around the door of Harlow's hospital room.

Wade, whose shoulder had been reset and was feeling much better, squeezed Harlow's hand. "Thawing."

"And no one will lose any fingers or toes to frostbite. That's a blessing," Harlow added, then her expression sobered. "What about Chris? Did she live?"

Fletcher hesitated, then shook his head. "No. She, of course, stayed in the lake longer than either of you and apparently had a preexisting cardiac condition, which made her heart more susceptible to failure."

Harlow sighed. "While I'm glad that she can't terrorize or threaten me anymore, I'm sad that it ended so tragically. She was hurting and lost after the death of her sister. I know that doesn't excuse her actions, but with help, with proper counseling or medical intervention—"

"You're awfully forgiving, considering all the trouble she caused you." Wade creased his brow as he studied Harlow, marveling at her kind soul.

"Well." Harlow dropped her gaze to her covers and plucked at a loose thread on the blanket. "Forgiveness is the healthier option. Harboring a grudge just means hold-ing on to stress and anger and pain." She lifted her eyes to him. "Forgiveness doesn't excuse wrongdoing, but it frees you to move past the offense, not let the person *continue* hurting you. I mean, look what vengeance and anger did to Chris."

Wade considered her point, and with an exhale, nodded. "You're a wise woman, Harlow Jones." After a beat, he con-tinued, "Any chance you could forgive me while you're in this merciful mood?"

She tipped her head. "Forgive you for what? Wade, you saved my life. You got Chris out of the lake despite the risk to your own life and your injured shoulder. You did everything right."

"Agreed, brother," Fletcher said, folding his arms over his chest as he leaned back against the wall. "I couldn't have done better myself." Then with a lopsided smile, he added, "Oorah!"

Fletcher's approval and nod to Wade's career with the Marines warmed Wade better than any blanket or heated IV drip. With a lopsided grin, he chuckled and teased, "Thanks, but...that was the weakest *oorah* I ever heard."

Turning to Harlow, Wade brushed back a lock of her chestnut hair that had curled around her cheek as it dried. "I meant I want you to forgive me for breaking your heart after high school. I should never have broken up with you. Never hurt you. Never said the terrible things—"

"Wade..." Harlow's eyes filled with tears.

"Um." Fletcher pushed away from the wall and moved toward the door. "This sounds private. So... I'll go now. I only wanted to make sure you were both on the mend. The waiting room is full of worried Coltons needing a report."

Harlow gave a small wave. "Thank you, Fletcher."

The brothers exchanged a nod and smile, and when Fletcher reached the door, he paused and looked back over his shoulder at Wade. "I know this isn't the time for a full conversation about it, but…the Owl Creek PD could always use good officers…if you'd be interested."

Something akin to an electric shock zipped through Wade, and he sat taller as he stared at his brother. Join the OCPD? He'd never considered law enforcement as a career, but…the idea had merit. The suggestion…felt right. "I…maybe. Yeah."

Fletcher's face brightened. "We'll talk."

When he faced Harlow again, her eyes were bright with tears, and a smile tugged her lips. "You'd make a great policeman, Wade. And don't miss what Fletcher was really saying just then. He believes in you and your abilities."

Wade's chest tightened with emotion, and he had to clear his throat before he could speak. "I know. And that means…a lot." He exhaled and took both her hands in his, careful not to squeeze the IV needle in the back of her hand. "But more important, this morning has made something else starkly clear. The idea of living without you for even another day scares me more than any nightmare, or stalker, or explosion ever could. I never stopped loving you, Harlow, despite what I said as a confused and hurting teenager."

Fresh tears bloomed in her eyes. "Oh, Wade, I love you, too. And I'm sorry for pushing you away instead of embracing your dreams of the Marines."

"You're forgiven. And I should have seen how important having a place to call home was for you. I should have listened better, been more understanding."

Harlow wiped a tear from her cheek. "You're forgiven."

She touched his cheek, adding, "I thought I needed a town to call my home, but the truth was *you* were my home. You were what I needed to feel rooted and secure. And you still are."

Wade's heart stilled, and he sat taller, his gaze narrowing on Harlow's dark eyes. "What exactly are you saying? Because… I don't want a misunderstanding or selfish argument to ever come between us again."

She gripped his hand tighter, a clear sign her strength was returning, and she smiled. "I'm saying I've decided not to sell my parents' house. I want to live in Owl Creek and do *Harlow Helps* from here. I want to wake up every morning next to you and never let you out of my life again."

A grin bloomed on his lips, and he chuckled his joy. "Same here. You are everything to me, Harlow Jones, and I made a vow this morning that I intend to keep," Wade said, and a shudder rolled through him as he remembered the terror he'd felt earlier when Harlow was in the frozen lake.

"A vow?"

He nodded. "To do whatever it takes to be with you. I'll move to LA. I'll get PTSD counseling. I'll share my deepest secrets with you, so you'll know I trust you completely. I'll—"

She touched a finger to his mouth to silence him. "No to LA. Our family is in Owl Creek. Yes to the counseling and honesty between us. But—" she leaned in for a quick kiss "—there's one more thing I want you to do."

"Name it," he said eagerly.

"Marry me."

Shock waves more powerful than a blast of dynamite shook Wade to his core, and he took a moment to catch his breath. In a flash, he could see his future clearly—growing old with Harlow, raising a family, exploring a new career and making Owl Creek his home for years to come. Happiness coursed through him, and he threw his head back to laugh. "You have a deal, my love. It's you and me forever."

* * * * *

COMING SOON!

We really hope you enjoyed reading this book.
If you're looking for more romance
be sure to head to the shops when
new books are available on

Thursday 24th
October

MILLS & BOON

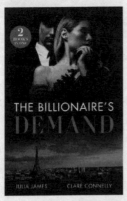
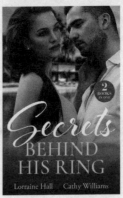

LET'S TALK
Romance

For exclusive extracts, competitions and special offers, find us online:

f MillsandBoon

X @MillsandBoon

⊡ @MillsandBoonUK

♪ @MillsandBoonUK

Get in touch on 01413 063 232